WID

HY

Please return/renew this item by the last date shown
on this label, or on your self-service receipt.

To renew this item, visit **www.librarieswest.org.uk**
or contact your library

Your borrower number and PIN are required.

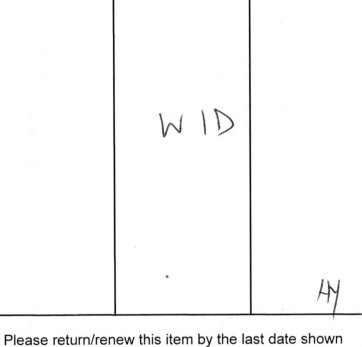

LibrariesWest

D0541070

Also by Donna Alward

Summer Escape with the Tycoon

Heirs to an Empire miniseries

Scandal and the Runaway Bride
The Heiress's Pregnancy Surprise
Wedding Reunion with the Best Man

Also by Ella Hayes

Her Brooding Scottish Heir
Italian Summer with the Single Dad
Unlocking the Tycoon's Heart
Tycoon's Unexpected Caribbean Fling

Discover more at millsandboon.co.uk.

MISTLETOE KISS WITH THE MILLIONAIRE

DONNA ALWARD

THE SINGLE DAD'S CHRISTMAS PROPOSAL

ELLA HAYES

MILLS & BOON

First Published in Great Britain 2021
by Mills & Boon, an imprint of HarperCollins*Publishers* Ltd,
1 London Bridge Street, London, SE1 9GF

www.harpercollins.co.uk

HarperCollins*Publishers*
1st Floor, Watermarque Building,
Ringsend Road, Dublin 4, Ireland

Mistletoe Kiss with the Millionaire © 2021 Donna Alward

The Single Dad's Christmas Proposal © 2021 Ella Hayes

ISBN: 978-0-263-29997-7

10/21

MIX
Paper from
responsible sources
FSC C007454

This book is produced from independently certified FSC™ paper
to ensure responsible forest management.
For more information visit www.harpercollins.co.uk/green.

Printed and bound in Spain using 100% Renewable Electricity
at CPI Blackprint (Barcelona)

MISTLETOE KISS WITH THE MILLIONAIRE

DONNA ALWARD

MILLS & BOON

To Boo and Romeo,
who never fail to let me know when it's dinnertime,
and give the best head-butts and purr-rubs.

CHAPTER ONE

SOPHIE WALTHAM LOOKED at the couples turning on the dance floor and pursed her lips. A Pemberton social function hadn't been on her "must attend" list in her diary, but her parents had decided to go to Prague for a week to celebrate their anniversary and had insisted Sophie represent the family at the event. She tapped her toe impatiently, wondering how long she had to stay before she could politely leave. It was an engagement party for Bella Pemberton and Viscount Downham. So why was she expected to "represent" as if this were a business function?

The dress she'd chosen had been a mistake. Her go-to little black dress was fitting a bit too snugly these days, and she wasn't comfortable in it or in the stilettos on her feet. Her dark hair was down around her shoulders, and a Waltham original piece graced her neck—a narrow, glimmering necklace of pearls and diamonds that she'd designed herself. She'd deliberately chosen it instead of an Aurora Gems piece. If she wanted to build her name as a designer, she should be wearing her own creations.

What had begun as Waltham Fine Jewelry nearly a century ago was now simply "Waltham," the name alone synonymous with quality on Bond Street. It was also one of the exclusive distributors of Aurora Gems, the jewelry line for the Aurora, Inc. dynasty. Which was why she was standing here, on the sidelines of the party, sipping club soda and lime and wishing she were home with her feet up, reading. She was tired. And her feet hurt.

She sighed and went back to the bar to refresh her drink. Just as she picked it up, a smooth voice sounded behind her that eased some of the tension in her shoulders.

"Well hello, stranger."

There was still a hint of French accent in Christophe Germain's voice, despite being brought up at Chatsworth Manor, the family home of the Earl of Chatsworth. She smiled and turned, happy to see his smile, his curly dark hair, and his right eyebrow. For as long as she could remember, he'd been able to lift that eyebrow just a tad when teasing, giving him a roguish air.

Christophe Germain was secretly her favorite member of the Pemberton family. He was also newly in charge of Aurora's jewelry division. Despite that important fact, she hadn't seen him for several months.

It was lovely to see that, unlike her, he hadn't changed.

"Christophe!" She leaned forward, and they bussed cheeks. "I'm so glad you're here."

"You are? How delightful." He looked her up and down and grinned. "You look like Holly Golightly."

"Thank you... I think?" Her hairstyle certainly wasn't the short, gamine look of Audrey Hepburn in *Breakfast at Tiffany's*, but she supposed the dress fit the bill and the necklace, too.

"It's a compliment. You are elegant, as always."

She knew some women would find the compliment boring and colorless, but not her. Understated, classic elegance was her preferred style; avant-garde wasn't. She saved the creativity for her gemstones and precious metals.

They moved away from the bar so as to not interrupt the flow of thirsty guests. "I've been meaning to pay Waltham a visit," he continued. "The last few months have been so busy, though. Maybe I can set up a time in the next few weeks. Before the holidays, for sure."

"My father would love that. And so would I." Though she'd never admit it, she'd always had a bit of a crush on Christophe. Oh, she'd never acted on it—she appreciated their friendship too much. Besides, if he knew, he'd tease her mercilessly about it. "He and Mum are on their anniversary trip this week. Thirty-three years."

He lifted his glass in a salute. "Now that's something to celebrate."

It certainly was, especially after her mother's illness a few years ago. Time was no longer something they took for granted. She looked at Christophe. Her mum had survived, but he'd recently lost the man who'd been a father to him most of his life.

She put her hand on his arm. "How are you doing, since Cedric's passing?"

The Pemberton family had been left grief-stricken and reeling since Cedric's death. Sophie had attended the funeral but hadn't had the opportunity to really chat with Christophe since.

"I'm all right. Tante Aurora is a strong woman. I still miss him and his advice, though. And the last few months have been a bit crazy on the family front."

"I heard about William's marriage, and Charlotte's, too." She'd offered congratulations to both of Christophe's cousins earlier. Charlotte looked ready to pop, expecting her first child with her husband within a few weeks. Seeing her glowing and happy had made Sophie's heart soften with wistful wishing. It wasn't often she let down her guard, let emotion override her determination. But seeing a very pregnant Charlotte had made her realize that by the time January rolled around, none of her dresses would be fitting anymore. She had already made her decision about her baby, but no one seemed interested in hearing it.

"Yes," Christophe said, "and now Bella and Burke. Very happy for them, of course. As long as the marriage bug doesn't bite me, I'll be fine." He winked at her, and she laughed. It was no secret that Christophe was a die-hard bachelor.

"Come, now. You're one of France's most eligible, aren't you?"

"That does not mean I have any desire to settle down." His voice held a touch of humor, and he offered her a bland look. "There's been more than enough drama at Chez Pemberton for a decade." He winked at her. "I suppose it does keep the days from being monotonous, though. Or, you know. Makes me look up from my desk now and again." He pretended to adjust his tie. "Put on a tux now and again."

"What about the woman you were dating last... What was her name? Elizabeth or something?"

Christophe lifted his eyebrow. "My, you've been paying close attention. Lizzy, yes. That ended a while ago." He sighed. "Suddenly she was all about marriage and babies."

Sophie watched him closely. "And you're not that guy?"

He shook his head. "I'm very much not that guy. Besides, I'm too busy for a social life right now. Company functions are about it."

She linked her arm through his and they walked to a nearby table. "Has the workload been daunting? With Aurora semi retiring?"

"A bit. I still run the jewelry section, but I've taken over some of Bella's cosmetics division, as well." He laughed and shrugged, his shoulders rising and falling in his perfectly tailored tuxedo. "Me, in cosmetics. There's been a learning curve."

She laughed, too, and the night suddenly seemed

brighter. She had known Christophe for several years, and she'd never been as intimidated by him as she had been by his cousins. She knew that he'd gone to live with the Pembertons when he was nine and had been brought up as one of the children with the same advantages and love. And yet she knew, too, that he still felt the difference. He was Aurora's nephew, but Aurora had also come from humble beginnings. Stephen, William, Charlotte, Bella...they were all Cedric's natural children, born into English aristocracy. Stephen was the new Earl of Chatsworth.

Once she'd heard Christophe refer to himself as "the bastard cousin," and she'd told him firmly that he was never to refer to himself as that again. As she looked him over, she remained convinced that there was absolutely nothing wrong with Christophe Germain. Nothing at all.

"Your necklace is lovely. And not one of ours, I don't think."

She took a sip of her drink and met his gaze. "I've been doing some designing. This is one of mine. Though one of the simpler ones." The small double strand of pearls was joined together by a glittering diamond clasp in the shape of a honeybee.

"I like this." He reached out with a finger and touched the clasp. A shiver skittered over her skin. She hoped he didn't notice the reaction. The last thing she needed was for him to clue in that she was attracted to him in any way. That would remain her little secret. Besides, he'd just admitted he wasn't into marriage and babies, and Sophie was a package deal now. That would be enough to send him running for the hills. No, he need never know of her crush.

"I—I've been using some elements of nature in my latest designs," she admitted, trying to regain the slip in her composure. "Flowers, leaves, fruit, bees."

"Fertility," he mused, and she choked on her sip of club

soda and began to cough. She wasn't showing yet. It was too early. There was no way for him to know she was pregnant. But had she been, subconsciously, bringing those elements into her work because of what was happening in her personal life? It was an interesting observation, and something she wanted to think about more later, when she considered what direction she wanted to take her new designs. As a gemologist, she oversaw Waltham's inventory. Each stone had to be of the highest quality to meet Waltham standards. She was good at that, but what she really wanted was to create her own original pieces.

He patted her back gently. "You all right?" he asked, that silly eyebrow puckered now in concern.

"Oh, yes. Of course." She cleared her throat. "Sorry about that."

"Don't be silly."

The song changed and he smiled at her. "Come on. Let's dance. You've been standing on the sidelines for the better part of an hour."

He'd noticed. What did that mean?

He held out his hand and she took it. How could she refuse? Besides, they'd danced together lots of times before. This was no different. He led her to the floor and brought her into the circle of his arms, moving smoothly, leading her effortlessly.

For a poor boy from a little French village, he had moves. In some ways, he was Pemberton through and through. His hand was strong and sure as it clasped hers, and he smelled delicious…hints of bergamot and sandalwood, perhaps. Whatever it was, she liked it.

His light chatter put her more at ease, and by the time the song was half over, she'd relaxed substantially, even laughing at some of his anecdotes about the family's mishaps over the past few months. He managed to take some of their hardships—the media storm after Stephen was left at the altar, the sabotage of the Aurora line at New York Fashion Week—and make them into colorful stories. His face had softened as he told her about his Aunt Aurora's heart troubles and how wonderful Burke had been. In addition to being Viscount Downham, Burke was a highly regarded cardiologist. And now he was marrying Bella, who, Christophe said, was so deserving of a happy ending.

What struck Sophie was the obvious affection he had for his family. She only had her brother, and as she'd been off to boarding school when he'd still been very young, they hadn't really grown up together. It made her the smallest bit lonely, hearing Christophe talk about his cousins in such a way. She thought about the tiny bundle of cells growing within her belly. She didn't want him or her to grow up as an only child. Which made her decision of last week even more…well, not confusing, really. But she could understand why some would think she was making a big mistake.

When the dance was over, Christophe led her to a table and held out a chair. She sank into it thankfully; the shoes were killing her feet and she was ready for bed. The baby was the size of a strawberry. How it could make her so exhausted was unbelievable. She stifled a yawn, then blushed as Christophe's keen gaze held on her face.

"It looks like someone is putting in extra hours at work." He frowned, then raised that quizzical eyebrow again. "Either that or there is someone keeping you up all hours of the night. Is there someone new in your life, Sophie?"

His teasing was going to be the end of her. "Wouldn't you like to know," she responded, offering a smile. One of the waitstaff stopped by and offered champagne. Christophe took a glass and she asked for iced water, hoping he wouldn't notice and ask why. Worse, however, was when the circulating waitress approached with her tray of hors d'oeuvres. Sophie took one look at the salmon and trout tartare with pressed caviar and felt her stomach do a slow, sickening roll.

No raw fish. No soft cheese. The first she could do without; the second was more of a hardship. She adored cheese. Now she felt Christophe's eyes on her again, so she smiled and chose an onion tartlet. She hadn't had dinner yet, and right now just wanted to go home to her flat and make a cheese toastie.

Her water arrived. She smiled at Christophe and nibbled on the tartlet, while he smiled back and bit into smoked salmon on some sort of brioche.

The fishy smell hit her nostrils and she tried valiantly to swallow the tartlet. The onion, however, caught in her throat and she hastily reached for her water. Christophe had put down the rest of his brioche and was watching her curiously now. "Sophie, are you all right? Is there something wrong? You don't seem yourself tonight."

Because I'm not, she thought, but kept the words inside. Instead, she jumped from her chair and headed for the closest powder room. The onion had been a mistake, and the salmon smell had only made it worse. She couldn't think about Christophe's alarmed expression right now. She had only one thing on her mind—get to the bathroom before she embarrassed herself.

Christophe stood as Sophie rose from her chair, but he wasn't even all the way upright when she dashed away, making a beeline for the ladies' room. She definitely wasn't okay. Hopefully it wasn't food poisoning. The family would be appalled if such a thing happened at one of their events, and so would the hotel. Not that he particularly cared about that—about appearances. He was more worried that his friend had suddenly run off, ill. If she were truly sick, she should go home. Be in bed and sleep off whatever it was.

Christophe abandoned his champagne and the tiny plate of food and followed her, waiting just inside the ballroom where he could see the door to the bathroom. Several people passed by and said hello; he greeted them cordially but never lost sight of the door. When Sophie finally appeared, her face pale and eyes looking bruised, he grew even more concerned. He stepped forward, noting the surprise in her eyes when she looked up and saw him there.

"You…you're waiting for me." She bit down on her lip, and her eyes slid away from his. Something was very off with her, and the more time went by, the more concerned he became. He'd known Sophie for probably seven, eight years. The relationship between her family's company and Aurora went back a very long way. And in all that time, he'd never seen her act so strangely. She was always warm, upfront, and easygoing in a way that was intimate.

"You're not feeling well. I wanted to make sure you were okay and offer you a way home if you want to go."

"It's still so early." But there was a tinge of relief in her tone, too, that belied her words.

"You saw Burke and Bella, didn't you? You don't need to stay longer if you're worried about any sort of obligation. Everyone will understand."

"I doubt it," she muttered, low enough he barely caught the words. What on earth did that mean?

"Soph?"

She finally met his gaze and let out a sigh. "I'm sorry, Christophe. I know I must seem all over the place. To be honest, I'm not feeling well, and I think I'll grab a taxi and head home."

"Let me drive you."

She glanced up in surprise. "You have a car here?"

Christophe was generally based in Paris, and he didn't keep a flat here in London. But this trip was a little longer in nature, and the cars at the manor house sat idle too often. "I'm using one of the family's cars," he explained. "I hate being driven everywhere. This gives me more freedom."

"And London traffic. Brave man." She smiled slightly.

"So, what do you say? I think we could both sneak off and no one would even notice. I'll give you a lift home and make sure you're okay, and then I can have a little of my own downtime. It works for me, too."

She looked as if she might refuse, so he added, "I love my cousin, but to be honest, all this romance lately has got to be a bit much. You'd be saving me."

Her shadowed eyes lightened, and she laughed a little. "All right, then. I think I left my clutch at the table, though."

They walked back into the ballroom, Christophe following just slightly behind her, and the smile on his face faded. Sophie wasn't herself, and there was no denying the grayish pallor of her skin when she'd come out of the bathroom. He hoped it wasn't anything more serious than a twenty-four-hour virus.

In no time at all they were on their way. Sophie gave him directions to her flat in Chelsea, and he navigated the streets easily. London was truly a second home, even if he didn't have a property here. He generally stayed at his Paris flat, or at the manor house when he was in England; the commute to the city wasn't horribly long, and the manor house was the only home he really remembered. Sophie was quiet in the seat next to him, her pale face illuminated by the lights from the dash. Christophe glanced over at her several times before speaking.

"Are you sure you're all right?"

She nodded. "I'm fine, really. My stomach is just a little off."

He stopped at a traffic light and spared a longer look at her profile. "If you're sure…"

"It was the fish. The smell didn't agree with me tonight, that's all. And I'm tired, so I think it's just a case of needing some rest. I'm sure I'll be fine tomorrow."

Something about her words didn't sit quite right. And yet they made perfect sense, so it wasn't like he could press the issue. His concern wasn't allayed, however, and he caught himself frowning several times before they arrived at her flat.

"I'll see you in," he said, parking the car in a surprisingly free spot in front of her building.

"Christophe, you don't have to do that. I'm fine." She smiled at him then, her eyes soft. "I appreciate the concern and the lift home. I truly do."

"Then indulge me. Let me make sure you're all right and settled. That's what friends do, after all."

"You're not going to let this go, are you?"

He grinned and unbuckled his seat belt. "See? You do know me. Come on. Let's go in."

The night was soft and quiet as Sophie let them into her flat and flicked on a light. He'd never been inside; the last time they'd hung out together she'd been living elsewhere with a flatmate, and before that she'd been at her family's home when she wasn't away at school. He liked the look of this place. It reflected her personality more than the previous apartment, which had been comprised of a varied assortment of furniture belonging to both her and her flatmate, a scuffed hardwood floor, and some sort of chintz curtains on the windows.

This place was decorated with intention and looked like

a bit of country home inside an eight-hundred-square-foot space. The small foyer opened up into the living room. There was a fireplace surrounded by a white scrolled mantel, a Turkish rug on the floor, and a comfortable-looking sofa flanked by two chairs. A television was above the mantel, attached to the wall. Graceful tables flanked the sofa, and a glass-topped coffee table sat on the rug, a novel on its otherwise flawless top.

"This is different from your last place," he remarked.

"I finished school and started working full time. It made a difference."

It was an expensive flat for someone on a regular salary. But the Walthams had money. It only made sense that some of that had found its way to their only daughter.

She shrugged out of her coat and hung it in a small closet. "Do you want to come in?" she asked. "I can offer you coffee or tea. Sorry I don't have anything stronger."

"I had a glass of champagne and I'm driving. But I'll take tea."

"Do you mind if I change first?"

"Of course not." Though he had to admit, it wasn't a hardship seeing her in a little black dress. He and Sophie were friends, but that didn't mean he was blind. She was ridiculously beautiful.

"Make yourself at home," she suggested, and disappeared down a small hall into what was presumably her bedroom.

Christophe ambled into the living room and stopped to glance at a few photos that were framed and around the room. There was one of her family, all four of them smiling with the Waltham garden in the background. The other, which sat on an end table, was a black-and-white photo of Sophie and her brother, Mark, making silly faces. He smiled at that one. For all Sophie's quiet elegance, she had a goofy side that he admired. Putting it on display in a framed photo told him she didn't take herself too seriously, either, and wasn't afraid to show that side now and again.

Which made her awkwardness this evening very out of character.

A meow sounded and Christophe looked down to see a long-haired tabby padding over the rug. "Well, hello," he said softly, kneeling and holding out a hand. "What's your name?"

The cat came forward, purred, and rubbed along the side of Christophe's hand.

"That's Harry," Sophie said, and Christophe looked up to find her changed into a pair of black leggings and a long gray sweater.

"You look much more comfortable," he said, then lowered his gaze to the cat again. "This is a very handsome kitty." He scratched beneath the cat's chin, earning more purrs and rubs.

"Oh, that's his favorite scratchy spot. You've earned a friend for life, now. And you're going to have cat hair all over your tuxedo."

He chuckled. "That's what the cleaners are for." He stood again and put his hands in his pockets. "Your color is better. I'm glad. I was worried."

She smiled and turned away, going to the kitchen. "Oh, you don't have to worry about me," she called. "I'm fine."

He wasn't completely reassured. Something was still off. She'd meet his gaze but not hold it for too long, as if she didn't want him looking too closely. He watched as she filled the kettle and set it on the burner to boil, then went to a cupboard and opened it. "What would you like? I have a decent selection of herbals, and some decaf black tea." She looked over at him expectantly. Harry twined himself around her legs, and she took a moment to croon at him and dig a few treats out of a cupboard.

His brows puckered. Okay, something was definitely wrong. She'd been drinking club soda tonight and didn't have any alcohol in the house. Now her teas were all herbal and decaf? Was she on some sort of health kick or something? Because the Sophie he knew loved champagne and would mainline coffee if she could. She never started her day without it. And she was too young to worry about it keeping her up at night.

He looked at the package of peppermint tea in her hand and then met her gaze. "You'd better tell me what's going on, Soph."

Her eyes clouded with indecision for a moment, and, if he guessed correctly, a bit of panic. Then her lips set, as if she'd come to some sort of decision.

"I might as well tell you, since I won't be able to hide it forever. I'm pregnant, Christophe."

CHAPTER TWO

THE KETTLE BEGAN to whistle behind her as she heard the words leave her mouth. She hadn't intended to say anything this soon, and certainly not to Christophe. They were friends but not overly intimate. They saw each other a few times a year, hung out now and again like they had tonight, at industry functions, that sort of thing. She hadn't even told her brother about the baby yet. And by the staggered look on Christophe's face, she wished she could take back the words. What had she been thinking, confiding such a thing?

Instead, she turned, removed the kettle from the burner, and poured the boiling water into mugs. Without asking, she dropped a bag into his, knowing that he'd drink the tea anyway after a bombshell like that.

There was a quiet *thunk* as she put the kettle back on the stove and turned to face him again.

"That explains a lot," he said weakly, and his gaze dropped to her belly and then back up to her face. He blushed when he realized what he'd done. "Sorry," he offered.

"Nothing to see there yet. I'm not quite through my first trimester. So yeah, it explains the dash to the ladies' tonight and why I didn't eat." She fought through her embarrassment. "Do you want milk in your tea?"

"No, thank you," he replied, and she dipped the bags out of the mugs with a spoon and put them on a saucer before handing him his cup.

"Let's go sit," she said quietly. "And I'll explain."

She led him into the living room and took a seat on the sofa, cradling the warm mug in her hands. The soothing scent of peppermint wafted up, and she took a cautious sip. Peppermint tea seemed to be the one thing that settled her stomach these days.

He sat next to her, but not too close, holding his steaming mug but not paying it any attention at all. "You're how far along?"

"Eleven weeks or so. Hopefully the morning sickness, or all-day sickness, rather, will ease up soon."

Silence fell between them for a moment, and then Christophe asked the question she'd been waiting for. "And the father?"

"Eric."

She didn't have to say more. She'd dated Eric for nearly two years, and occasionally the stockbroker attended events with her. Eric Walsh was practically perfect, as her mother continually reminded her.

"So are congratulations in order? I mean, how do you feel about it? How does Eric feel? Does this mean you two will finally be getting married?"

She took a sip of tea to buy herself some time. He'd fired out four questions and none of them were easy to answer. She'd already gone through all of this—with Eric, with her parents.

Sophie was quiet for so long that Christophe reached out and took her hand, a sheepish grin on his face and that eyebrow doing its quirky thing again. "Sorry, was that too much?"

"A little," she admitted.

"Then maybe I should just say, what are your plans?" He sat back against the cushions.

She put the tea on a coaster on the coffee table, pleased that he'd kept his fingers linked with hers. It was…reassuring. Kept her grounded, which was a nice feeling since she almost always felt her life was spinning out of control. "Well, that's a good question, really. I mean, I'm sort of happy about it? Clearly it wasn't planned, and it's taken me a good bit to wrap my head around the idea, but I like children, and wanted them someday, so this is really just moving up the timeline." She smiled, hoping it was convincing. Truthfully, she was still getting used to the idea. At times she was awed and amazed and even excited. That euphoria was generally offset by panic and worry. She knew nothing about being a parent.

"And Eric?"

"We broke up in September."

"Befo—?"

"Yes, before I knew about the baby." She met his gaze with her own. "We're still broken up, Christophe."

His lips firmed into a line and his throat bobbed as he swallowed, but to his credit, he didn't say anything.

"You're silent. It must be killing you." She offered a small smile, and to her relief, he smiled back.

"Not killing me. It's just…"

"I know." She squeezed his fingers. She was one of the few who truly knew Christophe's history. Despite them not being super close, he'd confessed it one evening years ago when he'd come 'round to her flat for pasta and wine and they'd had a little too much to drink. They'd played "two truths and a lie," but his had been easy to spot; he couldn't conceal the pain in his voice even though it was clear he'd tried. The truth of Christophe's life was that his father had abandoned him and his mother when Christophe was a toddler, and when he was nine, his mother had sent him off to live with his aunt, the great Aurora Germain Pemberton. He'd gone from living in poverty in a small French town with few opportunities to being part of an incredibly rich and powerful family.

"So you're not going to marry him."

She shook her head. "I'm twenty-nine and financially independent. I can do this on my own, you know."

His jaw tightened. "Of course you can. Still, I can't believe he didn't ask you. What kind of man doesn't take responsibility for his own kid?"

Her heart gave a heavy thump as she stared into his face. She knew his wounds ran deep. A small child didn't get over being abandoned. Because she understood his history, the next part was even harder to say.

"Christophe, look at me." When he did, his dark eyes stormy, she felt the contact right to her core. He was a paradox right now, with his rigid posture expressing his outrage but his eyes vulnerable and hurt. She wanted to soothe the furrows off his brow, bring back his smile. She took the mug from his hands and placed it beside hers on the table, then turned and took both his hands in hers. "You are a good friend, Christophe. You always have been, even though we go months between seeing each other. I have always felt comfortable with you, and protected. But you can't get protective now because you need to realize that this is my choice. I'm the one who broke up with Eric, and I did it before I knew I was pregnant. He did ask me to marry him, and I refused. Carrying his baby doesn't miraculously change my feelings for him. I don't want to spend the rest of my life with him. And I certainly don't want to put the pressure of a marriage's success or failure on a tiny, innocent baby."

He sighed. "But—"

"No buts," she said firmly. "Listen, I know how hard a subject this is for you. I know you have a lot of lingering feelings and that's okay, but it's not okay to judge me because of that, all right?"

His eyes finally cleared. "Sophie, I would never judge you."

"Wouldn't you?" She could practically hear him judging her right now, even though she knew he didn't want to.

He sat back. "Not intentionally." He sighed again. "You're right, though. I'm sorry. Being abandoned by my father, and even my mother, has left a mark. I can hardly be unbiased in this situation."

"I know that. I just…" She trailed off, picked up her tea and took a drink to hide the sudden rush of emotion. "My parents think I'm crazy. Eric is being persistent. No one seems to want to listen to what I have to say."

"I'm listening," he said softly.

She looked up at him, and the moment seemed to pause in time. Sophie had eyes in her head; it was easy for her to admit that he was astoundingly good-looking. But more than that, he had *depth*. He felt things. Cared about things. Even the small chip on his shoulder was understandable. His greatest quality was his loyalty. She knew without a doubt that she would only have to ask for his help and he would be there. To ask for his support and it would be granted. Friends like that were as rare as a Burma ruby. Tears formed in the corners of her eyes. Of course she'd trusted him with the news. Even if Christophe didn't agree, he'd offer his support regardless. It had nothing to do with her secret crush. She'd invited him in tonight and told him the news because she'd known he'd be on her side.

"Hey," he said, leaning forward. "Don't cry. It's all right."

"I know it is. It's everyone else who thinks I'm making the biggest mistake of my life."

He nodded. "Are you? Are you sure you don't want to be with him? I know how stubborn you can be, Soph. And how you resist being told what to do." He smiled a little, the curve of his lips making her smile despite herself.

"I'm sure," she said, starting to feel better. "I don't love him, not the way I should. I loved him out of habit and not passion. Out of complacency and not joy. We'd been together long enough that it made sense to start looking at our future. When I did, I knew I couldn't marry him. My feelings haven't changed just because I'm pregnant. If anything, I'm more sure now. I…" She hesitated before voicing her biggest objection. "Honestly, I can't imagine us raising children together. He works so much and frankly, we don't have a lot in common. I can't picture us being a team when it comes to bringing up kids. Or sticking together during thick and thin."

Christophe nodded. "I can understand that. I still…well, you know me. I still believe a child needs two parents."

"It's funny," she mused gently. "I had two parents and I'm positive I can do this myself. You didn't and you're sure it takes two. And somehow, I think the answer is in between somewhere. I will say, Eric agrees with you. He wants to marry me and make things 'legitimate.' The problem is that legitimate is a concept on a birth certificate. It wouldn't extend to the marriage, you see?"

"It would be easier if you loved him."

"You're telling me!"

She said it so emphatically that they both ended up laughing a little.

Sophie sighed. "I know he'll support his child. And Christophe, just because I'm positive this is the right thing, doesn't mean I don't have guilt about it. Misgivings. Nothing about this is perfect." She put her hand on her still-flat tummy. "And none of this is my baby's fault. Talk about innocent and caught in the middle."

Christophe tried to make sense of the thoughts swirling through his head. Of all the things he'd expected tonight, hearing that Sophie was having a baby was so far off the mark it didn't even register. And yet here he was, in her cozy little Chelsea flat, drinking horrible tea and getting all the sordid details.

Well, not all the details. Thankfully she'd left out any account of conception. He'd met Eric before and he'd seemed like a nice enough guy, but the last thing Christophe wanted to think about was Eric and Sophie in bed.

He shouldn't be thinking about her in that way at all, considering she was his friend. Especially since she was carrying another man's child.

She was right about one thing, though. The baby was innocent in all this.

He tamped down all his personal feelings—she'd been right on that score—and simply asked, "What do you need from me right now?"

"You've given it," she said softly, her eyes shining in the lamplight. "You listened. You didn't say I was being stupid and foolish. And you haven't given me a laundry list of Eric's attributes to try to convince me to change my mind."

"Your parents?" he guessed.

"And Eric, as well. But Christophe, all those things don't matter if the love…if that certain something just isn't there. You know. Your Aunt Aurora had it with your Uncle Cedric. And your cousins… Look at Bella and Burke. You can tell they think the sun rises and sets in each other. They're so devoted." She sniffed. "Am I wrong to want that for myself?"

"No," he replied, touched. She wasn't wrong about Tante Aurora and Oncle Cedric. Perhaps that was part of his resentment. They'd taken him in but as a result he'd seen what a real, committed love looked like. It was something he'd never witnessed before. Certainly not from his parents. "No, you're not wrong. I want that for you, too. I just don't want you to throw this away if it might be it."

"It's not," she answered, her voice definitive. "I just look at my mum and dad and know Eric and I will never have what they do. When Mum was ill, Dad's devotion was so beautiful. I can't settle for less than the example they've set."

Christophe merely squeezed her hand in understanding.

A gurgling sound interrupted the moment, and they both looked down at her stomach. She laughed a little, a blush tinging her cheeks an adorable pink. "I really should have eaten, I guess," she mused.

"We could order something in."

"Honestly? I've been dying for a cheese toastie."

He laughed. *Dieu*, she could be so adorable. Earlier she'd been in a killer dress and stilettos wearing thousands of pounds worth of gems, but what she really wanted was the simplest comfort food.

"Then a toastie you shall have. And I will make it."

"Oh! You don't have to. I can—"

"Shh." He lifted a finger and put it against her lips. "Let me look after you. This is a simple thing. I promise I won't set off any fire alarms, and it will be delightfully edible."

Her blush deepened and he removed his finger, suddenly disconcerted by the innocent-meaning touch. It had felt... intimate. And that was a new sensation where Sophie was concerned.

He covered by getting up from the sofa and going to

the kitchen, where he could think without being so near to her. As he took a copper pan off a hook and found bread, cheese and butter, he took deep breaths. He could understand why Eric was determined to marry her, and not just because of the baby. After having a woman like Sophie, who would willingly let her get away?

CHAPTER THREE

SOPHIE PUT DOWN her loupe and the engagement ring she'd been studying and stretched on her stool, arching her back to ease the constant ache that plagued her lately. The stones in the ring were of impeccable quality; the cushion cut center stone was ideal, and she rated the clarity at a VVS1. It was a new addition to the Aurora line, and she should be excited about it, but engagement rings just weren't doing it for her lately. For obvious and not so obvious reasons.

She'd been working on a different design lately, one that she thought had great potential. The stones had to be perfect for the colors to work exactly right. Clear, bright aquamarines, deep sapphires, golden citrines, and sparkling diamonds set in waves of color reminiscent of Van Gogh's *Starry Night*. The more she looked at the design, the more she considered an entire line inspired by works of art. She pictured perhaps Monet's *Bouquet of Sunflowers* or *Artist's Garden*, Degas's *Dancers in Pink*. She reached for her sketchbook again and started sketching out ideas.

Working at Waltham was a wonderful job, and she was happy she'd followed in the family footsteps and become a gemologist. But she didn't want to sit at a desk and appraise all day. She wanted to create. Anytime she brought it up, her parents brushed it off. It was fully expected that she'd simply take over Waltham when they retired. Many looked at Sophie and saw a life full of opportunity. She saw a box, hemming her in with expectations.

And it wasn't that she was against taking over, necessarily. It was that she wanted more. She wanted to be able to explore her career a bit first before settling in a permanent spot of her choosing.

Her pencil paused over the paper. Maybe that was it. Maybe that was the way to frame the discussion…taking time to spread her wings within the industry, to learn outside of Waltham. She stretched her back again and sighed. Well, whatever that plan was, it would have to wait a while. In six months, her world was going to shift substantially. She'd have a child to consider.

She continued sketching. The movement of the pencil tip on the paper was soothing, focusing her mind on the shapes in front of her rather than her troubles.

Eric had called again last night. He'd pointed out the life she'd be giving up, as if money were an enticement. When she'd replied that she had plenty of money of her own, he'd gotten angry and hung up.

The shape on the page became reminiscent of a ballerina's skirt and Sophie worked away, fashioning it into a pendant. Oh, she liked this one. Pink sapphire would do nicely, with diamond accents and set in warm rose gold.

She was deep into the sketch when her mobile buzzed, the vibration on the table making her jump in surprise and dread…was it Eric again? A quick look at the screen showed Christophe's ID, and she smiled as she picked it up. Right now, Christophe was the calm in the middle of a storm.

"Hello, you," she said into the phone, correcting her posture once again.

"Hi yourself. Busy?"

"Doing some designing. Why?" She tapped the pencil on the pad as she cradled the phone to her ear.

"I'm in town for another few days. I wondered if you'd like to catch some dinner tonight. No raw fish. Promise."

"I thought you'd gone back to Paris after the party."

"Well, there's been a development. Charlotte had her baby girl on Monday. Everyone stayed at the manor to be able to visit. Even the staff is aflutter."

"The first grandchild. Aurora must be in heaven."

"She is. And has already started sending Will and Gabi pointed looks. Anyway, I wasn't going to be the jerk who abandoned the family, even if I'm not quite as excited as Bella and Gabi. I've been holding down the fort with Will and Burke and Stephen."

"Sounds delightful."

"It's not. They're horrible company. Definitely not good-looking and boring conversationalists. You'd be saving me. Truly."

She laughed, utterly charmed. "How can I refuse?" The day suddenly looked much brighter. Definitely better than going home to a silent flat and scrounging for something appetizing.

"What do you fancy? I mean, other than bread and cheese."

"Pasta. I would love a plate of pasta and warm bread and salad. If that works for you."

"I know just the place. Pick you up at yours or from work?"

She checked the clock. How had it got to be four o'clock already? "I think from work. I'm not ready to leave yet, and by the time I go home and change... Is it too much trouble to come here?"

"Of course not. What time's good for you?"

"Six?"

"Perfect. See you then, Soph."

He hung up and Sophie put the phone down. How was it that her day went from blah to brilliant in a few moments, all because the charming and sexy Christophe Germain asked her out for dinner? Surely it wasn't just the company. It was the prospect of carbs and Bolognese, certainly. She was hungry. Lunch had been crackers, hummus, some veg, and fruit. Tasty, but not overly substantial.

No matter, there wasn't time to think about it too much. She still had a number of pieces to assess before she could leave for the day, and she'd faffed about with her sketching instead of sticking to her job.

At quarter to six she finally shut down her computer and locked everything away for the night before going into the bathroom and touching up her hair and makeup. Just because they were friends didn't mean she shouldn't put in a little effort. The fall day was cool, so she'd paired narrow trousers with heels and a collared blouse, and then a cashmere shawl as a wrap against the chill. With her hair up and a refresh of her mascara, her skin glowed and her eyes shone as she stared into the mirror.

This was not a date. It was Christophe and pasta. Nothing more. No reason to be excited or flushed.

He arrived precisely at six, just as she was walking out of Waltham's and onto the dark street. He rounded the hood to open her door and met her on the curb, stopping to buss her cheek with his lips. "You look better," he said warmly, stepping back. "Roses in your cheeks this time."

She was certain the roses took on a pinker hue at his words and hoped he didn't notice. He wore jeans and a bulky cream sweater that made him look both cuddly and incredible masculine, and the little bit of neatly trimmed facial hair was downright sexy. It occurred to her that for the first time she could remember, neither of them were dating anyone…

This was ridiculous. She shouldn't be thinking this way about Christophe. Particularly since she was pregnant and the idea of dating was now very, very different. There was no such thing as casual dating when a child was involved, was there? Even if that child wasn't yet born. "I'm feeling much better, thank you. And I'm hungry." She grinned at him, and he grinned back, and the old comfort between them returned.

He shut the door behind her and then got in the driver's seat. "Where are we going?" she asked.

"An old favorite of mine in Pimlico. Glad you're hungry. You won't be when you leave." He glanced over and grinned, then turned his attention back to the traffic. She marveled at how he weaved in and out with no anxiety whatsoever. She relaxed back against the seat, enjoying that for the second time in a week she was out with Christophe after months of not seeing him at all.

When they reached the restaurant, the street was packed so they parked a few blocks away and walked. A raw chill had descended with the darkness, and Sophie guessed that they were in for a bitter fall rain sooner rather than later. At the restaurant, Christophe opened the door for her and then chafed his hands as she passed by him. Once they were inside, though, all thoughts of the weather disappeared as the most gorgeous smells touched her nose. Tomato, garlic, the starchy scent of pasta and bread. Christophe came up behind her and put his hand lightly on her waist as a hostess approached. "Table for two?" she asked, and at Christophe's nod, she led them to a secluded corner.

It was every Italian cliché in one spot: the candle in the Chianti bottle, the checkered tablecloths, the music that could barely be heard above the happy chatter of the patrons. They'd been seated only a few moments when their server arrived to take drink orders.

"Still water for me, please," Sophie said.

"I'll have the same," Christophe ordered.

"Just because I'm not drinking doesn't mean you can't," she said once the server was gone. "It's okay. Truly."

"I'm driving again, remember?"

She laughed. "Oh, right. I'm so used to not having a car that it's usually not a consideration."

"Besides, it wouldn't be fair for me to enjoy a nice robust red while you're stuck with water."

"Ouch. You know how to hit a girl where it hurts."

He laughed. "Does it help if I remind you it's not forever?"

"No." She was gratified when he laughed at her flat response.

They looked at their menus. "I still want the spag bol," she said, closing it again. "I can't help it. I've been thinking about it ever since you called."

"Interesting. You've been thinking about pasta, and I've been thinking about you." His dark eyes held hers across the candlelit table and she bit down on her lip. Was he...flirting? Of course not. Why would he? They were friends, and she was pregnant with someone else's kid. But it felt nice anyway to be the center of his attention. Nothing would ever happen between them, but she could still enjoy the attention, couldn't she? Was that so very wrong?

"I highly doubt that," she returned, placing the menu on the table. "But I appreciate the compliment anyway."

He took a few moments to stare at her, and she was just getting to the uncomfortable stage when he spoke again. "I have been thinking of you, you know. About what's going on with you. About what you said the other night."

"Not you, too," she said with a groan. "You're not going to try to get me to change my mind about Eric, are you?"

As if on cue, her mobile rang. She fished it out of her purse and her stomach sank at the number on the ID. She rejected the call and put the phone down, but a few seconds later it rang again. Christophe raised his damnable eyebrow and she sighed. "Give me a sec," she muttered.

Eric's voice came on the line as she put the phone to her ear. "Sophie. I need to see you. We need to talk about this."

"Hello to you, too," she said, frustrated and embarrassed that this was happening in front of Christophe.

"I mean it, Soph. You can't keep avoiding me. I'm the baby's father."

"Yes, you are. And as I told you, I'll keep you updated on everything that's happening. You don't need to call me every day."

"I wouldn't have to if you'd quit this ridiculous... I don't know what to call it. Marry me. I can provide for both of you."

She closed her eyes against the repetitive argument. "I don't need you to provide for me. I can provide for myself. This isn't the 1950s, Eric."

"That's not what I meant."

But it kind of was, and they both knew it.

"Can we discuss this later, please?"

"Where are you, anyway?"

"I'm having dinner."

"With a man?"

He sounded so appalled she wanted to smash her phone on the table. She took a deep breath instead. "Eric, I'm going to say this just once more. You are the father of this baby and I wouldn't dream of keeping you from him or her. But I'm not going to marry you. I don't love you, Eric, not the way someone should if they're going to get married. A baby won't change that. So please, please, stop. This is bordering on harassment."

She felt Christophe's intense gaze on her and fought back the urge to cry. She refused to be the stereotypical emotional pregnant woman. Instead, she hung up the call and turned her phone off.

"Sorry," she said quietly.

"You have nothing to be sorry for." He reached across the table and took her hand. "Are you all right?"

She nodded. "A little anxious. His calls always do that to me."

"He calls a lot?"

She nodded again. "He doesn't like to take no for an answer. Oh," she continued, as Christophe's expression grew alarmed, "he'd never harm me. But he thinks he can convince me that marrying him is for the best. I'm sure he thinks he can wear me down. Have me come around to his way of seeing things."

"Ha. You're far too independent for that."

His simple words sent a warmth through her chest. Their server returned and Christophe ordered for them, choosing family-style servings of the Bolognese and salad. When the server departed, Christophe rubbed his thumb over the top of her hand. "I'll confess that I've been having trouble with this myself," he said. "I understand completely what you said to me the other night. I think you're right. And there's still a part of me that wonders if your little boy or girl will wonder why Dad isn't around. If they'll wonder if it was something they did."

Her heart melted a little. Christophe was still that little boy sometimes, unwanted and an afterthought. "I'll make sure that doesn't happen," she assured him. "And Eric plans to be involved. He's taking this responsibility seriously." *Too seriously*, she thought, but didn't say it out loud. "Honestly, I wish he'd just accept what I'm saying so we can work out what parenting is going to look like. I don't want to have him as an adversary. His constant pressure isn't helping."

"Maybe he really still loves you."

She shook her head. "But that's not enough, don't you see? He would have us marry for the sake of our child, but what about us? What about me? Don't I deserve to be happy, too?"

His face softened. "Of course, you do. I'm sorry, Sophie. I've been pushing where I shouldn't be. You get enough of that from Eric."

"And my parents."

"Then I promise I'll back off on the Eric thing. You're the best judge of your own happiness."

His willingness and openness took a weight off her shoulders. Their salad arrived, and Sophie dived at it both as a distraction and because she was so hungry her stomach was starting to get queasy again. She served them both helpings of the greens and then swirled a little olive oil and balsamic vinegar over top. The first bite was crisp and flavorful—a perfect choice.

When they'd eaten for a few moments, she asked, "Have you seen your new little cousin?"

"I have. Her name is Imogene and she's red and wrinkly."

Sophie nearly choked on a leaf of rocket. "You don't mean that!"

"Well, she was at first. She's not as red now. And her nose is like a little button." He smiled and touched the tip of his nose. "Hey, I have zero experience with babies and children. But I do have pictures."

He pulled out his phone and brought up his photos. "Here. There are three or four there."

She took the phone and stared down at the little sleeping face. Heavens, she was an angel, all long lashes and pouty lips and a fuzzy little cap of dark hair. Her heart did a big thump. In a few months she'd have her own little baby. She was so not prepared! And yet she was excited, too. There were other pictures of Charlotte with her sister, Bella, and sister-in-law, Gabi, and for the first time in a long time, Sophie wished she had a sister or two to share this with.

"She's gorgeous. Please send Charlotte my congratulations."

"You should call her yourself. She'd be delighted to hear from you."

Sophie wasn't so sure, as she wasn't as familiar with the other members of the Pemberton family. But it was a nice thought just the same.

"I have six months before this happens to me, and a lot to figure out by then." She frowned and handed him the phone back. "Life is going to change so much. Every now and again that sinks in and I get a tad stressed about it."

"I'm sorry it's not been easier for you. I mean, it's a big deal. It would be a big deal even if the two of you were still together, you know? Is there anything I can do to help?"

She smiled and picked up her fork again. "You're doing it. You're a lovely distraction, you know."

"Ouch. A distraction?"

"In the best possible way, darling." It was impossible not to smile back at him when he was so obviously teasing her. "You entertain. You're easy to look at and you feed me. And you don't ask me for answers I'm not ready to give. You're the perfect date, actually." Well, not quite perfect. There was still a missing ingredient, but she knew better than to look for it in Christophe.

"You're forgiven. And by the by, I have an idea. Do you know what you need?" Christophe pointed his fork at her, a slice of avocado stuck on the tines. "You need to get away for a bit. Take a few days off, have some time to escape and think and unwind. Give yourself some real self-care, as Bella would say."

She laughed. "You're forgetting my parents are on vacation. I can't leave Waltham without a captain at the helm."

"When are they back?"

"Saturday."

He speared some more salad and shrugged. "So next week, then. When *was* your last vacation, anyway?"

He had her there. She'd thrown herself into work after breaking up with Eric and had been so determined her pregnancy wouldn't affect her job that she hadn't missed a single minute. Even if some of those minutes had been spent in the employee bathroom.

"May," she admitted.

"I've got it." He sat back in his chair, a satisfied smile on his face. "It's perfect. You can come back to Paris with me. I'll be working, so you can have the days all to yourself. You can do whatever you like. You can visit Aurora, too, if you want, and I can show you next season's designs. But only if you want to. How can you say no to Paris?"

"And I'd be staying…with you." They were friends. There shouldn't be any sort of undertones. She'd always managed to keep her attraction to him tamped down. So why did the idea suddenly seem so intimate? Why was she looking at Christophe and appreciating all his attributes with new eyes? Pregnancy hormones? She'd heard of such a thing but hadn't believed it…until now. Christophe wasn't just charming and handsome. He was desirable. She resisted the urge to hide her face in her hands. He must never find out the thought had even crossed her mind.

"My flat's more than big enough. There's an extra room and a big kitchen and you'd have your own bathroom. You'd hardly have to see me if you didn't want to." He winked at her. "But I can be rather charming company."

She laughed then. He'd made her laugh more in their two evenings together than she had in weeks, and it felt good. Normal. She almost said *What will people say*? But that went against everything she believed in...mostly, minding your own business. She didn't have to explain herself. Especially not to staying with a trusted friend for a few days to decide exactly what steps to take next. Nothing would happen because whatever attraction there was, it was completely one-sided. And as long as Christophe never knew, it would be fine.

Besides, she did love Paris.

"I'd have to make sure my cat sitter is available to look after Harry."

Their pasta arrived then, and the conversation halted as they placed servings in bowls. It smelled absolutely heavenly, and she twirled some pasta around her fork and popped it into her mouth...delicious.

"I told you this place was good," he said, twirling his pasta expertly and taking a bite. "Mmm."

Spaghetti was a messy dish, and not one she'd generally order if this were a date. There was too much potential to get sauce on her face or have a piece of pasta take on a will of its own. Yet with Christophe she didn't mind. It was the strangest thing. One moment she was noticing all sorts of things about him and then next, she was the most comfortable she'd been in weeks. She picked up her napkin and wiped her chin.

That she was actually considering going to Paris told her that she'd been going full tilt for too long and needed some downtime. Work was one thing, but the breakup had been hard to begin with. The pregnancy complicated that a hundred times over. Emotionally she was worn out. Physically she was exhausted.

"You're serious about your offer? To stay with you for a few days?"

He nodded. "Of course. There's more than enough room. What are friends for?"

Friends indeed. As they continued their meal, Sophie wondered how everything could possibly work out the way she wanted…peacefully. Maybe she'd come to some conclusions when she had a chance to remove herself from the situation a bit. And if she got a chance to get an early look at the new Aurora Gems line, all the better.

Christophe wasn't sure what had prompted him to suggest Sophie get away to Paris, and now the idea of having her in his flat sent a strange sort of hollow feeling to his belly. Had he been wrong to offer?

He hadn't liked seeing the strain on her face as she'd taken her ex's call. He'd met Eric and thought he was a decent guy, but clearly he wasn't handling this situation well. Christophe also appreciated Sophie's assertion that she would never try to keep the child away from their father. It seemed that Eric's problem wasn't about being a dad, it was about letting Sophie go. Whether it was love or pride, it didn't matter. Harassing her wasn't okay.

He also knew Sophie would be justifiably angry if he approached Eric on his own. That left giving her space and time to sort some things out and get some rest.

"Dessert?" he asked, when their pasta bowls had been removed.

"I couldn't possibly. I haven't eaten that much since my morning sickness began." She smiled at him, and he noticed the edge of her top lip was slightly orange from the sauce. He lifted his napkin and wiped the smudge away while her cheeks pinkened.

"Good. I'm glad." He took out a card to pay the bill and

then sat back in his chair. "I was planning to go home on Sunday, and back in the office on Monday. We could travel together if you like."

"This all feels quite spontaneous," she said, and she frowned, a tiny wrinkle forming between her brows. "I'm not sure…"

"It's up to you. If it makes you feel better, you can make it a working trip with a light schedule." He smiled at her, knowing she was more likely to agree if he appealed to her practical side. "Waltham distributes our Gems line. You'd get a firsthand look at the new designs. Give some feedback, even."

Her eyes sparkled at him. "You mean have input into Aurora's jewels? That's a big deal, Christophe."

"Unofficially, of course. Unless you're looking for a job. Are you?"

Was that temptation he saw on her face? She looked as if the word "yes" was sitting on the tip of her tongue, and that surprised him. Waltham was the family business and she'd always seemed happy there.

"I'm not, but this is certainly a wonderful opportunity."

"You must take it easy, though. Get rest. Relax. It would be good for you and the baby, too."

"I thought you didn't know much about babies," she pointed out, picking up her water glass and taking a sip. There was a teasing glint in her eye. That hadn't changed. They still loved teasing each other. Not quite flirting, not quite not. His gaze dropped to her lips and he wondered what it might be like to kiss her.

The idea had his blood running hot and he tamped the response down. If she knew what had just passed through his brain, she certainly wouldn't agree to stay at his flat. He couldn't think of Sophie that way. It was just *wrong*.

Besides, he wouldn't endanger their friendship by messing it up with sex.

"I don't need to know a lot to know that taking care of yourself is good for both of you."

She nodded. "You're not wrong." After a moment or two, she nodded again. "All right. Let me run this past my parents first, as they'll be returning in a few days and will have to take up my slack while I'm gone. And like I mentioned, I have to make sure Harry's sitter is available."

"That's all fine. You can just text me to let me know either way, and I'll send you the travel arrangements. We're flying out of Gatwick."

"We?"

He grinned. "Why, Bella and Burke, of course. They're returning, as well. Stephen and Will already went back this morning."

"So your whole family will know."

"They don't need to know anything," he assured her. "Just that I've invited you to have a look at the new line. They know we're friends, Soph. You don't need to tell anyone about the baby if you don't want to. That's entirely your call. I won't say a word."

The server brought back his credit card and as he was tucking it back into his wallet, Sophie spoke again. "Why are you doing all this, Christophe?"

He pondered for a moment, and then thought back to his own childhood, and his mother, and even Charlotte and Jacob's new baby. "Because you need a friend. Because maybe if someone had been kind to my mother, she might not have been forced into a marriage with a man who abandoned her anyway." The truth hit him square in the chest, opening old wounds, but somehow eradicating the infection within. "My parents married because she got pregnant, and it ended in disaster. She married him because she didn't have options and he still left her without a penny. You do have options. And you deserve to be happy, Sophie. You deserve that so much."

He swallowed against a lump in his throat. For all of his charmed life, at least since he'd been nine, there'd always been the knowledge that he wasn't a true Pemberton. He was the poor relation. He worked hard to earn his place in the family ranks, and of course everyone had always been good to him. His cousins loved him and he loved them. But that small difference held on stubbornly, like a splinter under the skin that tweezers just couldn't reach. As if somehow his acceptance and worth was tied into his value at Aurora, Inc.

He had so many conflicting feelings about his upbringing that he wasn't sure what to think. A child deserved two parents who loved each other. But love couldn't be forced, so what was the alternative?

The answer was suddenly clear. Two parents who were, if not in love, at least committed to being parents.

No matter what happened, Sophie was going to be tied to Eric forever. He hadn't actually considered that before. They were broken up, but their relationship had simply changed. The last thing he wanted to do was get in the way of that.

Which meant his earlier thought of kissing Sophie could never be realized.

He helped her put on her wrap, swallowing tightly when his fingers brushed her shoulders. They walked quietly back to the car, a light drizzle hurrying their steps. "You were right about the rain," he said, trying to shift any conversation back to safe, uncharged topics.

"It's not bad yet," she said, and then, fifty yards from the car, the drizzle changed to icy droplets that clung to his hair and the wool of his sweater.

"You were saying?" he asked, and then they dashed for the car, Sophie's heels clicking on the pavement in a rapid staccato. He hit the locks on the key fob, and they flung open the doors and hurried to get in, shutting the doors again and laughing.

"I tempted fate with that one," she admitted, brushing some damp strands of hair off her face.

If she only knew. Looking at her now, beneath the light of the streetlamp and with rain droplets clinging to her face and hair, Christophe made a startling discovery.

Sophie had been right in front of him all along. And it was his bad luck that he'd waited until now to notice. Or perhaps it was for the best, because the last thing he wanted was to hurt her. Which he surely would if they were to get involved.

Sophie Waltham wanted what he could never give her: love and commitment.

CHAPTER FOUR

SOPHIE WAS AT her parents' house in Kensington when they arrived back from their trip, happy and tired. She was full of anxiety about the visit, as she didn't want a repeat of past conversations of late. Most of which concerned the baby and Eric and basically pigeonholing her into a marriage she didn't want. Wasn't it enough she was taking over the family business? Shouldn't she have some choices left?

The sharpness of the thought took her by surprise, and she let out a breath before moving forward to give her mum a hug. She loved Waltham. She did. She was only feeling cornered just now, that was all. Like nothing in her life was within her control.

"Hello, darling. How are you feeling?"

Sophie smiled. "I have my moments, but everything's okay. How was your trip?"

Her father came in with the cases and stopped to give her a kiss, then kept on toward the bedroom. "It was just lovely," her mother said. "Prague is so gorgeous. We had a marvelous time."

"I'm so glad."

"And how about you?"

"Well, I want to talk to you and Dad about that. How about I put on some tea?"

"I'd love a good cup. I shall need to put in an order from the market. There's nothing in the house."

"Oh, but there is. I picked up a few essentials on my way. We can have tea and biscuits at least, and I grabbed an entrée for you to heat up for you and Dad tonight, as well."

"You're so thoughtful." The praise was punctuated by a loving squeeze on her wrist. "And how is Eric?"

Sophie rolled her eyes and took a full breath. "I wouldn't know, since we're still not together."

"Sophie."

She put the kettle on and got out the package of biscuits. "No, Mum. And to be honest, he's putting a lot of stress on me right now, so I'd rather not talk about him."

Her mother pursed her lips, but thankfully said nothing more about Eric.

"Do you know who I did run into, though? Christophe. He was at the engagement party. It was very nice to catch up after so long."

The mention of Christophe Germain was a deliberate plant in order to get her mum off her back. Christophe was gorgeous, rich, and part of the Pemberton family. He wasn't an aristocrat, but he was related, and heaven knew he checked all the right boxes where her family was concerned. More than that, the Walthams had always liked him. Easy to see why. He was incredibly likable.

"How is he? So sad about Cedric, but lovely that the family seems to be getting settled. This is the third engagement this year."

"The wedding isn't until spring, or so Bella said. I'm sure it'll be a grand affair."

"You're due in the spring," her mum said. Because of course, every topic of conversation should somehow make its way back to her pregnancy.

Sophie prepared the teapot and before long they took a

tray to the living room. Her dad had reappeared, changed into casual trousers and a fresh button-down, and she poured him a cup of tea. "Here you go, Dad. Fresh cup, one sugar, no milk."

"You're a blossom."

She laughed, then continued pouring. "Actually, I came to talk to you both about something. I know you're just back, but how would you feel about me going to Paris for a few days this coming week?"

Her dad hesitated with the cup halfway to his mouth. "Paris? What's in Paris?"

Christophe, she thought, but pushed the thought away. "I've been invited to have a look at Aurora Gems' new line for next year and offer some feedback." She figured it was far better to take the first approach from a business angle. "It puts me out of the office just as you're back, but everything is caught up on the schedule and the shop is managing just fine. I'll be back before we reset the store-front for the holidays."

Her mother reached for a biscuit. "I suppose Christophe invited you?"

"He did. He's running the division now. All the children have director positions, actually. I have expertise that he doesn't. We've been friends a long time, Mum. And truthfully... You know I love Waltham, but I'd like to get out in the industry a little more before the company becomes my responsibility. Knowledge can never hurt, and this is almost like acting as a consultant. It's an incredible opportunity."

"It's a grand idea," her dad said, taking a hearty sip, then smacking his lips as the tea was still piping hot. "I'm sure we can manage just fine for the week." He looked at her closely. "After all, we're going to have to manage when you have the baby, aren't we?"

Her mother was far less enthusiastic. "Shouldn't you be more worried about making plans for the future?"

Meaning, patching things up with Eric. Her mother was nothing if not consistent.

"I am planning for the future. The future of Waltham. Besides, it's not a grueling schedule while I'm there. Getting away from London and having a little time to think might give me the clarity I need."

Boom.

"It might not be a bad idea," her mother admitted. "When do you leave?"

"I'd fly over tomorrow with Christophe, Bella, and Viscount Downham." When it came to her mother, it never hurt to throw in a title.

"It's short notice. But I suppose it will be fine. What about Harry?"

"I have my service taking care of him for the week. I'll be back by Friday." They were getting into a busy season, with the holidays right around the corner, and it wasn't unheard-of for the Walthams to spend time behind the counter during a busy retail season. "I know it's a hectic time of year. I won't stay away long."

She took a sip of tea, telling herself the tiny bit of caffeine in a single cup wasn't going to do any harm and was worth it for family harmony.

"And you're feeling all right?"

"I'm fine, Mum. Truly. But I should get back so I can pack for tomorrow. If you need me, I'll have my mobile on."

"Oh, that's good. I'll be sure to check in—"

"No, you won't," interrupted her father, who aimed a stern look at his wife. "We agreed to give Sophie space. She can figure this out on her own."

Sophie's lips dropped open in surprise as she stared at her dad. She honestly hadn't expected the support as he'd also put in his two cents about reconciling with Eric. It seemed now, though, he was backing off, and it took a substantial weight off her shoulders.

"I truly can," she assured them. "I just need some time and space to do that. I appreciate you giving it to me."

Her mother didn't look pleased but said nothing more. As Sophie said her goodbyes and headed home to pack, she realized she was more than ready to leave London, and all its pressures, behind for a few days.

Christophe waited impatiently for Sophie to arrive. Bella and Burke were already here, and their departure was supposed to be in twenty minutes. He checked his phone again—no call, no text. He hoped she hadn't changed her mind.

A few moments later he looked up to see her rushing down the corridor. "I'm so sorry," she called, her heels clicking on the floor. "There was an accident and traffic got backed up. I planned to be here thirty minutes ago!"

She reached him, slightly out of breath, pulling her suitcase behind her. Her cheeks were pink from the jog and her normally tidy hair was coming out of its anchor, some sort of bun on the back of her head. But she was smiling, as if she were truly happy to see him.

"Better late than never," he said, leaning over to kiss her cheek. "I see you've come prepared." He sent a pointed look at her rather large suitcase.

"Clothes for casual, different clothes for visiting the offices, and one nice dress in case something formal crops up. I am indeed prepared for anything."

He got the sense she always was. Prepared, that is. Sophie always seemed to have herself together. It made her current predicament all the more unusual.

"The pilot is ready for us to board," Burke called over. "Hello, Sophie."

"Burke. It's good to see you again."

"I'm delighted you're joining us."

Bella waved and gave her a big smile. "Me, too! It's been too long."

They all boarded the jet and got settled, and before long they were in the air for the short flight to Paris. Christophe had made sure there was a ready stock of beverages on board so she could have her choice, including peppermint tea. She chose orange juice, though, while the rest of them drank strong coffee and nibbled on biscotti.

"So you're joining us for work and pleasure, I hear," Bella said, looking between Christophe and Sophie.

"It looks that way. I'm dying to get my hands on the Aurora jewels."

Burke burst out laughing and Sophie blushed, while Christophe grinned and reached for another chocolate-dipped biscotti.

"You guys and your dirty minds," Bella chided, but chuckled. "Sorry, Sophie."

Sophie was laughing too, her face half covered with a hand. "I walked right into it. Anyway, when Christophe asked if I'd like to see the new line, I couldn't resist. I haven't left London for months. It'll be good for me."

They chatted a while longer about the business, but the flight got a little bumpy and the pilot asked them to put their seat belts on. Christophe looked over at Sophie and realized she'd turned that gray color again. He leaned over and whispered, "Are you okay?"

"I think so," she replied. "I don't usually get air sick…"

He reached into a compartment and took out a bag. "Here, just in case."

"I don't want to…in front of…"

"I know. It's just for insurance. Hopefully we'll be through it soon."

He kept an eye on her for the next ten minutes, saw her close her eyes a few times and swallow convulsively. Sympathy welled inside him. He hadn't really talked to Charlotte about her pregnancy and didn't think she'd been particularly unwell. But this was different somehow. Charlotte had Jacob. Sophie had…well, Sophie was well-loved, but it wasn't the same as having a partner there to share it with.

The turbulence finally cleared, and then it seemed no time at all and they were preparing for their approach. When they landed, Christophe shouldered his single bag and then reached for Sophie's suitcase.

"I can manage that," she said.

"But why would you, if you don't have to?" He gave her a shrug, and she pursed her lips but didn't respond. He didn't mind pulling her case along and would have felt like a heel, walking along with his small carry-on and leaving her to tug her full bag. "I've got a car waiting to take us to the flat. We'll be there in no time." He gave her elbow a nudge. "Hopefully you won't get car sick."

He was teasing but she sent him a wry grin. "I put the bag in my purse just in case."

She was so practical. He kind of loved that about her. The drive to his flat on Avenue de Wagram was a half hour, give or take. Traffic was light since it was Sunday, and as they zipped along, Sophie told him about her conversation with her parents. "It's strange," she said, "but when I said I was taking a few days away I got the sense they were hesitant. As soon as I used the word 'consultant,' though, they brightened right up."

"Maybe they're just used to you being a bit of a workaholic," he suggested. "You've dedicated a lot of your time to your studies and then to the company. When do you ever spontaneously take time off with no reason?"

She seemed to ponder his words. "You think I'm a workaholic?"

"I think you're driven. And organized. And because of it, taking time with no purpose seems strange to you, and therefore probably to them, too."

"That's very insightful."

"I live in a family of driven women. It's not such a stretch to recognize it." He lifted a shoulder. "Maybe breaking up with Eric was the first nonpractical thing you've done in a while. Having a baby complicates it, though." He frowned. "You're going to be tied to him forever."

"I know." She sighed deeply, and the sad sound reached in and touched his heart. He hated seeing her so distressed. He was sure he was right about the work thing, though. While he admired her work ethic, the all-work-and-no-play thing couldn't be sustained forever. Perhaps she was starting to realize that.

He recalled the comment she'd made about Eric working all the time. One thing he knew for sure: Sophie would put her all into motherhood the same way she put it into everything she did.

"Sorry. I didn't mean to bring you down. How do you feel about ordering something in? I will cook for you this week, though. I'm actually very good in the kitchen." He really wanted to treat her; let her relax and be cared for.

"I'm game for whatever," she answered. "Except seafood. It's killing me, too. Normally I love it."

"Noted. And…we're here."

The car pulled up outside his building and he sent Sophie a smile. For the next five days, they were roommates.

Sophie tried to calm the nerves in her stomach as she exited the car and Christophe retrieved her bag. He was right about one thing. She didn't do spontaneous things. Her life was planned and orderly, though perhaps not quite as rigid as he'd made it sound. Still, agreeing to stay with him at his flat for the better part of a week and leaving work behind was definitely more adventurous than normal.

Four and a half days. With Christophe. In his flat.

She hadn't had a roommate for a few years now and it showed, she realized, as she followed him to the lift that would take them to the fifth floor. Without someone else to balance her out, she'd become a creature of habit, only accountable to herself and her cat, who also liked to be fed on time and was very vocal if his schedule wasn't adhered to. The elevator hummed as it ascended, and she tried to quell the butterflies that had taken up residence in her belly. This would be fine. Christophe was wonderful and he wasn't interested in her *that* way. And why would he be? Being pregnant with another man's child had to be a pretty big turnoff. This really couldn't be any safer.

And why was she thinking this way, as if she wanted him to be? Maybe she needed to get out of her own head a bit.

"Here we are," he said as the lift door opened.

The wheels on her suitcase echoed in the hall as she followed him down the corridor to his door. He opened the door and stepped inside, pulling her case in and making room for her to enter. "Welcome to your home away from home," he said warmly. "Consider whatever I have yours for the duration."

"This is lovely." Indeed it was. The small foyer led to an open concept room with large windows facing the street, letting in tons of natural light and giving the entire space an airy appearance. His furniture was simple yet comfortable looking, with oak floors and golden draperies dropping in columns at the side of each window. To the left was the kitchen area, with all sorts of natural wood and gleaming appliances, including a double wall oven. Above the breakfast bar was a rack that held at least a dozen wineglasses. She glanced over to the working area and said, "Does that door open onto a terrace?"

"It is. I grow my own herbs out there."

"You...grow your own herbs?"

"I told you I liked to cook, and herbs are actually quite easy. In the colder months, I bring them in, see?" He gestured to a large, sculpted iron stand holding several plant pots.

She'd known Christophe for years but had not known this about him. She realized suddenly that she'd never visited him at any of his homes over the years other than the manor house, and she'd only been there a time or two. A person's home was key to their personality, and she realized this space reflected Christophe perfectly: warm, bright and without the need for affectation. She loved it.

"Come with me. I'll show you to the guest room."

He led her down the hall to where the bedrooms were. Presumably his room was on the left, and hers on the right. Her window was smaller, at the end of the room, but it still provided lots of natural light. Tawny beige curtains hung to the floor, and the bed was plush with an upholstered headboard and a duvet the color of the sand she remembered from the beach in Cornwall, where her parents had taken them in summers long ago. Simpler, easier days filled with the ocean and ice cream.

"This is perfect," she said, turning around to look at Christophe. "It's so relaxing and serene."

"I hope you'll be comfortable." He smiled at her and stood her suitcase just inside the door. "Over here is your bathroom."

He opened a door and she stepped into her own bath. Beige tiles and white fixtures kept up the light, airy feeling of the bedroom, and there were fluffy towels sitting on a table, waiting for her. A huge tub promised long, relaxing soaks, and there was also an oversize, glassed-in shower. The potential for relaxation was huge.

"I feel so pampered," she finally replied, facing him. "This is gorgeous. Your whole place is."

"Thanks. It's the first place that has been all mine, so I'm glad you like it."

"You chose everything?" She hadn't really considered him the decorating type, but maybe he truly did have a keen eye.

"Oh, no." He laughed. "I had help. I had a decorator help me pick the pieces. I had a strong hand in it, though. I knew what I wanted, and she knew how to make it happen."

Sophie loved every square inch of it so far. It was completely different from her flat in Chelsea and nearly twice the size, but it was absolutely perfect for Christophe and for the space.

"Why don't you get settled? Come out when you're ready, and we can decide on dinner. You're going to love the view from the terrace, too. Paris at night is too good to miss."

"Thank you, I will." She wanted to unpack and perhaps take off her heels.

He left her then, and she let out a breath. Christophe was going to be the perfect host, she could tell. Charming, polite, accommodating...perfect. So why did she feel uneasy? Was it simply because she was doing something a bit out of character, or was there something more to it? Like a six foot one with curly hair something?

CHAPTER FIVE

WHEN HER CLOTHES were hung in the closet and tucked away in the dresser, Sophie changed out of her dress and heels and put on leggings and an Irish wool sweater—perfect for relaxing in. She'd brought a book with her, too, as she didn't expect Christophe to entertain her every moment. But he did want to have dinner tonight, and as she'd unpacked the sun had slipped below the horizon, shadowing the city skyline. She supposed now was as good a time as any to venture out.

She opened the door and went to the living room, which glowed from the light of a pair of lamps. "Hello again," she said.

"Hi, yourself." Christophe was in the kitchen, pouring something into glasses. "Cocktail?"

"Um…" She couldn't imagine he would have forgotten she was alcohol-free, but it certainly looked like he was using a shaker.

He came around the corner with a pair of glasses. One had a slice of lemon, the other, orange. He handed her the one with the orange. "Don't worry," he said, treating her to that warm smile again. "Yours is a variation. I looked up how to make it without alcohol and I had all the ingredients, so…"

She looked into the drink. "What is it?"

"A French 75. Mine's the gin and champagne version. Yours is tonic and bitters and lemon juice. A little sugar." He was watching her hopefully. "Try it."

She tried a sip and found it to be tart and refreshing. "Oh, that's nice."

"And it won't put you on your ass."

She burst out laughing, nearly spilling the drink. "Fair enough. Thank you."

"I thought about dinner and there's a restaurant I like a few streets over that will deliver. If I promise no seafood, do you trust my selections?"

She blinked, unsure how to answer. This whole trip was out of her comfort zone, but she wasn't sure how much control she was willing to relinquish. It was only a menu selection, but it was still one more decision, however small, out of her hands. Still, perhaps she needed to learn to be more flexible and trusting.

"I promise that if you don't like it, I'll make you whatever you want."

She laughed. "How about if I pick dessert?"

"That sounds like a fair compromise to me. I trust you." He handed her his phone, with the dessert menu up already. She scanned the offerings—so much deliciousness—and chose the lemon tart, a particular favorite.

"Hmm. Lemon. I had you pegged as a crème caramel kind of girl."

"Anything lemon. I love it." She held up her drink. "Which is why this is particularly tasty. Thank you."

"You're welcome."

He placed the order and while he was on the phone, Sophie went to her room and took her sketch pad out of the dresser. If she wanted to set the tone for the visit as platonic and businesslike, it made sense to talk shop. No one had seen her drawings yet, but she trusted Christophe to be honest and fair. Besides, he was the head of Aurora's jewelry division. It made sense to get his input before casting a wider net. Hopefully they were good, and she wasn't about to embarrass herself.

"What have you got there?" he asked, crossing an ankle over his knee.

"The stuff I've been working on. You said you liked my pearl and diamond piece, but I've got a lot of ideas in here that I'd like to run by you. Not just if they're aesthetically pleasing, but if they're even marketable."

"Exciting. I love that you've been designing a little."

"Just a few pieces as samples and for myself. If these have any potential, I'd like to look at doing my own collection or something."

"Someone is spreading their wings," he mused, his tone approving. "Let's have a look."

Her heart stuttered as she handed over the sketchbook. It took a lot of trust to let him see what she'd been up to for the past few months. He opened it and gave each drawing a solid perusal before flipping to the next page. "I like this a lot," he said, lifting the book to show a sketch of a slim gold bracelet with a bumblebee held in place by two honeycomb-shaped pieces. "It's simple and youthful. What do you think for the gems? Onyx and yellow diamond?"

"I was thinking more a yellow tourmaline for a deeper color."

He nodded thoughtfully, turning the page.

"These next few pages are a different concept. I got looking at classic paintings and how to translate those into—"

"Smaller works of art," he finished for her. "I get it. This is gorgeous. Tourmaline again?"

"Citrine. With diamond, sapphire, aquamarine."

He kept looking, pursing his lips occasionally, nodding as well. She held her breath, waiting for his verdict.

"You've been busy," he said, closing the book and handing it back to her.

Her heart sank. That was it? "It hasn't felt like being busy at all. It's been more like a treat to myself." She was determined not to let him see her disappointment. "A chance to be creative. It's no big deal."

Christophe patted the cushion beside him. "Sit down. You're all tensed up. Did you think I wouldn't like them? I do. Very much. You should show them to François, our head designer."

She sank onto the sofa. "Wait. I thought you didn't like them."

He laughed. "Of course I like them. You're talented and inventive, with a great sense of color and balance." He turned a little sideways and looked into her eyes. "It's not like you to be insecure."

His insight was startling and accurate. "Maybe because it's different, and it's…creative. I'm not so sure of my abilities in this area."

He flipped open the pad to the page where she'd pasted a small pic of Monet's *The Artist's Garden* and pointed at the sketch below. "Your use of color here, and shape. It's perfect for an open neckline and yet not too deep."

"I envisioned it as a Princess style, as the stones and settings are substantial. It'd be heavy."

"Exactly. And amethyst is perfect here, with peridot and emerald above and chocolate diamonds below. So unusual and yet it absolutely works." He tapped at the picture. "I'm not a designer, but my instinct is the balance at the bottom might be off a bit. I love the concept, though." Then he flipped to the pink sapphire in the shape of the ballerina gown. "This is lovely, too. I can see it repeated in earrings with a marquise cut diamond above. What do you think?"

She could see it clearly. More than that, Christophe was showing genuine interest in something that meant a lot to her but that she'd kept to herself for fear of looking foolish. She doubted he'd understand how grateful she was, so she nodded and merely said, "Yes, I agree. I hadn't thought of the diamond above, but shaped right it absolutely mimics the dancer's body. I like it."

Then he turned back a few more pages to the Van Gogh. "This," he said, "is perfect as it is. The ring and the necklace."

"I'm partial to that one, too," she replied. "Thank you, Christophe. I was so afraid to show them to you, but I don't want my ideas to sit in a drawer, either."

He patted her hand. "I'm thrilled you trusted me with them."

"I trust you with a lot," she admitted, and their gazes clung for a few charged moments. She must trust him, for she was here, wasn't she? He was the only one outside her parents to know about the baby. Truthfully, she was putting a lot of faith in him, and it frightened her.

His phone rang with a call from the lobby, and he grinned at her. "Food's here. I hope you're hungry."

The interruption banished her thoughts, and within a few minutes they were seated at his dining table. Christophe had lit candles and got them each sparkling water to drink, then plated the food from the restaurant and served it to her with a flourish. "Madame," he said, putting the plate before her.

Her mouth watered just looking at it. A delicious pinwheel of rolled pork Florentine, plus a puffy and perfect cheese and herb souffle and *haricots verts amandine*. "Christophe, this looks amazing."

* * *

The food was superb, and so was the company. Over the course of the dinner they chatted and laughed, and Sophie got caught up on all the Pemberton family happenings of the past year. It was hard to believe how much had happened since she'd sat in the chapel at Chatsworth Manor for Stephen's wedding that wasn't. Despite the coverage in the tabloids, several details had been kept quiet. She realized, as they chatted, that as much as she trusted Christophe, he trusted her, too. Otherwise, he wouldn't be so open about his family and the intimate details.

She liked that. It made her feel as if they were equals, something that had often been missing in her past relationship.

After he removed the plates, he returned with the lemon tart. At the first bite, she closed her eyes and simply savored the tart smoothness of it, the buttery, flaky crust. "Oh, my God. This is perfection."

When she opened her eyes, he was smiling at her, his dark gaze warm and amused, but with an edge of something more. She quickly dotted her lips with her napkin and hoped she wasn't blushing.

Now she'd created atmosphere, all because she'd groaned over her dessert. She started another conversation, hoping to dispel the moment, but the way he'd looked at her sat in the pit of her stomach, a delicious, scary sort of something that she didn't want to feel when it came to Christophe. She needed a friend right now. She didn't need her crush getting in the way this week. Or him getting any ideas. One of them was bad enough.

She insisted on helping him clean up, so they went into his kitchen and she rinsed plates while he put them in the dishwasher. She was just handing him the flatware when her mobile rang.

She took it out of her pocket, looked at the display and ignored it, shoving it back into her pocket again.

"Eric?"

"Right on cue."

Christophe took the cutlery and put it in the rack. "He really doesn't know when to give up, does he?" Christophe's eyes took on that stormy look again, which she was learning was his "protective" look.

"No, he doesn't. I think he's sure he'll wear me down. If anything, it's just making me resent him more. I wish he could just accept that I won't marry him so we can move on and sort out what co-parenting is going to look like."

Her phone vibrated in her pocket, announcing she'd received a voice mail.

Christophe paused his tidying up and leaned back against a counter. "I can make myself scarce if you want to listen to that."

"No, it's fine. You might as well hear. Unless it makes you uncomfortable, in which case I'll go into my room."

"Not uncomfortable, exactly. I just don't like seeing you distressed. I want to help."

"Why?"

He tilted his head a little as he looked at her. "Because I've known you a long time, and we're friends, and I really don't like to see anyone bullied."

"I'm not sure I'd call it bullying. It's more desperation on his part, and a lack of understanding about what I really want."

"And what do you want?"

She met his gaze. "Love. I won't marry for anything less. My child will see a happy marriage with two people who love each other and are totally devoted to each other, or they won't see a marriage at all."

She took out the phone again and hit the buttons to play the voice mail.

"Sophie, it's Eric. You need to start taking my calls. This is ridiculous. I stopped by your work today and your father said you'd gone away for a few days? And you didn't think to tell me? Sophie, come on. It's time to stop being foolish. You know marrying me is for the best. I know you don't want our child being born a bastard. Call me, please."

The message ended and Sophie lifted her gaze to Christophe's. His mouth was hanging open and his eyebrows—both of them—were raised. And not in a teasing fashion.

"If you're looking for romance, you're not going to find it there," he said. "Wow."

"Our relationship was always comfortable. Not a great passion, if you know what I mean."

One eyebrow came down, the other stayed up, and she started to laugh. "Well, okay. I mean, passionate enough I got pregnant. But you know what I'm saying."

"I do."

"I don't like that he's pestering my father." She put the phone on the countertop and then twisted her fingers together. "I have to do something, but I don't know what. Nothing I say makes him give up. I've tried over and over to tell him that I want him to be a part of the baby's life, I just don't want to marry him, and it's like he doesn't hear me at all."

"Maybe he regrets losing you. Even so, I can't believe he said what he did about his kid being a bastard. Who does that?"

Her heart melted a little. Who, indeed? Christophe knew more than anyone how horrible that must feel as a child. "If you're going to tell me he's right, I'm going to stop you right there," she warned.

"I'm not going to tell you anything of the sort. But you can't marry him."

"I can't?" She looked up in surprise.

"No," he said firmly. "Because you're going to marry me."

CHAPTER SIX

"YOU'VE GOT TO BE JOKING," Sophie said, stepping away. "Didn't you hear what I just said? That I would only marry for love or not at all?"

Christophe nodded, his posture still relaxed and in control. She, on the other hand, wasn't sure if she wanted to run or cry, but every muscle in her body had tensed. She'd expected a lot of things from Christophe, but this wasn't one of them. Marry him? It was impossible. He was suggesting the exact same solution as Eric, just substituting himself as the groom. How did that solve anything?

"I did," he answered, "and I agree with you."

"Christophe," she said slowly, not wanting to be cruel in any way, "we are not in love." She would admit to herself that she was attracted to him, but that wasn't love. She was smart enough to discern one from the other.

A smile spread across his face. "Well, I know that, and you know that, but no one else knows that."

"I'm confused."

"I'm suggesting we get engaged for appearances. Think about it. It'll get your parents off your back, and Eric won't have any choice but to accept your refusal if you're engaged to someone else. With that out of the way, your conversations can focus on the baby and how you want to share custody. Meanwhile, I have a date for the Aurora,

Inc. holiday party." He winked at her, as if he had it all figured out.

"Wait. I need to sit down for a moment."

"Of course. Do you mind if I have a glass of something?"

"Not at all." She went into the living room, leaving him in the kitchen, and sank onto the plush sofa. He was proposing a fake engagement. It was the craziest, most outlandish idea, so why was she even hearing him out?

Engaged. To Christophe Germain.

For the flash of a moment, she had an image of what it might be like if they were actually together. There'd be laughter for sure, and lots of wonderful conversation. But passion? Would there be that?

Then she remembered how he'd looked at her at the restaurant last week, his dark eyes smoldering across the table, and her stomach tumbled. Yes, she decided, there would be passion between them.

This was ludicrous.

He came in with a glass of what looked to be cognac and put it on the coffee table as he sat down next to her. "You all right?"

"I'm still trying to wrap my head around what you just said," she admitted. "You want us to pretend to be engaged."

"Yes. For appearances only. Just to buy you some time to deal with everything you need to deal with."

Sophie bit down on her lip. "You realize this sounds like some archaic way of offering me your protection, right?"

He chuckled. "Are you saying I have a knight in shining armor complex?"

"If the shoe fits, Germain."

He was quiet for a moment, then his eyebrows dropped and his lips sobered. "Perhaps I do. It just disturbs me to see you upset every time he calls. Like I said, if you and I are engaged, he'll have to stop proposing."

She couldn't believe she was considering it. "We'd be lying to everyone."

"Yes, we would. So it's okay if you say no. I'm throwing it out there as an option to solve your current problem." He put his hands over hers. "Sophie, I hope you know you can trust me."

She did know that. "It's the only reason I haven't said no yet. I trust you to keep your word. I've never known you not to."

She was transported back several years to that night of too much wine and shared confidences. They'd been young and foolish, and she in particular had overindulged. She'd awakened the next morning snug in her bed, still in her clothes but tucked under the covers, a glass of water and a bottle of paracetamol on the nightstand. She didn't remember going to bed. After, her roommate had told her the story of how she'd draped herself over Christophe, clearly flirting, and when she'd passed out, he'd carried her into bed and taken care of her. He could have left her sprawled in the living room, but he didn't. He'd made sure she was safe and comfortable before sleeping in a cramped chair. He hadn't even slept on top of her covers. That night was the beginning of Sophie really developing feelings for him. He was the most gentlemanly man she knew.

Her phone buzzed again, still on the kitchen counter, but she heard the notification and tensed. If pretending to be with Christophe would get Eric off her back, then maybe she should just do it.

"What if it doesn't work?"

"Then we call it off, no harm, no foul."

"And how long would we pretend?"

"As long as you need. As I told you in London, I have

no desire to join my cousins in their pursuit of matrimony. You won't be cramping my style at all. In fact, you'd conveniently give me a plus-one to events. You'd be my cover and I'd be yours." He sounded completely happy with the idea.

"I see." But she didn't, not really. She still couldn't quite understand what was in it for him. It didn't make sense. She'd seen him with Lizzy. He'd looked contented and happy. Maybe their breakup had affected him more than he wanted to let on.

"Why don't you take your time to think about it this week? You can still get some relaxation in and come to the office. I meant what I said about the designs and about looking at our new spring additions. If you say no, you go back to London and that's that. If you think the ruse will help your situation, consider me your accomplice and we can announce our engagement on Friday."

"I'd like to take the time to think about it," she said, and the fact that she wasn't outright refusing took her by surprise.

"That sounds perfectly reasonable."

But there wasn't anything reasonable about it at all. So why was she seriously considering it? Was she that desperate?

Christophe wasn't quite sure what had prompted him to propose, even if it was just a fake engagement. Marriage wasn't a game and even if it were, he was determined not to play. His few memories of seeing his parents' relationship disintegrate was enough for him. Being left behind, with no support from his father, had made their lives a hardship. Maybe his aunt and uncle had had an idyllic union, but he knew many more who didn't. As much as he thought a child deserved two parents, he knew that without love, a marriage wouldn't survive.

He'd made his position on marital bliss crystal clear to Lizzie, or at least he'd thought he had. She'd seen it differently.

He sat on the sofa now, absently flipping through Sophie's sketchbook again. She'd gone to have a relaxing bath. He knew his proposal was a silly idea, and yet if it meant her ex would back off...

He hesitated on the Van Gogh drawings again. It was far and away his favorite of the designs, and he wanted to get François's opinion. This week was going to be an interesting one for him, both on the personal and professional front. Depending on how things went, he'd consider making Sophie an offer for the designs. After months of playing it safe, Bella was after him to expand and do something new with the division. He tapped the cover of the pad and pursed his lips. Sophie could be just the person to help him do that. She wanted her own collection. What if Aurora could give her the opportunity?

When she came out to the living room again, she was dressed in soft sleep pants and a T-shirt, her hair wet against her shoulders. "Better?" he asked.

"A little. My mind is still spinning, though." She sat beside him again and tucked her legs so she was sitting cross-legged on the cushion. "I have a few more concerns that popped up while I was soaking."

He tried not to think of her in the tub surrounded by scented bubbles and reminded himself that she was his friend. If she knew what direction his thoughts had just taken, she'd not only say no to the engagement, but she'd be on the first flight back to London. Still, the image remained...her long legs, sleek with water, the bubbles hovering just below her breasts as the steam curled into the air...

"…and I'm sure they won't appreciate being lied to. Are you listening?"

"Hmm? Sorry. Who won't appreciate it?"

"Your family."

"Don't worry about them. Stephen and Gabi were all set to have a fake marriage, remember? We're not even planning to go through with it. We'd just be pretending to be engaged."

"And then I thought of the tabloids. The Pembertons do find themselves in the gossip rags quite often at the moment. Any engagement will surely make it there, and it has the potential to get ugly, especially if they find out about my pregnancy. What if Eric talks to them?"

He thought for a moment, then remembered all the damage control they'd done after Stephen's failed wedding and how they'd mostly controlled the story by selectively feeding tidbits to the press. "They'll tell the story we give them," he answered. "And the one we show them. Eric won't say anything."

"How can you be sure?"

"Because he won't risk custody of the baby. It's in his best interest to stay quiet."

She nodded. "This is a lot."

"I know. Take your time, and no pressure. Like I said, take the week to think about it. In the meantime, I truly, truly want you to relax and enjoy yourself. How about a movie? There's got to be something streaming that's good."

So in the end, they spent the evening with tea and a flick, and when Sophie started to get tired, he got her a throw blanket and she drooped against his shoulder.

It was entirely too domestic. Too…settled. And yet it was perfect. And that was what scared him the most. Not fake engagements or the paparazzi or her persistent ex. But this warm bubble of contentment stirring inside.

He couldn't embrace it. Because the last thing he would ever do was let himself get hurt the way his mother had had her heart broken.

Sophie woke to bright sunlight streaming through her window. The flat was silent except for the rustle of her sheets as she rolled over and checked her phone charging beside the bed. It was almost nine! She sat straight up and pushed her hair off her face, and then a smile blossomed. When was the last time she'd actually slept in? She couldn't remember. Even on weekends, she tended to be up no later than seven. Frequent trips to the bathroom meant that she woke early and then didn't really get back to sleep. But today…she'd slept a remarkable ten hours.

Maybe this Paris trip really did have some merit.

She threw off the covers and got out of bed, and once she'd gone to the bathroom and then brushed her teeth, she headed for the kitchen. Christophe was nowhere to be found, obviously gone to work already. There was a note on the table scrawled in his handwriting.

Soph,
Have gone to work and should be back around six.
Help yourself to what's in the fridge—I know, I know,
I need to go to the market.
Have a great day.
PS I left a key for you on the table in the foyer.

The fridge revealed sparse contents for breakfast, probably because Christophe had been away for a week. She found some yogurt that was still good and some apples and oranges, which made for a healthy start to her day along with her vitamins. She made a tea and then ventured out onto the terrace for a moment. He was right; the view was spectacular, and she imagined how fragrant it would be in the summer with all of his herbs growing.

When she was done and had tidied her dishes, she texted him and let him know she'd pick up some things today and that she'd cook for them tonight.

Which meant peeking in his cupboards and making a shopping list.

Her purpose set, she brushed out her hair and braided it, then changed into another pair of leggings with a tunic-style blouse over top. Even though she wasn't showing yet, her waist was thickening, and her usual tailored clothes were uncomfortable. Pairing the outfit with boots and a soft scarf made the look a bit smarter, and she left her face bare save for the rich moisturizer she used. It was freeing to know that she was on her own today to do whatever she liked, with no responsibility to anyone. Perhaps before the market she'd go for a walk in the Jardin des Tuileries, only a short distance away. Whenever she visited the city, she rarely had time for leisurely strolls. In the southwest part of the garden was the Musée de l'Orangerie. Considering her recent interest in Monet, visiting the museum could be an additional sort of inspiration. She tucked her sketchbook and pencils into her handbag just in case, feeling absolutely decadent in her day's schedule.

The late morning air was cool but surprisingly mild for November, and the light jacket she wore over her tunic kept out the cold. She took a moment to get her bearings and then started her walk. The journey took her along the Rue du Faubourg St-Honoré, past the Canadian embassy, and then down the Avenue de Marigny, past the president's palace. The time of year meant fewer tourists about, and she took her time, soaking in the precious sunshine until she reached the Jardin des Champs-Elysées and the opportunity to leave the traffic behind.

The tree-lined paths offered a respite from the rush of cars, and burbling fountains partially masked the sounds of traffic rushing along the broad Champs-Elysées. Sophie let out a breath and felt the tension of the last three months melt away. Why had she waited so long to get away? Her troubles seemed smaller somehow, just by stepping back from them for a moment. She rolled her shoulders and slowed her steps; there was no one rushing her to get from one place to the next today.

The *jardin* bled into La Place de la Concorde and its stunning Luxor Obelisk. Intrigued, Sophie took a moment to retrieve her sketch pad from her bag and did some rudimentary sketches, then snapped a few photos on her phone. Not all of her inspiration had to come from paintings. The Egyptian monument was also a stunning work of art. She could do a lot with the shape of it, envisioning a gold and platinum pendant.

The Jardin des Tuileries was beautiful even in the off-season, and she spent a good hour walking through, the crowd a little thicker now the closer she got to the Louvre. She'd perhaps make another visit to the iconic museum another day; it had been a few years since she'd indulged in a trip. Instead, she made her way to the Musée de l'Orangerie and the paintings waiting for her there, and she spent two hours studying and sketching, letting her creative side out to play.

When her stomach growled, she left the museum and stopped for a quick ham and cheese baguette at a café in the gardens, and then started her walk back to Christophe's, looking for a good market along the way to purchase what she needed for dinner.

It wasn't until she was halfway to his flat that she realized she hadn't spent her morning agonizing over decisions that needed to be made or stressing over her situation. Nor had she felt ill, which hopefully meant her morning sickness was abating. She was so relieved to know there was still life outside of the bubble she'd unconsciously put herself in. And she had Christophe to thank for that. He'd been the one who'd seen she needed to get away, and he'd been so right.

Was he right in his proposition, too? Could she fake an engagement with him?

She thought of her mother's constant pressure. Sure, her dad had silenced her mum the other day, but it wouldn't last. Mum and Dad were old school; they, too, thought that marriage was the natural step. It amazed her that they couldn't see how she wanted a marriage like theirs—built on love. And Eric, too. She suspected what Christophe had said was true. If they got engaged, Eric wouldn't speak to the tabloids because he was concerned about their child's future. Something inside her softened. Even though he was driving her crazy, at least he was taking the responsibility of fatherhood seriously. If she said yes to Christophe's idea, maybe he was right: she and Eric could start a dialogue about how to navigate their relationship as parents and not partners. It was worth a shot.

Still, she had a few more days to decide, and she was going to take them. She'd needed today desperately; a few more days of no pressure and no decisions might actually deliver the clarity she was actually missing.

The market shopping took a quick thirty minutes and then she was back at the apartment, long before dinner needed to be started. Sophie picked up her book, curled up on the sofa with the throw she'd used last night, and within ten minutes had fallen asleep, the fresh air and day's exertions catching up with her.

CHAPTER SEVEN

THE NEXT MORNING, Christophe entered the kitchen to discover Sophie already there, cooking eggs and pouring coffee from his French press. "Good morning," she said brightly, and he blinked.

Never had he been in the position of having a woman in his kitchen making breakfast. Not even if she'd spent the night, which was rare. Having a woman in his space... there was nowhere to go.

He reminded himself that Sophie wasn't any woman, and their relationship wasn't like that, so he could just dismiss the panic that seemed to have settled in his chest and the sudden domestic image before him.

"You didn't need to do this," he said, stepping into the kitchen. "You're my guest, and you made dinner last night, too."

The Moroccan stew had been delicious, and he'd mopped up the juices with fresh bread from the *boulangerie*. They'd chatted about their respective days, and she'd told him she'd totally indulged and had a nap. The conversation had stayed light, and Eric hadn't called, though he had sent a text message. Christophe had to give the guy top marks for effort and persistence.

"I was awake at six, and not queasy. I'm taking advantage of it. Yesterday I slept until nine and then had a nap! I never do that. I feel wonderful."

She looked wonderful, too. Today she'd put on an off-white sweater dress with a wide brown belt at her waist and beige knee-high suede boots. Her hair curled around her shoulders, the thick waves inviting. If they weren't friends...

But they were. And he wouldn't play with her. Not ever. There were lines a man didn't cross. Any woman he dated knew the deal. He was not in anything for the long-term.

"So you're coming into work with me today?"

"If you're okay with that, I'd like to. I've never actually had a tour of Aurora HQ, you know. But only if you have time."

"I'll make time. Bring your sketch pad. I'll see if François has time to see you today, too."

Her eyes lit up. "Really? I'd love that. I added more ideas yesterday, though they're very rudimentary."

"This excites you. I like it."

"Know what else excites me? Scrambled eggs." She took the pan off the burner and spooned them onto two plates. "I don't know how you like your eggs, so I made them the way I eat them right now. Scrambled and fluffy, not creamy. I can't do soft eggs at the moment, especially yolks." She shuddered.

He laughed at the face she made. "As long as they're not raw, I'm fine," he replied. She'd also put a bowl of mixed berries on the table, and his coffee was strong and hot, just the way he liked. He wouldn't read anything more into this or let his own neuroses bring down the mood. She was his friend and she'd made breakfast. That was all.

After breakfast they took a taxi to the Aurora offices, a few blocks closer to the Seine than Sophie had walked yesterday. This area was home to the big names: Dior, Valentino, Vuitton, Saab. That Aurora could hold its own was a testament to his aunt's savvy and determination. It was also a lot of pressure. He was a boy from the outskirts of Orléans. What on earth was he doing managing a whole division of this company?

His aunt had sat him down a few years ago and had given him a stern talking-to. "Don't forget," she had said, her gaze steady. "We come from the same place. Never use it as an excuse. Use it as an asset."

Sophie carried a hobo bag the same color as her belt, and together they walked through the glass doors into the black-and-white lobby, a testament to the signature Aurora colors.

"*Bonjour*, Monsieur Germain," said the receptionist.

"*Bonjour.* I'm signing in a guest for today, Giselle. Could you give her a pass, please? All access."

"*Bien sûr,*" she replied. She retrieved a swipe card from a drawer and prepared it. "*Bonjour, madame. Voici votre carte-clé.*"

"*Merci,*" Sophie replied, and then to Christophe's surprise, proceeded to have a brief conversation with Giselle in flawless French.

"Well done," he said moments later as they walked to the elevators. "I didn't know you were so fluent."

"I'm a bit rusty. But I can manage."

"Come on. Let's give you a tour. I don't have any meetings until ten thirty."

For an hour, Sophie toured Aurora HQ, her head swiveling back and forth as she met tons of people, and she caught a glimpse into the well-oiled machine that was Aurora, Inc. By the time they reached the top floor and executive offices, her head was swimming. Everything about it screamed elegance and luxury, from the white-veined marble floors to the stylized black "Aurora" logo prevalent in each section. Glass and chrome kept the atmosphere modern and professional, and everyone offered a friendly *"bonjour"* or "good morning" to Christophe as he passed. Often she saw people smiling and laughing—this looked like a happy workplace.

He showed her his office, a moderate-sized room with a stunning view of the Seine. "This is gorgeous," she said, going to stand by the window. "How do you get any work done with that view?"

He grinned. "It's a good thing I have it. The work is pretty intense, and sometimes I need to look up and see the weather or just the outdoors, and remember this office isn't my whole world."

"Ah yes. The rich and privileged."

"I am, and I know it. But it doesn't mean I don't work hard. With jewelry and cosmetics, I feel like I'm having to spend a third of my time researching and getting up to speed."

"You just need to surround yourself with knowledgeable people you trust," she said, trailing her fingers over a glass-topped table. The office was incredibly neat, even neater than his flat. She looked up at him, a smile teasing the corners of her mouth. "Christophe Germain, I just realized that you're a neat freak."

He lifted his eyebrow. "You're not the only one with control issues, apparently."

She laughed. "I'm surprised. You're so chill most of the time."

He joined her by the window. "Yes, but I find it easier to concentrate and stay 'chill' if my environment is tidy." He hesitated for a moment, then added quietly, "The house where I lived before, it wasn't very neat. My mother worked long hours just to keep the rent paid. She was too tired to worry about our place that much. I suppose I associate mess with insecurity."

"And if everything is tidy and organized, then everything is all right."

"It probably sounds silly."

"I think that some experiences shape us, especially when we're young and process it differently than an adult. But thank you for sharing that with me."

"You trust me," he said, "I trust you."

This trusting each other thing was nothing new, but there was an added element now, since his unusual proposal, and she fought back the sense that she was getting in too deep. She was just about to reply when Bella poked her head in the door. "Meeting in the boardroom in ten," she said brightly. "And hello again, Sophie. Christophe, I didn't know it was bring your friend to work day."

He turned around and aimed a million-dollar smile at his cousin. "That's because you have no friends."

"Ouch!" She laughed and threw Sophie a wink. "I love teasing Christophe the most, you know. He knows how to give it back."

"I do have a better sense of humor than Stephen," he mused.

"Did I hear my name?"

Stephen Pemberton, Earl of Chatsworth, halted in the hallway and joined Bella at the door. "Oh, hello," he said when he saw Sophie.

Christophe stepped in. "Sophie, you remember my cousin, Stephen, don't you?"

Yes, the new earl. Her tongue tangled in her mouth as she scrambled to come up with the appropriate address. Should she actually call him my lord? It sounded so antiquated! But he was actually an earl...

Stephen stepped inside, a tall, formidable kind of man with dark hair and eyes, and a face that didn't have the easy humor of Christophe's. "Sophie, it's nice to see you again. Call me Stephen," he said, as if sensing her quandary.

She let out a relieved breath. "Lovely to see you, as well. Christophe was giving me the tour this morning."

"Are you in Paris for long?"

Christophe stepped in smoothly. "I invited Sophie to look at the new spring selections. I was just going to take her to meet François before joining you in the boardroom."

Stephen snapped his fingers and smiled. "That's right. Sorry, it slipped my mind. You're the gemologist."

"I am. Waltham is thrilled to be one of your distributors."

"Sophie's got a fabulous eye. She's going to be here for the week, offering some thoughts and taking a little time for relaxation."

Speculative looks were exchanged between Bella and Stephen, then Stephen looked at his watch. "Better get going. I'll see you in there, Christophe. Sophie," he added, giving a nod and disappearing.

"Me, too," Bella said. "Will's probably already there. The department heads are joining us at eleven, so we need to get a move on."

Christophe took his cue, and when Bella left, he turned and squeezed Sophie's hand. "I'm sorry. I let time get away with me. I'll run you to François's office, and then I'll have to dash. You'll be all right?"

"I'm sure he'll take excellent care of me. And if he's occupied, I have my sketchbook. Never fear."

"We should be done by one. I'll text you and we'll grab some lunch?"

"That sounds lovely."

He led her out of the office and down one floor. The

area was quiet, and he swiped his card for access into the department. All of Aurora's gems weren't on-site, but there was enough inventory that security measures were tight. The appearance here was far more utilitarian and less showy, scrupulously clean and neat. François's office was in the middle, and it was like a dream. Gone was the sterile environment outside the door and inside was a mishmash of equipment. A laptop with a much larger monitor, a workbench with an array of equipment, a drafting table, and books. Lots and lots of books. On the wall were photos of some of Aurora's finest pieces, including a stunning sapphire teardrop necklace surrounded by diamonds that Sophie remembered from maybe three years ago. It had been a one-of-a-kind bespoke piece for a member of the royal family.

Behind the desk sat a small man, squinting at something on the desk and then up at the monitor, as if his eyes couldn't adjust fast enough.

"François, this is Sophie, the gemologist I told you about."

François jumped, then pressed a hand to his chest. "*Mon Dieu*, Christophe, you scared me to death."

"Sorry. I'm late for a board meeting. I wish I could stay for a longer introduction."

"Do not worry." He smiled up at Sophie. "We are big kids, eh? We can handle it."

She was already charmed. When he stood, she realized he was a good two inches shorter than she was, and his head was three-quarters bald. He reminded her of a little chipmunk, with a wrinkled shirt and yet a precisely knotted tie.

"I'll text when I'm done," he said to Sophie. "Okay?"

"Big kids. I'm good. Go to your meeting."

He flashed her a smile and then disappeared.

François clapped his hands. "Perfect. Christophe says you're to have a look at the spring catalog. Let me get you a copy of what we're planning to send out."

"That would be lovely. And your office... I love it."

"The chaos drives Christophe mad, but it's my space, not his." François looked up at her with a sparkle in his eye. "I had my reservations when *madame* put him in charge of the division, but he's a good kid. He knows he knows nothing, and is not afraid to learn or ask questions."

He rummaged around in the mess and then took out a mock-up of the catalog. "Ah, here you go." He looked at her keenly. "You're a gemologist at Waltham. You, you know something. Your reputation precedes you."

She got the feeling it was high praise. "Thank you so much. Where would you like me to go? I don't want to be in your way or distract you from your work."

"Not at all." He gestured toward the drafting table. "It's not the most comfortable spot, but you're welcome to it."

"Are you joking? I spend most of my day on a twenty-year-old stool hunched over a microscope. This is lovely."

He laughed then. They both knew the ins and outs of the job and embraced them. As his eyes twinkled at her again, she got the feeling she'd just met a kindred spirit.

While she knew François didn't construct the pieces here in this space, she also knew that he was the final word in each design and oversaw the process. Every stone had to meet his standards, and each setting must be perfect. Design was nothing without craftmanship. She settled on the chair and opened the catalog.

She spent a long time poring over each page, from the ever-popular engagement rings to pendants, earrings, bracelets. There was a high jewelry section with gorgeous diamond collars, but there was something missing.

It was all completely on brand. Timeless, elegant, flawless. But also lacking an energy and inventiveness. How could she say so to the man who was the chief designer?

"You look displeased, *mademoiselle.*"

"Oh? No, not at all. It's just…"

François had slipped on a pair of reading glasses. He now took them off and put them on his desk. "*Oui?* Do not be afraid of me. I can take the bad news." He put his hand over his heart, as if she were wounding him, and she smiled. She liked him very much.

"Each design is stunning. Classic, elegant. Everything Aurora stands for."

He tilted his head a little. "But?"

She sighed. "But it's…" She tried to search for the gentlest word. "Oh, François, never mind."

He got up from his desk, grabbed a stool, placed it beside her, and sat. "Christophe brought you here for your feedback. He wouldn't do that unless he trusted you. So tell me. Be honest."

"All right. I'm sorry, François, but it's…boring. I can't see anything that really sets it apart from the previous year."

Her cheeks heated and she waited for him to express his disapproval. Instead, a broad smile overtook his face.

"*Merci!* Thank you! That was what I've been trying to say for months!"

Sophie was startled and turned to look at him. He seemed almost joyful. "You have?"

"*Oui.* The last eighteen months have been very hard. First with the earl passing, and then all the executive changes, and then Aurora's semi-retirement. *Mon Dieu*, it has been enough to drive me…" He made a swirly motion around his ear and she laughed. "I tried to do something different with these designs last summer, but Christophe just kept saying to 'keep it on brand, keep the ship steady.' He was afraid and with everyone else adjusting…" He suddenly stopped talking and his cheeks colored. "Oh. I have said too much. I admire Christophe very much, but he's new and lacks confidence. That is all."

"He should have trusted you, though. You're a wonderful designer. We carry the Aurora Gems line. I know." She pointed at the photo of the sapphire necklace. "That is a gorgeous, gorgeous piece."

"Thank you."

She sighed. "There's nothing wrong with these pieces, but they're not going to cause a stir or be accused of being innovative. You've used the tried-and-true gems—ruby, sapphire, emerald, with a few yellow diamonds thrown in. But there are so many other colors and combinations. Citrine. Tanzanite. Pink sapphire." Her brain was racing again. "Asymmetrical settings, too. Something really unique. I'd love to see your other designs sometime."

"I'd like that very much." He patted her hand. "Christophe mentioned yesterday that you've started designing, as well. You're serious about it?"

She nodded. "I think I am. It feeds a part of me that assessing and selling just doesn't. We got on the subject because I wore one of my designs to Bella's engagement party."

"Do you have a picture of it?"

She nodded. "Of course." She grabbed her phone and logged into the cloud, retrieving the picture of the necklace on a black velvet stand. François took the phone from her hand and examined the photo, then used his fingers to enlarge it. "The clasp is lovely. A bee?"

"I've been fascinated with nature."

"It adds a bit of whimsy to a very classic pearl choker."

"That was my intent."

He gave her back the phone. "I'd like to see your designs, Sophie. Perhaps tomorrow you can come back, and we can meet in the afternoon?"

"You'd really like to see them?"

"Of course. When someone accuses me of being boring, I'm curious as to what they find exciting." He winked at her. "I have high expectations, you know."

Nerves centered low in her belly, but they were the best kind. "I'd like that very much. I'll warn you though, some sketches I've just done in the last week so they're rudimentary."

"I can see past that, as you can imagine."

Her phone buzzed and she looked down. "Oh. The meeting is over."

"Just on time, then. I shall go mend my wounded pride and you shall go to lunch. And tomorrow we will meet and be creative, *oui*?"

"Oui," she answered. "Thank you, François."

"No, thank you," he responded. "I think you're just what was needed around here."

CHAPTER EIGHT

CHRISTOPHE TOOK A few moments to clear his head before collecting Sophie from François's department. The meeting had taken a toll. Department managers had attended as well, and it was clear that Aurora's retirement, Charlotte's maternity leave, and the general inexperience of the rest of the Pemberton siblings in their new roles was taking a toll. Will was back and in charge of fashion, and he had a good staff, but with Charlotte out they'd had to hire an outside PR consultant and assistant, and they were still getting up to speed. Stephen was head of acquisitions and now operating as COO, while Bella had left cosmetics behind to move into the vacated CEO position. She left some of those duties to Christophe in addition to his workload, and delegated others to their former head of fragrance, Phillipe Leroux. But Phillipe's background was in chemistry, not business, and he was going through his own learning curve making the leap to management. It was enough to give Christophe a headache.

But when he stopped by the elevators and found Sophie waiting for him, the stress melted away. "You're beaming," he said, unable to hold back a smile.

"I had a lovely morning with François. He is incredibly charming and wonderful."

"How charming? Should I be worried?"

She laughed. "Maybe. He has opinions. You should listen to them. But not today. François and I are going to look at my designs tomorrow, and then I'll fill you in."

"You two are in…what's the term? Cahoots?"

She laughed. "Yes, we are."

"And your thoughts on the spring line?"

"Tomorrow," she said, dimples popping in her cheeks. "Right now, I'm starving. Let's lunch. When we come back, I can find a corner where I can sketch until you finish. Unless you'd rather I went back to the flat."

"You are more than welcome to find any nook or cranny that captures your fancy." He took her hand and pressed the button for the elevator.

He took her to a restaurant with cozy alcoves, where they wouldn't be rushed, and the noise would be minimal. He knew the menu here and what normally would have been a typical hour for a meal ended up spread out over nearly two. Still, he didn't feel the need to hurry to get back. It was too lovely watching Sophie chatter, talking with her hands. He'd never seen her this animated.

"You," he said, gesturing with one of his *frites*, "are lighting up the room. You're very excited."

"I truly am." They'd started the meal with onion soup and now she was picking at her entrée of duck breast, which smelled heavenly and had him regretting his choice of roast chicken. "This was something I was tinkering with, but suddenly it matters so much." Her smile faded. "Which I don't think is going to be good news for my mum and dad."

"You're still poised to take over Waltham."

"I am."

He shrugged. "Sophie, you can own a business and still hire someone to manage it."

"I know that's not what they have in mind."

He held back the response that had immediately come to the tip of his tongue. What did it matter what they envisioned after they were gone, and it was Sophie's? She couldn't tailor her life to their expectations forever. But he expected that if he said so it would seem like piling on, so instead he thought about her brother. "What about Mark?" Her brother was younger and just finishing his MBA from Brookes at Oxford. "What are his plans after he graduates?"

"Not Waltham, I don't think."

"Hmm. Well…" Christophe thought for a moment about the merits and burdens of carrying on a family business. Was there something he'd rather be doing right now? He didn't think so. He'd done his studies in business as well and had worked various jobs within Aurora over the years, as they all had. It had always been assumed that they would all take their place one day, even Christophe. He loved the business. The past year had been tough, but the only thing he'd change would be having Cedric back with them once again.

"Anyway, how was your meeting? You were looking a little stressy when I met you." She changed the topic smoothly.

"Intense. We covered a lot of ground. Many of us are new to our roles, so we've really got to rely on each other as a team. That includes the family, of course, but also the management we've put in place." He went on to talk about Phillipe and how much he liked him. "I think we're going to get along just fine."

It was long past time they went back to the office. The afternoon had taken on a raw chill and he held Sophie's wrap for her, his fingers brushing her shoulders as he tucked it around her. She stilled beneath his casual touch, and his stomach tumbled. Was she as aware of him as he was of her? The soft scent of her perfume wrapped around him, disturbed by the movement of her clothing and hair. Awareness was one thing. Acting on it was another. Besides, if she took him up on his offer, he'd have to get used to being this close to her. Casual touches would be more frequent, at least in public. They'd have to appear as a couple.

He was probably crazy to even suggest such a plan, in hindsight, but when he thought of how upset Sophie got when dealing with Eric, and how innocent her baby was, he knew it was the right thing. He'd support her no matter what. This little awareness that kept cropping up was just an annoyance. Nothing to really worry about.

"Ready?" Sophie asked, peering up at him. "You look like you're a thousand miles away."

"Just thinking." He smiled down at her. "Sorry."

"It's all right. Occupational hazard." She led the way back outside. The overcast sky pressed down on them, making the November afternoon seem bleak and drab. "Oh, it's so gloomy today. The sun's completely disappeared."

"Christmas lights will be out soon, though," Christophe said, and he cheered a bit. He really did enjoy the festive season. "Have you been in Paris at the holidays? There are lights everywhere. The entire length of the Champs-Elysées is lit, and of course the storefronts, and all sorts of other areas. It's magical. Chases any gloom away, guaranteed."

"I haven't been at Christmas. But can it rival London?"

"If you're here this year you can compare."

She got strangely quiet, and he expected she was thinking the same thing he was. Would she be? Here? If she said yes to his fake proposal, perhaps. And then he could show her the Aurora storefront dressed for the holidays, as well as the other luxury shops along the Avenue Montaigne. He imagined holding hands with her as they strolled along... it didn't bother him as much as it should.

Which meant he'd have to remind himself to keep her at arm's length. It would be far too easy to get caught up in things and forget this was a temporary solution to help a friend.

"You feeling all right?" he asked, when she continued to be quiet.

"Oh...oh, yes." She shook her head slightly and offered a small smile. "Sorry. Got into my own head there for a moment." The heels of her boots echoed on the sidewalk as they headed back to the office. "I'm feeling quite well, actually. I think you were right. I did need this week away. I mean, I'm still tired most of the time, but I haven't been sick since Sunday morning."

He wasn't sure she realized that her hand had drifted down to cover her tummy.

"I guess my book was right. Once you start moving into the second trimester, the sickness often eases."

"Your book?"

She nodded. "Of course. Did you think women are born with some internal knowledge bank that we can just search when we're pregnant?"

He laughed. "Okay, fair enough."

"I mean, certainly I knew how it happened, and what happens at the end, but all the in between stuff...there's a lot."

"That's what Charlotte said, too. Maybe you two could chat. I'm sure she'd help."

Sophie's face softened. "Actually, I might like that. I don't know anyone with small children just now. My life's revolved around my job and other social occasions that are more scheduled than, I don't know, spending time with friends. Present company excepted…"

"And I'm hardly a good source of information on having babies," he added, chuckling. They reached the Aurora doors and he stopped, taking her hands. "But I am your friend. I hope you always remember that."

A puzzled look blanked her face. "Why wouldn't I?"

Christophe held the door open and they entered the building. He got the sneaky suspicion that he was the one who needed reminding, not her.

Sophie had chosen a little alcove next to the on-site café with a large window and a comfortable chair, but after an hour of sketching she'd nodded off. When she woke, she found the afternoon had disappeared, the sky was dark gray, and her pencil had dropped onto the floor.

She reached down to retrieve it and let out a sigh. She supposed her nap was the result of a morning of excitement and then a full stomach after their delicious lunch. But she had wanted to work on her designs a lot more before tomorrow. Tonight she would, after she and Christophe went home.

She stopped herself. Not home. His flat. She had to remember that and not get too used to having him around. It had been so easy, being with him the last few days. Comfortable in a way she'd never experienced before. She'd almost say brotherly, but that would be a lie. There were times when he looked at her that she would swear there was fantastic chemistry simmering beneath the surface. And today, when he'd helped her with her wrap, the light touch of his fingers had sent a frisson of longing down her body. She'd wanted him to touch her. Thankfully they'd kept clear heads and had gone back to chatting as they returned to the Aurora building.

But before she'd fallen asleep, she'd imagined what it might be like if he kissed her. Her *tendre* for him wasn't going away. If anything, being with him more, getting to know him even better, put her more in danger of liking him far too much. If the objective of a fake engagement was to get Eric to see reason, then she had to be aware that the result also had to be that she was able to walk away unhurt. The only way to ensure that was to pretend that this crush didn't exist.

She packed up her things and made her way to his office, prepared to wait for him to finish for the day. Instead of Christophe at his desk, however, she popped in the door and discovered Aurora herself.

"Oh!" she exclaimed, before she could think better of it.

Aurora looked up, reading glasses perched on her nose.

"Aurora! I mean, Lady Pemberton." Her cheeks flared as she wanted to swallow her tongue. "Oh, bother."

Aurora slid off her glasses and offered a small, elegant smile. "Aurora is fine, Ms. Waltham."

Aurora knew who she was. While she was still absorbing that fact, Aurora stood and held out a hand. "I don't know if we've ever been properly introduced."

Sophie reminded herself to be calm and graceful. She stepped forward and took the hand offered. "It's lovely to finally meet. Officially." She smiled at the older woman and hoped she didn't sound as awkward as she felt.

"You're looking for Christophe. He's just down the hall and let me use his desk for an hour or so. I can show you where he is, if you like."

"I don't mind waiting. I don't want to interrupt his meeting." Her cheeks remained stubbornly hot. "I'm visiting this week, you see, and we were going to go back to his flat together."

Aurora's sharp eyes assessed her coolly. "Yes, I've

heard." She stepped back and leaned her hips against the desk, crossing one ankle over the other in a relaxed yet commanding pose. There was no question who owned the room.

Sophie found Aurora incredibly intimidating. Not because she was domineering in any way. Simply because she was so successful and so…composed. Always. A woman in complete control. It made her incredibly resilient and a formidable negotiator. "I didn't realize you were in Paris," she said, clutching the strap of her bag.

"I wasn't, until this afternoon. Bella rang me after the meeting and asked if I'd mind spending a few days helping her with some transitional things. Since my schedule these days is flexible, I was happy to help." She smiled then, a truly warm smile. "Besides, I missed Paris."

"It's beautiful, isn't it? I haven't been in so long, and yesterday I spent the whole day walking and taking in art and visiting a market…ordinary things, but then, nothing is ordinary in Paris, is it?"

Aurora shook her head. "No, it's not. Come, let's sit and wait for Christophe. Would you like a glass of wine? Tea, perhaps?"

"Tea would be lovely," she admitted. When she was at work at home, she almost always had a cup on the go. She missed it. Even if she was now drinking herbals more often than not.

They sat in the more comfortable chairs in the corner, and Sophie put down her bag and told herself to relax. Aurora was a big presence, but she didn't have to be frightening. "Congratulations on your first grandchild, by the way. Christophe showed me pictures. She's gorgeous."

"She is, isn't she? You know, for all the success of the company, I do miss the days when my babies were small."

It was hard to imagine Aurora as the mother of small

children. Her bob-length blond hair—colored, of course—was always perfectly coiffed, her clothing impeccable.

The tea arrived and Aurora thanked the assistant and then took on the job of pouring. "The most fun was Cedric playing tag with them in the garden. They would run and run and run and then when he got caught, he'd freeze in the most ridiculous postures." She smiled in remembrance. "There were always dirty faces and hands in those days, but I wouldn't trade them for anything."

"It must have been hard trying to balance motherhood with building the company."

"Oh, it was. Cedric was such a support, both with the children and financially, too. My name might be the company, but it is every bit as much his as mine."

"I'm so sorry," Sophie whispered.

"Thank you, dear." Aurora picked up her tea. "We had a wonderful life. I couldn't ask for anything more." She laughed. "Well, except more grandchildren. With Will married and Bella on her way to the altar, perhaps I won't have to wait too long."

Sophie hid behind her teacup. If she and Christophe went through with their ruse, they'd be deceiving Aurora as well as everyone else. They would have to be very convincing, because Aurora was sharp.

"Christophe tells me you've been doing some designing." Aurora changed the subject. "I'd love to see your ideas."

Sophie paused. It was a great compliment and opportunity, but she wasn't as comfortable showing Aurora as she was Christophe, who was a friend, or even François, who she knew understood her sketches were concept only and not a formal design. She put her cup back on the saucer and tried a nervous smile. "I'm very flattered, of course, but I'm not sure my concepts are ready for your eyes, Lady…

er… Aurora. They're only sketches at the moment, and really need refining. In fact, I'm meeting with François tomorrow. They may not even be any good. But I know he'll tell me the truth."

"You don't think I will?"

Oh, heavens. "Of course, ma'am… I'd just rather go through the proper channels. If there's anything in my concepts that is worthy of exploring, I look forward to a much better presentation to Christophe, and Bella, and you, of course…"

"Because I'm no longer the CEO."

"That hardly matters. You're Aurora, ma'am."

"If I insisted?"

Sophie rather thought she was being tested, and while she wasn't overly confident about her designs, she was no fool. "I'm afraid I'd have to decline at this time. Not until they are ready."

Aurora smiled then, and her eyes warmed. "I like you, Sophie Waltham."

"Thank goodness, ma'am."

They shared a laugh while Aurora reminded her, "No ma'am-ing me. You call me Aurora as everyone else does."

By the time Christophe returned to his office, Aurora had moved her chair closer to Sophie and was showing her pictures of baby Imogene. While delighted at the way the meeting had turned out, Sophie couldn't help but wonder what Aurora would say if she knew Sophie was pregnant. And she was sure Aurora's opinion would change if they announced their engagement and then news of the baby. A tension headache started across her forehead and she smiled faintly as Christophe strode back into his office, his curls mussed from presumably running his fingers through it. He looked tired, she realized.

"Maman," he said, and Sophie realized that despite

being Aurora's nephew, he'd just addressed her as his mother. It was a telling detail about their relationship. "Are you showing off the baby pictures again?"

"Naturally." She stood and took a few steps and kissed Christophe's cheek. "Thank you for the use of your office. Everything all right?"

"Yes, I think so." He smiled. "You've met Sophie."

"Indeed. She refused to show me her drawings."

Christophe turned startled eyes to Sophie, and Aurora laughed, a rusty chuckle that Sophie was starting to enjoy. "That is her prerogative. She is a smart woman, Christophe."

"Don't I know it."

Aurora looked from Christophe to Sophie and back again, putting two and two together. Neither of them spoke to disabuse her of the thoughts running through her head.

"Well, I'm spending the night at Bella's, so I'd better get on. And you look tired, darling. You should go home. Tomorrow is another day."

"I am. We are," he amended. "Heading home. Will we see you tomorrow?"

"I'm going to stay until the end of the week. Charlotte begged me to give her some peace and as I was telling Ms. Waltham, I've missed Paris."

"Then we should have dinner before you return. Perhaps all of us together?"

Sophie could see where this was going, and it felt as if she were on a runaway train. A family dinner, where they could possibly make an announcement? She wasn't sure she could go through with this, even with pressure from Eric. It was a foolish idea. No one would believe them anyway.

"I have a better idea," Aurora said. "Let's all head to the château on Friday afternoon. We can have dinner there, and a little family time. I'll run it past the others." She looked at Sophie. "You're invited of course, Sophie. If it fits your schedule?"

Christophe sent her such a pleading look over his aunt's shoulder that she smiled and nodded. "I just need to make a call to my pet service," she said. "And extend my stay by a day or so. Thank you so much for including me."

And thank goodness she'd packed the cocktail dress in case of a more formal occasion. A family dinner at the famed château in Provence?

As her mother would say, out of the frying pan and into the fire. She just hoped she could take the heat.

CHAPTER NINE

BY THE TIME Thursday arrived, Christophe still hadn't spoken to Sophie again about the engagement. Tuesday night
she'd disappeared to bed early with a headache, and he'd
been tired, as well. Then she'd spent all afternoon Wednesday with François, the two of them with their heads together, and he found he was jealous. Not of the two of
them, but knowing they were, as he'd put it the other day,
in "cahoots." Nor had she heard from Eric in that time. Perhaps the engagement wasn't going to be necessary after all.

He shouldn't feel disappointed, not even a little bit. If
he wanted to spend time with Sophie, to be closer friends,
all he had to do was keep in touch and make an effort.

And yet when he returned home on Thursday, and saw
her standing out on his terrace, he couldn't imagine her
not being here in his flat. She added something to his life
that he hadn't realized was missing. When this was over,
he was going to miss her.

"Soph? I'm home." The kitchen light was off and he
could see her form silhouetted in the darkness, looking
out over Paris at night. She had the throw from the sofa
wrapped around her and looked small and vulnerable.
Without thinking about it, he stepped out onto the concrete terrace and put his arms around her, tucking her
close in a back-to-chest hug. She looked as if she needed it.

But when he heard her sniff, he let go and turned her around by the shoulders. "What is it? What's wrong?" A look at her tearstained face sent alarm skittering through his veins. "Is it the baby?"

She shook her head quickly. "No, the baby is fine and so am I. It's just…" She sighed, turned away and put her elbows on the terrace railing. "How do you get through to someone who sincerely just keeps hoping they'll get a different answer?"

Ah. The fear slid out of his veins and understanding took hold. So the two days of respite from her baby's father had ended. "He called?"

She nodded. "And I answered. I thought maybe the last time I'd got through to him. Instead he…" She sniffled again. "I know he's frustrated and he won't let go, and that's not okay. But he also has good intentions, even if he's not handling it in the best way. He told me that he's been looking at country properties, where a child could have room to run and play, outside the city. That he's researched schools and health care and he just wants us to be a family. That all that's missing is me saying yes. Christophe, I feel like I'm destroying his dreams. Am I just being selfish?"

"Do you love him?"

She turned back and met his gaze. He watched her steadily, waiting for an honest answer. Somehow her answer was very, very important. Like something was hanging in the balance and would slip to one side if she answered no, and to another if she answered yes.

"Not anymore," she answered truthfully. "But I think he loves me. And that makes me feel horrible."

"You're not responsible for someone else's feelings," Christophe said, lifting his hand to wipe away one of her tears. He hated seeing her cry. Was pretty sure she wasn't the crying type. But tonight she seemed…forlorn. Worn out. As if all the ebullience and effervescence of the last few days had disappeared, like a glass of flat champagne.

"I know that, in my head. It's just hard. It's easier when I think he only cares about the baby, but I'm not sure that's true. I was the one who broke up with him, you see. I was the one whose feelings changed. They are what they are, but I still feel awful if I've truly hurt him."

"I don't know what to say."

"There's nothing to say. I'm torn between being gentle with him and ripping off the bandage. I don't want to give him false hope."

"The man has been, for lack of a better word, harassing you and not taking no for an answer." He felt duty bound to remind her of that fact. "A broken heart doesn't excuse his methods."

She sighed. "I know." Then she sniffled again. "Could you just hug me again? That felt awfully nice."

What could he say to that? He opened his arms and welcomed her—blanket and all—into his embrace. She sighed and rested her head on his shoulder. "Thank you. For all that you've done this past week. For putting up with my back and forth."

"You've met my cousins, right? Drama comes with the family. This is nothing."

She chuckled against him, her breasts lifting and falling against his chest. She felt good. Too good. If it were anyone else, he'd tip up her face and kiss her. But this was Sophie. It was a line they dare not cross. Especially because he found himself wanting to so very badly. She needed him to be strong and steady. Not muddy the waters with his own desires.

"Better?" he asked, rubbing his hand over her back.

"Much." She pulled back and looked up at him. "And I think I have my answer. If you're still up for it, I'll say yes. Perhaps the kindest thing to do right now is to let Eric think I've actually moved on, so he can, too. No more false hope. Rip off the bandage."

His throat closed over as his gut tightened. He couldn't rescind his offer now, and besides, he didn't really want to. It was a short-term, temporary thing that would help out a friend. More than that, there was her baby to think of and the ultimate goal: a safe, secure home filled with love. It was all he'd ever wanted for himself as a child. He knew what it was like to be a kid and feel like a burden. To have his mother look at him and see failure. If he could help Sophie provide that for her baby in some way, it would be worth everything.

"Let's hold off and tell the family tomorrow night, at the château."

She pushed away, taking a few steps back. "That will make it a big family thing, though. I'm...wow. I'm not sure."

"But it also means only having to tell people once, because we'll all be together."

"There is that."

"And it'll give me time to get you a ring tomorrow."

She bit down on her lip. "I didn't think about that. It's not necessary, really..."

"It will be expected. It's no big deal, Soph." But it was. He knew it and he knew she felt the same.

"Are you sure this is the right thing?"

"No." He could tell his response surprised her. "I've thought about it all week, to be honest. But I keep coming back to how he just won't let you go." Her eyes held his in the darkness of the terrace. "I wouldn't either, if you were mine."

"Christophe..."

Was that longing in her voice? Doubtful.

"The thing is, this is the soft tactic. The other option is getting lawyers involved, and I don't think you want to do that."

She shook her head. "I really don't. I don't want this to be combative in any way."

"This gives you time to have him come around." He put his hand on her shoulder. "You're not alone in this. As antiquated as it sounds, having the Germain-Pemberton name behind you gives you some protection and influence."

She smiled faintly. "Ah, yes. Using your powers for good."

"Something like that." He smiled back. "There is a third alternative, I suppose."

"Which is?"

"I go back to London and meet with him to make him see sense."

Her eyes widened. "You wouldn't."

"Only because you'd hate it."

"All that would be missing would be pistols at dawn. No, that's not what I want."

He laughed at her quip and she visibly relaxed. He pulled her into a hug again. "It's going to be okay. Promise. Come on, let's order some dinner and relax in front of the TV or something."

"I'd like that."

"Good. We can worry about tomorrow when the time comes."

He led her back inside where it was warm and suggested she choose their last meal in his flat. For now, anyway. She was about to become his fiancée. Who knew how much more time they would spend together here before the deception was over?

Sophie found herself on the Aurora, Inc. company jet for the second time in a week, this time transporting most of the family from Paris to Avignon. Christophe had explained that they would be picked up in two separate limousines in Avignon, and then make the drive to the château from there.

She'd lived a privileged life, but this sort of thing was a definite novelty. She'd brought her suitcase—she planned to head home tomorrow afternoon now—and found herself joining the jovial atmosphere of the family in private, rather than the slightly more formal Pembertons in the social sphere.

There were eight of them all together: Gabi and Will, Bella and Burke, Stephen and Aurora, and Christophe and Sophie. Charlotte was still resting and adjusting to motherhood back in Richmond, but once they were in the air Aurora set up a video call so they could all say hello and see Imogene, who was definitely looking less pink and wrinkled and more plump and adorable. Sophie stared at her tiny nose and nearly translucent eyelids, and Charlotte's tired but blissful expression. In a few months this would be her, holding her precious baby in her arms. Her heart melted a bit, and she surreptitiously touched her tummy. Her baby was in there. Growing, developing, becoming a little person. She'd been so caught up in her body's changes and the situation that she hadn't had much time to really think about how miraculous it all was. And how scared but excited she was, too.

She looked over and caught Christophe watching her, a tender smile on his face. For the first time, she let her hopes have their freedom. She wished this was different. Wished that he were the father and that this wasn't all for show. He was so kind, so funny, so supportive. And the way he'd hugged her last night… She'd felt safe, comforted. It had reminded her of those tough times her parents had shared when Mum had been going through chemo, and how she'd often come across her father offering a supportive embrace.

There'd been something else, too.

For a moment last night, she'd thought he'd been about to kiss her, and in that moment, she would have let him. But she couldn't let those thoughts in. They were friends. And he'd made it very clear that marriage and a family life weren't for him.

Any thoughts of Christophe had to be put aside, no matter how much she might want them to come true.

Once they landed in Avignon, Sophie and Christophe shared a limo with Gabi and Will. The pair had been married since the summer, and still snuggled up in the buttery-soft leather seats like newlyweds. The conversation between the two couples was light and fun, and it was Will who finally brought up the subject of Sophie's designs.

"I heard you spent time with François yesterday. Christophe has been raving about your designs all week."

She blushed and turned to look at Christophe, who bore an innocent expression. "Oh, he has, has he? Well, everything is preliminary. There might be a few pieces worth pursuing."

Christophe shrugged. "To hear François tell it, you have definite opinions that he agrees with." He lifted his eyebrow at her. "Like how you agreed with his assessment of the spring line."

"He told you that?" She wanted to sink through the seat. "Oh, I…uh…"

"Go ahead," he urged. "Tell me what you told him." His smile widened. "I mean, you don't usually have trouble telling me what you think."

She lifted her chin. "It's a very careful choice. And it lacks innovation."

"See? That wasn't so hard." He patted her knee while Gabi and Will laughed.

"Says you. Well, I guess if I'm honest at least you can't fire me."

"Maybe you should work for us," suggested Will.

Sophie sat back, taken by surprise. Work for Aurora, Inc.? It would be a dream job, for sure, but leave Waltham behind? She just didn't see how that was possible.

They changed the topic back to the current Aurora Gems line, debating the strengths and weaknesses, until they arrived at the château.

Sophie had never been, and when the driver opened the door and she stepped out, it was like stepping into another world. The château was three stories of glorious stone, white and elegant with windows that winked at her from the setting sun. It was slightly warmer than Paris, too, without the raw edge to the cold that they'd experienced the last few days. Sophie breathed in the air and let it out again. She was here, at the family château, and tonight she and Christophe were going to announce their sham engagement.

A lot had happened in the past few months, but this was as surreal as it got.

"Come in! There's lots of time to get settled before dinner. Drinks in the library in an hour?" called Aurora, her step lively as she made her way to the front door.

"She's not as terrifying today as she was on Tuesday," Sophie whispered, and Christophe chuckled.

"She likes having her family around. And to be honest, semiretirement suits her. After her heart difficulties this past summer, we're all glad to see her slow down a little bit."

Once inside, Sophie was shown to a spacious bedroom with walls the color of the lavender that grew in the nearby fields. White moldings and ornate trim contrasted with the purple hue, and the rich, silk spread was a paler shade of mauve. Pillows covered in embroidered silk dotted the bed, and a vase of fresh flowers added contrast and a delightful scent to the air. "This is absolutely stunning," she breathed.

Christophe rolled her suitcase inside. "I'm glad you like it. There's a bathroom right in there." He pointed to the right. "I'm down the hall a few doors."

She was glad he was close by. This was far grander than she'd been prepared for, and as the minutes ticked by, she felt more and more like an interloper. "Are you sure this is okay?" she whispered. "Your family is going to think I'm... I don't know. A gold digger."

"They'll think no such thing. Besides, Sophie, you have money of your own. You don't need me for that."

She smiled. "You're right. I don't have a château, but I do have a rather nice Chelsea flat."

He let go of her suitcase handle and quietly closed her door. "So, before we go down for drinks, I think we need to make this official."

Her heart pounded so heavily she could hear it in her ears, but she tried to remain nonchalant. "Oh?"

He nodded, and the easy look slid off his face as he reached into his pocket. "Sophie Waltham, will you marry me?"

He didn't mean it. She knew he didn't, that it was all for appearances, so why did that single sentence from his lips send her brain and heart into utter confusion?

"Honestly, Christophe, you don't need to propo—"

The word was cut off when Christophe took the black velvet box with the stylized *A* on its lid from his pocket. Oh, goodness, he had a ring. An Aurora ring. This felt too real. And at the same time, like the world's biggest farce.

He opened the lid and she gasped.

"It's a little unconventional," he said softly. "Like us. I thought that when this is over you might just resize it and, well, there's a matching necklace and earrings. No sense in putting it in a drawer and never wearing it again, you know?"

His practicality popped the bubble of what had become a surreal moment, and she pushed away the wave of sentimentality that had washed over her. "It's gorgeous, Christophe." Indeed it was. Apparently he'd listened to her comments about predictability and uninspired designs, because this one was unlike anything she'd ever seen. Diamonds and rubies set in platinum, different cuts and an asymmetrical design. An offset troidia-cut diamond touched points with a princess cut, while two baguette-cut rubies flanked each side and another baguette diamond sat parallel on the band. The gems glittered and sparkled in the light as he took it out of the box.

"I don't remember seeing this in the collection," she murmured, holding out her hand, trying to keep her fingers from shaking.

"It wasn't," he replied, sliding the ring over her knuckle. "François designed it, and it was one of the ones I held back last spring when I was determined to play it safe."

Oh, that last phrase had the potential to mean so much more, but they had to remember that this was just for appearances.

"Remind me again why we're doing this?" she asked.

"For your baby. For your happiness. A little ruse to reset everything to just the way you want it." He smiled at her, the cheeky grin she'd come to love. Suddenly she wanted more, though. She wanted to slip past the facade, the wall he erected to keep people from getting too close. She'd been attracted to him for years. She could definitely categorize her feelings as a crush. But this was more. There was a wounded soul behind the flippant comments and charming smile, and she wanted to know that part of him, too. Not just because of a drunken game of two truths and a lie, but because he chose to let her in.

"And what's in it for you?" She resisted the urge to wiggle her finger and set the stones sparkling again.

He lifted her hand and kissed it. "I can't go back and help the boy I was. But maybe I can help another child." His dark eyes dimmed with sadness. "And maybe that child's mother, too, so she's not as unhappy as mine was."

"You felt your abandonment very deeply," she murmured, her hand tingling from his lips and her heart aching for his confession, not only for himself but for his mum. What a gentle soul was beneath all the charm. Perhaps he would let her in after all...

"I saw what can happen when two people who don't love each other try it for the sake of the child. One parent left me. The other loved me in her way, I suppose, but I was a reminder of what her life had become. She resented me. She never thought twice about me going to Cedric and Aurora's. It would kill me to see the lovely light go out of your eyes the way it went out of hers."

"Oh, Christophe." Tears had gathered in the corners of her eyes. "You felt so unlovable and unwanted. I can't understand that, not when you're—" She stopped, afraid of saying too much.

"When I'm what?" he asked softly. There was barely any space between them now, even though they had the entire room to themselves. Sophie's pulse hammered heavily in reaction to his nearness.

"When you're so wonderful," she whispered. "I don't know what I did to deserve your loyalty, but I'm very grateful for it. This goes above and beyond the bounds of friendship."

He leaned forward and kissed her forehead. "Soph, you shouldn't marry him if you don't love him. If this can help the two of you have a productive discussion about what is best for the baby, then putting a ring on your finger and hanging out with you for a while is easy." He smiled again, a bit wistfully, she thought. "You're actually kind of nice to have around."

She jostled his arm, needing to break the intimate spell. "You know I have to go back to London."

"I know. But all you have to do is call, and I can be there in a couple of hours on the train." His face lit up. "And you can come for Christmas at the manor house. You should see it when it's decorated for the holidays." He squeezed her fingers. "Do say you'll come."

A yearning swept over her as she pictured it. Of course there'd be a giant tree, and garlands on the railings. Perhaps a dusting of snow if they were lucky, walks through the village and mincemeat tarts and mulled wine…cider for her this year, she supposed. Already she felt as if this might be going too far, and they hadn't even told his family yet. What would happen then? "I'll think about it," she promised. Heck, she was already thinking about it.

Christophe checked his watch. "Are you ready? It's nearly time for drinks."

"Do I dress for dinner now?"

"A bit later. Drinks are more casual."

She took a breath and let it out. "Well, it's now or never."

They were almost to the door when she reached out and tugged on his hand. "Christophe, wait."

When he turned, she lifted up on tiptoe and gave him a hug. "You're an amazing friend," she whispered, knowing it was true, wishing it was more than that. Wishing, though it went against every instinct, that this wasn't fake. That their feelings were deep and true and sure.

But that wasn't Christophe. He'd made it clear back in London that he was not in the market for marriage or a family. He might want to help a friend, but this wasn't a life he wanted for himself.

And for better or worse, Sophie was now a package deal.

CHAPTER TEN

DRINKS WERE HELD in the library, and Sophie tried not to goggle at the sight of the floor-to-ceiling bookshelves along two walls and the paintings above a fireplace that had logs burning briskly, throwing off a delightful heat. Even though they were close to the Mediterranean, temperatures here were only a few degrees higher than Paris, and the warmth was welcome as she and Christophe made their way to a table with assorted decanters and bottles.

"Anything for you?" he asked, his voice low, and she took a wobbly breath.

"Not at the moment. Everything is…alcoholic."

"I can arrange for something."

"Not yet."

He grabbed a cut crystal decanter and poured some amber liquid into a highball glass. "Let me know," he answered, then lifted the glass for a sip. His jaw was tighter now than it had been upstairs, and she wished she could soothe the tension away with her fingers. Instead, she clasped hers, hiding her ring beneath her right hand.

Aurora was already in the library, wineglass in hand, and she came over to give Christophe a kiss on the cheek. "I'm so glad you both could join us for the weekend. It's wonderful to have the family together. Well, not quite the whole family, but that can't be helped."

"Charlotte will be sticking her nose in in no time," Christophe said, smiling at his aunt. "She does need to be in the middle of everything."

"As opposed to Bella, who bides her time," Aurora agreed, nodding toward the door where Bella and Burke were just now coming through, their faces happy and flushed, and Bella's hair not quite perfect. Christophe nudged Sophie's arm and cocked his eyebrow. She wanted to laugh but just barely held it in. It was easy to see that while Christophe had been proposing, Bella and Burke had indulged in a late afternoon pre-drinks interlude.

"Oh, my," Aurora murmured, dropping her gaze to her glass and sipping. Sophie couldn't help it; she let out a tiny snicker at Aurora's dry tone and was delighted when the other woman's lips tipped up in a discreet but amused smile.

"We're just missing Stephen now," Aurora said, as Will and Gabi entered the room and helped themselves to drinks. She looked at Sophie. "My dear, did Christophe not get you a drink? What would you like?"

"Oh, um, I just wasn't sure so..." She hated how she sounded ambiguous and unsure. Thankfully Stephen entered then, and Christophe reached down and took her fingers.

"Actually, Sophie and I wanted to talk to everyone for a moment once Stephen gets his drink."

Aurora's head snapped up, and her sharp gaze landed on Sophie. "Oh?" she asked, but Sophie couldn't tell if it was a good "oh" or a bad one. Nerves skittered up from her stomach and down her limbs. What was his family going to think? Would they be able to pull this off and make them believe it was genuine?

"Patience, Maman," Christophe said softly. "All is well. I promise."

It was another five minutes before the family was set-tled on the sofas and chairs surrounding the fire. Sophie took a chair and crossed her legs, wondering if she should have changed out of her trousers into a dress or something a bit more remarkable. Christophe perched himself on the arm of the chair, clearly pairing himself with her, and she was buoyed by his presence.

She could do this. She could pretend to be in love with Christophe. It wasn't that hard, after all. Or even much of a stretch. Her feelings for him grew by the day.

The chatter had started to focus on the business, and it was no time at all before Bella spoke up, addressing So-phie. "Christophe says you spent time with François, and that you showed him some designs. I'm very intrigued, Sophie."

Ah. Comfortable territory; her field of expertise. "Fran-çois is utterly lovely and generous. He liked some of my designs and told me the truth, that some others were not worth exploring. He knows the business as well as any-one I've ever met."

"What are your plans, then?" Stephen asked. "Are you looking to bring Waltham under the Aurora umbrella?"

She stared at him. Such a thought hadn't even crossed her mind, and she certainly wouldn't speak of it without having broached the topic to her parents. But Stephen was in charge of acquisitions, so it was interesting to note that this was on his radar. "That's very premature," she said honestly. "I've just started exploring designing and find I enjoy it immensely. Where that takes me in the future is still very much undecided."

Christophe put his hand on her shoulder. "But speaking of the future," he said, his voice confident, "Sophie and I do have an announcement to make." There was a beat of silence as all eyes fell upon them, and then he said, "I asked Sophie to marry me, and she said yes."

The moment of silence drew out as shock rippled through the room, and then as one the family seemed to collect itself and react with the appropriate well wishes and decorum. "Congratulations!" exclaimed Will, who put his arm around Gabi and squeezed. "I can tell you firsthand that marriage is wonderful, cousin."

"Congratulations," echoed Gabi, her eyes soft and loving. They were like a dart into Sophie's soul. Gabi and Will's love was so true, and here she and Christophe were in this sham of an engagement.

She reminded herself that this was not the Pemberton family's first experience with a sham engagement though, and it helped a little. Precious little, but still.

"Darling." Aurora got up and went to Christophe and kissed his cheek. "This is wonderful news. And Sophie." She rose and Aurora pulled her into a polite but still warm hug. "Welcome to our big and crazy family."

"Thank you," she whispered, her eyes pricking. She didn't deserve this. She didn't deserve any of it.

"Come on, then," said Bella. "Let's see the ring." She looked at Christophe with an accusatory glare. "You did propose with a ring, didn't you?"

Christophe laughed, looking far more at ease than she felt. "Of course I did."

Sophie held out her hand. "Oh…" Bella said, rising from the Louis XIV settee and coming forward. She took Sophie's hand and lifted it so that the light reflected off the brilliant stones. "I haven't seen that one before."

"It's one of a kind," Christophe said, beaming. "François helped me choose just the right one." He looked over at Sophie, his face perfectly adoring. "Nothing ordinary for my extraordinary fiancée."

God, he was such a good actor. She almost believed him…and she knew the truth! She could practically hear the internal *aww*s coming from his family.

"Christophe really knows me," she said shyly. "He did a wonderful job picking the ring. It's beautiful and yet unusual…just like our relationship." She laughed a little, knowing she had actually managed to tell the truth somehow in all this farcical sentimentality.

"When's the big day?" Stephen asked. He was the only one not to rise from his seat for a better look, but if what Christophe said was true, Stephen wasn't a big fan of matrimony at the moment, either. He'd had one engagement broken off and Gabi had left him at the altar. Even though that had all turned out for the best, Sophie could understand him not being the most excited person in the room.

"Um, we haven't really discussed it. It, uh…"

Christophe pulled her in close to his side and leaned over to whisper in her ear. "We might as well tell them. It's going to come out anyway."

She swallowed against a massive lump in her throat, a rush of cold panic racing through her veins. She nodded briefly, gathering herself together. *In for a penny, in for a pound*, she thought, and with all the courage she possessed, she lifted her chin and faced his family.

"We're not sure," she said clearly, "because I'm having a baby."

Bella gaped. Aurora sat down. Gabi and Will stared at each other, and Stephen kept his steady gaze on the two of them, rubbing an index finger across his lips as if deep in thought. That unsettled her the most. Stephen didn't even look surprised. How could that be, when she was?

Burke, bless him, recovered first. "Well. This family never does anything halfway, does it? How are you feeling? When's the happy event?"

Sophie sat down again, and Christophe resumed his perch on the arm of the chair, but he kept his arm around her shoulders, a firm show of support. "I'm due in the spring," she said quietly. "And I'm feeling much better, now that the sickness seems to have eased."

"I was sickest with my first," Aurora said. "I'm glad you're over the worst of it. It's so very unpleasant."

She was trying, Sophie realized, and she smiled at Aurora in gratitude. "It wasn't fun. But you should know…"

Christophe's fingers pressed into her shoulder. "The baby isn't mine. Sophie and the father had already split up when she found out she was pregnant."

"Dammit, Christophe, it's just bombshell after bombshell," Bella groused. "I think I might need another drink."

"Sorry," Sophie said, her voice small. It was a lot for them to take in. There was asking for support and then there was just…whatever strange thing this was.

"Don't be sorry." Christophe's voice was firm as his gaze touched hers. "It does nothing to change how we feel about each other."

Again with the wordsmithing. He'd managed to imply love without actually saying the word. *Well done*, she thought, her admiration for his quick thinking and fortitude growing.

"Of course it doesn't," Gabi added staunchly. "If I've learned anything over the past year, it's that love plus this family equals complicated. It also equals worth it. You've got our support." She nudged Will, who added his agreement with a nod, as if he didn't dare contradict his wife.

"And ours," Bella said, sounding slightly less convinced but holding Burke's hand just the same.

"Absolument." Aurora let a smile touch her lips although Sophie thought perhaps her eyes weren't as warm

as before. "This family sticks together, and now you're one of us, Sophie."

She appreciated the solidarity, but how much support would she have when they found out the truth?

Christophe clapped his hands, hoping to maximize the felicitations and make the scene joyful in order to avoid more questions. In hindsight, he and Sophie should have laid out a game plan. Still, it could have gone worse. Much worse. Thank heavens for Gabi.

"I think we should have a toast," he suggested, keeping his tone light and jovial. "Champagne?"

Aurora rose and smiled again, and he recognized it as a forced expression. She patted his arm and said, "I'll arrange it and be right back."

While they were waiting, Gabi and Bella offered their congratulations and surrounded Sophie to look at the ring and ask all sorts of questions about their courtship and her pregnancy. Thankfully, he heard her say that while it seemed sudden, they'd been friends for a very long time. What touched him especially was when she said, "In the past weeks he really has shown me he's the very best of men."

God, he hoped he was. Was this even the right thing? He wasn't sure. It was a crazy idea that made some sense, but certainly it wasn't the only solution to her problem. So why had he stepped in? Why had he taken the extraordinary step of suggesting an engagement, when the very word had sent him running in the past?

The question gave him a great deal of discomfort, so he ignored it and instead kissed her temple before turning back to his glass of Scotch and draining it in one gulp.

"So, fatherhood." Stephen's dry voice came from beside him and he turned around. Of all the family, Stephen would be the toughest to fool. Probably because he was the least trusting of all of them.

"Seems like," Christophe answered, clapping his hand on Stephen's arm and smiling widely.

"Are you sure about this?" Stephen's dark brows pulled together, but at least he kept his voice low so Sophie wouldn't hear. "Someone else's baby? And it's been such a short time."

Christophe met his eldest cousin's astute gaze. "We've been friends for a very long time, Stephen. I can't imagine anything better than marrying a friend, can you?"

He said it to appease Stephen, but when the words came out he realized that they were true. If he ever did marry—not that an actual wedding was in his plans—he would want it to be with someone he was friends with. Who he could be himself with. Who saw beyond the Pemberton and Aurora, Inc. façade.

"I thought I was going to marry a friend. Then she married my brother."

"Perhaps it has to be both," Christophe suggested. "A friend but also a…a lover." He stuttered over that last bit. His fingers were still twined with Sophie's even though they were facing opposite directions. And for a flash of a moment, he thought about being her lover and his blood ran hot.

No, no, no. This was not part of the plan. That sort of thinking had to be nipped in the bud.

"Perhaps," Stephen acknowledged, but he didn't sound convinced. Christophe was saved, though, by Aurora returning with a chilled bottle and a maid following behind with a tray of crystal flutes.

There was a general bustling around as glasses were filled and handed to everyone, even Sophie. Christophe noticed she took the glass with a wobbly smile and shrugged.

As head of the family, it was up to Aurora to give the toast. She took a breath and then lifted her glass as they all gathered in the center of the room, the fire crackling behind them.

"To my son, Christophe, and to Sophie, his bride-to-be. May your lives be filled with blessings and your hearts with love."

Christophe's throat tightened as her words hit home. Not her nephew, not someone she loved as a son, but *her son*. No qualifiers. He called her Maman, but in his head she was always *ma tante*, not *ma mère*. He did love her. But there would always be one other woman who held that place, whose love he craved more than anything. How stupid was that, when he hadn't even seen the woman in five years?

"To Christophe and Sophie," Stephen said, lifting his glass, and the other couples echoed the words.

Everyone touched glasses and drank. Christophe noticed that Sophie touched the rim to her lips and tasted the fizzy champagne, and then lowered it again, taking part in the toast but abstaining from consuming any alcohol. He drained his glass and then took hers from her hand and put both on a nearby table.

"Well, aren't you going to kiss your fiancée?" asked Stephen.

Christophe looked into Sophie's eyes and saw confusion beneath the dark depths, but also acceptance. If they were going to convince everyone this was genuine, they had to get used to touching each other. It was one kiss, and it could be a chaste one, really. They were in front of others, and it didn't need to be a big display. Just believable.

Christophe channeled all of his charm and let a slow smile lift his lips as he gazed into her eyes. It wasn't hard to act attracted to her; she was utterly gorgeous, and he cared about her deeply. Indeed, in another time or place this might have been the natural progression of things. "That sounds like a wonderful idea," he murmured, just loud enough for everyone to hear. Then he lifted his hand and cupped her neck in his palm before dipping his head and touching his mouth to hers.

He hadn't been prepared, though, for the contact to rocket through his body. He hadn't expected her to be so responsive, either. As their lips met, hers parted slightly, softly touching his with shyness and uncertainty but definitely with participation. Sophie, who had never been shy in her life from what he knew of her. Her breath came out on a small sigh and the muscles in her neck were tense, but a quick check showed her eyes were closed, the dark lashes lying innocently on her cheeks. He moved his mouth over hers, taking a few precious moments to taste the supple flavors of her before drawing away, but not before the contact shook him to the soles of his feet. It was the smallest of kisses, without any dark promise of the night that lay ahead, and yet he was completely and utterly undone by it.

Sophie. His Sophie.

Where had she been his whole life?

Sophie ran her tongue over her lip to make the taste of him last a little bit longer. Her heart was knocking about in her chest as if she'd just run a marathon, and she was sure there were stars in her eyes. What in the world was wrong with her? It was a celebratory engagement kiss in front of his family. So why had her whole world just tilted?

He was smiling down at her, a private smile that did nothing to quell the conflicting feelings racing through her mind. She had to get ahold of herself. Keep up the pretense, act as if kissing him was the most natural thing in the world. She had to push away the need to kiss him again. Forget the other desires running through her body right now, and her heart, too. This had been such a bad idea. There was absolutely no way she was going to come out of this unscathed.

"Aw, you two are so sweet." Gabi's voice reached Sophie's ears and she reluctantly turned away from Christophe's magnetic gaze.

"What can I say?" She laughed lightly and waved her hand, the jewels in her ring sparkling in the light. "It's been a whirlwind time, really."

"But when you know, you know," Christophe added, and Sophie thought maybe he was laying it on a little thick. He couldn't mean such a thing. For the millionth time, she reminded herself that Christophe didn't do love or commitment. He'd said it himself—his last relationship had ended because he'd been unable to commit.

Sophie's glass was replaced with one of sparkling water, but she noticed that Christophe picked up her champagne and drained it, too. That made three drinks in the thirty minutes they'd been in the library. Perhaps this was more difficult for him than he let on, and for some reason it felt as if someone had let the air out of her happy balloon. This wasn't real. Why did she have to keep reminding herself of that?

The cocktail hour wound down and Christophe reappeared at her side, ready to escort her back to her room as everyone went to change for dinner. "Shall we?" he asked, his voice low, and it shivered along her nerve endings.

He dropped her at her room, with promises to come back in twenty minutes to collect her again, lest she get lost in the hallways of the château. Once inside her room, Sophie turned on a soft lamp and sat down on the edge of the bed.

The ring sparkled in the light and she held her hand

aloft, studying the gems and the way it looked on her hand. It was unlike anything she'd seen before, but it suited her, too. Funny how Christophe had been able to see that when no one in her life seemed to get who she really was. It was as if the people who cared about her put her in their own private box of expectations, but with Christophe, she could just be Sophie—her own version of herself.

After a few minutes, she got up and went to her suitcase to take out the cocktail dress she'd brought along. Tonight she would eat dinner with the Pembertons. Tomorrow she would have to go back to London to face the music—and Eric.

The Pembertons might be the first test, but seeing Eric was going to be the hardest one.

CHAPTER ELEVEN

DINNER WAS ABSOLUTELY divine and in a number of courses that boggled Sophie's mind. First a small salad of cucumber and apple in crème fraiche, then a fish course of seared scallops, a main course of guinea fowl and steamed vegetables, followed by a cheese course. Sophie avoided the soft and blue cheese varieties, but it was no problem, as she was already stuffed. The cook at the château was clearly very talented. She hadn't had such a meal in a very long time, and that included the fine dining at exclusive restaurants she'd experienced while dating Eric and during the past week with Christophe.

"This was amazing," she said, after touching her napkin to her lips. "The guinea fowl was perfect."

"It's not often so many of us are together," Bella said, sipping on the last of her glass of white wine. "And tonight we had a real reason to celebrate."

"Hear, hear," said Will.

"Thank you all. For the lovely welcome and the support."

Stephen studied the rim of his glass, then met her gaze. "What you need to understand, Sophie, is that once you're one of us, we all come with the package. That means you're not alone. You have the Pembertons behind you."

Her lips fell open in shock at the unexpected support.

"Thank you, Stephen." Christophe acknowledged his cousin with a nod.

The jovial mood had sobered quite a bit, and it was Aurora who finally voiced the question that Sophie had been waiting for. "And the father…is he in the picture?"

"Yes," she answered, determined to keep her voice clear and strong. "He intends to be a father to the baby, and for that I am thankful. He's…he's a good man. He's just not the right man for me, that's all." She looked around the table. "But I do hope you'll understand if I leave tomorrow to go back to London. I'd like to tell him and my parents the news before there's a chance of it leaking." She looked at Christophe. "And I think it's only right I do it in person."

"Of course, *ma chère*," he said, picking up her hand and kissing her fingers.

The gathering broke up after that, and Sophie was more than ready for bed. Dinner had gone on until well after nine, and it had been a long and emotional day. Keeping up pretenses was exhausting work. She wasn't prepared for one last edict from Aurora, however, as she and Christophe were leaving the dining room.

"Christophe, while I appreciate you putting Sophie in a guest room for appearances, now that everything is official, you don't have to have separate rooms."

Oh, Lord. Sophie was sure her ears were flushed bright pink as the two of them stopped and stared at his ever-calm aunt. She laughed, that rusty laugh that Sophie had admired earlier but now…now it made her feel incredibly awkward. "Good heavens, you two. You've been staying at the flat all week anyway. It's not exactly been a secret." She gave a wink. "Besides, I knew it was like this when I first saw you together. It's in the way you look at each other. It reminds me of me and Cedric."

The teasing expression softened into one of sentimentality. "Your lives together will sometimes be complicated," she offered, "but if you face it together, as each other's best friend, and with commitment, you'll be just fine. Good night, darlings."

Christophe took Sophie's hand and they escaped to the stairs and the upper floor to the bedrooms. It wasn't until they got to the empty hallway that he let go of her hand, halted, and let his head drop.

"Are you all right?" she asked, immediately putting her hand on his arm in concern. "I'm so sorry about that last bit. I knew pretending would be hard, but—"

"Shh," he commanded, and they turned their heads together toward the sound of Will and Gabi coming up the stairs, talking and laughing. Christophe took her arm and spun her toward her bedroom door, turned the knob, and hurried them both inside.

"Sorry," she whispered.

Gabi's and Will's voices sounded outside their door; there was a little giggle and Will's deeper response, and meanwhile Sophie was pressed against Christophe's front while he had his shoulder against her door. It was utterly dark in the room; not even the lamp was on. They were cocooned in blackness, and all Sophie could hear now was the sound of their breathing, rising and falling quickly.

And still she did not step away.

"Soph," he murmured. "This…dammit."

He kissed her then, and it was as different from the kiss downstairs as day was from night. This was dark, seductive, passionate. It ignited something deep in her core, and her brain simply stopped working as she wound her arms around his neck and kissed him back fully.

Nearly a decade she'd known Christophe, nearly a decade she'd wondered and occasionally fantasized. And yet she hadn't ever realized he had this dark, intense passion about him. Having it focused completely on her was a glorious revelation. He shifted his weight and she found herself pressed against the door, sandwiched between the heavy wood and the hardness of his body. And it was hard, she realized, as his lips slid from hers and skittered over her neck. A gasp erupted from her throat, calling his mouth back to hers.

A welcome heaviness centered in her pelvis, and she knew that either they had to stop or he was going to have to take her to bed. Her body cried out for the latter, but common sense had to prevail at some point.

This was a fake engagement. Christophe didn't want marriage or a family. This could go nowhere.

"Christophe." How she managed both syllables of his name was a miracle, because his mouth was a wicked, wicked thing as he kissed the tender spot just below her ear. "We have to stop. We can't do this."

It might have had more effect if she hadn't pressed her breast into his palm. She wanted him so badly. Wanted the heat and passion of him, so different from—

The comparison that popped into her brain had the desired cooling effect. She put her hand on his wrist and moved it off her breast, then slid out from between him and the door. Her breath was coming heavily, and her lips felt deliciously swollen, but they really did have to stop. It wasn't fair to her or especially to him to start making comparisons. Exploring whatever this was would only complicate things. And potentially harm their friendship, which was far too important to jeopardize.

"I… I'm sorry." Christophe ran a hand through his rumpled curls. She could just make out his features in the moonlight coming through the window now that her eyes had adjusted to the dark. "I don't know… I mean…"

"I know. There's our friendship to consider."

"Yes," he agreed emphatically, taking a step toward her. "I don't want to mess anything up. And yet..." She saw him swallow, and there was still this tense energy radiating from him, as she was certain must be from her, as well. They were turned on...by each other.

"I know. I didn't expect it. Didn't... Please, don't be too sorry. We just can't let it go any further."

"Which is a damned shame," he replied, and the desire in his voice nearly had her reconsidering. Her whole body was crying out for him, craving satisfaction. Over the past two weeks she'd noticed things about him, certainly. She'd been able to explain them away. But this... there was no denying that in addition to being wonderful friends, there was amazing chemistry between them. She'd always wondered. Now she knew. It was almost impossible to walk away from, even knowing it would blow up in her face in the end.

"A damned shame," she echoed.

"I'll be right back."

He disappeared into her bathroom and she heard water running. Then he returned with a glass of water in his hand and a little moisture clinging to his hair. "In lieu of a cold shower," he explained. "So I can attempt to have working brain cells when we talk about this."

"I agree." She passed by him and headed to the bathroom, as well. At the sound of his muffled laugh, she pointed out, "You're not the only one who needs cooling off."

The cold water didn't really work, however. When she returned to the bedroom, he was still standing there, in his trousers and shirt and tie, looking devastatingly sexy and rumpled. Need pulsed through her. Pretense was gone. For the past week, they'd carefully avoided too much touching, hadn't crossed a line. Now it had been crossed and she'd had a taste of him. Was it wrong that she now wanted it all?

"Sophie, if you don't want this to happen, you have to stop looking at me like that."

She bit down on her lip while a war raged within her. Once again, she reminded herself that the engagement was fake. That Christophe couldn't give her what she truly needed: love, security, a life together. A partner to see her through the rough times, because there would definitely be hardships. The only thing he could give her was this moment, right now. Was it enough? She didn't know. She wasn't sure of any of her decisions over the past few months. And yet a singular thought persisted...if she walked away tonight, that would be it. She would never know. And she would always regret it.

They'd already crossed a line. There was no more pretending that attraction, chemistry didn't exist. Three minutes against her bedroom door had told her exactly what she needed to know.

"This," she said softly, taking a step toward him. "What do you mean by this?"

"I mean..." The words were taut, bound tight by the restraint he seemed desperate to maintain. "I didn't mean for this to happen. And then we kissed downstairs..."

"And we had to stop pretending?" She took another step closer, her heart thundering.

"You're my friend. This is wrong. I shouldn't think of you this way."

"Think of me how?" she asked.

"You need to stop asking me questions."

A small smile touched her lips. The closer she got to him, the more certain she became. She was about to leave her past life behind. No more twenty-something young professional. She was going to be a mother, with new responsibilities. One night. One night with Christophe to hold on to. She'd had a thing for him for so long, and here he was in front of her. Could she really pass up what was likely to be her only chance?

"Then let me answer," she said softly. She was now only inches away from him, and she saw a muscle flex in his jaw. She reached up and loosened his tie, sliding the end out of the knot. "I've been thinking of you this way for the past four days. I've thought of you this way long before this, but I didn't want to let it get in the way of our friendship. But the moment you pressed me against that door and said my name, well, that ship sailed, *mon ami*. This engagement might be fake, but my need for you isn't. I want you, Christophe." She let the tie fall to the floor.

He let out a breath, as if she'd just ripped the rug out from beneath him. "You. Need me."

"Touch me again and find out," she said, daring.

"I can't make promises," he said, the words strangled. She busied her fingers with the buttons on his shirt now, slowly releasing each one from the buttonhole.

"I know that. I'm not asking for any. I'm not asking for a thing besides tonight, in this bed, with me." She pressed her lips to his chest, just below the hollow at the base of his neck. "Tell me you won't always wonder if we don't."

He made a sound in his throat that rumbled beneath her lips.

"Tell me you don't want me, and you can go to your room and I'll stay here and that will be it. That's all it takes, Christophe. Just say the words. *I don't want you, Sophie.* Say it."

She looked up into his hot, dark gaze. Every nerve ending in her body was begging for stimulation and release. *Touch me*, she silently begged. *Love me.*

"I can't say it, because it would be a lie. I want you so much I'm dying with it. Sophie…" He curled his hand around the nape of her neck. "I want you so much right now it scares me."

Victory.

"One night. The only promise I want is that tomorrow we'll still be friends."

"Always," he said. "That's an easy one."

She wasn't so sure, but he was stripping out of his shirt and she moved her fingers to the zipper of her dress. It caught and he turned her around by the shoulders, working at the zip in the dark, sliding the dress off her shoulders while the hot skin of his chest grazed her back.

This had escalated so quickly. Her crush had been one thing. This explosive desire was another. Downstairs she'd kept her response to his kiss sweet and shy, playing a part. Now, though, now she wanted so much more. All it had taken to make that fire come to life was the way he'd responded to her moments before. As if he couldn't help himself, couldn't get enough of her.

She needed him, but being needed in return was the biggest turn on she could imagine.

"Sophie," he whispered, his breath warm on her neck. "Kiss me, Sophie."

He didn't have to ask twice. She turned around, dressed now in only her bra and panties, and slid her arms over his shoulders. Their mouths met, this time without the uncertainty of the first time and the frantic passion of the second, but with mutual acknowledgment and desire. His lips were demanding and she answered the call, then slid her hands down his hard chest to his belt buckle. Hands working quickly, she undid the button and zip on his pants while he flicked open the clasp on her bra. She shimmied it down her arms and let it drop on the floor, then hooked her thumbs in her panties and skimmed them down her legs.

"You are so unexpected," he said, reaching for her.

"I'm surprising myself," she admitted, and was glad that in the midst of the scramble to disrobe they'd found a way back to their easy banter.

But Christophe had his own surprises. He swept her up into his arms and crossed the room to the bed, then with one hand, flipped the covers down to the bottom and laid her on the silken sheets. He joined her there, lying beside her, braced on an elbow so they could kiss and touch and explore. There was a moment when his palm covered her belly and wishes filled her heart, but then his hand slipped lower and she let the wishes flutter away on her sighs.

And when the touches grew desperate, she reached for him. "Don't make me wait," she whispered.

There was a moment where they paused, as if realizing that birth control was not a concern, and then he was there, joined to her, and the world stopped turning.

Sophie arched her neck and said his name.

If this was one night only, he was making it one she'd never forget.

Christophe woke with the sun in his eyes. He squinted, then realized the walls were purple. A glance to his side showed Sophie, still asleep on her belly, her hair spread out in a cascade of chocolate silk.

They were both gloriously naked.

God. He should never have slept here. Images of the previous night raced through his brain, causing both arousal and panic in his blood. What had they done? At the time it had seemed the most natural thing in the world. Kissing her the first time had been the mistake. He should have left her at the door and that was it.

And yet…it was hard to regret something so amazing.

She'd been so confident. So sure of herself. Had he ever met anyone who knew their own mind more than she did? When Sophie went after something, she just did it. No second-guessing. She made decisions and moved forward. He admired that about her. And he couldn't complain. Making love with her had been spectacular.

There'd been a moment, just beforehand, when his fingers had trailed over her belly. He'd remembered then that a life grew within her, just beneath his palm, and he'd been awed and humbled at her trust in him. She wasn't showing, but he'd noticed the small, firm bubble where her child grew. It had unlocked something in him that was so uncomfortable he'd nearly stopped and walked away.

Instead, he'd done what he always did: pushed the thought aside and ignored it. He was rather good at that.

Which meant this morning he'd have to compartmentalize the feelings crowding his chest, strangling him. Tenderness. Protectiveness. Need. He had to get up now, get out of this bed, because if she rolled over and touched him, he wasn't sure he'd have the strength to turn her away.

One night. That was what she'd asked for and that was what he'd given. Friendship. Her one condition.

It was going to be hell, but he would give her what she asked for. Because if nothing else, Christophe kept his word.

He slid out from beneath the covers and gathered his clothes on the way to the bathroom. When he returned, fully dressed, she had rolled over in bed, the sheets gathered beneath her armpits, her eyes sleepy. "Good morning," he said softly.

"Indeed," she replied, but he noticed her eyes were more guarded than usual. Interesting. Maybe he wasn't the only one who could compartmentalize.

"I thought I might go back to my own room and shower. I don't have any of my things here."

"Sure." She sat up a bit. "Christophe, are we okay?"

"Of course we are." He took a chance and went to her, perching on the side of the bed, though not too close. She was naked and tempting and this was not the plan—even if they'd thrown out the playbook on the first night.

"Okay. I just wanted to be sure. I don't think we should act as if it never happened."

He chuckled. "I don't think that's possible, *ma chère*. It was pretty amazing."

"It just can't be repeated."

"That's right."

"For obvious reasons."

"Exactly."

She nodded at him. "I know that." She reached for his hand. "I would never ask you to compromise your own needs. I know you don't want marriage and children. I'm not looking for you to change. It's the one thing I truly love about our relationship. We each get to be exactly who we are."

Then why did he feel so let down? Why did he feel as if the man he was was somehow wanting?

"Last night was unexpected," he acknowledged. "But I will keep my promises, Soph. One night only, friendship firmly intact."

She lifted her hand to his cheek, the ring he'd given her sparkling on her finger. "You are the best of men," she murmured, meeting his gaze. "I said it to your sister last night and I meant it. I trust you, Christophe. You have honor and honesty."

He kissed her forehead, but that was all he dared, and with a smile of farewell he got up and left her bedroom. Once alone and in his own shower though, the hot spray sluicing down his body, he put a hand along the tiles and hung his head.

He didn't have honor or honesty. An honorable man would have done the right thing and turned down her invitation. And an honest man would have admitted that one night with her would never be enough.

CHAPTER TWELVE

SOPHIE SPENT THE morning feeling entirely off balance. On one hand, the effect of good sex left her body relaxed and still humming with pleasure. On the other, navigating a new normal with Christophe, while under the watchful eyes of his family, took some mental and emotional finesse.

Thankfully, breakfast was a casual affair with people eating at different times and picking and choosing something light. Pastries, Greek yogurt and fruit fit the bill for her, as well as tea instead of the bottomless coffee service. She'd dressed in a long skirt and boots, as well as a sweater and belt, as she wanted to be comfortable on the flight back to London. Her flight left at noon, and it was nearly an hour to the airport at Aix-en-Provence, which had a daily direct flight to London. She'd be home early afternoon, leaving France and Christophe behind, but his ring still on her finger.

Christophe was always there, making sure she wasn't alone, being supportive and kind. It seemed to her that he had an easier time of regaining his equilibrium than she did, but she let it steady her. Before long, she was putting her suitcase in the limousine. She'd said goodbyes to most of the family, and thanked Aurora for her hospitality, and now there was just Gabi and Bella, who had followed her outside, and Christophe—the hardest of all to say goodbye to.

She'd turned down his offer to go with her to the airport. Instead, he'd return to Paris with the rest of the family that evening, on the company jet out of Avignon.

"I'm sorry you couldn't stay longer," said Bella, giving Sophie's elbow a squeeze. "But we'll see you soon, I'm sure. Either in Paris, or for sure at the château for the holidays. It's only five weeks away."

Five weeks. Christophe had asked her to join him…perhaps their relationship would be back to somewhat normal by then.

Gabi nodded. "I had my first Christmas there last year. You'll love it." She smiled her soft, sweet smile and said, "One of the best things about becoming a Pemberton is that I keep gaining sisters. I quite like it, really."

Sophie struggled to keep smiling. Oh, they were going to hate her when the engagement suddenly ended, weren't they? This had to have been the most foolish idea on the planet.

"Get going, so I can say goodbye to my fiancée, and so she doesn't miss her flight," Christophe chided, shooing them away.

With a last wave the two departed. Christophe turned back to face her, and her pulse jumped. It was good she was leaving. They needed some space to deal with what happened. To put it in perspective.

"Will you call me tonight? Let me know how things are? I'll be worried about you."

"Of course. Or at the very least, I'll text, okay? Depending on how I feel."

"I wish I could be there with you. Not because you can't handle it. Just because I feel like I'm leaving you alone for the hardest part."

She met his gaze and squared her shoulders. "This is my life, my parents, my ex, Christophe. It's not up to you to make things better." She softened her voice. "But knowing you're supporting me helps. I know you're there. I know you have my back."

"All right. And if things get to be too much, in any way, you call. I can be there in a few hours. Or you can come to me." He held out his hand. "You gave this back to me yesterday, but I want you to keep it."

He dropped the key to his flat into her palm, still warm from his skin.

"Christophe, I don't know what to say."

"Last night changes nothing," he said. "One night only, friendship intact, remember?"

"I remember. Thank you."

He leaned forward and kissed her forehead for the second time that morning. She was starting to hate that, actually. A gesture that implied intimacy but was guarded. Still, she said nothing, gave him a smile, and slid into the limo.

"Goodbye, Christophe. I'll be in touch later."

"Safe travels," he said, and shut the door.

The tires of the limo crunched over the drive, and she turned for one last look at the château. She'd hoped Christophe would be standing there still, but when she looked, he'd disappeared back inside.

She let out a breath and sat back against the plush seat. Then she took out her phone and started making plans for the day. A message to her pet service that she would be home this afternoon. One to her parents that she would like to have breakfast with them in the morning, and finally, a third to Eric, asking if they could talk later today, at his place. His because she wanted to be able to leave if things didn't go well.

Security was not overwhelmed midday on a Sunday, and it took very little time before she was at her gate, ready to board. Every minute took her farther and farther away from Christophe and the past week. Boarding was called and she made her way to her seat, then took her sketch pad and colored pencils out of her bag once they'd taken off. Working on her designs would surely ease some of the anxiety settling in her gut.

She picked a blue pencil and stared at her hand. She hadn't got used to the ring, and it stayed there as a reminder of the previous evening. Now instead of a family dinner stuck in her mind, she had Christophe's kisses, the feel of his hands on her body on replay.

They'd agreed to one night. He'd seemed completely fine with that this morning. She wasn't, though. She finally could admit it to herself now that there were several miles and twenty-odd thousand feet between them. It wasn't fair to compare; she knew that. But being with Christophe…it had been different from anything she'd ever experienced. And if she ever admitted that he was the best sex she'd ever had, she could just imagine how he'd laugh at her.

She smiled despite herself. Here she was in the biggest mess she'd ever been in, and he didn't even need to be present to make her laugh.

She wanted to go back to Paris. Back to his flat. Back to Aurora, to François, to all of it. The entire week had been perfect. Life altering. It had made her question everything she thought she knew.

Once she'd landed and collected her bag, she took a cab to her flat and asked the cabbie to wait. Eric had messaged back that he was home all afternoon and would be available. There was no sense putting it off. She took a moment to give Harry a quick cuddle and a promise she'd return soon, and then she went back to the cab and gave the cabbie instructions to Eric's executive flat in Canary Wharf.

He greeted her at the door with a wide smile. "Darling! I'm so glad you messaged. Come in. I've made tea."

She stepped inside and he removed her wrap, but she kept her gloves on, not wanting him to see her ring just yet. Maybe she should have taken it off, but it would add weight to what she was about to tell him, and she could use all the help she could get. He looked good, she realized. Not a strand of his dark blond hair was out of place, and even on a Sunday he was perfectly groomed. Clean-shaven, neat trousers, collared shirt under a sweater.

She thought of Christophe coming out of his room for his morning coffee, dressed in sweatpants and a rumpled T-shirt. She knew which she preferred.

He hung her coat in the closet. "Thank you, Eric."

"Did you have lunch?" he called as he headed toward the kitchen. She closed her eyes. It would be so much easier if he were less likable. She reminded herself that he'd said his share of hurtful things over the past two and a half months, and that he'd been pressuring her unfairly. She had to keep perspective here.

"I'm fine, thank you." She followed him into the kitchen area. "Tea is lovely, though."

He poured from a pot—no bag in a cup for him—and hit the button on his espresso machine, making himself a coffee. "When did you arrive back in town?" he asked.

"About an hour ago."

"I see."

She knew he didn't, but that was fine. She took the cup from him and had a sip, just to keep her hands busy while he waited for his coffee.

"I was in Paris. At Aurora, doing some…consulting."

His eyebrows went up. "Wow. Nice gig for you." His beverage finished and he took the cup from the machine, then waved her into the living room overlooking the river.

She'd spent many hours in this room, and now he would buy her a place in the country if she wanted it. Somewhere to raise their baby. She almost wished she could say yes; it would be so much more uncomplicated, but it would be a lie. When she looked at him now, she had no hard feelings or regrets about the time they'd spent together, but it was over. If she'd had any doubts, last night would have laid them to rest. She could never accept anything less than...love.

Her throat tightened, and she was afraid she might burst into tears. It was love, then, this feeling that filled her heart to bursting, that made her anxious and sad and thrilled all at the same time. To find it in a good friend was even more shocking. And knowing she could never have it was devastating.

"Are you all right? Is it the tea? What do you need?" He reached for her hands.

She brushed his hands away. "No, I'm fine. So is the tea. Please, Eric, sit down. I came here to tell you something and I don't want to put it off."

His easy, friendly expression turned wary, and he sat on the sofa across from the chair that she chose. Nerves tightened her muscles as she stiffly tugged on her gloves, first taking off the right, then the left, before laying the soft leather in her lap.

Then she put her left hand over her right, looked him in the eye and made herself say the words. "Eric, I came here to tell you that I'm engaged to marry Christophe Germain."

Eric jumped to his feet and stared down at her. "I beg your pardon? Who the hell is Christophe Germain?" He frowned, a deep furrow appearing between his eyebrows. "I know I've heard that name. Who is he? And engaged? We've only been split up a few months! Does he know about the baby?"

"Sit down, Eric, and stop shouting, or I'll get up and walk out. I would rather stay and talk."

He sat, but looked remarkably unhappy about it.

"Christophe is the cousin of the Earl of Chatsworth and one of the heirs to the Aurora fortune. I've known him for years." The engagement might be false, but that much at least was true.

"Years. Of course. He's the French one, right?"

"Obviously." She resisted the urge to roll her eyes. "You met him once or twice, I think. And he was at Stephen's wedding." Eric had gone as her plus-one.

"Ah yes, the wedding that never was." He didn't bother hiding his disdain. "But engaged. When did this happen?"

She swallowed and forced herself to remain calm and still and tell as much truth as possible. "Well, he asked me on Monday, and I answered him on Thursday night, and we told his family last night. I flew back this afternoon because I wanted you to hear it from me in person, and Mum and Dad, too."

He sat back on the sofa, still scowling. "This is ridiculous. For two months I've been asking you to marry me. Offering you an amazing life, and you…you never once thought to tell me you were seeing someone else?"

Ah, now it was becoming sticky. She looked him in the eye and considered her words. "I wanted us to discuss our future as parents. I already told you I wouldn't marry you. I shouldn't have to qualify that with whether or not I'm seeing someone else." She didn't bother to gentle her words. "This is between you and me, Eric. I truly don't want this to be acrimonious. I want us to figure this out together. But we can't do that if you won't accept that marriage is not in our future. I'm marrying someone else."

He got up again and paced to the window, then turned back again, his hands on his hips. "You told me that you could never marry unless it was for love. You're telling me that you love him? That you are undeniably, forevermore, head over heels and every other cliché in love with him?"

She wouldn't cry. Even though his words were meant as an accusation, they effectively echoed everything going on within her right now. It didn't matter what boundaries they set or what Christophe was or wasn't capable of. Feelings were feelings, and she had a lot of them. But her lip wobbled just a little as she nodded. "Yes, that's exactly what I'm telling you." She lifted her hand and wiped away the one small tear that had escaped.

When she did, he noticed the ring, and his face fell. "You really are engaged."

She nodded.

"You accepted his ring."

"I did." She fiddled with the diamonds and rubies, nerves still jumping about.

"Dammit, Sophie."

Silence fell in the flat, a resentful, awkward silence that had her shifting on the chair. She would give anything to be back on Christophe's sofa right now, watching a movie with a throw blanket over her and a bowl of popcorn between them. But that wouldn't happen again. At least it was improbable. She focused instead on the baby, and the future she would provide for them, and how this moment was going to lay the groundwork for that.

It would be enough.

"You really won't marry me."

She shook her head. "I'm sorry. You deserve someone who loves you better than I can. Someone who can make you happy. That wouldn't be me, Eric. But we can work together to make sure our baby is loved. I meant what I said. I want you to be a part of their life, to be a father. Let go of this fantasy of the life you had laid out for us and try to picture a new one. We can make it work."

He turned back to the window again, his posture stiff. "You broke my heart, you know."

Her eyes stung. She knew it wasn't just words. "I'm sorry for that. Truly. I don't know what else to say."

"There isn't anything to say."

Her tea was cold now and she left it on the table; it had only been a prop anyway. "We can talk about arrangements another time," she suggested softly. "There's almost six months before the baby is born. We have time."

"I don't want to have to fight you for custody," he said, turning to face her once more.

"Me, either. I would like for us to come up with our own workable solution. But I'm also happy to get that in writing. I think it would make us feel better."

"When did we get to be strangers?" he asked, pain in his voice.

"I don't know," she answered, but she knew deep down they'd always been strangers of a sort. There'd always been a barrier between them; their relationship had been comfortable but merely adequate. Routine. But she'd hurt him enough. She would never say so and hurt him further.

"I should go," she said then, standing. "I do have a scan in a few weeks, and if you'd like to go, I can send you the appointment information."

"I'd like that," he answered stiffly.

It wasn't great, but it was a start. And Christophe had been right. Being engaged to him was a big signal that marriage was off the table. Now they could focus on their child's future. The plan had worked.

But there'd been a cost she hadn't anticipated. As she slipped on her coat and said goodbye, she felt pity for Eric, looking adrift and alone in the doorway of his flat. After all, she now knew exactly what it was like to love someone who could never love you back.

CHAPTER THIRTEEN

THE NEXT WEEK passed in a blur. Sophie hadn't been up to talking to Christophe the first night, so she'd merely sent a text and said she'd keep him updated, but she was fine. The conversation with her parents had also been tense. They were far more skeptical of her relationship with Christophe, as if they sensed something wasn't quite right. It wasn't until Sophie had tearfully brought up her mother's illness that her mum came around. "The way you and Dad came together, the strength and love you showed even though we were all afraid we were going to lose you…"

"Oh, darling."

"It's true. It's your fault for setting such a perfect example," she accused through a watery smile. "Mum, how can I settle for anything less?"

Her mother had then shifted her focus from wanting Sophie to marry Eric to fretting over how they'd manage co-parenting. Then there were the professional questions to which she had no answer. What were her plans where Waltham was concerned? Where would they live? How could they have a marriage based in two different countries? It had given her a whopping headache, and she'd spent the entire Sunday on her sofa watching *Pride and Prejudice*, eating ice cream, and feeling like she could relate to Lizzy very closely when it came to Mrs. Bennett's poor nerves.

Monday she was back at work but distracted. Every time she moved her hand, the ring glittered, reminding her not only of their bargain but of that night. The proposal, the kiss…making love. She missed most of Wednesday afternoon because of an obstetrician appointment. She texted Eric with the date and location of her sonogram. And Charlotte phoned, asking if she'd like to meet for tea the following week, as she was going to be nearby doing some early Christmas shopping.

By Friday, word of her engagement had leaked, and she started getting messages from acquaintances who'd seen the news on the internet.

She went home Friday night utterly exhausted. And she hadn't had the time or the energy to even work on any designs this week. By seven p.m., she'd turned off her phone and was debating either taking a soak in the tub or putting on some music and reading. Anything to relax.

When there was a knock on her door, she let out a massive sigh and tiptoed to the entry, where she could peek through the peephole and see who could possibly be on her doorstep. When she saw Christophe's face, her relief was so great she nearly wilted.

Instead, she opened the door. "I wasn't expecting you."

"I tried calling." He held up his phone. "Then I got worried." His normal teasing expression was uncharacteristically serious. "Is it okay that I'm here?"

"Yes. God, yes." And she surprised them both by bursting into tears.

"Whoa, hey. What's wrong?" He stepped inside and shut the door, then pulled her into his arms. "Whatever it is, it'll be okay."

"I'm so sorry," she said, her voice a half-wail. "I don't know why I'm crying. It was just such a week."

He chuckled and tucked her head under his chin. He was so strong and reassuring. She hadn't truly realized how much she missed his steadying presence until he was here again, holding her. That he wasn't really hers made the moment bittersweet, but she stayed where she was, needing the solace in the moment.

"You were so quiet all week I couldn't stop worrying, but I didn't want to blow up your phone. Today, though, I couldn't wait. When your phone kept going to voice mail, I knew something had to be up. It's not me, is it?"

For the first time, he sounded insecure, and she sniffed back her tears and looked up at him. "No, it's not you. Not really. I didn't mean to ghost you."

"We're supposed to be engaged," he reminded her.

"I know. I just didn't know what to say and so I turtled. It's been a lot. And now it's online…"

"Come on, let's get out of your doorway and you can tell me about it."

He hung up his coat and followed her into the living room. She'd left last night's mug and plate on the coffee table, and her favorite blanket was in a heap on the end of the sofa. Her purse was thrown in a corner, and she'd left her laundry in a basket on the hall floor. What on earth had come over her this past week? The mess was totally unlike her, and she rushed around, trying to pick up.

"Hey, stop. You don't need to tidy." He grabbed her hand and she looked up. His eyes were troubled.

She let out a long, slow breath. She really was wound rather tightly. "I wasn't prepared for this week, that's all. Talking to Eric, then my parents, and then work was crazy with me coming back after a week away and then resetting the storefront for the holidays. I had a doctor appointment, and the news came out and it's just…too much."

He led her to a chair, gently pushed her into it, then went behind her and started to rub her shoulders.

"Oh, God." His fingers were strong and sure and felt so good. "I really am wound up."

"Yes, you are. Your shoulders are a mass of knots. Do me a favor and drop your chin a little."

She obeyed; his fingers worked their magic, easing so much of the tension she was carrying in her upper back and neck. "I'm sorry I didn't answer your calls today," she murmured. They'd agreed they were in this together, but she'd kept him out of the loop most of the week. She knew why. Because after spending the night together everything had changed, and she hadn't wanted to deal with that. Because she'd realized she loved him. What she was realizing now, though, was that she needed him. She needed his friendship, and she'd just have to find a way to deal with her deepening feelings.

"We all get overwhelmed sometimes." His thumbs dug into her muscles and she began to unwind. A sigh escaped her lips.

"So what has you so tense? Is it work? Or is it Eric and your parents?" He hesitated. "Is it me?"

"All of the above?" she said, but gave a small laugh. "I think it's a bit of everything. I guess we never really prepared for what would happen, you know? What we would tell people. Eric was hard, but he took my words at face value, thank goodness. Ripping off the plaster was the right call. I think he's ready to accept that the two of us aren't going to happen. But my mum and dad…they were harder to fool. And they started pressuring me about the business, and I didn't have any answers."

He let go of her shoulders and came around the chair,

squatting in front of her and putting his hands on her knees. "Pressuring you how?"

"Like what this means for me taking over Waltham. Where we're going to live. Did we really think this through?" She lifted an eyebrow. "News flash—we thought we did, but we really didn't."

A grin crawled up his cheek. "No, I guess we didn't. What did you tell them?"

"That we hadn't decided any of those things yet, but that it would all fall into place."

"Nice."

"Except my mum knows me. She knows I always have everything planned, so she didn't really buy it."

The smile on his face grew. "She's right. You do always have a plan."

"Well, maybe this time I don't want to." She sounded so petulant that she couldn't help but laugh. "Oh, my. How much did I just sound like a four-year-old?"

"You had a hard week because nothing was in your control." He offered that wise bit of insight without the smile. She was glad, too, because it meant he wasn't teasing her about her need for control but accepting it as part of who she was. Because he understood her.

But he didn't love her.

Ugh.

"You're right. I hate it that you're right, but you are."

He patted her knee and stood. "I'll try harder to be wrong sometimes. But for now, you need to relax. How were you going to spend your evening?"

"I was debating between the tub and a book. Exciting, right?"

"Why don't you run a bath? Have you eaten yet? I haven't. I can order something in for us."

That sounded perfect. "I'm not fussy. You know the drill for me. No seafood or soft cheese but otherwise I'm good."

"Then we have a plan."

Because he understood how important it was for her to have a plan. To have some sort of control over the situation. She'd been sitting here twenty minutes ago in an emotional mess, and suddenly he appeared just when she needed him most. Like a true and valued friend.

As she went to the bathroom and started filling the tub, she wondered if that could ever really be enough.

Christophe did a quick search and ordered ramen to be delivered. He was starving; he'd eaten a dry sandwich on the train while working on his laptop. He'd also checked into a hotel, since he didn't want to presume to stay at her flat and he really didn't want to show up at her doorstep with an overnight bag.

The truth was, he didn't need to be in London this weekend. He was only here because he'd sensed something was wrong. They'd come up with this plan, and then he'd left her to execute it all on her own. In hindsight, he should have come with her a week ago. Sure, it was best she spoke to Eric alone, but he could have been here for moral support after, and with her family, too.

He'd been a coward when all was said and done. The night they'd spent together had scared him to death, so he'd let her face things by herself. And she'd become overwhelmed.

That wasn't being a good friend or showing support.

There was a strange chirping sound followed by a meow, and suddenly Harry was up on the sofa beside him, head-butting his arm. "Well hello, Harry," he said, adjusting his posture so he could pat the cat. "Look at you. You're so fluffy."

Another plaintive meow and Harry was on his lap. The cat kneaded his paws a few times and then, calm as you please, curled up in a ball and started purring. Christophe tried not to laugh. He'd never really been a cat person. Cedric had always kept a few dogs at the manor house, though there hadn't been any there for several years. But never any cats. It was beyond strange that Sophie's pet had taken to him so suddenly, but here he was, stroking Harry's head while the cat's purrs vibrated against his stomach.

"Oh, heavens. Harry, what are you doing?"

Christophe turned his head. Sophie was standing at the juncture of the hallway and living room, bundled up in a plush pink robe with her hair wet and her skin flushed from the hot water. She was so beautiful. So lovely. Christophe imagined he could undo that tie at her waist to reveal the soft skin beneath in about two seconds. The scent of her bath salts reached him, and he imagined what that skin would taste like. Lavender? Rose? His groin tightened, and he hoped to God the cat didn't decide to start kneading again.

"He made himself comfortable," Christophe answered, hoping his voice didn't sound as strangled as he felt. "Feel better?"

"Much."

"I ordered us some ramen. It should be here soon."

"That sounds absolutely perfect."

When she came back to the sofa, he noticed the ring on her finger. "I see you're still wearing it."

"Well, we are still engaged. At least to the world." Then she smiled as if sharing a secret. "And to be honest, I like it."

"I'm glad."

When the meal arrived, he moved Harry off his lap and went to the door, and once they'd eaten, he also tidied up the empty containers and put everything in the bin. He was just rinsing off his hands when Sophie came up beside him. "Thank you for that. There's not even any mess to clean up."

"It was my pleasure. Honestly, it's a breeze to make sure you're fed and pick up a few things. It's the other ways you need me that I'm unsure of."

"How do you mean?"

He didn't particularly want to have this conversation, but figured they had to. "We never really talked about what happened last weekend, other than agree it couldn't happen again. But it's not quite that simple, is it?"

She bit down on her lip and her gaze slid away. "No, I suppose it's not."

He put a finger beneath her chin and lifted it up. "It changes things when friends see each other naked."

Her lips twitched. "I shouldn't find that funny, but..."

"I know. The thing is, Sophie, we were really good at it. I don't think either of us expected what happened or the force of it, either. And on Saturday morning, your departure made it easy for us both to retreat."

She nodded. "It did. Part of why I didn't call you all week was because I didn't want to rely on you too much. And I thought you probably regretted what happened."

"Not in the way you think."

Now his pulse was hammering, from anxiety more than anything. He made it a practice not to be too vulnerable with people. He tried to be kind, charming, easygoing, so no one could find fault. So people would want him to be around. It was wearing sometimes, but he'd been doing it for so long now it was simply who he was. But Sophie... she pushed so many buttons. She made him open up when he'd rather remain a closed book. And God help him, there was a part of him that wanted to reach for that robe and have a repeat of last Friday just so he wouldn't have to talk about himself.

But something Cedric had said to him years ago had stuck in his brain. Cedric had sat him down to talk to him about girls, responsibility, and consent. "Grown up people have to have grown up conversations," he'd said. "And if you're old enough to take a woman to bed, you're a grown up. Be sure you act like one."

He certainly wasn't the fifteen-year-old youth he'd been during that lecture, but the lesson had stuck.

"What do you mean?"

"Let's sit. I think we need to talk."

He led her by the hand back to the living room and they sat next to each other. Her hair was nearly dry and curling around her shoulders, and her skin… He'd heard someone tell Charlotte once that pregnant women had a glow, and he realized how true that was. He lifted a hand and touched her cheek, a soft, tender touch that made his heart clench. She deserved so much better than him. Someday someone was going to come along who could give her all the things she wanted. The thought caused a pain in the center of his chest.

"I do not regret last weekend," he said softly. "It was amazing. You were…" He let the thought hang. "There's only one thing I regret, Soph. And it's why I asked you to promise we could stay friends. I can't offer you what you want. You want love and a family and I… I decided a long time ago that marriage wasn't going to be for me."

"I know that. You said from the beginning that you're not the marrying type."

"You talked about false hope. The last thing I want to do is give you the wrong idea."

"And what would the wrong idea be?" She leaned forward a little, looking up into his eyes.

"That I might change my mind and decide I'm the marrying kind."

Her gaze clung to his, and she nodded slightly, a tiny movement of her head that acknowledged his words. "Christophe, tonight you understood my need for control. That's because you know who I am. I like to think I know who you are, too. I know you're not interested in marriage. And the last thing I'd ever do is try to convince you to change your mind."

Of course not. Because she didn't love him, either. Which was fine. It was exactly what he expected and wanted. It was better to know than to hold on to a little bit of hope that someone might care enough to fight for him. To come back for him.

There were no disappointments that way.

She cupped his face in her hand. "One of the best things about our friendship is that we understand and accept each other just as we are. I never want that to change."

"Me, either."

"I'm sorry I shut you out this week. You were right. I was hiding."

"I was, too, so let's not worry about it. Instead, why don't you tell me how I can support you this weekend?"

"You're staying?"

He grinned. "Have laptop, will travel. If I need to do something, I can. But otherwise, I was going to be spending the weekend at my flat." He shrugged. "I don't even have a Harry to keep me company."

As he heard his name, the cat came around the corner and gave a sad meow.

"It's his bedtime," she said, laughing a bit. "He's very particular about things like that. So now he's telling me it's time to go to bed so he can get up on the covers, too."

Lucky cat.

"And you're tired. I should go."

"You could stay," she suggested. "On…on the sofa."

She couldn't know how difficult that would be. Knowing she was so close, knowing how she looked in sleep, wanting to pull her close against his body. Part of what had shaken him so much last weekend was that he couldn't remember the last time he'd slept as well as he had holding her in his arms.

"We'll see."

The cat meowed again, this time a bit more insistently, and even Christophe laughed. "It really is bedtime."

"I kind of want to chat a bit more, though." She paused, and then said, "If I promise nothing will happen, you could lie on the bed and we could talk for a while."

She really, really didn't know.

"You don't think Harry will be put out that I'm taking up some of his space?"

"I don't know. He's never had to before."

Christophe considered. It was playing with fire, going into her room, lying on her bed, whispering in the dark. But if he could do that, maybe he could actually make it through the next time, and the time after that, and eventually he wouldn't want her so much.

"Come on, then. I'll tuck you in."

He waited while she brushed her teeth and changed into pajamas, and then after she'd crawled into bed, he lay on the top. With another chirp Harry jumped up, stared at Christophe for a solid minute, and then settled down by Sophie's feet on a folded-up blanket. "His bed," she whispered. "Or His Lordship's throne. However you look at it."

"He's a good companion."

"The best."

Their voices were low. Christophe rested his head on an elbow while she rolled to her side and cushioned her head on her hands. "So," he said, trying to keep the mood light, "what should we talk about?"

It wasn't as difficult as he might have imagined. She told him about her visit to Eric, and about her parents' pointed questions, and how she'd felt seeing her name paired with his online. "We kind of expected that to happen eventually," he said. "Don't worry about it. I'm not Stephen or Bella or even Will. I'm the nobody in the family. Trust me, we'll get a mention online and probably on page ten of some gossip rag and that'll be it."

"Don't say you're nobody. You are. You are Christophe Germain. You heard Aurora last weekend. She called you her son. She loves you like her own. You are smart and successful and run an entire division of a multinational billion-dollar company. Don't ever let me hear you say you're nobody again."

His heart swelled. No one ever came to his defense like that. "My head knows that. But it's different. Different when other people call you stupid and in the way. Then you feel like you don't matter. It sticks with you, even when logically you know it shouldn't."

"You matter to me," she whispered, and he thought again that she would be easy to love…if he let himself.

"Thank you for that," he replied.

"Your mum said that to you, didn't she?"

That and so much more, but Sophie didn't need to know all about that. "Mum was single and trying to provide for us both…and incredibly unhappy." That was something else he could rationalize, but it still didn't take away the sting of hearing that she'd wished he'd never been born. "That's why I want to help you, Soph. I know you're going to be a wonderful mother. But it's hard on your own."

"I would never say those things to my child. Or even think them."

His eyes stung, and he hoped she couldn't tell her words had made him well up. "I know that. You're stronger than she was. When Tante Aurora came and offered to take me away, I think I had my backpack ready before she'd finished her sentence."

But it had still been difficult. He'd left because he'd known he wasn't wanted. He'd heard his mother and aunt arguing, too. "My mother was drinking too much," he murmured, and Sophie reached out and took his hand in the dark. "Aurora got angry with her and said if she put her mind to it she could make something of herself. And my mother yelled back that she wasn't going to whore herself like Aurora had."

"Oh, Christophe."

"My aunt and uncle had a deep, strong love. My mother was wrong about them. She's stayed bitter and resentful."

"How long has it been since you saw her?"

"Five years."

Five years, and she lived barely an hour away from him if she was still in Orléans. Sophie's hand felt good on his, and she rubbed her thumb over his knuckles in a soothing gesture.

He cleared his throat. "Anyway, I made sure I put my mind to it. I figured if my own mother could send me away without a thought, why would Aurora and her husband keep me? So I studied hard and did what I was told and learned that being charming got me a long way."

"Aurora would never send you back."

"I know that now. Nine-year-old me did not."

"That's fair."

"Anyway, that's a lot about me. How did we get on this topic, anyway?"

"You said you were a nobody, and I disagreed."

He smiled. "My champion." He twined his fingers with

hers now and changed the subject. "So, back to what we were talking about before. What can I do this weekend to be supportive?"

"I don't have much planned. I have tea tomorrow afternoon with your sister, actually. She invited me earlier this week."

"Lots of baby talk. Count me out."

She giggled and he smiled in response to the sound, so much nicer than her tears than when she'd first opened the door.

"I was going to do some Christmas shopping. That probably bores you."

"Not at all. I can carry your bags."

"You're ridiculous."

"Probably." They were bantering again, and it was far more comfortable than revealing details of his past, which he hadn't intended to do but somehow had been persuaded by her gentle questions. "How about we take your parents for brunch on Sunday? My treat. Give me a chance to win them over."

"You don't think they'll see through it? I mean, us?"

He thought for a moment, but remembered the past weekend. "We completely fooled my family, didn't we?"

She nodded. "Yes, we did. Somehow."

"Because we're friends. Because we do actually care about each other, even if we aren't in love."

She was quiet for a moment, a moment during which he wondered if that was actually the truth or if he was lying to himself. And wondered if it even mattered, since the end result was going to be the same.

"We do care about each other," she whispered. "Okay. I'll message them in the morning."

"Feel better now?" he asked, noticing her eyelids were starting to droop.

"Yeah," she answered, and she blinked. It took a long time for her lashes to come back up again.

He should get up right now, put on his coat and go back to the hotel. He'd just wait until she was asleep and then he'd sneak away.

Just as soon as she was asleep.

CHAPTER FOURTEEN

WHEN SOPHIE OPENED her eyes, she found herself staring at Christophe's face.

There was a hint of stubble on his jaw and chin, and his hair was pressed to one side, the curls sticking up. He was still in his jeans and shirt, and Harry, the traitor, was curled up right against Christophe's chest, his ears just below Christophe's collar.

He'd fallen asleep on her bed, and he was cuddling her cat.

She held in the sigh that was building in her chest. Seeing Christophe on her doorstep had been the answer to a prayer she'd never made. All the stress and anxiety of the week melted away when he put his arms around her. She'd relaxed, and then she'd felt a new energy. He made her come alive. And she'd wanted him, so much. It was only the fear of messing things up even more that had kept her from touching him. Instead, she'd run a warm bath, put in scented salts, and touched herself.

It had relieved some tension, but not for long. Eating ramen, talking, listening about his childhood…just when she thought she could maybe not love him, he had to make himself vulnerable and trusting like that. Burying her feelings had to be her only option, because right now he was her lifeline. The one person who knew everything, who kept her secrets, who supported while asking nothing in return.

He would never accept her love or return it. So she'd just have to hold on to it for safekeeping until she didn't need it anymore.

His lashes flickered and she put a smile on her lips as he woke. "Good morning, sleepyhead," she murmured.

He shifted, then seemed to realize he was curled around the cat. "Harry. Thanks for keeping me warm, buddy."

"If you were cold you should have…" She let the thought trail off as she searched for a different phrase. "Should have got a blanket."

"Naw. But I do need a shower and a change of clothes. Everything's back at the hotel."

"Right."

"You can come with me. We can do that shopping you wanted before your tea this afternoon. What time are you meeting?"

"At three, at Fortnum & Mason."

"Brilliant. There's a bookshop nearby, and I can hide there while you talk about baby things. How do you feel about walking?"

"I suppose it's fine if it's not raining."

"Let's spend a day like tourists." His smile widened. "If you were new to London, where would you go?"

She scowled. "I am not going to Harrods."

He laughed. "Point taken. Selfridges? It's an easy walk to Fortnum's from there, and it has everything."

He really was ridiculous, but it was one of the things she really liked about him. "Hmm, shall we take one of those bus tours around the city, as well?"

He tapped his lip. "We could. It's hop on hop off, and would save you walking."

She swatted at his arm, which sent Harry scurrying. "Stop it. I'll say yes to Selfridges but no to guided tours."

He sighed. "Fine."

Harry let out a pitiful howl.

"Breakfast time?" Christophe asked.

"Indeed." She stretched and crawled out of bed. "Give me thirty minutes to get cute. You can make tea if you like."

He scowled and she picked up a pillow and threw it at him. "Decaf tea or nothing," she said. And then she left the bedroom to feed Harry.

She took the full thirty minutes to get dressed and style her hair, which was floofy on one side from sleeping on it while it was still damp. If they were walking, she'd need to wear comfortable footwear, so the suede boots came out again. She tried a pair of skinny jeans with them and after three minutes gave up trying to fasten them. But before she grabbed a pair of leggings she stopped in front of the mirror and placed her hands on her growing belly.

"Hello, in there," she whispered, and a smile bloomed on her face. It was the first time she'd actually talked to the little one growing inside her, and her heart expanded. "I'm going to be your mum. And look at you. You're right here." She looked at the just-noticeable bump. "We're going to be fine, us two," she promised.

"Did you say something?" Christophe's voice came through the door, and she scurried away from the mirror.

"Just talking to myself!" she called back, feeling slightly foolish but with a new sentimentality where her baby was concerned. Somehow things had changed. The baby had gone from being a concept to something suddenly very tangible and real.

The lovely feeling carried through the morning. After

her decaf tea, they walked back to Christophe's hotel where she took the time to message her parents about brunch and they set a time and location. When he returned to the lobby in pressed clothes and a fresh shave, she had to stop herself from staring. He was so…everything. *It's enough he's on your side*, she reminded herself. It was hard, though. Even her very discriminating cat loved him! And Harry hardly ever liked anyone.

She liked, too, that he didn't put on airs or flash his money around. His first demand of the morning was to find coffee, so they sat in a café while he drank his dark roast and she ordered orange juice. They got bacon butties and ate them on a bench in the sunshine, folding the waxed paper around the bread to avoid any sauce drips. After that they headed to Oxford Street.

"I'd like to get something for Charlotte and the baby," Sophie said, squinting up at him. The day was uncharacteristically bright, and Sophie noticed that many of the holiday decorations were out now, brightening the shops. It put her in a holiday mood for the first time. "Can we go to the baby section?"

"Of course we can. The day is yours. I'm just here to carry your bags, remember?"

She wiggled her eyebrows. "You might regret saying that. When I'm in the mood to shop, it can be dangerous."

He replied with an eyebrow quirk of his own. "I'm part of Aurora and have two cousins who are champs at it. I have experience. Bring it on."

The warning was timely, as she found an adorable set of soft shoes and then a package of bamboo swaddles and a stuffed rabbit that was the softest thing she'd ever touched. At the bookstore she added a copy of *Jemima Puddleduck* to the gift, as well as a new paperback for herself and a travel book for Iceland, which was her parents' next trip, planned for the summer, and would be part of their Christmas gift. Noise-canceling headphones were purchased for her brother and went into another bag.

"You weren't kidding." Christophe looped the handles of the yellow bag on his fingers. "Who else is on your list?"

"Well, you, I suppose."

"You don't have to get me anything."

He said it so sharply her feet stopped moving and she stared at him. "I…what?"

"I just mean, I know we're keeping up appearances. But it's not necessary."

His refusal hurt her feelings, and she wasn't sure why. Maybe it had something to do with the fact that he seemed perfectly fine doing stuff for her but was hesitant to let her reciprocate. "Maybe I want to get you something."

"Well, I can hardly stop you." He smiled a little, as if making up for his previous sharpness. Maybe he wasn't that into Christmas. Either way, she wasn't going to press the issue and mar the day they had together.

Holiday music played in the background as they entered the Christmas area, chock-full of decorations and trees and everything one could possibly need to celebrate the day. Getting even more into the spirit, Sophie oohed and ahhed over beautiful table linens and chose a deep red damask tablecloth with a pattern of holly and berries, white napkins, and a set of napkin rings in silver with green holly leaves and red berries in crystal. "I've always wanted something this pretty," she said, holding the items close. "So I can set a real holiday table."

Christophe was even getting in the spirit a little, looking at Christmas ornaments. "Look at these," he said, and lifted up a small box. "They're pretty."

Indeed they were. Iridescent baubles were cradled inside, soft and pearly, and Sophie had a sudden urge to put up her Christmas tree. She usually didn't until the week before Christmas, but it was December already, and why not? "Let's get them," she said, adding them to her stack of holiday kitsch. They explored the section some more, and when they came upon a Paddington Bear ornament, Sophie stopped and got all broody again.

"You should get an ornament for the baby," Christophe suggested. He picked up the ornament and dangled it from his finger. "Look, he's in his little blue coat and red hat."

It was adorable. Sophie looked up at him. "I haven't done any shopping for the baby yet. It's been so surreal and confusing that I haven't thought about a nursery or anything." She realized she was in a one-bedroom flat. That wouldn't do, would it? For someone who always had a plan, she'd dropped the ball on this.

"So you start with a single ornament and go from there." His smile was understanding. "No wonder you're exhausted, Soph. This has got to have thrown you off so much. But you only have to figure out one thing at a time."

Which was true. But it didn't help that her feelings were all over the place. His support helped ground her, but realizing the depth of her feelings? Took all that progress and tossed it out the window.

"You're right. Starting with this Paddington bauble." She looked at her watch. "Are you ready for tea? We should probably head there soon."

"I'm ready if you are."

She paid for her purchases and just as he'd promised, Christophe carried the bags as they made the journey to Fortnum's. Charlotte was already there, and he kissed her cheek in greeting before putting down the bags. She held baby Imogene, and as Sophie took off her jacket, Charlotte pressed the baby into Christophe's arms.

When Sophie turned around, her heart exploded. Men

with babies was one thing, but Christophe holding a baby, while she was carrying her own precious little one, did something to her that she couldn't ignore. Imogene stared up at him with wide eyes and he looked so natural holding her there. Sophie imagined him holding her baby and felt a longing so sharp and deep it made her catch her breath. Why, why couldn't he see that they could be right for each other?

If she even suggested such a thing, he'd be gone in a flash. Christophe handed the baby back to Charlotte. "I'll be back in an hour or so," he murmured. "Enjoy yourself."

"I will," she replied, her insides fluttering as he pressed a kiss to her cheek.

Charlotte looked over at Sophie with a satisfied smile. "I never thought I'd see Christophe lose his mind over a woman, but here we are. I'm really happy for you two, Sophie."

Sophie didn't correct her, but the kindly meant words were another knife to her heart. Because maybe Christophe had lost his mind, but he'd never give her his heart.

Christophe spent the better part of an hour at a bookshop, and then returned to pick up Sophie from her tea with Charlotte. He was thankful he hadn't been expected to stay. Of course he hadn't been able to say no to Charlotte when she'd put Imogene into his arms, and to be honest, it hadn't been that bad. Imogene was a cute little thing, and she'd just stared at him with something that looked like wonder. No crying, no messy diapers…but he'd also been relieved to hand her back. Babies terrified him. Not only because he had no idea what to do with them, but because fatherhood scared the hell out of him. It didn't help that Sophie was too adorable today. For the first time, he'd heard her speak not of the pregnancy but actually of the baby. Her face when he'd held up the Paddington ornament had been beautiful. If he wasn't careful, he'd end up caring for her too much.

Sophie and Charlotte were still inside, the remnants of a pot of tea, sandwiches, and cakes littering the table. "It looks like you had a marvelous time."

"We did." Sophie held Imogene now, and she was glowing. Did she realize how great a mother she was going to be? His stomach clenched at the thought, and he turned his attention to the plate of sandwiches. "Is that Coronation Chicken?" He plucked it from the plate and popped it in his mouth. "Yum."

"I really should get back," Charlotte said wistfully. "This has been lovely. I needed to get out. But she's been so good she's bound to be cranky soon."

"She's an angel," Sophie said, tucking the blanket around Imogene. "I almost don't want to give her up."

"Do you want to borrow her for the evening?"

Sophie laughed. "Maybe not tonight, but… I wouldn't mind babysitting sometime. It would give me some practice."

"Be careful what you agree to. I'm liable to take you up on it."

"Please do," Sophie said. "And thank you for tea, Charlotte. It really was lovely."

"You're family now," Charlotte said simply.

The whole exchange made Christophe vastly uncomfortable. His family was accepting their engagement so easily. What were they going to say when they called if off? They all loved Sophie. They would blame Christophe for sure.

Charlotte packed up all of her baby things—there was a lot, he noticed—and left. "I suppose we should get back, too," Sophie said. "With all the bags, would you mind if we got a cab instead of walking all the way back?"

"That's a great idea. I'll go hail one while you get ready."

It took a few minutes and when she joined him on the pavement, her face was far more relaxed than it had been last night. "Today was good for you," he observed.

"It was. And do you know, I wasn't even tempted to go into work, even though we were so close."

"Hmm. Are you perhaps achieving…balance?"

"I'd better learn at some point." She touched her stomach. "Or this little one is going to make me learn."

He lifted his own bag with his bookstore purchases. "Actually, I got you something while you were at tea."

"You did?"

He nodded. A black cab pulled up and he opened the door. "Climb in and I'll give it to you."

They got inside and he gave the address, then handed her the bag.

"Christophe, what did you do?"

He smiled at her, loving what a simple gift did to her face. "You said you hadn't done any planning, so I thought you could use some ideas." Inside the bag were three baby magazines, all with features on creating the perfect nursery. He'd got her a book, too, something about chicken soup and expectant mothers, that the lady at the shop had suggested. Sophie held it in her hands and then looked up at him, her eyes shining.

He didn't deserve the way she looked at him. And he wished he could look at her with the same unreserved affection. But it wasn't who he was. She said he was lovable, but he knew differently. And it wasn't just that. It was that he didn't know how to love in return, as if there were a switch somewhere but it had never been wired in.

"They're okay?"

"They're perfect. And so thoughtful. Thank you, Christophe."

"It was my pleasure."

They were almost to her flat when she said, "Stay for dinner? I'll actually cook tonight."

He shouldn't. He should go back to the hotel, work a bit, meet her tomorrow for the brunch thing. Instead, he found himself replying, "That sounds great."

He didn't know how to say no to her. And yet he was going to have to learn, because the longer they carried on like this, the more potential there was that he'd hurt her. That was the last thing in the world he wanted to do.

CHAPTER FIFTEEN

SOPHIE SET THE TABLE with her new linens, still slightly wrinkled from the packaging but she didn't care. Her white dishes looked lovely against the rich color of the tablecloth, and the napkin rings were a festive touch. She'd put a small beef roast in the oven and surrounded it with little potatoes, carrots, and parsnips. A hint of bay leaf and rosemary scented the air, and the day with its Christmas atmosphere put Sophie in a holiday mood. As the meal cooked, she disappeared into a closet and came out with a long box.

"What is that?" Christophe asked.

"My Christmas tree," she said proudly. "Today really got me in the spirit. Will you help me put it up?"

He stared at her. "You want me…to put up a Christmas tree."

She nodded. "I know it's not as nice as a real one, but it's the perfect size for my flat." She tapped the box. "It's actually flat on one side, so it takes up less space."

He got up from the sofa and went to her. "That," he said, "is a travesty. It's bad enough that you don't have a real tree."

"Um…" She waved her hand around the space. "It's not like I have a lot of room. Not compared to Chatsworth Manor."

He pointed a finger at her. "There you will definitely

see a real tree. I think the one last year was around twelve feet."

"Twelve!"

He laughed. "All right. I'll help you set up your little tree. It shouldn't take long."

She moved a few items of furniture around to make room, and then while he was taking it out of the box, she found a Christmas mix on her phone and ran it through a wireless speaker. Christophe lifted his eyebrows as Bing Crosby came on, but said nothing, which made her smile. Maybe he was acting Grinchy, but she got the feeling he was secretly enjoying himself.

By the time the tree was up and she'd fluffed out the branches, the timer on the oven dinged and it was time to eat. "We can decorate after dinner," she said, arranging the vegetables on a platter and letting the meat rest before carving it. "You must be starving. I had tea, but all you had was a tiny sandwich."

"I could eat," he said, and they sat down at her festive table.

This was something new for her, she realized. Last year, she'd put up her tree alone, and she hadn't really done any other decorating. Eric had never been one for carols, either, so cozy meals for two with Nat King Cole in the background simply never happened. Christophe spent most of the meal telling her about the holidays in the Pemberton family, and she sat back and enjoyed the stories of when they were kids and how different Christmas was now.

"And a new generation will make things different again," she mused, putting down her fork. The beef was tender and vegetables flavorful, but she was stuffed. "Charlotte's baby, and I'm guessing there'll be more to follow. Aurora is going to love that."

"Nan Aurora. Has a special ring to it, doesn't it?"

"She's more of a *grand-mère*, I think," Sophie said, smiling.

"You might be right."

But neither of them mentioned that Sophie's child wouldn't be part of that circle. She certainly wasn't going to bring it up and mar the lovely vibe of the evening.

Christophe helped with the cleanup and then they plugged in the tree, the white lights gleaming in the darkened room. "What's next?" he asked.

"Ribbon," she said. She went back into the storage closet and took out a box of decorations. When she held up the first roll of wired mesh ribbon, Christophe put his hands up.

"I think that's going to be your job. I have no idea what to do with that."

She laughed. "Then just hold the end so it doesn't roll everywhere. If Harry gets his claws into it, we'll never get it back."

He held the end while she wound the strands around, anchoring each loop with a twist of the wire around a branch. The gold mesh reflected the glimmer of the white lights, casting a romantic glow in the room.

"How do you do that?" he asked.

"You like it?"

"It looks lovely."

"Good. Because that box over there has the rest of my decorations. It's your turn to help."

Together they put the baubles on until each empty space was filled with something sparkly and shiny.

Sophie looked over at Christophe and her heart swelled. The lights gave off a glow that highlighted his face, and the soft smile on his lips made her feel so secure and happy. They could be happy, couldn't they? If she could just show him that he was lovable...that he was deserving of love and happiness. It seemed impossible that he didn't already know so, but he'd also had a very different childhood from hers. She tried to think of how she'd feel if she were rejected by her own parents, the two people in the world who were supposed to love her no matter what. She understood that such a thing would leave an indelible mark.

But even indelible marks could heal. Scars would remain, but only as reminders of bad times. The bad times themselves didn't last forever.

The song on her playlist changed to one she hadn't heard in a very long time, and as Tony Bennett's crooning voice started to sing about what he wanted for Christmas, Christophe turned his head, discovering she was looking at him and not the tree. Something hummed between them, something good, and she held out her hand. "Dance?" she said simply, but her heart seemed to freeze for a moment as she waited for his answer.

He took her hand and they moved toward each other until she was in his embrace, his feet moving in small steps in her tiny living room as they swayed to the music. To say anything would break the spell, so Sophie kept all of her words inside and let her body tell the story as she shifted slightly closer and rested her head in the hollow of his shoulder. His chest rose and fell as he let out a breath, and then he turned his head slightly so that his chin grazed her head, a subtle acceptance of their closeness. This moment was beautiful in its perfection and in its imperfection. Their relationship was complicated. Their engagement was a lie. But these feelings were undeniably real, and she didn't want to hide them anymore.

She shifted her head, just a little, nudging his chin with her temple, lifting her face a tiny bit closer to his as butterflies winged their way through her stomach. Their breaths mingled as their faces drew closer, tempting, hesitant, wanting. When she couldn't wait any longer, she rose up on tiptoe and brushed her lips along the corner of his mouth.

He turned his head the last bit and met her kiss, softly, sweetly, sending a line of joy straight to her heart.

The song ended but still they remained, kissing in the middle of her living room. He lifted his hands and cupped her face like a precious chalice, sipping from her lips and making her throb with need. She slid her hands over the hard wall of his chest, wanting to feel the warm skin beneath her fingertips, but needing him to take the lead. He needed to come to her willingly, completely.

"Soph," he murmured, but she put her finger over his lips as her gaze met his. There was fire there, the same flame that had burned for her back at the château. Desire. Passion. If that was what he needed, then she would give it to him. She would give him that and so much more.

But he shook his head, nudging her finger away. "We said one time." His voice was rough, and it slid over her nerve endings. Did he have any clue at all how sexy he was when he left his carefree self behind and let his intense side take over?

"Once didn't cure me of wanting you," she answered. "Once wasn't enough."

His stormy eyes searched hers, and then he reached for the buttons on his shirt. A thrill zipped up her spine as she pulled off her sweater. She reached behind her for the clasp of her bra, and when it let go, she realized how much fuller her breasts had gotten over the past month. With a low growl of acquiescence, Christophe came forward and cupped one in his hand as he kissed her again and again and again.

I love you. She tried to show him the words as she knew he'd reject them if she said them out loud. Instead, she put all of her attention into worshipping his body with hers. They made love there, on her living room floor, their skin golden by the light of the fire and the tree, and Sophie hid the tear that slid out of the corner of her eye at the sheer wonder and beauty of it.

Tomorrow she would tell him. But for tonight, she'd do everything to show him that friendship would never be enough. She'd show him that he was everything.

Christophe straightened his tie and tried to get his head on straight. Sophie was sitting on the end of the bed in his hotel room, looking beautiful and remarkably calm. Considering her parents had been skeptical of the whole engagement, he thought she'd be more nervous.

But the exertions of the night before might have served to relax her. And there had been exertions. Unlike last weekend at the château, once truly hadn't been enough. She was looking rather well-rested, considering they hadn't had much sleep.

He was in this far too deep, but it wasn't the time to go into it. He had another two hours of pretense to keep up before he could let down his guard. It didn't help that she was watching him tie his tie.

"Okay?" he asked, dropping his hands and letting her inspect it.

"Perfect." She placed her hands flat against his chest. "You look dashing, as always. Even your curls are on their best behavior today."

Which was miraculous, as he'd showered at her place… with her in the shower with him. If it were anyone else, he'd chalk it up to a pretty damned good weekend. But this was Sophie. He couldn't be flippant about it.

He checked his watch. "We should be going. Our reservation is at eleven."

He'd picked Aurora's favorite spot for brunch, thinking it might also appeal to Sophie's parents. He'd never done a "meet the parents" event before, and this was even more pressure as there was a fake engagement to uphold. And yet pretending wasn't the most difficult thing. The hardest thing was reminding himself that it was all a ruse. Especially after last night.

It was glorious and terrifying, how consumed he was with her.

Mr. and Mrs. Waltham were already there when they arrived at exactly five minutes before the hour. "My parents are sticklers for punctuality," Sophie whispered, as they were guided to the table. "Five minutes early means we're off to a good start."

Great.

Mr. Waltham stood as they approached. "Hello, blossom," he said, a warm smile on his face. "Christophe. It's good to see you again."

"And you, sir," Christophe replied, shaking his hand. He smiled at Sophie's mother. "Mrs. Waltham, you're looking lovely today."

"Yes, well," she answered, and it set Christophe back on his heels a bit. Sophie was frowning, too. It seemed he had his work cut out for himself.

So he held Sophie's chair for her and then took his seat, reaching under the table to take her hand for reassurance.

Sophie took up the challenge, and after greeting her parents ordered champagne. "Champagne for three, please, and may I have something nonalcoholic? I'll leave it to you to come up with something special."

"I have just the thing," the server assured her. "I'll be back with your drinks momentarily and take your orders."

"Wow," Christophe remarked. "You're leaving your drink to chance. This is big progress."

She smiled up at him. "I try," she said. "I'm learning that sometimes unexpected things happen and they can be really great. I'm trying to go with the flow more."

Mr. Waltham coughed and covered his mouth to hide a laugh. Even Mrs. Waltham's tight lips had relaxed a little at Sophie's pronouncement.

"Sophie, you have never been a go with the flow person," Mrs. Waltham remarked. "But I can't deny, it looks good on you. You're feeling better, aren't you?"

A delightful blush tinted her cheeks. "Um…yes. I suppose I have been feeling rather well lately."

Her foot touched his under the table.

She was playing footsies with him. Unbelievable.

Their drinks arrived and once they'd ordered, Mr. Waltham offered a toast. "To Sophie and Christophe. And to unexpected blessings. Congratulations, you two."

It was spectacularly generous, considering that until just over a week ago her parents had wanted her to marry Eric. But they loved her. Approval or not, she would always have their support.

"Thank you," Christophe said, and they all touched rims before drinking. Sophie's glass held a pinky-red liquid with some sort of bubbles in it. "Good?" he asked.

She nodded. "I think it's the raspberry and pear juice, with something it in for sparkle. It's just right."

"Have you set a date yet?" This was from Mrs. Waltham, and Christophe let Sophie field the question.

"Not yet, Mum. We're not in a big rush."

"But with the baby coming…"

"I was thinking we'd wait until after he or she is born." Sophie took another sip of her drink. "My clothes are already starting to not fit. Trying to fit a dress and constantly needing alterations would be a nightmare."

There was a silent beat of disapproval.

"Mum," Sophie said, "we've only been engaged a week. There are a lot of things to sort out. We have time, though. Let's just enjoy brunch and celebrate. It's a chance for you to get to know Christophe a little better. Besides, wedding plans would just bore the two of them," she said with a nod toward Christophe and her father.

That drew a reluctant smile from her mother. "You're right, Sophie. I just want to see you settled and happy."

Sophie laughed. "You mean you want to know I have my ducks in a row. I did inherit my organizational skills from you, you know."

Despite herself, Mrs. Waltham laughed. "Fair, darling. Fair." Her attention turned to Christophe. "My daughter does like to have things just so."

"Don't I know it. It's one of her most endearing qualities."

Mrs. Waltham flapped at hand at him as if to say "go on," and Sophie nudged his arm. Charm points: one.

Their starters arrived then: Porthilly oysters and caviar, and fruit with lemon verbena for Sophie. Christophe watched her carefully, and she turned her nose a little at the oysters but gave him a small smile. "It's a lot better," she whispered, leaning close to his shoulder.

After the oysters came a full English breakfast complete with black pudding for Mr. Waltham, eggs Benedict for both Mrs. Waltham and Christophe, and French toast with blueberry compote for Sophie. "No eggs, darling?" Mrs. Waltham asked. She looked at Christophe. "Sophie loves eggs Benny."

"I believe soft yolks are a firm no at the moment," Christophe stated, picking up his knife and fork. "But that looks delicious, Soph."

"Christophe has taken very good care of me," Sophie said, looking at him adoringly. "He always makes sure I eat and take downtime. We had a lovely day yesterday. We did some holiday shopping and then I had tea with Charlotte, his cousin."

"Ah yes. She just had a baby, didn't she?"

"Indeed," Christophe said. "And she is just as beautiful as her mother."

"I got to hold her yesterday, Mum. She's the sweetest thing."

The conversation seemed to loosen after that, and by the time brunch was done, Christophe felt he'd done his duty playing the doting fiancé. There was a bit of unease since the fiancé bit wasn't true, but he'd been honest in everything else. He did care for her, so very much. He wanted her to be happy. It just couldn't be with him. And yet the thought of her sharing that sweet smile with anyone else…of sharing her body and passion with someone else…it tore at his insides.

"Will you be around for Christmas, Christophe?" They were getting up from the table and getting ready to depart when Mrs. Waltham asked the question.

"The family has invited Sophie to join us at the manor house for Christmas. I'm happy to extend the invitation to you both, if you'd like to join us." He knew Aurora wouldn't mind two more, and the house was more than big enough.

"Oh, my… Christmas at Chatsworth Manor. We'll definitely consider it, won't we Sam?"

They parted ways outside the restaurant, and Christophe looked down at Sophie. "I think that went well, don't you?"

"You totally got my mum with the invitation to the manor. She's not above being seduced by spending Christmas with the Earl of Chatsworth and family at the country estate."

He rolled his eyes. "That doesn't impress you, though."

"As long as you're there." The words were said lightly, but there was something about them that sent alarms ringing. He lifted his arm, hailing a taxi.

"When do you have to go back to Paris?" she asked.

"This afternoon. I have meetings with Phillipe in the morning."

"Could we talk before you go?"

"I can drop you at home first. Anything important?" She didn't meet his eyes, which sent another ripple of unease through him.

"A little."

A cab pulled up, and they said nothing else as they climbed in. But Christophe felt the walls closing in around him. Last night had been too good. This morning too easy. Whatever was coming wasn't going to be as pleasant. It occurred to him that during the entire weekend she hadn't mentioned Eric, either. But if she'd already achieved her objective, why would she have made a point of perpetuating the lie of their engagement?

CHAPTER SIXTEEN

SOPHIE FELT AS IF her heart was sitting at the base of her throat. She was so nervous about the conversation to come but determined to see it through. Today had shown her all she needed to know; Christophe was perfect for her. She loved him, and if he could trust her with that, they could have a future together.

The cab dropped them off at her flat, and they were both unusually quiet as she unlocked the door and led the way inside. There was no sense procrastinating by offering him a drink or something to eat; they'd just had brunch. She took off her coat and draped it over a chair, then twisted her hands in front of her. She had never had such difficulty saying three simple words before, and it occurred to her that it was because never before had they been this true. There was also the chance that he would hand them back to her, and the thought of him turning away was crushing.

"Are you all right? Is it something about the brunch?" He came up behind her and put his hand on her shoulder.

She placed her hand over the top of his and gathered strength. "No, it's not about the brunch. You were perfect." She took a deep breath, corralling all of her courage as she turned to face him. "You *are* perfect, Christophe."

His face changed. Oh, he still looked pleasant enough, but she knew him well enough now to know when he was erecting walls. "Don't do that," she whispered. "Don't shut me out."

"Sophie…"

"No. I need to say some things and you really need to hear them. You need to believe them."

He shook his head and stood back, and she realized that he suddenly looked very much like a scared boy.

Love scared him. It scared the crap out of him. And maybe she should wait, but what would be the right time? Just like she'd needed to rip off the bandage with Eric, she felt like she needed to put one on Christophe so he could start to heal. "Don't be afraid of it," she said softly. "This thing between us…last night…we both know it's not always like that. I was there. I know you felt it, too. It's not just chemistry, Christophe. It's love."

"We're friends, Sophie." He said it firmly, as if reminding himself as much as her.

"That's what makes it so much better, don't you think? That we trust each other? That we take care of each other? I know this scares you, Christophe, but I can't pretend not to feel something when I do. I love you. I know because this is so different from anything I've ever felt for anyone before." Her voice shook, but she forced herself to keep on. "A few years ago, my mum had leukemia. We weren't sure she was going to make it. But my dad…the way he loved her, the way he could still make her smile, the way they loved each other through all of that…it showed me what real love looks like. And Friday night when I opened the door and saw you there, I knew. You were here when I needed you, even though I didn't even call."

He turned away, his posture stiff, rejecting her words. Her heart took the hit, but she wasn't ready to give up. "I know you feel you're unlovable, but nothing could be further from the truth. Your parents abandoned you. How could you not feel that way? And you said that you always felt as if your aunt's and uncle's affections were contingent on good grades and hard work, but you know that's not true now. They would have loved you anyway. Aurora does love you. She thinks of you as a son."

"You don't understand." He turned back to her, his jaw tight, his eyes dark with hurt and strain. "Until you've had someone say out loud that they wish you'd never been born, you don't understand. Don't you think I know I was deserving of love? That's not what scares me, Sophie."

"Then tell me what does."

He ran his hand through his curls, leaving them rumpled and agitated. "It's believing that someone does, and then having them leave. I don't trust anyone to stay, you see. Not even you."

She fell quiet, any argument she'd formulated in her brain rendered silent.

"A parent's love is supposed to be unconditional. If I can't trust a mother to stay, a father to stay, how can I trust anyone else?" His lips thinned as his voice strengthened. "Eric loved you, and you left him."

The jab hit its mark and she gasped. "That's not fair."

He softened slightly. "I'm not accusing you. If you don't love him anymore, you don't. But it does go to my point that nothing is guaranteed. And it's not a risk I'm willing to take. Not knowing how much it hurts."

"So all of this—the last few weeks—means nothing to you?" She swept out her hand, knowing she was losing the battle to reach him and desperate to regain ground. "We trusted each other with things we haven't shared with anyone else. We became lovers. We were vulnerable with each other, and now that's it?"

"This isn't what we agreed," he said calmly, "and I can't

offer you more than that. It was why we laid ground rules to begin with."

"Ground rules that have already been broken!"

"Yes, you're right. We said one night only. But last night…"

"Last night you weren't such a stickler for the rules."

This time he was the one who was silent.

"I don't want it to be this way," she said, her voice breaking. "We also said always friends, but I can't just be friends with you, Christophe. I love you. And that means all of you. Not as just a friend."

"Are you saying you want this engagement to be real?"

The implications swirled around them. The ring on her finger. Marriage. Christophe as a partner and father. Yes, she thought she wanted those things. And it was clear by the tone of his voice, by the accusation behind it, that he did not. She should have known better. He'd already told her this had ended his previous relationship. Why had she thought she'd be any different?

"I love you," she whispered. "But if you don't love me, then this conversation has no point."

"I'm sorry, Sophie. You have no idea how sorry. I wish I'd never come up with this stupid idea."

And that cut most of all, because it meant regretting everything that had happened between them, and she would never do that. She'd cherish it, not regret it.

She moved to take the ring off her finger, but his voice cut into the silence. "Keep it. I won't say anything for a while and if we break off the engagement now, you'll have to deal with Eric again."

"I don't care. I can deal with him. I didn't need a ring when I told him the truth anyway."

"You told him the engagement was fake?"

"No. I told him that I was in love. He had no argument

against that." She lifted her chin. "I love you. A ring isn't going to change that." She wrested it off her finger and held it out.

"Keep it. It was always meant to be yours, even after the engagement was over. And it'll keep you from having to answer questions right away." He turned away, refusing to take the ring from her. Her hand trembled as she dropped it down to her side. She'd thought she'd be able to get him to see he didn't have to be afraid, but he didn't love her. Cared for her, yes. She believed that, at least. But he didn't love her. Maybe he wasn't capable of it.

He looked back at her. "I'm sorry. You have no idea how much. This wasn't how it was supposed to happen."

"We were fools to think it wouldn't," she said. "To think we could pretend like this and there not be consequences. I know what mine are now."

"I can't lie to you and give you what you want. You said from the beginning that you would only marry for true love. It would be unfair of me to let you believe in something that doesn't exist."

She hadn't thought he could wound her further, but that did it.

"Just go," she whispered.

"I'm sorry," he said, one last time.

And then he walked out her door.

Christophe kept the door shut to his office and focused on the spreadsheet in front of him. For four days he'd buried himself in work, trying to forget the hurt look in Sophie's eyes on Sunday afternoon. It was no use. He'd hurt her and he'd lied to her. Not about everything. He didn't believe in love, or at least didn't believe in it lasting. But he did feel it, and he felt it for her. She'd been a friend for years, but in the space of three weeks she'd become his lover and his everything. And that scared him to death. She was the control freak, but she was willing to relinquish that for something unknown and risky. He, on the other hand, was supposed to be so easygoing, but he was the one who was terrified of his out-of-control feelings.

It was better to stop the charade now, when they could both still recover and move on. And maybe someday they'd be friends again.

The last three weeks, well, they felt like a runaway train and he'd had to get off.

But God, he missed her.

His office door opened, and he looked up in irritation... didn't anyone knock anymore? When he saw it was Aurora, he bit back his annoyance. Snapping at her wouldn't do anyone any good.

"You're working late again."

"As are you, Maman. And you're supposed to be retired."

"No one is retired during the holiday season. Not in our business." She smiled at him, then came over and perched on the corner of his desk and reached out to smooth a piece of hair on his forehead. "Tell me where it hurts, *ma petite*."

She hadn't spoken to him like that in years, and his heart ached with it. It suddenly got difficult to swallow and his vision blurred. "I'm fine," he managed to say.

"No, you are not. I've seen this look on your face before, Christophe. Twice, to be exact. The first time was when we drove away from Orléans and brought you to Paris. The second was when I told you Cedric was gone." Her voice was soft but held a hint of steel. "Did she break your heart?"

He shook his head. "No, Maman. I broke hers."

Aurora sighed. "Oh, Christophe. I rather feared that was the case. You got scared and ran, didn't you?"

He looked up sharply, annoyed by how quickly she'd put that together. "Am I so transparent?"

"I've known you since you were a little boy. I will always maintain that bringing you to be part of our family was the best thing, for you and for us. But it is not without its scars. When I saw you with Sophie, I'd hoped you'd put those fears behind you."

"I don't know how to talk about this with you without seeming ungrateful."

She laughed, a small chuckle that was filled with affection. "Darling, I know you love me, just as I love you."

"You and Oncle Cedric...you raised me. You took me in when I wasn't wanted anywhere else."

"That is what you think? That we did it out of duty? Christophe. You were such a wonderful little boy. Your mother was struggling. She wouldn't let us help her, even though Cedric offered to. She was angry at me and angry at your father and at the world. We didn't 'take you in.' We saw an opportunity to give you the kind of life you deserved. We saw the opportunity to add to our family. I don't know how to explain it better than that. But you were wanted, Christophe."

Tears stung again. "I'm such a mess."

"We all are. We all have something. Bella's scars were on the outside. But so many of us...ours are on the inside. Facing them is torture. But happiness usually lies on the other side. You are miserable without her. The question is, does she love you?"

"She says she does."

"Why don't you believe her?"

He didn't answer at first. Then he reached over and took her hand. "I do believe her. But I'm afraid to hope. To trust. Because if she leaves me... I don't know if I can go through that."

"Not everyone leaves people." She reached out and touched his cheek. "If you marry her, you will be a father to her baby. Would you ever abandon him or her?"

"Of course not!" He was horrified at the thought.

"How do you know?"

He stared at her, confused.

"You trust yourself, but you don't trust someone else, and I understand why. You're willing to sit here right now and pledge that you would never abandon a child not your own flesh and blood. Not everyone is like your father, or even your mother, Christophe. But you will never know if you don't give them a chance, and you will never find happiness if you are determined to go through your life alone. If she loves you, and you love her, you're a fool to let her go." She lifted his chin. "And I did not raise you to be a fool."

"I'm still scared."

"Of course you are. It's a big thing, falling in love. Taking that leap." She frowned. "I just have one question. If you were this uncertain, why did you propose in the first place?"

"That is a question with a very long answer that will be a great anecdote someday."

They sat there for a long moment, and he was glad she was with him. Unconditionally. He looked up and his throat tightened again. "Thank you for being my mother," he said, his voice rough with emotion. "Sophie told me that a mother's love is unconditional, and she was right."

Aurora blinked rapidly and leaned over to kiss his forehead. "It is. Whatever you decide, I just want you to be happy. I saw you with Sophie at the château. It is extra special when you marry your best friend, Christophe. Don't throw that away because of fear. Work through it together. It's the only way your relationship will survive."

She left him sitting there and shut the door behind her as she left. Christophe stared at the spreadsheet but couldn't make heads nor tails of the columns and numbers. Instead, he searched his heart for the answers he needed. And when they came, he picked up his phone and called François.

Sophie stared at the email and felt an anger overcome her that was quite uncharacteristic. "Is he serious?" she asked the empty room. Empty except for Harry, who was perched on a cushion in the chair next to her. He looked up, gave a squeak, and put his head down again.

She stared at the email once more. What was his end-game? She hadn't heard a peep from him in two weeks. He'd walked out and…silence. Not that she'd expected anything. It had taken some serious verbal tap dancing around her parents to explain his absence. She'd framed it as both of them being extra busy during the holiday retail season, but it was hard to keep up the pretense of happiness. Harder to keep that up than the lie of the engagement.

Now he was making an offer on her jewelry collection. He'd sent through François's notes, too, and the CAD designs the designer had done of her drawings. He wanted them for a collection within the Aurora Gems line. And he wanted her to go to Paris for a meeting.

She hit the reply button and typed two words and then halted.

Aurora, Inc. would produce her collection using her name. It was a dream come true.

It was also a consolation prize, or at least it felt like it. As if he were saying "sorry, I don't have any love to give you, but here's a contract to make up for it." If she were going to sell the designs, she damned well wanted it to be on her own merit and not because Christophe felt guilty.

She fiddled with the ring on her finger. She'd been

wearing it to work to avoid questions, but suddenly now she wanted to take it off. Sophie twisted and pulled, but it stuck on her knuckle. "Oh, for God's sake!" she exploded, and then, for the millionth time since he'd walked out, she caught her lower lip wobbling.

It was hormones. It could only be hormones because she never let herself cry over a man like this.

When she composed herself again, she sent a quick email back. If he wanted to keep this business, so be it.

I'm interested in your proposal. Please send over the contract so i can review it, then I'll be in touch.

Short, to the point, no emotion. Perfect.

An hour later, she got an inbox notification. It was seven at night—eight in Paris. What was he still doing at work? Maybe, like her, he was working extra hours to fill the void.

We would prefer to meet in person before drawing up the contract. My assistant will contact you to set up a meeting at your convenience and will look after your travel arrangements for you. Best, Christophe

She briefly considered saying no, but as her mother would say, that would be cutting off her nose to spite her face, wouldn't it? If he could be utterly professional, then so could she. She'd show him that he might have broken her heart, but he hadn't broken her.

I'll look forward to her call.

CHAPTER SEVENTEEN

SOPHIE WALKED INTO the Aurora offices alone this time, and when she stopped at the front desk, she was greeted with a smile. "Oh, Ms. Waltham. We've been expecting you." Giselle's smile was wide. "Here's your card for the elevator. You remember the way to Monsieur Germain's office?"

"Oui, merci, Giselle." She offered a smile and fought of the sense of belonging that came over her when she entered the building. It wasn't right that she felt so at home here.

Maybe it was enough that her designs would be produced by Aurora. There was no better way to launch a career than with Aurora's backing. But not if Christophe was offering it as a token or to assuage some sort of guilt. He was a great one for gestures of that sort while refusing to accept anything in return. Well, not this time.

The elevator hummed quietly as she ascended to the executive offices. She pressed a hand to her stomach—it was growing by the day now, it seemed—and let out a breath to calm her jittery nerves. She had to keep her composure when she saw him again. Use her best poker face. She'd had enough practice the past month that it shouldn't be that hard, right?

She stepped off the elevator and went to main reception. "Ah, yes, Ms. Waltham. If you'll follow me. Monsieur

Germain has asked that you join him one floor down, actually. I'll take you there."

They went into the elevator again for the short trip, and the receptionist led her along the familiar hall. Perhaps they were meeting with François first? She should be glad; the designer would provide a welcome buffer during that first meeting.

A swipe of the key card and she was inside.

"Ah, Sophie! I heard you were on your way down." François approached, smiling broadly, and kissed her cheeks. "What did you think of the drawings?"

She was honest. "They turned out beautifully."

"I'm looking forward to working on them with you. Come with me."

He took her past his inner sanctum to a smaller office, set up similarly to his but on a smaller and neater scale. "What's this?"

"Your own space, for when you are here."

"François, I haven't signed anything."

"I know, *cherie*. The day is young."

"Where is Christophe?"

"Right here."

His voice came from behind her, in the doorway, and she spun around. He looked so good, so perfect, in a dark gray suit and pale blue shirt, open at the throat. She remembered how he hated ties, how he'd worn one to brunch and wrestled with the knot. She also remembered exactly how the hollow of his throat tasted. This had been a mistake. She should have insisted he send an agreement to her in London.

"This is kind of you, but I'll be working in London, remember? Waltham is there." Her anxiety kicked up a notch as she pointed out, "My baby's father is there."

"It is wonderful how convenient travel is between the

two cities," he pointed out. He stepped inside the room and François discreetly made himself scarce, leaving them alone. She realized belatedly that she'd mentioned the baby, something only his immediate family knew. "Don't worry about François. He adores you. He won't say a word."

She nodded and took a step back. "Do you have an offer for me? François didn't say which of the concepts you were interested in."

"Yes, I have an offer for you."

She waited, growing frustrated with his calm and patience. "Well?"

He took his hand out of his pockets and spread them out to his side a little. "Forever. My offer is forever, Sophie. If you can forgive me for being a total ass."

She stared. Surely she hadn't heard him right. "This isn't funny, Christophe. I came from London because you said you wanted to offer for my designs. Do you or don't you?"

"I do, and the paperwork is upstairs in my office. You're free to take it with you and have your lawyer look it over. The contract will stand no matter how you answer my next question."

She looked for signs he was joking, but there were none. No half smile, no teasing lift to his eyebrow. Instead, there was apology in his eyes, and something else, too. Something she'd wanted to see for a long time, only now she was too afraid to believe it was real.

"What's your next question, then?"

He didn't move. Just looked her square in the eye and said, "Will you marry me for real?"

It was amazing how she could stand so very still while inside it was all chaos. "I don't understand," she said slowly.

"You were right, about everything. About me being afraid. But I've come to understand that I am not my father or my mother. I would not abandon those whom I've claimed to love. And if I am not my parents, it is unfair for me to project my fears on you and expect you will leave me as they did. I was so afraid that I couldn't step back and see that for myself."

"What changed?"

"Aurora," he said simply. "Maman did what the best mothers do. She offered love and guidance…and a soft place to fall. I am blessed to have her. I only hope I am not too late with you. I never wanted to hurt you, Soph. I was just trying to protect myself."

"I know that," she said. "I could see it all along, but I didn't know how to get through to you."

"You couldn't. I had to figure it out myself. I would be a fool to throw away the love of my best friend. And I do love you, Sophie. I love you so much."

She'd never expected to hear those words in a hundred years, and she bit down on her lip because she didn't want to cry right now. "I was so mad at you for demanding I come here," she said. "Burning with rage because I thought you were offering me a consolation prize. A contract but no you. I was going to sign it just to spite you."

"And now?"

"Why would I want to spite my fiancé?"

His eyes widened. "Is that a yes?"

"Yes, Christophe. Yes, I'll marry you." She went to him and put her arms around his neck, holding him close. Oh, it felt so good to be in his arms again. Like coming home. "We have things to work out," she murmured, "but I really want us to do that together. The last two weeks have been horrible without you."

"For me, too. There were times I was fired up to get you back. And then other times I was sure it was for nothing and I'd lost you." He squeezed her tighter. "You're really here."

"Of course I am. I love you. Even when I'm furious with you."

He laughed then, and they pulled back to gaze at each other. His eyebrow twitched, and it gave her so much happiness she thought she might burst with it. "Are you planning to be furious with me often? It could be an interesting marriage."

"Only when you deserve it," she answered. Then she sobered and held his face between her hands. "Love means working through your problems and not walking away. I love you, Christophe. I know trust is so hard for you, so I'm just going to have to remind you every day that I'm not going anywhere."

"Nor am I," he replied, and he kissed her finally, long and deep, for the first time with their spoken feelings between them, and it was the sweetest thing she'd ever experienced.

Someone cleared their throat at the door and Sophie and Christophe broke apart. Her cheeks flushed as she saw François standing there with a lopsided grin on his face.

"Is there a reason you're interrupting me and my fiancée?" Christophe asked.

"Yes, sir. *Madame* herself is on the way down. I thought you might want to know before things got too...uh-huh." He wiggled his eyebrows and Sophie laughed.

"Thanks, François."

"We must look out for each other," he said wisely. "Welcome to the team, Sophie."

"Yeah," Christophe said, pulling her close to his side. "Welcome to the team."

Sophie couldn't believe she'd agreed to a Christmas Eve wedding. When Christophe had first suggested it, she had told him he was crazy, but it had taken maybe an hour for her to come around to the idea. The other alternative was the two of them spending the next several months traveling back and forth while her pregnancy progressed, and then trying to plan a wedding when the baby was small. Christophe's suggestion was to plan the wedding and then work out all the other logistics step by step: where they'd live, her role within Aurora and Waltham, and of course, shared parenting with Eric. They'd gone to see him together, and Christophe had asked his blessing. He'd even spoken to the other man about his childhood, and how he was determined that they all work together for this baby to feel loved and secure.

If she hadn't loved him completely before, that would have sealed it.

Her next step had been to sign the contract with Aurora. The Masterpiece Collection by Sophie Waltham was going to be a real thing.

Now she was standing in a guest room, wearing a stunning dress designed and tailored by Aurora's team. Christophe was down the hall in his own room, getting ready in his tuxedo. The wedding was going to take place in the grand hall downstairs, with only their families present...and François. He'd personally designed their wedding bands, and he'd come to mean a lot to her.

Bella and Gabi circled her, fluffing her skirt, smoothing a button. "You are stunning," Bella said, standing back and admiring.

"I feel like this is all a fairy tale and I'm going to wake up and find it's all been a dream," she admitted.

"Oh, it's real." Charlotte came in, beaming as usual. "Christophe is so smitten it's ridiculous. Never expected him to be the next to settle down." She sent a sarcastic look in Bella's direction. "Some people like long engagements, apparently."

Gabi laughed. "All right, Sophie. Here's your bouquet." She handed over a bouquet of crimson roses. Sophie had chosen it for its simplicity and for the season. The hall had been decorated for weeks for the holiday. They'd hardly had to do anything. Evergreen boughs and ribbon hung from every banister and railing. Arrangements of flowers and greens were everywhere, and white folding chairs had been brought in for the guests. While the family tree was in the drawing room, an arch had been constructed as an altar for the ceremony in the grand hall. It had all been in place when Sophie had left to get ready.

"We do need to get downstairs, girls," Gabi said, giving Sophie's gown one last fluff. "Happy wedding day," she whispered in Sophie's ear, giving her a little hug.

Sophie had quite fallen in love with the whole family over the past few weeks, everyone chipping in to hastily throw together the simple wedding—even the garrulous Stephen, who seemed determined to retain his bachelorhood, despite the fact he was the heir and the oldest of them all. He wasn't nearly as scary as he'd first appeared and had told Christophe that he'd just acquired the most precious gem in the Aurora dynasty. It was an uncharacteristically sentimental thing for him to say.

The sisters departed, and Sophie had a few moments to herself. She took a large breath and went to stand in front of the mirror. Her little bump didn't show in the empire-waisted gown, which she adored. A low scoop neck showed a hint of cleavage, but delicate cap sleeves gave the gown an innocent look, and the lace overskirt was divine, ending in a small train at the back. Aurora had loaned her a tiara, too, the one that she had worn at her wedding to Cedric, and Sophie had been particularly touched.

Christophe had even invited his mother, though she'd declined the invitation. Sophie knew it had hurt him terribly, but she'd tried to make him see that his mother was the one losing out.

Either way, within the hour Sophie and Christophe would be husband and wife. He would be a father to her child. They would be…a family.

There was a knock on the door and her father peeked inside. "Are you ready, blossom? It's time."

"I am, Dad," she said, clutching her bouquet. She'd moved the diamond and ruby ring to her right hand for the ceremony, and just this morning Christophe had gifted her the matching necklace and earrings, which glittered at her throat and ears.

"I'm so happy for you, Sophie," he murmured, kissing her cheek. "I don't want to mess your makeup."

"You won't. We used setting spray." She laughed and kissed him on the cheek. "You and Mum…you like him, don't you?"

"We do. And he loves you, and that's all we ever want for our children." He stopped, choked up for a moment. "I didn't think it would be this hard, giving you away."

She got misty-eyed too, and took a moment to say, "Thank you, Dad. It's because of you and Mum that I know what love is, and why I wouldn't settle for less."

"Well, now that's done it." He reached inside his pocket for a handkerchief and wiped his eyes. "Sophie, one more thing you should know. Your mother and I have been talking, and it's unfair of us to expect you to take on Waltham when you have your own life to live. We're nowhere near ready to retire, mind you, but we'll support you in whatever future you choose. You have a family to consider now, after all. And family means everything."

"Oh, Dad." She sniffled and kissed his cheek. "I love you."

"I love you too, blossom. Come now, let's get you down the aisle."

They descended the stairs, Sophie careful to let her toe peek out from beneath her hem before taking each step. When they reached the end of the hall, every eye turned to look at her, but she had eyes only for Christophe. Pristine, black tuxedo with a white cravat and a red rose at his breast; curls freshly cut but barely tamed, and one damnable eyebrow lifted—the same one that had started all this trouble. A smile curved her lips as she made her way to him, growing the closer she got, until she reached his side, and they were both grinning like idiots.

To her right, Aurora gave a sniff and dabbed her eyes with a tissue.

The officiant took one look at them and declared, "I don't think I've ever seen a happier couple."

As Sophie looked into Christophe's eyes, she had a feeling the officiant was right. And after the vows were spoken and the rings exchanged, Christophe pointed to a spot above her head.

Mistletoe. He'd hung mistletoe from their bridal arch. And as they shared their first kiss as husband and wife, it was with the promise in her heart that each year they'd revisit this tradition and renew their vows to each other, no matter where the future took them. Whether it was Aurora or Waltham, Paris or London, it didn't matter. Their love was forever, and they would spend each and every day proving it.

* * * * *

THE
SINGLE DAD'S
CHRISTMAS
PROPOSAL

ELLA HAYES

MILLS & BOON

For my brother, Steven,
and all the other fearless ones…

PROLOGUE

'YOU'RE OFTEN DESCRIBED as fearless. Are you?'

Dax D'Aureval felt a string of nerves tightening in his ribs. Was the microphone clipped to his jacket picking up the quick beats of his heart? He could feel his blood rushing, pounding in his ears. He drew a slow breath, allowing the familiar feelings to settle, then he looked past the camera lens and into Pierre's expectant face. 'Really? You're asking me this again?'

Pierre's nod was slight, but his eyes held a gleam.

Dax let out a slow sigh. Pierre filmed all his snowboarding exploits for the sponsors, but for the documentary features action shots alone weren't enough. They needed interview material to use as voice-over, talking head stuff because his fans liked to see his face. The whites of his eyes! They wanted to know what made him tick. As if he even knew! All he could ever do was answer Pierre's questions, in whichever moment they came, as honestly as he could, dialling up the charm, of course. He had over a hundred and seventy thousand followers on social media and his job was to keep the brands he represented in the spotlight. If that meant schmoozing to camera, coming out with little quips that could be used as teasers for the documentaries, then that was fine. It was part of the sponsorship gig, part of the life he'd created for himself. Free riding was his passion so talking about it wasn't a hardship, except that at that moment his insides were chaos, and his throat was dry. He was about to take on a Chamonix classic—the Mallory Couloir on the north face of the Aiguille du Midi—and what he needed was to be taking a moment, sifting through his fear, sorting it into good and bad, not answering questions about it.

He flicked a glance at the lift. His support team was hovering by the doors, waiting for him. His guides. His friends. *Crazy steep-skiing machines!* They all spent their lives romancing the slopes. He wasn't the only one.

He took a breath, strapping on his game face. 'I wouldn't describe myself as fearless… Not at all. You can't do what I do and not be scared.' He swallowed. 'Like right now I'm really scared, but I don't try to block my fear because it's useful, even if it's annoying.' He smiled, principally to loosen the tightness in his cheeks. 'Fear primes you for danger. It keeps you on your toes. It's a strange fear, though…' A tingle moved along his spine. 'I kind of love it.'

The camera moved closer. 'Love is a strong word, Dax, but is it love, or could it be an addiction?'

He could see his own reflection in the lens, could see the intent in Pierre's eyes. Yes, the lines he rode looked reckless… Yes, it might have seemed to a casual observer that he was in the grip of a dangerous addiction, that he was a man who liked flirting with death, but free riding was about living not dying, and Pierre got that because Pierre was an extreme snowboarder too. Pierre was only prodding him because he was on a crusade to debunk the myth that extreme sports were the domain of cavalier, thrill-seeking adrenaline junkies. Usually he fell in, but today, for some reason, he didn't want to. Maybe it was because the lens was too close, or because the guys by the lift were getting restive, or maybe it was because his stomach was gnawing a hole in itself. He could feel himself sliding into the *Why the hell am I doing this?* headspace and he had to shake it off before it took hold. He needed to get onto the mountain, face his fear, find the beauty on the other side of it.

He shifted slightly. 'I don't know if it's an addiction… but it *is* an obsession.' He paused. 'When I'm riding there's a spirit inside me that *is* wild, definitely a little crazy…' He could sense Pierre stiffening, but he was invested now. He had to keep going. 'I don't understand it, but it drives me, keeps me wanting more. Higher. Harder. Faster. I'm always chasing something…' He shrugged, holding in a smile. 'Is that addiction?'

'Dax!' The camera tilted in Pierre's hand. 'That's the wrong answer.'

He felt a pang of guilt. 'I'm sorry, man. It's all I've got today.' His veins were thrumming, chemicals flooding in, preparing him for what he was about to do. He unclipped the microphone, handing it back to Pierre, then he picked up his pack. 'You should use it anyway because it's the truth, even if you don't want to hear it.' His insides were boiling, turning to liquid. 'I mean, yes, we plan for risk. We've got the experience, the skills, the equipment. We take every precaution, but there's no denying it: we seek out impossible lines, lines that have never been ridden before and we ride them hard.' He shrugged. 'It follows that we must be a little bit crazy.'

CHAPTER ONE

Paris, December 5th, one year later...

SIMONE COSSART HURRIED across the Place du Palais Royal, squinting through the spiralling snowflakes, resisting the urge to lift her face and catch some on her tongue. She loved snow, the way it transformed the city into a wonderland, but dallying wasn't an option. She wanted to get to the bistro first, ahead of Dax D'Aureval, so she could seem calm and collected when he arrived, 'seem' being the operative word, since she wasn't feeling remotely calm.

Maybe she was mad, bending over backwards to meet Dax at such short notice. It wasn't as if he'd ever bent over backwards for her. He'd never been to pick up his son, Yannick, from her apartment, and he'd never reciprocated a playdate for her daughter, Chloe, even though Chloe and Yann had been best friends from their first day in Cours Préparatoire. It was always Amy, Dax's au pair, who came to collect Yannick. It was Amy who'd warned her quietly before Yann and Chloe's first playdate that Yann's *maman* was dead and that she shouldn't ask Yann about her. Amy hadn't elaborated, and at the time Simone had been too preoccupied with her new job in the school's office—her first proper job in years—to give it much thought. She'd simply been glad that Chloe was settling in at school and had made such a nice friend, but now all the things she didn't know about Yann and his mysterious *papa* were weighing heavy. She was flying blind, meeting Dax to discuss a business proposal because Amy had asked her to, but she didn't quite know what to make of it!

She dipped her chin, bracing herself against the swirl. Why hadn't she brought a hat? Gloves? She'd seen the forecast! It was why she'd made sure that Chloe had been well wrapped up that morning but, somehow, she'd forgotten to wrap herself up and now she was paying the price. Her fingers were freezing, her nose was probably red, and she could feel snow settling in her hair and melting wetly on her cheeks. Calm and collected? *Not!*

She marched on, head down, until she reached the corner of the square and then she stopped. This was the place! Bistro Royal. Crimson canopies edged with twinkling lights, windows lushly decked with Christmas greenery, glowing interior. *Lovely!* She stood, staring, feeling nostalgic. This was what she'd come to Paris for a decade ago, to be a part of this…this city of lights and romance, this city of lively cafés and big dreams…

Broken dreams…

She bit her lips together. No point dwelling on that. There were more pressing things to think about, like getting inside, drying off and making herself presentable!

She hurried towards the entrance, brushing snow off her coat, going for the door handle just as a gloved male hand claimed it.

'Oh—' She drilled her toes hard into the paving, slewing to a halt, but somehow she was still moving, pitching forwards.

'Whoa!' A firm hand closed around her arm, holding it fast. 'God, I'm sorry! Are you all right?'

At the pulsing edge of her vision, she perceived a blue

jacket. She touched her chest, catching her breath. 'Yes, I think so.'

'Are you sure?' He was letting go of her arm, stepping back.

'Yes, I'm fine, really, and it wasn't your fault…' She gathered herself, looking up. 'I was rush—' Her tongue stuck. Monsieur Blue Jacket was devilishly handsome, and curiously familiar, the bit of him she could see anyway between the band of his dark green beanie and the turned-up collar of his jacket. He was clean-shaven, dark browed, and his large brown eyes were flecked with mischief, or maybe it was the canopy lights that were making them twinkle all the way to their warm seductive depths. It was hard to tell, hard to breathe.

A slow smile dented his cheeks. 'I was rushing too, to get out of the snow—' he closed one eye, scrunching his face a little '—which is weird because actually I love snow.'

'Me too…although…' He was dragging off the hat, releasing a dark mop of supremely touchable hair. She curled her fingers into her palms, 'Although I wish I hadn't forgotten *my* hat.'

'Here!' His hand shot out, dangling the beanie. 'Take mine.'

She felt her mouth falling open. Was he for real? Who offered their hat to a total stranger just like that? Her heart thumped. Was he hitting on her? *Oh, God!* She swallowed hard. 'It's extremely kind of you but I couldn't possibly—'

'Yes, you can. I want you to have it.' He dipped his chin, eyes half teasing, half serious. 'I have an endless supply of hats so I can definitely spare this one for a lady in need.'

Her heart pulsed. In need didn't come close! She was burning up with it, tingling from head to toe, and it was clear from the look in his eyes that he could see it, knew exactly what effect he was having on her. He was playing, flirting, and suddenly she realised that she didn't mind one little bit. She liked him, liked the way his eyes were travelling over her face, lingering on her mouth, then moving up and reaching into hers again. She could feel her body responding, liquid warmth spreading through her limbs. If she accepted his hat, would something happen? Maybe the hat was a sign...

Stop!

She broke away from his gaze. What was she doing, weaving silly fantasies? She wasn't looking for a man, and as for serendipity and dreams coming true, she didn't believe in all that. Not any more. She shivered, feeling cold. Her dreams had all been trampled. She'd lost her love and, with him, her rose-tinted view of the world. That was all this silly flirtation was. A rose-tinted moment, briefly warm.

'Go on...' His voice pulled her back. He was brushing off the hat, scattering drops, his eyes twinkling. 'Think of it as compensation for almost knocking you over.'

'You didn't! It was me, not looking where...'

His eyebrows slid upwards.

She felt the air softening, a sudden warmth filling her chest. He seemed determined to give her his hat and the light in his eyes was making it impossible to refuse. She pressed her lips together then reached out, smiling. 'Okay. Thank you! It'll make my walk back to the Metro much warmer.' She tucked it into her pocket. 'You're very chivalrous.'

A smile touched his lips. 'I don't know about that but, thank you.' His eyes held hers for a beat, and then he blinked. 'I should probably go inside. I'm meeting someone.'

A gorgeous girlfriend no doubt! She nipped off the thought with a smile. 'Me too.'

He yanked the door open, standing back, and then she felt the briefest light touch between her shoulder blades. 'After you.'

In the ladies' room she set her bag down, waiting for the ghost of his touch to fade, and then she looked in the mirror.

Oh, God! She was a mess, all damp and smudged. Still, she could fix her face and hair. Fixing the chaos she was feeling inside was a different matter. How could a fleeting encounter at the door have put her into such a spin?

She went to unzip her bag, then stopped, reaching into her pocket for the hat. Cashmere soft. She flipped the label. *Wow!* Actually cashmere! She lifted it to her face, breathing in his smell. *Clean!* He'd smell good, close up, she knew it. Fresh…like mountain air. *Yes!* He had that outdoorsy glow, the traces of a summer tan, oh, and those melting eyes, the unhurried way he'd looked at every part of her face… A tingle played along her spine and she hugged it tight. *Feeling!* How long had it been since she'd felt so aware of someone, so trembly and dizzy in all the right ways? Kaboom! He'd woken her up, just by looking at her.

She let her hands fall. Men didn't usually look at her like that, or maybe she just didn't notice them because André was always there, even though he was gone. No one's smile had ever matched his. No one's gaze had ever stopped her heart the way his used to. She'd kept his flame burning for Chloe, so that Chloe would know how deeply her *papa* had loved her, and for herself, because memories were all she had left. They'd kept her going through the silent weeping days, and the ranting inside days, and the day that his parents had turned their backs. She squeezed her eyes shut, pushing the thought out of reach. For the past three years all she'd thought about was making Chloe happy, and making ends meet, but now a stranger's gaze had stolen her breath away and her senses were ringing like Christmas bells, ringing for *herself*.

The door sprang open and she startled, stuffing the beanie back into her pocket. The girl coming in was beautiful, powdering the air with her instantly recognisable fragrance: two hundred euros a bottle! Was *she* the one he was meeting? They'd look good together...

Stop!

She slipped off her coat and dug out her hairbrush, working it upwards through her damp tangles. Why was she poking at jealous little fires? Didn't she have enough to poke at already: a hastily arranged meeting; an offer from a man she'd never even met? That was what she needed to be thinking about, even though it still didn't feel real...

Amy had come to the school office that morning ashenfaced. Her father had just been diagnosed with myeloma, she said. The prognosis was bad. She was going back to Melbourne just as soon as Dax could find her a flight. Simone had still been processing that news when Amy had dropped another bomb. Would *she* consider stepping in to help Dax look after Yannick over Christmas at his chalet in Chamonix? She'd asked the obvious question: wasn't there a relative who could help, or a childminder in Chamonix? Amy had said, no, it was complicated. She'd said Dax would explain everything if Simone agreed to meet him, and then she'd said he'd pay her whatever she wanted if she agreed to go. A well-aimed strike! Amy knew she was hard up. Amy knew that Chloe was only at Yann's expensive private school because of her job in the school office, and Amy had seen her apartment in all its miserable glory: the peeling paint, the torn kitchen lino. Amy had heard the incessant dripping of the kitchen tap.

She wound her hair up catching it with an elastic. Amy knew she hated the apartment, knew that she was planning to move as soon as she passed her probation period at the school and could count on her salary. In short, Amy knew that a cash injection would make a world of difference.

There! Her hair was done. She dampened a tissue, cleaning the mascara smudges from around her eyes. Getting paid to spend Christmas in Chamonix definitely wasn't a horrible idea, although her parents would be disappointed if she and Chloe didn't go to the farm. She breathed through a stab of the usual guilt. Maman and Papa didn't know how things had been for her since André's death, how strapped for cash she'd been. Telling them would only have led to questions that were too painful to answer and she wasn't ready, wouldn't be until she was properly on her feet again. She took out her lipstick and dabbed some on. But that day was coming—soon—and then she'd be able to let them in again. In the meantime, if she agreed to go to Chamonix, she wouldn't mention the money. She'd say it was an invitation she couldn't turn down for Chloe's sake. At least that part would be true!

She popped her lipstick away and zipped up her bag. The money was a magnet, but even without it the chance to give Chloe a magical Christmas in the mountains would have been tempting. Chloe loved snow, loved making snow bunnies. Wonky ears. Twigs for whiskers! Simone felt a smile coming. And 'chalet' sounded so cosy. She could see it in her mind, crackling fires, and fur throws. All the clichés! And even though Christmas was her worst time of year because of André, being somewhere different— somewhere where she wasn't having to dodge Maman's unsubtle attempts to fix her up with a lonely farmer— would maybe make things easier. And Yann wasn't hard work! He was deeply quiet, but he seemed to adore Chloe and Chloe adored him right back. No wonder! He was cute as, with his big eyes, and his dark eyebrows and his dark mop of curly hair…

Her heart pulsed. *No!* She gripped the sink unit, replaying the scene at the door. That feeling of familiarity. The shape of his nose, his mouth, his hair springing free… *Oh, God!* How hadn't she seen it straight away? Monsieur Blue Jacket was the spit of Yannick. The man who'd set her senses alight was Dax D'Aureval!

Dax glanced at the entrance, then scanned the interior yet again. Simone Cossart was due to arrive at any moment—skinny, according to Amy, with serious eyes and dark hair—but he couldn't stop perusing the tables, looking for the woman he'd almost knocked over at the door.

He'd been head down, churning away over Amy's sad news, feeling sorry for her, and—*yes*—feeling sorry for himself, and then somehow, she'd been there, his very own snow angel with snowflakes melting on her cheeks and nestling in her hair like confetti. For a few heavenly moments, her warm eyes and lovely smile had sent his spirits skywards. For the first time in months he'd felt alive, but now she was nowhere to be seen and he wanted to see her. A glimpse would do, from a distance, just something… anything…anything at all.

Stop!

This wasn't him, tangling himself up in the thought of someone. He never did this, ever! He squeezed his eyes shut. Maybe it was just another symptom of his disarray. His life was out of control, so why not his emotions too? That would be the cherry on top! He slumped back in his chair, feeling a drag of weariness. Was he really here, in a Parisian bistro, trying to solve a childcare emergency? Four months ago he hadn't even been a father, hadn't had an unfathomable six-year-old son who froze him out at every opportunity. Four months ago he'd been free as a bird, packing his gear for a new free-riding adventure in Alaska—

'Hello…'

His heart pulsed. *Snow Angel?* Grey dress, tidy hair, red lips. Different from before yet the same.

'You're Dax D'Aureval, aren't you?' She was looking at him carefully, blushing slightly. 'Yannick's *papa?*'

'Yes, but…' He blinked, trying to clear the confusion in his head, then he looked at her again. Dark hair. *Like Amy said.* Serious eyes. *Like Amy said.* For a beat, the room stood still, then a small spark of joy ignited deep in his chest. '*You're* Simone Cossart?'

She nodded. 'Yes.'

'Wow!' *What?* He shot to his feet, heart racing. 'I mean, hello, again!'

'Hi… Again!' A smile lit her gaze, but there was wariness behind it. Was she already planning her escape? *Hell's bells!* If he'd known who she was, he'd never have flirted with her at the door. He felt a fluttering panic. Too late to rewind, but he could hit the reset button, make her see that this was business, pure and simple. He *had* to get her on board. Yann's happiness and his own career depended on it.

'So…' He moved round the table, pulling out a chair for her, keeping his tone light. 'That was funny, us meeting like that. Not knowing…'

'Very!' Her eyes caught his, holding him as he sat down again. 'The thing is, I actually thought there was something familiar about you.' She was smiling now, wariness fading. He felt a wash of relief. Dealing with it up front had been the right call. 'I can't believe I didn't see it right away. I mean, Yannick is the spit of you!'

It was exactly what he'd thought when Yann's picture had pinged onto his phone. No DNA test required! He forced out a smile. 'Yes, he is, although his eyes are lighter.'

Like Zara's. He felt a lick of anger. It was wrong, thinking ill of the dead, but he couldn't not be furious with Zara. She should have told him he had a son. She'd known he was a D'Aureval, but, aside from his family's wealth and status, at twenty-two he'd been a public figure in his own right, a rising star on the world free-riding circuit. She could have contacted him so easily, but instead she'd kept Yann to herself, and now *he* was dealing with the fallout, messing up constantly, and that wasn't his style. Christ, if he'd been in the habit of messing up—

'Are you ready to order?'

Somehow a waitress was there, looking at him. He shook himself. 'Simone? What would you like?'

Simone smiled at the girl. '*Café au lait*, and a glass of water, please.'

'And for you, *monsieur*?'

'I'll take an espresso, thanks. That's all.'

The girl tapped at a device in her hand, and then she was gone.

He looked at Simone. 'So, we should probably start. Amy said you can't stay long…?'

'That's right.' She smiled apologetically. 'Chloe's at ballet. I have to collect her.'

'Okay.' He smiled to hide his nerves. He wasn't used to divulging information about his private life, but it was the only way. He had to make her see that she was the only one who could help him. He took a breath. 'So thanks for coming. Obviously, you know that Amy's leaving…'

'Yes.' Her eyelids fluttered. 'It's so awful about her father.' She shook her head a little. 'Why do bad things always seem to happen at Christmas?'

Had she been through something herself? It seemed as though maybe she had, but now wasn't the time to ask. He shrugged. 'I don't know, but it's terrible for her and, frankly, for me as well. She's been a big help.' Connecting with Yann in a way that he couldn't, in a way that he didn't even seem to be equipped for. He pushed the thought away, trying to sound upbeat. 'It was her idea to ask you, you know. She says you're good with Yannick.'

'Well…' She seemed to falter. 'Yann's easy…'

Easy? He felt an ache in his chest. Yann was quiet but there was nothing easy about him, not for *him* anyway.

Her eyebrows flickered. 'Most of the time I hardly know he's there.'

'There' being her apartment, a place he'd made a point of avoiding. His stomach churned. He might have planned a careful route into this conversation, but the guilt he was feeling about Yann's frequent playdates with Chloe was all too real, especially now that Simone was sitting right there in front of him.

'Simone…' It was hard to hold her gaze. 'Thanks for having Yann over so often.' He took a breath. 'I'm sorry we haven't reciprocated yet.'

She blinked. 'It's okay.'

'It isn't—' He could see a splinter of hurt in her eyes, could feel it piercing his own skin. 'You've been kind and I've been rude. I didn't mean to be. It's just that…'

'Just that what?'

He felt despair winding through his veins. 'I'm useless at the whole parenting thing, okay! Meeting other parents. Talking to them. Playdates!' He held her gaze, loading his voice so she would understand. 'It's all new to me.'

'New?' Her eyebrows drew in. 'But Yann's six.'

'Yes…but you see, he was with his mother—'

'Café au lait?'

He leant back, giving the waitress space, taking the moment to breathe. He'd got to base camp, but his nerves were fraying. Opening up wasn't his thing. Hiding behind a cut-out was his thing. Cut-out Dax was a thrill-seeker, a playboy. Cut-out Dax was always smiling, always upbeat. But Yann's arrival had turned him over, reminded him of what was on his flip side, and now, for Yann's sake, he needed to lay himself out for Simone, like cards on a table. No wonder his mouth was dry.

He took a sip of his coffee, steeling himself. 'Simone, Yannick only came to me four months ago, after his mother died. Before that, I didn't even know he existed.'

Her eyes flew wide. 'His *maman* only died four months ago?' And then the second thing he'd said seemed to find fertile ground. 'You didn't know about him?' Her mouth was hanging open just as his had been when Zara's father, Claude, had called, but he'd dropped his phone too, smashing the screen so that he'd had to peer through a web of cracks to see the picture of Yann that Claude texted through.

'No.' He swallowed hard, reining in his emotions. 'I had no idea. Zara and I weren't together. We had a fling. She never contacted me, never told her parents that I was Yann's father. Her *papa* found my name in her diary after she died.'

She was shaking her head. 'I don't know what to say.'

'You don't have to say anything. I'm just trying to explain why I'm struggling with the parent stuff.' The empathy in her eyes was tearing at something inside him. He sipped his coffee again, steadying himself. 'It was a shock, obviously, but after I'd come to my first thought was that I wanted to be a good parent...' Better than his mother, Colette, better than his anonymous, absent father. Admittedly, between them they'd set a low bar, giving him no template for exactly *how* to be a good parent! He pushed the thought away. 'I thought I'd have time to work things out, but Zara's parents had other ideas. They said they were too old to be running around after Yann…' Simone's eyes narrowed. She was doing the maths, but she didn't have the right figures. He sighed. 'Look, Zara was a lot older than me, and she'd been a late baby herself. Her parents are in their seventies, so fair enough. They love Yann, but they said his place was with me. They asked me to fetch him straight away.'

Simone was frowning. 'But that's—'

'I know.' At least they were on the same page! 'It seemed wrong to me too, but I was the absent father without a leg to stand on, so off I went to fetch him. No easing in. No getting to know each other.' He felt an ache in his chest, a sagging weariness. 'It's been a disaster.'

'No wonder.' She was shaking her head again. 'Yann's grieving. Displaced. And, yes, you're his *papa*, but you're still a stranger.' She looked down, toying with her cup, and then her eyes were on his again, her gaze searching. 'I wish I'd known Yann's loss was so recent. Why didn't Amy fill me in properly?'

He felt his heart shrivelling. 'Because I asked her not to. Yann's in a new place with new people. I thought not hearing Zara's name would make it easier for him to settle.' Something that looked like disagreement momentarily surfaced in her eyes but then it faded. He sighed. 'It seemed wise at the time, but probably wasn't, I don't know…'

For a long moment she was quiet, and then she sighed. 'I can see it's been difficult—'

'Difficult?' He felt something snap inside, and suddenly unrehearsed words were rising on his tongue and spilling out. 'Yann has no time for me, Simone. I can't reach him, can't seem to make him happy no matter what I do, and I don't like other parents and other kids seeing the way he ignores me.' Was he sounding pathetic, self-pitying? Probably, but she needed to know. 'It's why I don't do playdates, why I've never been to collect him from your apartment.'

'But that's—'

'Stupid?' He gulped a breath. 'Pathetic?'

'No.' Her eyes were filling, glistening. 'I was going to say, it's understandable.'

His throat went tight. She really was an angel, a kind, sweet, beautiful angel. Talking to her, confiding in her, was beginning to feel like a sweet release. He took a breath. 'I'm not used to failing, but I'm failing with Yann. I can't seem to connect with him. I don't know how. It's why I took Amy on, why I leave everything to her. Yann prefers her to me.' He closed his eyes for a beat. Final push! 'But now she's going, and I don't know what to do. It's our first Christmas together! I want Yann to be happy. If you and Chloe come with us to Chamonix then there's a good chance he will be, because Yann adores Chloe.'

Warm light filled her eyes. 'And she adores him right back, believe me.'

He felt his spirits lifting, hope kindling in his chest. 'He's fond of you too, Simone. That's what Amy says, so, you see, it has to be you... You, and Chloe. Yann isn't close to anyone else.' He rested his forearms on the table and leaned towards her, putting everything into his gaze. 'Please come with us to Chamonix, Simone. I'll make it worth your while, pay you whatever you want...'

Whatever I want...

Dax's gaze was intense, full of hope, too hard to hold. She looked down, staring past the skin on her untouched coffee. Talk about releasing the motherload. It was almost too much to process...an accidental father struggling to bond with a grieving son, losing his trusted au pair and turning to her, because of her daughter. Didn't he have family who could help? Presumably not, since he hadn't mentioned them. *Think!* If she and Chloe were to go, then maybe Yann would be happy, but would that really help Dax in the end? If he kept stepping back, using other people as intermediaries, he was never going to build a bridge to his son and he clearly wanted to. The money was a big, shiny magnet but taking it would prick her conscience if she didn't at least try to point him in the right direction first.

She took a breath and looked up. 'Dax, I'm not trying to talk myself out of a job or anything, but do you *really* need us?' His gaze flickered. 'I mean, wouldn't Christmas be the perfect time for you and Yann to be together, just the two of you, bonding?'

'Ah!' He sat back a little, looking sheepish. 'Sorry! I should have explained before. I have to work over Christmas. The hours are erratic, so I can't be with Yann all the time.'

'I see.' Now it made sense. This wasn't just about helping him with Yannick for the Christmas holidays. He needed an actual childminder. That was better in a way. More defined. She refocused. 'So what do you do?'

He took a breath. 'I snowboard, professionally.'

That made sense too. It explained his outdoorsy glow, the athleticism that seemed to underpin his every movement. It explained the chalet in Chamonix. She felt her shoulders inching upwards. 'Are you an instructor?'

'No.' A smile broke over his face, filling his eyes with twinkling light. 'I'm a free rider.'

'Right.' He clearly loved being a free rider, whatever that was. It had brought his smile back just like that. She felt her own lips curving up. 'And what do free riders do?'

'They find their own lines.'

'Lines?' She pulled the bug-eyed face that always made Chloe laugh.

He chuckled. 'Basically, we ride outside the resorts.'

'Okay…' She picked up her glass and took a sip of water. 'I love snow, but, as you can probably tell, I know nothing about winter sports. I know ice-skating, and skiing, oh, and luge, and I only remember luge because I saw it on television once and it looked terrifying.'

His eyebrows flickered. 'Terrifying, huh?'

Was he flirting again or was it just that she was involuntarily susceptible to the light in his eyes? She put her glass down. 'So, how does free riding qualify as work? I mean, it doesn't sound much like work.'

He laughed roundly. 'I can see how you'd think that, but actually it's quite involved. There's a lot of planning, and waiting for the right conditions.'

'And you get *paid*—' She bit her tongue, felt a blush tingling in her cheeks. 'I'm sorry. It's none of my business.'

'Don't be.' His hand covered hers for a warm second, his gaze deep and kind. 'I don't mind.' She felt her lungs emptying out, warmth rushing through her veins, and then his hand was back on the table and he was smiling as if he hadn't just stopped her heart. 'I do get paid, yes. I have sponsors, brands to promote. I'm what they call an influencer. It's why I have to go to Cham.' A shadow crossed his face. 'Since Yann came, I haven't been pulling my weight for my sponsors! I need to get back to it, honour my commitments. I'm planning a big expedition.'

The set of his jaw spoke volumes. The life he loved had been ripped away and he wanted it back. She knew how that felt.

His gaze sharpened suddenly. 'You know, if you want to see what I do, you could watch one of my films.'

She felt her mouth falling open. 'You're a film star?'

'No...' His eyebrows flickered. 'But they make films about me.'

Intriguing! 'Then you must be good?'

'I'm not bad.' There was mischief in his eyes, and something else that was making her heart flutter.

She looked away, catching the time on her watch. *Oh, God!* She sprang to her feet, grabbing her bag. 'I'm sorry. I've got to go—'

'But what about Cham?' He was getting up, chair scraping. 'We haven't finished...'

He looked strained, anxious, but all she could think was that she was going to be late for Chloe, and she was never late for Chloe.

She licked her lips. 'Look, I'm leaning towards yes, but I need to think about it a bit more.'

'Okay.' And then he blinked. 'I mean, of course.' He plucked a card from his shirt pocket and handed it to her. 'Here's my number. If you have any questions, please call.'

'I will.'

And then he was moving round the table towards her, leaning in, kissing each of her cheeks in turn, making her head spin. When he stepped back his eyes were full of warm light. 'Thank you for coming.'

She smiled, suddenly remembering. 'And thank *you* for the hat.'

His face lit up. 'You're more than welcome. Hopefully, I'll see you wearing it in Chamonix...'

She bit her lip, tangling inside. 'Hopefully.'

CHAPTER TWO

December 5th, later...

'So, VINTAGE ROSES, express delivery?'

'Yes. They need to go straight away.'

The pretty assistant—Marie, according to the badge pinned to the front of her apron—was pouting a little. *Flirting!* Usually, he'd have flirted back but instead he was drifting, sliding into the dark green depths of Simone Cossart's eyes. He couldn't see past her sweet face, that lush, kissable mouth—

'Did you have a colour in mind, *monsieur*?'

He blinked. 'What have you got?'

'Pink, mauve, cream, and apricot.'

Which colour would Simone like? Her coat had been black, her dress grey. That wasn't much to go on. What had Amy said about her apartment, that she'd made the best of it but that it was dreary and chilly and dated? Amy hadn't mentioned a colour, just a dripping tap! He felt his neck prickling. Landlords shouldn't have been allowed to let out places like that. They should have been forced to maintain things! In his line, things *had* to work. It was a life-or-death thing—

'Monsieur?'

Marie's face came back, instantly morphing into Simone's…that blush in her cheeks, the disbelief in her eyes when he'd offered her his hat. Such a small thing, and yet she'd looked as if he'd been giving her the world, a world she thought she didn't deserve. It was only a hat, one of many that his sponsors sent by the boxful on a regular basis. He took a breath. 'Let's go for ten of each and please send them as an arrangement in a cylinder vase.' Slicing and crushing the stem tips of forty roses would have turned his gift into a chore, and gifts weren't meant to be hard work. 'Plain crystal, I think.'

'Certainly, *monsieur*.'

'And I'll need a card.'

Marie pulled out a box of cards from under the long green counter. He thumbed through, picking a cream card with a simple tooled border. Nothing fussy. Simone wasn't the fussy type. She'd looked elegant in her plain grey dress and long black boots. No frills, no adornments, but she'd stolen his breath away all the same. He was still trying to get it back.

Marie tucked the box away. 'We can print the card for you—'

'No, thanks. I'm going for the personal touch.' He pulled out his pen, flashing his eyebrows. 'Means more, right?'

She nodded, returning a wistful smile.

He moved to the end of the counter and clicked the pen. What to write? How to translate his chaotic feelings into words?

He'd gone to the bistro with one thing in mind: to persuade Simone to be Yannick's childminder for Christmas. What he hadn't expected was to feel attracted to her, and he definitely hadn't expected to feel so moved by her gentle empathy. He'd thought that opening up was going to be one-way traffic, him pouring everything out, making his case, but what he'd seen in her eyes while he'd been talking, what he'd felt flowing back had drawn him in somehow and now he was in a tangle. Being drawn in—*where?*—was absolutely not his comfort zone. He didn't do intimacy, didn't want to dangle himself on the end of anyone's strings, or dangle anyone on the end of his. He'd felt enough pain in his life to know that he never wanted to inflict it on anyone else. It was why he always kept his encounters with women honest—purely physical—only ever going with women of the same mindset, like Zara. No strings, no ties. *Ironic!*

And yet, talking to Simone had felt like being in a kind of comfort zone. She'd made things easy, made him feel safe and he was so, so grateful. It was why he was here, why he'd sprinted all the way from the bistro to catch the florists before they closed. He wanted her to feel his gratitude, wanted to give her something that would light up her lovely face, and cheer up her dreary apartment. Tenderness bloomed in his chest. He'd always felt guilty about being rich and privileged, even though he'd exploited it, but now he was glad that he could afford to send Simone forty vintage roses in a crystal vase, express delivery.

He ran his eyes over the buckets of colourful blooms. His mother, Colette, had always filled their apartment with exotic lilies and richly scented roses. Always the best, the most expensive. Maybe he'd inherited the gene! Hopefully, it was the only one, or was that unfair? A sharp ache lanced him between the temples. Who knew? Colette had always confused him. *Hurt him!* Capricious. Generous. Selfish. Which label fitted her best? All of them or none? He swallowed hard feeling a familiar stab of resentment. He hadn't bothered asking her to help him out over Christmas. She wouldn't even have considered it. For some inexplicable reason, Colette hated Chamonix, and her sentiments had always overruled his needs. He clenched his teeth. Why was he even thinking about her? She didn't merit the energy, whereas Simone…

He closed his eyes, felt his pulse climbing. Kissing her goodbye, feeling her skin against his lips had almost undone him because he'd wanted to pull her close and kiss her mouth instead. He'd wanted to take down her hair, wreak some havoc—

'*Monsieur!*' Marie's gaze was firm. 'I'm sorry but if you want delivery today, then I'm going to need the card.'

'Of course. I'm sorry.'

He squared up the card. Whatever Simone was doing to him, for Yann's sake, and for the sake of his career, he had to stow it. He needed her to say yes to Chamonix, and that meant staying focused, using everything in his power to persuade her. She was a good parent, dashing off so she wouldn't be late for Chloe, putting Chloe first. He clicked the pen. He didn't know how that felt, to be put first, but it was what he was trying to do with Yann…

He felt an ache in his throat. He didn't love Yann, but he wanted to, wanted to give him love, and attention, and time, all the things he'd never had. And he wanted to feel love flowing back, see Yann's eyes lighting up when he came in. He wanted to feel Yann diving into his arms as kids did with their *papa* in movies. He wanted to be a good father, and Simone could help him. She *had* to come to Chamonix.

He anchored the card with his fingers, drew in a long breath and wrote.

Thank you! Dax.

Simone gazed at the roses, flexing the card in her fingers. Pastel perfection! The most gorgeous flowers she'd ever received from anyone, including André. And already in a vase so there was nothing for her to do but look at them! She felt her eyes welling, a smile wobbling onto her lips. *Dax!* First his hat, and now this…

She looked at the card again. Handwritten. Big generous loops. Not the florist's writing. His, surely. He must have gone to the florist himself, straight after, picked out the colours, the card, everything. Thank you for what, though? For meeting him? For considering his proposal?

She propped the card against the vase then buried her hands into the sleeves of her cardigan. The proposal was simple enough. It was everything else that wasn't. It had been hard watching Dax wading through all that personal stuff just to explain why he needed her and Chloe to go to Chamonix. His eyes had been full of hurt and frustration, desperation, determination and then, as they'd said goodbye, hope.

She sighed. She'd carried his hope all the way back to the Metro, had felt its weight pressing down on her as she'd watched Chloe pointing her pink satin toes through the final moments of her ballet class. It was here now, mingling with the fragrance of his roses, shimmering through the air around her, but she couldn't let it cloud her judgement. Yes, for Chloe, a snowy Christmas in the mountains with her best friend would be a huge treat, and yes, the money would be great. The problem was that even though Dax seemed nice—more than nice—she didn't *know* him, and, even taking into account the extenuating circumstances, going away for Christmas with a man she'd only met once seemed rash.

She bit her lips together. Except she wouldn't be *going away with a man*. That was the wrong emphasis, her own feelings tangling things up because of what had happened between them at the bistro door, the thing that they'd somehow glossed over and tucked away. She sighed. It was what she needed to do now, tuck away the flutters and the tingles and weigh things up objectively. Dax was offering to pay her whatever she wanted for taking care of his sad little boy in Chamonix, and Chloe would love to go, definitely! The alternative was faking Christmas cheer at the farm, pretending to Maman that life in Paris wasn't paper-thin.

She felt a cold lump shifting in the pit of her stomach. If Maman and Papa hadn't been tied to the farm, they'd have come to visit, seen the apartment, seen how unhappy she was. *There!* She'd admitted it, and if she could admit that Paris wasn't the same without André, that her dreams had died with him on that crossing, then, where did that leave her? Where did she want to be? Definitely not in Charente, married to a farmer, which was what Maman wanted for her. Avoiding that fate was one of the reasons why she'd come to Paris in the first place!

She pulled her hands out of her sleeves and rubbed her temples. Could she find the magic in it again? She wanted to, desperately, because Paris was André's city. She wanted Chloe to experience it, to live it and breathe it as he had. André *was* Paris. All her memories of him were here, memories she wanted Chloe to feel. Happy memories! Life *had* been good before. Yes, falling pregnant with Chloe had scuppered her own musical ambitions, and yes, they hadn't exactly planned on getting married at twenty-two, but they'd been in love, and so incredibly happy. Her in-laws had helped them out with the rent on a decent apartment and, just months before he died, André had been accepted into the Paris Orchestra. They'd been on their way…

She swallowed hard, tuning in to the drip of the tap. *Bloody thing!* But this apartment wasn't for ever! Things *were* getting better. The school job meant regular money and a place for Chloe, a place she'd never have been able to afford otherwise! A better apartment was on the cards too. She was turning a corner. Selling her violin to help make ends meet had felt like a body blow, but soon she'd be able to buy a replacement and get back to giving lessons. Having a proper job was only the start! It was opening doors. It had already opened Dax's…

'I haven't been pulling my weight for my sponsors. I need to get back to it, honour my commitments.'

Free riding was as important to Dax as playing the violin had been to her, even if she couldn't quite visualise what 'lines' were or why sponsors paid him to ride them.

'…if you want to see what I do, you could watch one of my films.'

Of course! How could she have forgotten? She felt a tingle travelling along her spine. When Chloe was in bed, she'd fire up André's old laptop and find out exactly why Dax D'Aureval was a movie star!

She typed Dax's name into the search bar. Instantly the screen filled. Articles. Photos. Dax, tanned and smiling, making her pulse flutter. She went to a profile piece, speed reading. He had a lot of sponsors. Snowboard manufacturers; winter sports clothing brands; a Swiss watch maker… tracking devices… GPS phones…a climbing equipment crowd. *Why?* Surely snowboarding was about coming down, not climbing up!

She shrugged inside her head, clicking links. *What?* Was that him spooning dollops of yoghurt into a bowl? She cranked the volume, feeling a giggle starting. He was smiling into the camera, completely gorgeous in a plain white tee. *'If you're as active as I am, you need to pack in the protein…'* She giggled, watching as the picture cut to him somersaulting on his board. He *was* good! No wonder he was getting advertising deals. *Films!*

She settled the computer on her knees, clicking through to a video site. *Wow!* They really *did* make films about him, lots of films! *Ice Rider*; *Taming Alaska with Dax D'Aureval*; *Free-Riding Hacks with Dax*; *Whispering Slopes* and *Frozen Line*. That would do!

She clicked play. A tense, tingling refrain started as blackness faded up into a breathtaking aerial shot of snowy slopes and jagged peaks, edged pink by the rising sun that beamed its rays out of the screen as the camera panned round. *Chamonix!* When the camera—it could only have been a drone—breached an edge and dropped, her stomach dropped with it, and then she was travelling along the splintered side of an icy cliff. The music dipped, and suddenly Dax was speaking, his voice low and calm.

'I've studied Mallory Couloir many times, looking for a way to make it mine, to find a line that no one else has found. And now, I have...'

She felt her mouth falling open as the camera closed in on a figure—*Dax*—sliding his board sideways down a face that looked near vertical. He was wearing a helmet, and he was roped, anchored to a place higher up, letting out the rope as he went, his board scraping ice.

Suddenly his face filled the screen, eyebrows flashing, a smile twitching on his lips. *'Intense, huh?'*

The picture zoomed out, and her breath caught. He *was* on a vertical face, him and the crew that were filming him. Were they all mad?

His face filled the frame again. He was blowing out quick breaths, grimacing a bit, talking to the camera but maybe also to himself.

'Whew, whew! Breathe!'

And then the camera tailed him as he slid his board along a narrow ice shelf, digging a pair of sharp axes into the face above as he went. *Axes!* What if he fell on his axe? She curled her fingers into her palms.

The shimmering music shifted into a lower key as the view changed. He was riding now, weaving tightly over powder snow, axes in his hands, but the slope was still sickeningly vertical. When the view switched back to aerial, she bit her knuckles. He was like an ant against the white colossus of the mountain. Small. *Vulnerable.* And then he was wearing ropes again, lowering himself down another impossible face. Suddenly the mountaineering equipment sponsorship made sense!

And then he was on snow, a bullet in a red jacket hurtling down a vertical gully, free falling metres at a time before catching the slope again. The music faded and there was his voice again, slightly defiant.

'When I'm riding, there's a spirit inside me that is wild, definitely a little crazy...'

A *little* crazy? He was certifiable! But she couldn't look away, even though her heart was racing, and her mouth was dry. Dax's power and agility were mesmerising. He looked sexy as hell. She *had* to keep watching.

The music was growing jauntier, matching the rhythm of his quick weaving movements. He was throwing up flurries, launching himself off spurs, sailing through the air with joyful hyena cries, and then he was hammering down the mountain, the view switching to his helmet camera and she was right there with him, feeling the rush of the slope, hearing the scrunch and swish of the board, feeling white blinded, blue dazzled, snow and sky flying towards her at breakneck speed.

And then the picture changed to a wide view from a lower angle. Dax was racing down the corrugated mountain, racing mini avalanches that were exploding into life on either side of him. He stayed ahead, slicing across the snowfield, somersaulting—sky rotating into snow, snow rotating into sky—whooping and hollering, and then he was coming in fast, slewing to a halt inches from the camera. He ripped off his goggles, eyes bright as fever. 'Now, *that's* what I'm talking about!'

She slumped back, blowing out a long breath. So *that* was free riding? It was amazing, and terrifying, and— The air in her lungs solidified. *This* was what he was going to be doing in Chamonix? *This* was why he needed her to be there? She felt a band tightening around her chest, a fluttering panic. He'd said something about an expedition. Was it going to be like the one she'd just watched…ropes, axes, vertical cliffs? She looked at the screen. Another film was playing, more of the same. She hit the cross. He couldn't do this, couldn't *keep on* doing this! It was too dangerous. One slip, one wrong move…

She shoved the computer off her lap and rocked forwards, pressing her fingertips into her forehead. What was he thinking? He was a father! That meant changing, making sacrifices. Carrying on was selfish. Completely irresponsible! For pity's sake, Yann had already lost his mother!

She squeezed her eyes shut, anger rising. He'd been kitted out and roped up. He'd seemed confident, but accidents happened. By definition they were unexpected. He could lose his balance, fall into a crevasse, slide off an edge. A rope could snap, a karabiner could sheer… Those mini avalanches could have turned themselves into giants. Dax could be buried alive. He could die, and then what? What would happen to Yannick?

Suddenly she couldn't breathe. Her throat was burning, clogging with bitterness, the old pain searing her insides all over again. She got to her feet, gulping breaths, tears scalding her eyes. André had been killed three Christmases ago by a driver who'd been texting instead of watching the road. His life had been snuffed out, and a good part of hers with it, and there was Dax, a father as well, asking her to look after Yannick while he spent Christmas risking his life for the sake of what, an adrenaline rush?

No! A sob felled her. *No way!* It was wrong. *Wrong!* She wouldn't do it; wouldn't facilitate it.

She swallowed hard, sitting back on her heels, shuddering breaths, smearing the tears into her cheeks. All that hope in his eyes…and the hat…and the flowers… But she couldn't sanction the thing he loved, and she'd have to tell him, just as soon as she was calm enough to make the call.

Dax tapped the arrow key, rotating the satellite image on his screen by degrees. Aiguille du Plan looked scary from the top, and scary from below, but its ambivalence was magnetic. He wanted to conquer it, look out from its splintered sides, see views that few had the privilege to see. He felt a sudden tearing ache in his chest. He missed the mountains. In the mountains his senses had meaning, his mind was free. Here everything was chaos. He had no control. He couldn't make Yann like him, couldn't make him happy. Why couldn't he find the right line with Yann?

His phone jumped, vibrating on the desk. An unfamiliar number. He swiped right. 'Hello?'

'Dax?'

'Simone!' Warmth streamed through his veins, apprehension galloping behind. Had she made a decision about Chamonix? He leant back in his chair, trying to sound mellow. 'How are you? Did you make it to Chloe in time?'

'I'm fine thanks and yes, I made it.' Her voice filled with a smile. 'Thank you for the roses, Dax. They're so, so beautiful.'

'You're welcome. I'm glad you like them.' He couldn't help smiling. Dashing to the florist's had been a happy distraction from worrying about Yannick, and his career, and his sponsors. All the obligations he was going to have to juggle from now on.

'So, Dax…'

His heart pulsed. Her voice was downshifting. He swallowed, trying to keep his tone even. 'Yes?'

'I…erm…'

He squeezed his eyes shut, bracing himself.

'I've been thinking about Chamonix, and, on reflection, I've decided that, much as I'd like to say yes, I can't disappoint my parents.'

Parents?

'Chloe and I always go there for Christmas. They farm in Charente. It's very tying so they never get to visit us in Paris, which means they don't see much of Chloe. Us going there is important.'

No! Her parents had each other. They didn't need her, not as *he* needed her, not as Yannick needed her.

Her voice was catching a little. 'I came to meet you because I promised Amy I would. I wanted to give you my consideration…but I just feel that I can't let my parents down. I'm sorry.'

He felt his heart shrivelling. What was he going to do now? Some of his Chamonix friends had kids. Maybe he could ask… *No!* They were *his* friends, not Yannick's. To Yann they'd be strangers and no way was he leaving Yann with strangers! Not leaving his son with strangers was exactly why he'd laid out his whole sorry history for Simone, so she'd see that she and Chloe were the only ones who could help him. But now…? He stared at the rocky pinnacle on his computer screen. He was going to have to shelve Aiguille du Plan, let everyone down, as he'd let them down over his Alaskan adventure. His stomach cramped. Letting people down wasn't him! It was Colette's way, not *his*.

'Dax?'

He blinked.

'Are you still there?' There was an anxious pause. 'I feel bad. I *am* really, really sorry…'

She really *did* feel bad. He could hear it. He felt his pulse gathering. Maybe this wasn't over. It wasn't as if she'd called him as soon as she'd got home. He flicked a glance at his watch. Nine-thirty! She'd been thinking about it for almost five hours. And she *had* come to meet him, hadn't she? She'd known what he was proposing because Amy had already told her. She hadn't been thinking about her parents *then*. What had she said as she'd been leaving? *'I'm leaning towards yes…'* How close had she been at that moment? He ran his tongue over his lower lip. Was there still a chance he could change her mind? There were still a few days to play with. There was nothing to lose…

He inhaled slowly, sliding behind cut-out Dax. 'Please, Simone, don't feel bad. It's my problem, not yours.' He squeezed his eyes shut, hating himself for being disingenuous. 'I'm only sorry that you and Chloe won't be with us in the mountains. It's truly magical at Christmas.'

CHAPTER THREE

December 8th...

'RUE VICTOR-HUGO, PLEASE.' Simone sat back, drawing in a slow breath. Her heart was drumming and, in spite of her big coat and the muggy warmth inside the taxi, small shivers were running up and down her spine.

Stupid nerves!

She glanced at the meter then looked through the window. A taxi was the only way to get to Dax's apartment and back in her lunch break so torturing herself about the cost was pointless. She scanned the boulevard, trying to distract herself, but it was no good. She couldn't stop turning it over. Dax had finally done it, pushed her into a corner, and now she had to push back, spell it out face to face once and for all: she was not going to Chamonix for Christmas, no matter how many flowers and gifts he sent. The plumber who'd arrived at stupid o'clock that morning to fix her tap had been the last straw. If Dax wasn't listening, she'd have to make him.

She chewed her lips, watching the pale elegant buildings slip by. How had she got herself into this impossible situation? She sighed. By being too soft, that was how! If she'd been honest from the start, told Dax exactly what she thought of his risk-taking, instead of trying to soften the blow with the whole *We always go to my parents for Christmas* routine, adding extra layers of, *I feel bad… I'm so sorry*, then none of this would have been happening.

She sighed again. It was just that by the time she'd calmed down, it had felt too harsh to be calling Dax out on his lifestyle choices. After all, she barely knew him, and he *was* the father of Chloe's best friend. It had seemed best to give him a credible excuse that wouldn't sour things for them, or the kids. *Mistake!* All she'd done was leave him a gap to squeeze through!

The next day a lavish arrangement of sugar-pink roses and stargazer lilies had arrived. This time he'd written, by hand:

Thank you for thinking about it at least. Dax

She twisted the strap of her bag around her fingers, watching the windows of the fancy Champs-Élysées boutiques spinning by. *Dax!* So gorgeous. So generous. So transparent! He hadn't been thanking her; he'd been forcing her to engage.

'Hi, Dax.'

'Simone!' Brimming warmth. 'How are you today?'

'I'm fine. I'm just calling to say thank you—again—for the beautiful flowers.'

'My pleasure.'

'You really shouldn't have sent them—'

'But I wanted to thank you.'

Small hesitation.

'You said you felt bad about Chamonix and I can't have that. The Chamonix situation is for me to deal with, not for you to feel bad about.'

Small hesitation, confessional tone.

'To be honest, I feel bad for asking you in the first place.

*I was desperate, but it was unfair of me to put you in that
position. I hope you can forgive me?'*

'*It's fine, Dax, honestly.'*

Long sigh.

*'I'm relieved...because Yann really does love Chloe. I
wouldn't want my mistake to change anything. She's all
he has.'*

'*Nothing's going to change, okay, but please, don't send
any more flowers.'*

Lighter tone.

'*Okay. I promise. No more flowers.'*

She freed her fingers and opened her bag, taking out
her lipstick. *Warpaint!* She applied it carefully, checking
her teeth, then slipped it back.

If Dax had stopped then, things would have settled,
but he hadn't. The next day a pink goose-down ski jacket
had arrived...for Chloe! One of Dax's sponsor's brands,
top of the range.

His handwritten note had said:

*Hope you don't mind me sending this. It was sup-
posed to be blue, for Yannick, but they sent the wrong
colour. I thought Chloe might like it.
Dax*

She'd felt blindsided. Chloe had pounced on the jacket,
parading around in it like a mini catwalk model, flicking
up the fur-trimmed hood then flicking it back with a giggling head toss. Simone had had to laugh, even though she
was furious. Sending Chloe a gift was a calculated move,
and, of course, it had meant calling him again. She'd made
Chloe say thank you first, then she'd taken over.

'*Dax, it's a really beautiful jacket so thank you. Chloe's thrilled, but if you think that it's going to change anything, then I'm afraid you're wrong.'*

'I'm sorry?'

Confused tone.

'It's a winter jacket. For winter sports. It's the kind of jacket a little girl would wear if she were going to, let's say...hmm... Chamonix?'

'Simone!'

Incredulous tone laced with amusement.

'Are you accusing me of bribery?' Heavy sigh. *'Look, it's a winter jacket because my sponsors make winter jackets!'*

Low, mischievous tone.

'If I'd been trying to bribe you, I would have been far more imaginative.'

Her neck prickled at the memory. Had the jacket really been an innocent gift? Even now she didn't know. She'd apologised for the misunderstanding and ended the call in a haze of confusion.

She closed her eyes. *Dax!* Confusing her at every turn. She didn't approve of him, but there was something undeniably warm about him, something about him that was pulling her this way and that, night, and day. She couldn't stop remembering the way he'd looked at her at the bistro door, the sensuality that shimmered around him like phosphorescence. In his eyes, in his smile, in the way he held himself, even in the way he sipped espresso. She couldn't stop imagining how his lips would feel on hers, warm and perfect, how his skin would feel next to hers if they were naked, wrapped together warm and close and—

The taxi lurched. She came to, cheeks burning. What was wrong with her? André was the one she ought to have been fantasising about, André, who'd snatched her heart away under the enigmatic gaze of the Mona Lisa. Dax didn't come close! Dax was a practised charmer, a player, a selfish adrenaline junkie, and she needed to remember that! It was why he'd sent the plumber, but it was one plumber too many. She'd had enough of being toyed with. Telling him why she'd really turned down his proposal was the last thing she wanted to do, but if it came to it, she would, if he gave her no choice...

'Hey, Dax!' Amy's voice broke his concentration. 'Simone's here!'

Simone?

He twisted his head, felt his breath catching on a smile. She was standing next to Amy, looking up at him with red, slightly parted lips. He gripped the handholds hard, felt his heart pumping. Was she here to say that she was coming to Cham after all? Did he even dare to hope? He climbed down a notch, then jumped clear of the wall, dusting the chalk off his hands as he walked over.

'Hello!' He kissed her cheeks. 'This is a nice surprise.'

'Hi!' Her eyes locked on his. 'I'm sorry if I'm disturbing you.'

'You're not.' Not in the way she meant, anyway. Her steady gaze was wrecking his pulse and as for her ruby mouth... He swallowed, motioning to the wall. 'As you can see, I was just hanging around...'

'Without ropes!'

She looked so serious that he couldn't resist a little mischief. He flashed his eyebrows. 'I like to live dangerously.'

A smile ghosted on her lips and then it faded. His heart caved. If he couldn't stir a smile out of her, then she definitely wasn't here to accept his offer.

'Would you like some tea, Simone?' Amy was hooking his tee shirt off the bench press, handing it to him with a pointed *Cover yourself* look, and then she turned back to Simone. 'Or some coffee?'

'No, thanks. You're busy, and besides, I'm not staying.' Her eyes came back to his. 'I just need to speak to Dax for a moment.'

A moment? He toyed with his tee shirt. If that was all she should have phoned instead of getting his hopes up. It wasn't as if she hadn't called him twice already, about the flowers and about Chloe's jacket! *Oh, God!* Was this about the plumber? Had he gone too far? He hadn't meant to. It was just Amy had said the dripping tap got on Simone's nerves, and since things that didn't work got on his nerves too, he'd sent someone—

'Okay then…' Amy was backstepping. 'I need to get on with my packing.'

He gave her a nod, felt a knot tightening inside. She was leaving in the morning, leaving him at the helm, and he still didn't know what to do about Christmas. He'd held off booking flights, hoping that he'd be booking four seats not two, but something was telling him he was out of luck. He sighed and pulled on his tee shirt. 'Are you sure I can't get you anything, Simone, a soft drink maybe?'

'I'm fine, but thanks.' She took a step, looking past him. 'You've got your own climbing wall.'

'Hasn't everyone?'

Her eyebrows flickered but she didn't smile.

His chest went tight. What was wrong with her? Or… was it him? Flashing his eyebrows, making quips that effectively cut conversation dead? Classic cut-out Dax! He rubbed his arm, cleaning off a streak of chalk. The last time he'd been with her, he'd been himself, and she'd been warm and full of kindness. If he wanted that Simone back, if he wanted to know what was on her mind, then he had to drop the act.

He took a breath and went to the wall, curling his fingers around one of the holds. 'I put in my own wall because I can change the holds around whenever I want. I like to keep challenging myself.' He turned, meeting her gaze. 'I'm energetic by nature. Some would say hyperactive!' He shrugged. 'Bottom line, if there wasn't a climbing wall in here, I'd be climbing the walls anyway.'

The light in her eyes softened a little. 'You're very agile. I saw that in your film.'

'You watched one of my films?' For some reason he felt stoked. 'Which one?'

'Frozen Line.'

'Ah, Mallory Couloir! We made that last year!' When his life had been *his*. He pushed the thought away. 'Riding that line was crazy scary.'

'Is that why you do it?' Her gaze sharpened. 'For thrills?'

He felt a stab of resentment. Was she judging him? He didn't deserve that. He measured out a breath, keeping his voice level. 'Tell me, Simone, do you have a favourite food?'

Her eyebrows arched. 'Hasn't everyone?'

In spite of himself, he felt his lips twitching. *'Touché,* Madame Cossart!' And then suddenly there seemed to be a spark in her eyes too. This was better. Much better. He shifted on his feet. 'So what is it? What's your favourite?'

She gave a little shrug. 'I don't see the relevance.'

'You will.' He held in a smile. 'Please, just answer the question.'

She pouted a little. 'I like flan.'

'What do you like about it? Break it down.'

Her eyes widened. 'Really?'

Fighting all the way! He dipped his chin. 'Yes.'

She let out a sigh. 'I suppose it's the taste—vanilla—the sweetness, the smooth texture, the way the pastry crumbles. All of it!'

'Everything, then?'

She nodded.

'So it's the same for me with free riding.' He took a step towards her. 'It's thrilling, absolutely, but I don't only do it for thrills. It's bigger. It's the challenge. It's simply being in the mountains. It's the snow. It's the ice. It's that special silence, and the big sky. Up there, you feel the very tips of your senses.' He felt a smile loosening his cheeks. 'Free riding feels like nothing else on earth. I love it, and I'm good at it, and I'll always want to do it, like you'll always want to eat flan.'

Her eyes were glimmering. What was she thinking? Suddenly he couldn't stand it. 'Simone, why are you here?'

She blinked. 'To thank you for sending the plumber, and for your kindness.' Her gaze tightened on his. 'But I also want to know what you're expecting to come of it, because it seems to me that maybe you're expecting something…?'

His chest went tight. 'No, no, I'm not.' He felt a drag of weariness. 'I was just hoping, that's all, hoping to sway you…' Hoping to save Yann from having to suffer his presence over Christmas without a buffer, without a friend there to make him happy. Hoping to save his career, because leaving Yann with some random childminder while he went on the slopes was out of the question.

'There's nothing you can do to sway me, Dax.' She was shaking her head slowly, her eyes softer now. 'So please, stop trying.'

No! He felt desperation boiling up inside, taking him over. 'Please, Simone, please reconsider. I need to be on the slopes, not for the thrill of it, but because I've got obligations, commitments. It's how I make my living.' The only one that mattered anyway.

She was opening her mouth to speak, but he couldn't let her interrupt. Selling it hard was the only way, because if she didn't help him, he'd have to call everything off so he could be there for Yann twenty-four-seven. He'd do it, of course he would, but Yann would be miserable, and his own reputation would be ruined.

He took a step towards her. 'Look, what I'm asking you to do won't feel like work. It'll feel like a holiday!' A tiny spark lit her gaze. She was listening. He felt his love for his home rising like a tide. 'My chalet is on its own high up in the mountains. The views are awesome. And it's luxurious. All mod cons! There's a pool, and a hot tub. Oh, and in case you're wondering, I have a housekeeper who comes in to cook and clean, so no chores! And I can set up cool activities for the kids, like ski school…' Something flickered behind her eyes. Of course, Chloe was her Achilles heel, as Yann was his. He licked his lips. 'Has Chloe ever skied?'

She shook her head.

'So wouldn't this be the perfect opportunity for her to try!' Now she was really paying attention. He swallowed. 'And if she doesn't like skiing there's always tobogganing or ice skating. And there are things we could all do together if you wanted to.'

Would she want that? He just needed to keep talking.

'Dog sledding is fun! The kids would love it, and there's a Christmas market, and cool shops! Cham is magical at Christmas.' He took another step towards her, loading his gaze. 'Wouldn't you like to give Chloe a magical Christmas?' Her eyes were clouding, growing hazy. He looked at her mouth, felt his pulse quickening. 'I'll pay you whatever you want plus expenses, whatever it has to be to make it work. Just say you'll come. Please.'

For a long second her eyes held his and then she was stepping back, shaking her head. 'No.'

'Why?' It came out hoarsely. He swallowed hard. 'Because of your parents? Forgive me, but I'm struggling to believe that's the reason.' She was blinking, her throat working. 'For pity's sake, Simone, why won't you help me?'

She looked away for a beat, and then her eyes snapped back to his. 'Because when you kill yourself, Dax, I don't want to be the one who has to tell Yannick that his *papa* thought riding a snowboard down a cliff was more important than being a father!'

Her words hit him like a slap. For a moment he was breathless, disorientated. He'd never even thought of that! The mountains were dangerous. It was why he took every precaution but dying wasn't on his radar. It was a distant possibility. Unreal. As it was for anyone. He felt an ache bouncing between his temples. What would Simone have him do? Give up everything he was, everything he'd ever loved for a son he'd never asked for, a son who didn't even like him and probably never would? And would giving up even make Yann happy? It was too big to think about under the burn of her gaze.

'I'm sorry.' He stepped back, tasting the dryness in his mouth. 'I won't ask again.' He turned and went over to the water cooler, feeling despair aching through his veins. Was it so wrong, to want to carry on doing the thing he loved? Couldn't he be a free rider and a father? He tugged two paper cups from the dispenser, filling them in turn. Simone didn't think so, and for some annoying reason what she thought mattered. He sighed. Simone was a proper grown-up. She was strong and sensible and kind. And he was, what? He threw back a cupful of water. Without his snowboard, he was nothing.

He drew in a deep breath then went back over, offering her a cup. 'How about some water?'

'Thanks.' She took it, sipping slowly, and then she looked up, her gaze softer now. 'I didn't want to say it, you know, but you weren't giving up, so I had to.' She sighed. 'How you live is obviously up to you, Dax, but I can't not feel what I feel...' She drained her cup then handed it to him. 'I've got to go. I'm on my lunch break.'

'How are you getting back?'

'Taxi.'

'No, you're not!' The least he could do was take her back. Whatever she thought of him, she was still the mother of Yann's best friend, and he liked her, didn't want there to be any awkwardness between them. 'I'll run you back.'

She tilted her head, eyes narrowing. 'You're not still trying—'

'No!' No matter how devastated he was feeling about Christmas, he absolutely wasn't going to bring it up with her again. He smiled. 'I promise.'

'This is yours?' Simone was staring at the SUV with raised eyebrows.

Maybe she'd been expecting a sports car, something fast. Five months ago she'd have been right. He opened the passenger door, stepping back. 'I had something sexier before, but it wasn't family friendly, so it had to go.' He flicked a glance at the wing. 'I think it might have been better in red, but Yann likes blue.'

She was looking at him as if he'd said something profound, and then she smiled quickly and got in. 'The blue's nice.'

'It's okay.' He closed her door, tailing round to the driver's side. If Yann had ever enthused about the colour it would have felt like a win, but he hadn't. Yann seemed to be as ambivalent about the car as he was.

He got in, reaching for his seat belt.

'Wait!'

He turned, felt his breath catching. Simone was looking

at him softly, her eyes full of warm light. He felt it reaching in, turning him inside out. He swallowed. 'What's up?'

She pressed her lips together. 'I just wanted to say that, for what it's worth, I thought your film was amazing.'

Amazing!

'You blew me away, Dax. I don't like what you do, the risks you take, in fact, I think you're insane, but you're really good at it.' Her cheeks were colouring. 'I admire you.'

Her honesty was astounding. Humbling. He drew in a careful breath. Was there any mileage to be made—? *No!* He'd promised he wouldn't try persuading her again, and whatever his other failings were, breaking promises wasn't one of them.

He pushed the seat belt home and started the engine. 'Thank you.' He felt a smile edging onto his lips. 'It means a lot that you think I'm insane!' He pulled out, catching her smile in the wing mirror. Smiling suited her. Smiling made her eyes shine, yet most of the time she seemed serious, and a little sad. She was a widow, but Amy didn't know how she'd lost her husband. He was curious but asking didn't feel right. It wasn't as if they were proper friends, people who'd come together naturally—

'The taxi didn't go this way!'

'Really?' The note of indignation in her voice was too tempting. He looked over, felt his lips twitching. 'Maybe the taxi took you the scenic route.'

Her eyes flew wide. 'You think?'

He chuckled. 'No! I'm teasing. This is just the way I go. I grew up in Paris, so I know a few short cuts.' He looked ahead. Ribbons of snow still edged the bare branches of the trees lining the boulevard, but the gutters were thick with dirty slush. Parisian snow! So different from alpine snow. He felt a pang, a sudden need to keep talking. 'I haven't lived here for years. I don't like it really.' A memory flashed: Colette's soirées. He shuddered. 'I left when I was sixteen, took off travelling. In Alaska I hopped on a snowboard and that was it! I was smitten. After that, I was always on the move, chasing snow, then I built my place in Cham, travelled out from there…' He bit his lips together. 'Of course, that's all changed. Now I'm back.'

'Why?' She was twisting in her seat, angling herself towards him. 'Why did you come back if you don't like it?'

'Because I was in a flat spin, thinking about good schools, thinking that my mother would—' A knot yanked tight in his belly. Did he really want to be getting into this? *Yes!* Simone was a gentle ear and for once in his life he wanted to let it all out. He looked over. 'Because it's instinctive, isn't it, running home when you're in trouble, when you need someone to lean on?' He fixed his eyes on the road again, feeling the old bruise starting to swell. 'True to form, my mother hasn't exactly fallen over herself, unless you count giving me the apartment, which was, of course, *very* generous. Gifts always were Colette's forte! She wasn't so good at—' He bit his tongue. *Enough!* If he carried on bleating, maybe she'd think he was courting sympathy, trying to persuade her to help him yet again and he wasn't.

'At what?'

He looked over. Simone's gaze was soft, full of ready empathy. He gave a little shrug, going for a nonchalant tone. 'She just wasn't very hands-on.'

'What about your father? Was he—?'

'He wasn't around.' He looked ahead, felt the knot in his stomach twisting. 'I don't even know who he is.' He felt her silent question humming through air. 'Yes, I asked my mother, and no, she doesn't know.'

'I'm so sorry.'

He felt her hand on his shoulder fleetingly, her eyes

combing his face. If she was looking for tears, she was wasting her time. It didn't hurt. He wasn't curious. He had been once, but that was a long time ago. 'Thanks, but it's okay. It is what it is. Ironic!'

'What? That you don't know your father and nearly didn't know your son?'

'Yep!' He met her eye. 'At least Yann knows who I am and who he looks like. He knows I'm here for him.' He forced a smile out. 'I just need to crack the whole parenting thing and then we'll be fine.' He turned the SUV into the school road and pulled in by the gates. 'Here you go, back to school safe and sound.'

'Thank you.' She put her hand on the door, and then she turned, her eyes full of light and kindness. 'You'll get there with Yann, Dax, it's just going to take time, that's all.'

Time and a whole bunch of miracles! But it was his problem now, and his alone. He cracked his door open. 'Sit tight. I'll get your door.'

'There's no need.'

'Yes, there is.' Anything to delay saying goodbye, to delay being alone with his turmoil, to delay being without her. He held her gaze for as long as he dared and then he smiled. 'I might be insane, but I like to think I'm a gentleman too.'

CHAPTER FOUR

Later...

'MAMAN, DO YOU like snow? Because I *love* snow.'

Dax shimmered into her head. That moment at the bistro door, pulling off his hat, showering snow...that moment in his gym, half naked, dusting off his hands, showering chalk—

'Maman?'

She blinked, steadying the laptop on her knees. 'You know I do.'

'Snow makes everything Christmassy!' Chloe was drawing, leaning over the coffee table in a scatter of crayons. 'I *love* Christmas. You love it too, don't you?'

She slipped a smile into her voice. 'Of course I do. Everyone loves Christmas.'

Lying to Chloe about Christmas was second nature. Chloe didn't know the date of André's death, or the details, and she wasn't in a rush to tell her. She watched her daughter's fair hair swinging, her busy little hands moving over the paper. Maybe she never would.

Chloe looked up suddenly. 'Can we put the Christmas tree up tomorrow?'

'Absolutely!' The artificial tree she'd had to settle for because dragging a real one up seven flights wasn't an option! Maybe the access in their new place would be easier, then they could go back to having a real tree with all the nice piney smells. She smiled. 'We'll put it up as soon as we get back from school. It can be our way of celebrating the end of term!'

Chloe's eyes lit with a smile. 'I love you, Maman.'

'I love you too, *chérie*.' *So much!*

Chloe went back to drawing and she turned back to the picture on her screen: a team of frisky huskies pulling a laughing couple along in a sled through sparkling snow. Her heart twisted. Chloe loved dogs, would love riding behind huskies…

Impossible!

She shut the laptop. She'd given Dax her decision, and it was the right decision—wasn't it?—even if it meant that Chloe wouldn't get to go dog sledding or stay in a mountain chalet with all the mod cons!

She pushed the laptop aside and got up. 'Would you like some hot chocolate?'

'Ooh, yes, please!' Chloe was colouring in fiercely.

'Okay…one hot chocolate coming up!'

She went into the kitchen, set the milk warming, then leaned against the worktop, gazing at Dax's flowers, still fresh and lovely on the table. Why was she feeling so restless? Why had she spent the last half an hour looking at pictures of Chamonix? Was it because not going meant Chloe was missing out and she was feeling guilty about that, or was it because she couldn't stop thinking about all the things Dax had said in the car?

What was wrong with his mother? Couldn't Colette see that he needed her? Didn't she care about him, or about Yannick, her own grandson? Was she just like André's parents? She felt a cold lump hardening in her stomach. They hadn't helped her either. Instead, two weeks after André's funeral they'd turned on her. Suddenly, she was nothing but a provincial gold-digger who'd trapped André into marriage by getting pregnant! If not for her, he'd have made the Paris Orchestra at twenty-two! If not for her, he'd never have been lumbered with a child, would never have been carrying that child's Christmas present over that crossing! If not for her and Chloe—*Chloe?*—their son would have been alive! She felt tears scalding her eyes, bile stinging her throat. She'd lost it then, torn into them. How dared they implicate her own sweet, innocent girl, the apple of André's eye, their own flesh and blood? How *dared* they? She'd never hated anyone in her life, but she'd hated them then. Still did!

She took a shuddery breath, pushing it all down, feeling sadness flooding in. How could they not love Chloe? How could Colette not want to help Dax with Yann? What kind of people were these?

She closed her eyes, steadying herself. Thank God Maman and Papa weren't like that. They couldn't get enough of their granddaughter. After André died, they'd begged her to go home and for a moment she'd been tempted, but the thing was, she'd have been restless in no time. Paris had always been her dream, and with André gone it had seemed even more important to stay, because it was the city they'd shared, and she wanted Chloe to share it too. Struggling on her own with Chloe had been hard, keeping it from her parents, to stop them worrying, had been hard too, but just knowing that they were there, that she could have cut and run if it had all got too much, had helped her stay strong.

But no one had Dax's back. Colette wasn't helping, and Amy was leaving. He was all alone, and she couldn't bear the thought of it. When she'd turned down his proposal all she'd seen was his selfishness for wanting to keep riding dangerous lines, but now she was seeing a wider view, a more complicated view. Dax *did* care about Yann. It was why he'd come back to Paris, why he'd put him into a good school. It was why he'd swapped his sexy car for a blue brick, *blue* because Yann liked blue, and it was why he'd pursued her relentlessly to be Yann's childminder for Christmas, because Yann adored Chloe. His instincts, save the one that made him want to throw himself off mountains, were all good. She sighed. But that was the biggie! He *did* want to keep riding down vertical cliffs, and she wasn't fine with it.

She turned back to the stove, opening the hot-chocolate tin. Two scoops for Chloe, not three as it said on the label. Just one of the million things she knew about Chloe, because Chloe was hers, had been hers from that first indignant birth cry. Dax hadn't had that luxury, knowing his son from the beginning. Yann was a stranger. He didn't *love* him yet.

But what if he did?

Would he stop taking risks then?

She stirred in the chocolate, felt her pulse quickening. What if she could help Dax to fall in love with his son? If she went to Chamonix with that express aim, then her conscience could be clear, and Chloe could have her magical Christmas in the mountains with her best friend! Skiing! Dog sledding. All the things Dax had talked about. It was nothing less than she deserved, some proper fun, some happy indulgence. And the money would be such a boost. Enough to furnish their new place when they got it, enough to create a fairy-tale bedroom for Chloe? If she drove a hard bargain, Dax would think she was only going for the money.

'Maman! Look!'

She startled then turned, catching her breath. Chloe was holding up her drawing: snowy mountains cloaked in snowy pines and a little boxy house. She felt a smile loosening her cheeks. 'What a beautiful picture!' She turned off the hob and went over, cupping Chloe's face in her hands. 'Would you like to go to a place like that for Christmas?'

Chloe's face stretched. 'Could we?'

She felt her smile widening, a bubble of happiness exploding in her chest. 'You know, I think it could be arranged...'

CHAPTER FIVE

December 12th, Charles De Gaulle Airport...

'YOU'VE LOST WHO?' Dax was bending down, looking into Yann's face.

Lost? The last word any parent wanted to hear in the middle of a busy airport! She tightened her grip on Chloe's hand, looking Yann over: boots, jeans, blue jacket, orange backpack and...empty hands. *Uh-oh!*

She touched Dax's shoulder. 'He's lost Maurice.'

Dax looked up blankly. 'Who's Maurice?'

Chloe sighed dramatically. 'His bear!'

She touched Chloe's head. 'Dax knows that.' She widened her eyes at him. 'You just forgot for a moment, didn't you, because you're excited about Christmas?'

He blinked, then seemed to catch on. 'That's right. I forgot because I'm stoked for Santa!' He turned back to Yannick. 'So you've lost your teddy...?'

Oh, no!

Yannick bit his lip. 'He's a *panda*!'

Dax's face stretched then tightened.

She pressed her lips together. Hopefully, he was giving himself a roasting! One, for not knowing who and what Maurice was, and two, for not tying Maurice to Yann's backpack as she'd done with Chloe's monkey. She let go of Chloe's hand, dropping down so she could look Yann in the eye. 'That's what Papa meant! Pandas are just black and white teddy bears.' Yann's eyes were glistening, and his bottom lip was trembling. *Oh, God!* She wrapped her hands around his, trying to sound breezy and confident. 'Don't worry.' She flicked a glance at Dax. 'Your *papa* will find Maurice. He's a superhero!'

Yannick looked at Dax balefully.

She held in a sigh. Maybe it was a hard sell, but bigging Dax up to Yann was her job now, part of her plan to zip them together, but that plan was going to be all for nothing if they didn't find Maurice.

Think!

Yann had definitely had Maurice at check-in because while Dax had been hefting their luggage onto the conveyor, a smiling flight attendant had attached a 'special' label to his paw. They'd stopped on the way through Duty Free so that Chloe could examine a tower filled with rainbow sweets, then they'd gone for breakfast. *Bingo!*

She straightened. 'I think he might be—'

'On the bench in the café!' Dax was already shrugging off his pack, dropping it at her feet and then he looked at Yann. 'I *will* find him! I promise.' His eyes snapped to hers. 'Stay right here!' And then he was off, haring through the crowd.

She wedged his bag between her feet. This wasn't a good start! *How* hadn't Dax known who Maurice was? Maybe it really *was* excitement. He certainly seemed to have been high as a kite from the moment she'd said yes. His breath hadn't even hitched when she'd named her price. He'd taken her bank details then asked how soon he could meet Chloe. Would going out for crepes after school the next day suit them?

'Perfect!'

Then, all weekend, gifts had kept arriving. Pink bug-aboo pants for Chloe to match her pink jacket. Gloves. Goggles! Several hats. And for her, smart black ski pants and an exquisite red goose-down jacket. *'Expenses!'* And he'd kept calling. Would flying on the twelfth suit her? What did Chloe like to eat, aside from crepes smothered in chocolate? What, aside from flan, did *she* like to eat? Any allergies? Did Chloe prefer duck-down or goose-down pillows? Did she have a preference herself? When Dax had said he was naturally energetic, he hadn't been understating it. He was frenetic. *Kinetic!* Big on detail, and yet for some reason he hadn't known about Maurice!

She looked at the kids. Chloe was comforting Yann, talking to him in low, earnest tones. Chloe was all heart. She'd let Dax in right away, giggling at his jokes in the creperie, teasing him back when he'd teased her. Even Yann had looked on with interest. That was Chloe's gift, shining for everyone, but it had tugged a bit, seeing her shining so readily for Dax. Simone sighed. She'd tried so hard to keep André alive for Chloe, but Chloe was forgetting. These days, when she started telling Chloe how much André had loved the Louvre, how they'd met in front of the Mona Lisa, Chloe always said, *'Maman, I already know the story of you and Papa.'* For Chloe, André was an old story and Dax was a new one, a handsome, charming one, with a melting gaze and heart-stopping smile. Dax was alive. Vital. *Gorgeous!* No wonder Chloe was smitten… But better that than not, right, since they were all going to be spending Christmas together?

The speaker blared suddenly. 'This is the final call for flight AF1842 to Geneva. Would all passengers please go to the gate immediately?'

'Maman!' Chloe's eyes flew wide. 'That's Geneva! Are we going to miss it?'

Yannick was twisting his hands together, chewing his lips.

Oh, God! What *had* she got herself into? In her head, she'd imagined herself as Mary Poppins, snapping her fingers, oiling the wheels, but the wheels were wobbling, about to come off.

She plastered on a smile, putting a hand on each of their shoulders. 'No! Of course not. The announcements always sound dramatic, but they're used to people running late. They won't go without us.' She swallowed hard. If only that were true. If they didn't get to the gate soon, they wouldn't be allowed to board and then Yann would fall apart completely.

She rocked up onto her toes, heart going, scanning the crowd, and then a face flashed, a mop of dark hair. She locked on just to be sure. It *was* him! Relief streamed through her veins. Dax was sprinting towards them, dodging suitcases, and then his hand went up, and there was Maurice, looking like a crowd surfer, his label flying and spinning.

She felt her heart melting, a smile breaking her face apart. 'Look!' She squeezed Yannick's shoulder, hearing the excitement in her own voice. 'Papa's coming, and he's got Maurice! I told you he was a superhero!'

She took two sweets out of her bag and rose up, stretching across the aisle to hand them over. 'Kids? Suck these and they'll help your ears pop when we take off.'

Yann's face brightened, his cheeks suddenly bursting into Dax's irresistible smile. 'Pop, pop, pop!'

Chloe locked eyes with him, giggling. 'Pop-a-poodle-poo.'

Simone felt a smile coming. Yann was okay. *Happy!* Everything was fine. She dropped back into her seat.

'You're amazing!' Dax's eyes were full of admiration.

'You brought sweets.' His voice dropped to a whisper. 'And you made Yann smile!'

She felt her cheeks flushing. 'Thanks, but I'm not amazing, just well-practised, and, for the record, sweets and smiles tend to go hand in hand.' She stowed her bag, then fished for the two halves of her safety belt, taking her time. Sitting with Dax hadn't been the plan, but the kids had dived into the window seats, begging to sit together, and after all the shenanigans with Maurice they hadn't had the heart to say no. So now she was beside him, breathing in his cologne, trying not to melt every time he looked at her. At least the seats in business class were nice and wide!

'Sim...' He was leaning in, his voice low. 'You think I'm terrible for not knowing about Maurice, don't you?'

What to say? After all his heroics, she'd resolved to keep her thoughts to herself, but if he wanted to know her feelings, she wasn't going to lie. She turned to look at him, keeping her voice low too. 'I don't think you're terrible exactly, but at the same time—'

'There *is* a reason.' His eyes were holding her fast.

She felt a tingle travelling along her spine. Being this close felt rather intimate, but he clearly didn't want Yann overhearing. She swallowed. 'Okay. Go on.'

'Before I went to collect Yann from Tunis, I bought him some toys...' He paused. 'I probably went a bit overboard.'

That fitted! Flowers, clothes, plumbers. The hat off his head! Dax was nothing if not generous. *Kind!*

He shrugged a bit. 'I didn't know what to get. I asked Colette what I'd liked at Yann's age, but she didn't know so I basically bought the shop, including a menagerie of soft toys. Bears, rabbits, tigers, owls. A giant penguin! I put them all on his bed. So many eyes.' He pulled a mock terrified face. 'Staring!'

He was trying to make her smile, but she felt like crying. Lulu the rag doll, Jumpy the rabbit and Serge the monkey would be burned on her memory for ever because Chloe loved them. They were family! But Colette couldn't remember what Dax had used to like! Was that hands-off parenting? No wonder Dax didn't call her Maman.

He shook his head. 'I thought I was going to be like one of those movie dads, you know, propped against the head-board reading bedtime stories, but Yann didn't want me there.' He blinked and then his gaze tightened on hers. 'I didn't push it because I didn't want to cause him stress or make him unhappy. I figured he'd been through enough already. So I stayed out of his room, left bedtimes to Amy, and that's why I didn't know about Maurice.'

She felt her heart going out to him. Yann had shut him out. None of this was his fault. She took a breath, going for the silver lining. 'Well, you do now.'

He nodded. 'I do, and we're never losing him again because next time I'm going to chain him to Yann's bag, like you did with Chloe's monkey.'

He looked so serious that she couldn't help smiling. 'His name is Serge.'

'Serge the monkey...' He tapped his forehead. 'I'm locking it in. One day, you'll be proud of me!'

He was smiling but there was steel in his eyes. He was trying so hard, had been trying right from the start, smothering Yann with toys, expecting to get love back. It wasn't the way things worked, but he deserved Yann's love, he really did, because *his* heart was in the right place. More or less. Free riding aside...

Suddenly she couldn't stop herself from reaching for his hand, wrapping it in hers. 'How do you think I learned to tie Serge to Chloe's bag?'

For a beat he looked startled, probably because she was gripping his hand so hard, but then bemusement lit his eyes. 'I'm guessing maybe Serge got lost…'

'Lost?' She felt laughter bubbling up inside. 'Serge is a specialist. He's been lost in the shoe shop, the dry-cleaners, nursery school twice, the Square des Batignolles more times than I can remember, the Louvre and, ironically, the zoo. *That's* how many times I made the mistake of *not* tying him on, so please, don't ever tell me I'm amazing, or put me on a pedestal.'

His eyes flickered, and then she felt his hands moving, wrapping around hers, squeezing gently, making her feel all warm and tingly. 'It's too late for that, but you've made me feel a whole lot better about Maurice.'

'Dax's turn!'

He glanced into the rear-view mirror. Chloe was twinkling at him. Yann was smiling too. Maybe not *at him* exactly, but smiling all the same, joining in with the game, and talking, *actually* talking. Hallelujah!

He shot Simone a sideways glance. She was smiling too, her eyes warm. She seemed different, more animated, more…accessible. Maybe it was chatting on the plane—explaining about Maurice, hearing her funny story about Serge—that had softened the air between them. And there'd been her hands too, around his, then his around hers, that feeling of, what? Affection? Connection? Whatever it was, it was still there, flowing back and forth, doing strange things to his pulse.

He turned back to the road. Had she really changed her mind for the five months' salary plus expenses she'd asked for? Not that it mattered. The main thing was, she was here—thank God—making things flow, keeping Yann happy, keeping them all entertained. She'd got them playing a memory game, packing an imaginary suitcase with their favourite things. *Clever!* It meant they were all learning more about each other.

He adjusted his hands on the wheel. 'Okay, I'm going to Chamonix and I'm taking Serge the monkey, Maurice the panda...' He flicked a glance at Simone. 'My piece of flan, my snowboard, my pink woolly hat with the pom pom—'

A sudden throaty chuckle cracked the air. *Yann?* His heart leapt. Was Yann engaging? *With him?* He met Yann's eyes in the mirror, feeling a silly smile breaking his face apart. 'What? Don't you think I'd look nice in pink pompom hat?'

Yann clamped his lips together and shook his head, but his eyes were smiling.

Smiling eyes, proper eye contact! His heart leapt again. Milestone moment!

'You're cheating.' Simone was raising her eyebrows at him. 'You're buying time.' But she was messaging him too, with her eyes, telling him that she was seeing everything, feeling happy for him.

He felt another silly grin coming. 'No, I'm not! I'm simply responding to some oblique heckling from the back seat.' Her mouth quirked, sweet, and supremely kissable. He tore his eyes away, focusing on the road. 'Now, where was I? Pink hat, my *crôque monsieur*...' Funny that Yannick loved that; it was *his* favourite too! 'My...' he looked at Simone '...violin.' She nodded tightly. She played? So many things he didn't know about her and wanted to... *Focus!* 'And—' suddenly he couldn't resist hinting at the surprise he'd planned '—and my Christmas tree!'

'You haven't got a Christmas tree in your suitcase!'

He held in a smile. He'd expected this, Chloe jumping

right in. She'd been the same in the creperie, teasing him, but letting him in at the same time. She was adorable, just like her mother. He took a breath, squinting at her through the rear-view mirror. 'How do you know?'

She pouted. 'Because it wouldn't fit!'

'It does because it's a magic Christmas tree.'

Her mouth stiffened and then her face scrunched up. 'You haven't got a magic Christmas tree…'

He looked ahead, feeling her eyes on him, and Yann's, and Simone's, feeling his belly starting to vibrate. Two days ago, he'd hired a team of stylists to deck the chalet. He'd given them his ideas for the Christmas tree, told them to go large with it, create something that would make the kids' eyes pop! When he'd phoned his housekeeper, Chantal, that morning, to see how it was looking, she'd said it was magical! Hence 'magic' Christmas tree! Its magic was already working, sending festive tingles up and down his spine, or maybe he was tingling simply because he was going home, taking Yann to the place he loved most in the world, the place he belonged!

He felt his glow fading suddenly, a band tightening around his chest. Why had he gone back to Paris? Some misshapen instinct? Or panic, pure and simple. Whatever, he should have known better than to run to Colette because Colette had never been what he'd needed her to be. Her love, if that was what it was, had always felt insubstantial, loose around the edges. She'd always seemed more interested in her parties and trips than in him. She'd always let him do exactly what he wanted. At fourteen, what he'd wanted was to spend his days at the skatepark practising fakies, carving and grinding and getting air, enough air to hone his spins and grabs. He'd used to go off in the morning—*to school*—with his skateboard strapped to his pack, but she'd never said a word, never told him to stop playing hooky. She'd just kept on paying the exorbitant school fees. If she hadn't paid for his skateboard and helmet and shin pads too, he'd have wondered if she cared at all.

He looked at Yann in the rear-view mirror. His son was never going to have to wonder if he cared. Yann was going to know it one hundred per cent, even if the only way he could show him right now was with a bonkers Christmas tree. He looked at Chloe. Her little face was still taut, her eyes full of challenge. He felt the magic kindling again, his belly vibrating but laughing would give the game away. He tightened the corners of his mouth, flashing his eyebrows at her in the mirror. 'Well, Chloe, what can I say? You'll just have to wait and see.'

'Fifty-five, fifty-six, fifty-seven...' Simone paused for a beat, trying to keep her face straight. Was she really standing in the entrance lobby of the most gorgeous mountain chalet she'd ever seen, counting to sixty with pair of excited six-year-olds? Dax was inside, taking the 'magic' Christmas tree out of his bag. He'd said he'd need a minute, then they could go in. A ruse obviously, but it was completely impossible not to feel caught up in it. She took a breath, eyeing Chloe and Yann in turn, eking out the last seconds for effect. 'Fifty-eight...fifty-nine...*sixty*!'

The kids dived for the door, pushing it open, then froze. Her jaw went slack. Dax's tree was enormous, filling the stairwell and rising all the way to the galleried landing above. It was dense with silver and burgundy baubles, knobbly brown pinecones and...hundreds of felt animals. She felt a smile curving on her lips. Cheeky rabbits and bushy squirrels, cute mice and bespectacled badgers, wise owls, and wily foxes. A whole woodland carnival!

The kids unfroze suddenly and rushed over, peering into the branches, oohing and ahing.

She looked at Dax. He was watching them, eyes shining, a smile hanging on his lips. Warmth filled her chest. He'd organised this perfect Christmas tree on top of everything else! On the plane, he'd said to her that she was amazing, but *he* was amazing. Kind, thoughtful, good fun and, at that moment, the perfect father.

Suddenly his gaze shifted, catching her. For a moment she couldn't breathe, and then he smiled, and she couldn't breathe all over again. And then he motioned to the floor with a small nod of his head. She looked, stifling a giggle. His holdall was lying open, a length of organza ribbon trailing from its gaping zip, a scatter of pinecones, and woodland creatures, and baubles leading to the base of the tree.

Genius!

'So is this *really* a magic tree!' Chloe was nailing Dax with a look.

'Of course.' He was deadpanning like a pro. 'Did you think I was telling tall tales?'

Chloe's eyebrows knitted. It was her *I'm not sure* face. Dax needed a co-conspirator fast!

She went over, examining the tip of a branch detective-style. 'I have to say, I almost didn't believe it, but—' she turned to Chloe and Yann '—it was clearly a messy business getting it out.'

Chloe and Yann looked at the floor around Dax's bag, then exchanged deep looks.

She sensed Dax smothering a laugh but in the next instant he was dropping down, poker-faced.

'It was. I'm going to need some help tidying up.'

Chloe and Yann hesitated for a nanosecond then they were on it.

She stepped back. Dax needed this time, this kind of interaction with the kids, *with Yann*. He was doing fine, pointing to gaps, helping them hook things back on. Yann was watching Chloe, copying her, but he was also watching Dax. Was he seeing what she was seeing…a different Dax, a happier, more comfortable Dax? Was Yann getting curious about his *papa*? That was good!

She ran her eyes over the wooden balustrades. She was feeling different too. Maybe it was the warm, festive vibe in the hall, that lovely fresh pine smell and the feeling of home that was making her glow inside, or was it something else? She looked at Dax. Smiling. Merry-eyed. Coming to Chamonix for Chloe's sake, and for Yann's sake, had felt right, but at the airport there'd been a moment when she'd felt the weight of what she was doing, an acute awareness that Dax was an unknown. But then on the plane, exchanging parenting stories, she had started to feel that they were the same, just two people trying to be good parents and messing up sometimes. Holding hands, feeling that anchoring warmth flowing between them, had cemented that feeling. After that everything had felt natural and easy.

'Dax!' A smiling, silver-haired woman was coming through the hall towards them. 'I thought I heard voices.'

'Chantal!' Dax straightened, holding out his arms. 'I've missed you!' He gave her a hug, then stepped back. 'Yann, Chloe, Simone, this is Chantal. She's going to be looking after us while we're here.'

Chantal's gaze was warm. 'It's lovely to meet you all.' She turned to Dax. 'Lunch is ready when you are. Are you showing round first, or do you want to eat?'

'What do you think, Simone?' Dax's eyes came to hers. 'Eating or exploring?'

She glanced at the kids. Hopping like frogs! They

wouldn't settle until they'd looked round, and neither would she. The modern stone and timber exterior had taken her breath away as they'd driven up and she was dying to see the rest.

She smiled. 'Exploring!'

CHAPTER SIX

Later...

SIMONE SANK ONTO the bed and blew out a long breath. Putting Yann and Chloe to bed had been easier than she'd thought. She'd suggested to Dax that they read the bedtime story together and he'd been all for it, so they'd planted the kids in Chloe's bed and sat shoulder to shoulder, doing Goody the Elf and Big Bad Giant, Dax trying to rumble his part menacingly but mostly laughing. And then miraculously eyelids had started to droop and that had been that. Dax had taken Yann to his own room while she'd been tucking Chloe in, and moments later he'd reappeared, smiling, saying that Yann had gone out like a light!

It was a good sign, surely? A sign that Yann was relaxed about being here.

She got up and went over to her suitcase, taking things out, putting them in drawers. Something was definitely happening with Yann. All through dinner he'd kept shooting glances at Dax, and Dax had noticed. She'd seen it in his eyes every time they'd caught hers across the table. Maybe Chloe's easiness around Dax was reassuring Yann, making him see his *papa* differently, or maybe he was simply mesmerised because from the moment they'd come through the door, Dax had been all smiles.

He'd toured them round the house with delight strapped to his face. No wonder! His home was delightful, *no*, breathtaking! Large, light rooms. Vaulted timber ceilings. Polished wood floors. Stunning views! The kids had loved the TV den with its squishy sofas and cinema-sized screen. She'd loved the immense black and white photograph of Mont Blanc that covered a whole wall in his office, although she'd felt trembly too, looking at it, remembering his film, a speck of Dax on the vast white slope.

In the basement garage he'd shown them his snowmobile, and his camper van, and the four-by-four that was hers to drive, but it was his kit room that had really blown her away. So much gear! Regiments of snowboards, helmets, boots, goggles, and bindings, innumerable impeccable skeins of climbing rope hanging from dozens of pegs. Ice axes, harnesses, packs, and jackets, all tidily arranged. He kept the small stuff like karabiners in neatly labelled colour-coded plastic boxes. *Colour-coded!*

He'd said before that free riding was quite involved but seeing all his kit had brought home how technical it really was. He seemed so knowledgeable, and he was a total neat freak! He'd said keeping tabs on his gear was vital, maintaining it essential. It was reassuring in a way and yet there was that little knot tightening again.

All afternoon, he'd been on the phone, making plans. She'd heard him as she'd been unpacking the kids' things in their rooms. Later, when she'd been in the den watching a silly movie with Chloe and Yann, he'd still been walking around, phone in hand, talking excitedly. Dax was thrilled to be home, definitely, but that wasn't the only reason he was shining like the North Star. He was shining because he was going back out on the mountain, free riding…

Taking risks!

Just the thought of it was making her feel sick, sick for

Yann, and—*admit it*—sick for herself. She zipped up her empty suitcase and stood, staring at it. Twelve hours with Dax and she was already in a tangle. Holding hands on the plane, conspiring over the magic tree, playing Goody the Elf to his Big Bad Giant, feeling the hard swell of his shoulder against hers, laughing into his eyes. There was something irresistible about Dax, something that had flipped her over from the very first moment. He had a way of looking at her that made the floor slide, a way of looking at her that made her want something for herself…closeness, connection, the warm touch of someone who wasn't her daughter, but Dax couldn't be that someone. Whilst he was taking risks, the price of caring about him would be always waiting for *that* visit. Grim faces at the door, grim words coming out, that boneless feeling, lungs too tight to breathe, lungs so tight she'd thought she was dying too. She swallowed hard. She'd been through it once, and once was enough. Never again!

If only she could persuade him to stop taking risks, but she'd burned those boats the second she'd 'changed her mind' for money! And now she was here, enjoying his home and his company, getting her wires crossed and her feelings tangled. She had to draw a line somehow, compartmentalise! She was here to give Chloe an amazing Christmas, and she was here to bring Dax closer to Yann. If she succeeded, then hopefully, for the love of his son, he'd stop hurling himself off mountains. And that was it! She took a deep breath. Chloe and Yann *had* to be her sole focus. Making room for her own confusion wasn't an option!

Air! That was what she needed. To clear her head. She grabbed her cardigan, pulling it on as she slid the door open and stepped out onto the veranda. Dax had said that the mountains at dawn were 'sick' but these mountains, vast and ghostly under the stars, were 'sick' too. She leaned against the rail, breathing cold crisp air, listening to the singing silence, and then suddenly, her stomach dipped. Focusing on Yann and Chloe was all very well but they were in bed now. The rest of the evening stretched. Just her and Dax! Alone! And not just *this* evening, but every evening for the next three weeks! She tugged her cardigan tight, heart drumming. How come she was only realising this now? Saying yes, going for crepes, packing, taking Dax's endless calls… Things had moved so fast, she hadn't quite realised… A shiver forked through her shins. She huddled into her cardigan, jiggling. It was too cold to stand around but going inside would mean going downstairs and going downstairs would mean being alone with Dax, trying to stop her senses swimming every time he looked at her, every time he smiled…

She looked along the veranda. It wrapped all the way around the house under cover of the eaves, so the boards were dry and free of snow. Walking always helped, made her feel better. She set off, treading lightly past Chloe's window, and Yann's, then stepping out a bit, breathing deeply. This wasn't so bad. A teeth-chattering stretch in the freezing cold was just what she needed!

She turned the corner, loosening up. The rooms at this side of the house were empty guest rooms so there was no one to disturb. Such a big house for one person or…not! Dax had said he'd built a big place because he was always having friends to stay, free-riding buddies from around the world. It was what they did, hosting each other in one another's homes, spending their evenings planning adventures, looking for new lines.

Dangerous lines!

She swallowed hard. Knotting herself up was pointless. What she needed were strategies to fast-track the father-son bonding process, like…maybe getting Dax to do the bedtime story on his own next time and…maybe finding something that Dax and Yann both liked, something they could do together when Dax got in from the slopes. *Anything* to get them interacting!

She swung around the next corner and stopped dead. The swimming pool below was lit up and glowing like a turquoise jewel, and Dax was front crawling across it at speed, biceps glistening, his hair darkly plastered to his head. He flipped over, then he was coming towards her, arm over arm, head down. She felt the deck sliding under her feet, a sudden thick heat pulsing in her veins. He looked wonderful gliding through the water. She took a breath, tiptoeing nearer, then stopped. What was she doing? Being ridiculous was what! She took a step back, faltering. He was turning again, arrowing through the water, breaking the surface, water streaming off his shoulders and powerful arms. She swallowed a dry edge in her throat. It was impossible not to watch. He was poetry in motion, so graceful, so fast. She went forward again on slow soft feet. As long as he didn't look up… But what if he did? *Oh, God!* What was wrong with her? She was a grown woman, a mother and, at that very moment, his employee! She shrank into her cardigan, heart pounding. She couldn't *be* like this, couldn't let herself get tangled up in the thought of him. She'd told herself that just two minutes ago! He was just a man, swimming in a pool, and she was acting like a schoolgirl with a crush. *Enough!* She needed to say hello then walk on.

She drew a breath and went to the rail. He was midway through another length but then he turned onto his back, floating, staring upwards. She opened her mouth to speak, but suddenly he was turning his head in her direction and then his eyes found hers.

'Hey!' He broke into a smile that cost her a heartbeat. 'Are you coming in?'

'No way! It's freezing!' She rubbed her arms, trying to sound casual. 'I was just taking a walk.'

His feet disappeared then he was rising out of the water, pushing his hair back, his gaze unswerving. 'It *is* heated…'

Was he trying to persuade her? No matter. Talking to him, feeling the warmth in his eyes and his smile was way better than spying on him. She felt a smile unfurling. 'The pool might be, but the air isn't.'

'It's refreshing!' He sank to his chin, tilting his head back. 'Night swimming is the best. Just look at those stars!'

She looked up. 'Strangely enough they look amazing from here too!'

He grinned. 'Fair play, but you *should* try night swimming sometime, or—' he was rising out of the water again, torso glistening '—maybe you'd prefer the hot tub!' He flashed his eyebrows suggestively.

She held in a smile. He was playing with her, flirting for fun. She couldn't resist flirting back. She pulled a lock of hair forward, twisting it in her fingers. 'Ooh… Hot tub? Now you're talking.'

He laughed, then his gaze steadied, holding her fast. 'If you're not coming in, you should go inside. It's too cold for just a cardigan—'

She arched her eyebrows. 'But a swimsuit's fine?'

His eyes lit. 'Go! Before you catch a cold! I've got ten lengths to go then I'm done.' He dropped down into the water. 'What would you say to us warming up with a cognac in about twenty minutes?'

She could hardly say no and she didn't want to. She smiled. 'I'd say that sounds perfect!'

CHAPTER SEVEN

Twenty minutes later...

DAX POURED COGNAC into two glasses, then pushed the cork back into the bottle slowly. Fifty laps of the pool should have taken the edge off his jitters, but his stomach was still twisting itself into knots. Crazy! It wasn't as if he wasn't looking forward to spending the evening with Simone. He absolutely was.

He liked her, liked the way he felt inside whenever her eyes held him, liked the way her lips curved up so sweetly when she smiled. Maybe that was the problem! He liked her *too* much. She was stirring things inside him that he didn't recognise, things he didn't know how to process. Reading the bedtime story had tipped him over the edge. Feeling her shoulder against his, the small movements of her body, her warmth. He could have leaned away but something had kept him there, something he hadn't been able to control. He'd tried to swim it off but, somehow, suddenly she'd been there, smiling down at him, heating his blood all over again.

He blew out a breath. When Simone had said yes to Chamonix, it had felt like a chance for him to get his life under control again, but it wasn't feeling like that any more. It was so good to be home, but it wasn't the same.

He wasn't the same. Yes, he'd felt the same old excitement talking on the phone to his free-riding buddies, making plans for getting out on the slopes, but he'd also felt as if he was missing out on what Simone and the kids were doing, missing out on their laughter and happy chatter. He'd wandered around the house, talking on the hoof, just to see them, just to catch traces of Simone's perfume in the air...

His chest went tight. A feeling of home and family was what he'd wanted for Yann, to make him happy. It was why he'd begged Simone and Chloe to come but getting caught up in it himself was the last thing he'd expected. He didn't know what it meant, or how to feel about it. It was like dangling, mid-somersault, not knowing what the landing was going to be like, and feeling hopelessly attracted to Simone wasn't helping things, especially since there was something in her eyes that was making him think she liked him too.

He picked up the glasses and started walking. She was in the sitting room waiting for him, stunning in grey jeans and a soft black shirt, her hair loose for once and hanging darkly around her lovely face. He broke step, drawing in a steadying breath. She was lovely. He liked her in all the ways it was possible to like someone, but she was here for Yannick, and no way could he risk Yann's happiness, Yann's Christmas, by making a stupid move on her. It had been hard enough persuading her to come in the first place.

'I'm seeing a change in Yann.' Simone was dropping onto the opposite sofa, settling her glass on her knee. He felt his tension melting away. Talking about Yann would pull him out of his own head. Besides, he was keen to hear her thoughts. She smiled, 'I mean the way he's watching you all the time. I think it's a good sign.'

'I hope so.' Yann had definitely been watching him

more, making eye contact. He'd even seen glimmers of interest. Yann still wasn't talking to him much, but he'd let him tuck him into bed easily enough. It was progress, and if Simone was seeing it too, then it had to be real. He felt a sudden swell of gratitude. If he'd been on his own with Yann, it wouldn't have been happening. He shifted, stretching out his legs. 'I think Chloe's a big influence.'

She smiled, her eyes flickering with just a hint of mischief. 'Just as well she's on your side!'

'True!' He chuckled. Chloe was definitely on his side. She was something else! He sipped his cognac, suddenly wanting to let some of what he was holding inside come out. 'Chloe's a beautiful soul, Sim. She's like you…' Something flickered behind her gaze. Was he overstepping? It wasn't his intention. He just wanted her to know how grateful he was that she'd come through for him. Maybe a little humour would help. He smiled. 'She's kind, blisteringly honest, and willing to give a hopeless loser like me a chance.'

She blinked. 'Thank you! I think.' She sipped her drink, and then a spark lit her gaze. 'And you're not a *hopeless* loser. You're good at losing panda bears…'

He grinned. 'Like I said, blisteringly honest!'

She laughed softly for a moment and then her eyes became serious. 'Can I be blisteringly honest now?'

His heart panged, not out of fear but out of curiosity. He trusted her. Anything she had to say was worth hearing. He nodded. 'Of course.'

She drew up her legs, tucking them under. 'I think you should talk to Yann about his mother.' His heart panged again, this time with guilt and a confusion of other emotions that he couldn't quite pin down. 'I understand why you went for the fresh start, but you can't just wipe people away like that, not a mother, not a father, not if they've been loved…' The corners of her eyes were glistening. 'Yann's grieving. You need to open a door for him so he knows he can talk about her if he wants to.'

'But how?' He felt a wave of hopelessness. 'I only knew Zara for a couple of weeks, and we didn't exactly spend our time talking.'

'There must be something?' Her gaze was gentle, urgent.

'I don't…' He sipped his cognac, thinking. 'She was quite a bit older than me, ran her own business, Desert Jeep Adventures. It's how we met.' His chest went tight. 'It's how she died actually…rolled a jeep…knocked her head.'

Simone's hand flew to her chest. 'God…that's…'

'I know.' He swallowed hard. 'Anyway, I was on one of her tours. She knew the desert, knew the best parasailing places. That was her thing—parasailing. She was good on a horse too.' He felt a smile coming. 'She was action girl! A free spirit. She had these amazing amber eyes…'

'Did you love her at all?' Simone's gaze was hopeful.

'No.' What would she say if he told her that he'd never been in love, didn't know what it felt like?

'Right.' She drew in a little breath. 'Well…you could tell Yann how you met Zara…tell him that you thought her eyes were amazing. Share everything you have because Zara's your bridge. *Use* her, and let Yann *use* her too. Let him remember her through you.' Her eyes were glistening again. 'You need to keep her alive for him.'

He could feel her passion, see it blazing in her eyes. She was right. *Wise!* Zara was the path he should have followed from the start. Why hadn't he? He looked down, swirling his cognac, losing himself in its amber glow, and suddenly he knew. He hadn't wanted to talk to Yann about Zara because he'd been afraid that Yann would see that he hadn't loved her. Maybe Yann wouldn't have cared; maybe Zara had told him already, but what if she hadn't? He hadn't wanted to be the one to reveal the truth, because knowing that your origins weren't rooted in love was the kind of knowledge that gnawed at your soul, made you feel less... The feeling never went away, even if you told yourself that you were being stupid because it didn't matter, even if you told yourself you didn't care—

'Dax!' Her voice pulled him back. 'Are you okay?'

He blinked, saw concern in her eyes. For some reason it warmed him. He dug out a smile. 'Yes. I was just thinking about what you said, thinking that you're always right.'

'Don't say that.' She was shaking her head. 'I'm not always right. I'm only making a suggestion because I see a change in Yann, and it would be so great if you could build on it somehow...and quickly!' Her eyes flashed. '*Carpe diem* and all that!'

He raised his glass to her. 'It's always been my motto!'

'Figures!' Her glass went up too, and then she took a small sip. 'So... You're planning to go free riding tomorrow?'

'Yes.' He felt a buzz starting in his veins. 'Or, actually, no. Not free riding. If the conditions are right, I'm going out, but I'll be sticking to the resorts. I need to ease back in—'

'*Ease* back in?' She was arching her eyebrows playfully.

He grinned. 'Which for me obviously means I'll be tanking it, but it'll just be playing plus a little bit of work. My sponsors have sent me some bindings to test.'

'What do you mean *test*?' The playful light disappeared. 'Don't tell me you're expected to find out if something's going to break?'

'No!' She was jumping for the wrong stick! He drew in his legs and sat forwards. 'I don't test equipment to see if it works. It absolutely does work, okay?' She was biting her lips, holding him in an anxious gaze. He ran his tongue across his lip. This wasn't the moment to be thinking about kissing her worries away. He swallowed. 'It's more of a review, a question of how things feel, and it's subjective, of course. A binding might suit me but not you.' He couldn't resist. 'In the same way that you might prefer flan from one patisserie over another.'

A smile ghosted on her lips, but there were familiar clouds behind her eyes. He felt a knot tightening in his stomach. They hadn't revisited the sticky subject of risk since her outburst in his apartment. He thought she must have put her feelings aside somehow, because she was here, wasn't she? But they were still there after all, frozen into the ice, just visible. It was no good! She was helping him out. She deserved to have a nice Christmas, not one spent tying herself into needless knots. He couldn't bear the thought of that.

He parked his glass on the low coffee table and fastened his eyes on hers. 'Sim, I don't want you being anxious all the time. It's not necessary.'

She blinked, as if she hadn't expected him to be so direct, and then she swallowed, a glimmer of steel in her gaze. 'Why isn't it necessary? I want to know.'

Finally! A chance to lay it all out! He took a breath, feeling the words rising like a tide. 'First, because for me free riding is as natural as walking…or breathing. I do it without having to think about it. Secondly, the film you saw was a grand spectacle, a few high-octane minutes set to music, but you need to stop reacting and look deeper… *think* deeper.' The corners of her mouth started to tighten but her gaze held steady. He licked his lips. 'Look, every line I ride is earned in hours of preparation. I study the terrain from the top and from the bottom. I consult with expert mountaineers. I go on recces. You need to understand that when I'm up there on the mountain, I'm doing things I've done hundreds, thousands of times before. Every jump, every somersault you see has a thousand others behind it. I've been riding snowboards for thirteen years, and before that I was riding skateboards. All in all, it's a lot of practice!'

Something came and went behind her eyes. *Acknowledgement? Understanding?* He pushed on.

'In the beginning I made mistakes, of course I did, but every mistake is a lesson. You learn. You grow. You get better, but you can never get complacent. The mountain *is* dangerous. You have to give it your full attention, all of your respect, and I do—*always*—so the risk for me is small.'

She lifted her chin. 'Maybe the risk is small, but the consequences of something going wrong are huge, especially now.'

His chest panged. He couldn't argue with that, but he wasn't going to let anything go wrong. He had no intention of orphaning his son and he *needed* her to understand that, needed to see it register in her eyes.

He got up and went to sit beside her. 'You're right. The consequences would be huge, which is exactly why I'm not going to let anything bad happen. I don't want to die! Why would I risk my life when I have so many reasons to live?' Her eyes were on his, full of thoughts he couldn't read. Maybe if he told her the last thing, the thing he'd never told anyone before, it would ease her mind. He took a breath. 'You know, it's strange… I grew up in Paris, but the mountains have always felt like home. It's like they're in my blood. I feel…' How to explain? 'I feel I have a sort of *sense* for the mountain, like a sixth sense. When I'm out there, I can feel if something isn't right, and if it isn't right then I turn back.'

The light in her eyes softened. 'You turn back?'

'Always.' Her eyes were flickering, tugging at something inside him. He swallowed. 'Whatever impression you have of me from that film, the truth is that I'm not remotely reckless. I've never been reckless. I'm—'

'Meticulous!' A smile warmed her eyes. 'That's if your kit room is anything to go by!'

His chest filled. Simone's smile was already one of his all-time favourite views. He shook his head, chuckling. 'Meticulous is a polite way of putting it. I was going to say I'm on the scale when it comes to my mountain adventures.'

She took a sip from her glass then set it down. When she looked up again, her gaze was soft and full. 'So I can trust that your sixth sense is going to keep you safe?'

His heart thumped sideways. Her need for reassurance was turning him inside out. She seemed so vulnerable, so afraid and he couldn't stand it. He wanted to scoop her up, shield her from every terrible thing in the world, but at the same time he wanted to tug her out onto the ledge, show her some thrills, see her cheeks glowing and her eyes shining. More than anything, he wanted her to be happy.

He leaned towards her. 'Yes, you can.' He touched her hair without thinking, sliding his fingers down one smooth lock. 'I don't want you worrying, okay?'

Her eyes held his for a moment and then she looked down.

Oh, God! He dropped his hand. 'I'm sorry.' He swallowed hard, heart pounding. He hadn't meant to touch her; it had just happened, a tender impulse, a desire to sweep away her worries, and her hair was so lovely, the way it hung at the side of her face, glowing in the firelight. He touched her hand with one finger. 'I'm sorry. I shouldn't have done that… I wasn't trying to—'

'It's okay.' She looked up, blinking, and then her gaze settled. 'The truth is I liked it.' The tip of her tongue flicked across her lip. 'I haven't…' She took a breath, swallowing. 'No one's touched me like that for a long time.'

His heart pulsed. What was she saying? He looked into her face, running his eyes over the curve of her cheek, the soft pout of her lips, then back to her steady gaze and suddenly he knew. She was asking for more, asking him for something he desperately wanted to give.

He leaned towards her again, running the back of his index finger along her cheekbone, watching, giving her a chance to pull away, but she wasn't pulling away. She was leaning into his touch, her eyes hazing over, her lips parting. A voice in his head was saying no, was saying that he was crossing the very line he'd told himself he couldn't cross, but it was a small voice, close to noiseless and then it was gone. He looked at her lips, and then he moved in, taking them slowly, tasting cognac and warmth, feeling his pulse heating, gathering. And then her mouth was softening, moulding to his. She was kissing him back, pulling him closer and suddenly he was free falling, hungrier for her than he'd ever felt for anyone. He cupped her nape, deepening his kiss, exploring the sweet wet heat in her mouth, feeling desire blazing through his veins, feeling her hands in his hair, tugging him closer, deeper, and deeper…and then suddenly it wasn't enough. He broke off, heart pounding, kissing her neck, tasting her throat, moving his hands over the soft silk of her shirt, over her breasts, over her hardening nipples. She gasped, then her body was rising to meet him, and her hands were under his shirt, moving over his skin. It was too much sensation. He wanted her, right there, right then, and her body was telling him she wanted him right back. He went for her buttons but then suddenly she was fighting him off, pushing his hands away, her voice a sort of strangled whisper. 'Dax!'

'What?' He felt dizzy, momentarily blind, his heart pounding broken beats. 'What did I do?'

She was shaking her head. 'It's Yann!'

Yann! He looked round. *Oh, God!* Yann was bumbling towards them. He sprang to his feet, heart banging. Was Yann sick? He hurried across, scanning him from head to toe. He didn't look sick. He was yawning, and sleep rumpled, but still, he was here, wanting something or someone. *Him?* Couldn't be. Yann *never* wanted him.

He swallowed hard. 'Yann? Are you all right?'

Yann rubbed at his eyes, swaying slightly. He seemed so small, seemed as if he should be picked up and held on a hip, but they weren't on tactile terms yet. If he scooped Yann up, he'd probably frighten him half to death. A memory flashed. Simone, eye to eye with Yann at the airport. *Of course.* He dropped to his haunches, taking Yann's shoulders in his hands. 'Are you okay?'

Yann's eyes fastened on his, sleepy but direct. 'I want to see the snowboards.'

Definitely not what he'd been expecting! He licked his lips. 'Which snowboards?'

Yann blinked. 'In the room downstairs. I want to see them.'

His heart pulsed. Yann was interested in snowboards! If only he'd known, he could have talked to him about it before. Why hadn't he? He felt his chest tightening. Because he'd been too busy trying to be a movie dad, and failing, and then he'd backed off altogether. He gulped a breath. Too late to worry about that now! The main thing was, Yann was interested, and *that* opened things up! He felt a sudden rush of euphoria, a silly grin splitting his face apart. 'Of course you can see them—'

'After breakfast in the morning!' Simone was suddenly beside him, a noticeable flush in her cheeks. Her eyes caught his. 'Maybe you could treat us all to a demonstration tomorrow!' She smiled at Yannick. 'You know your *papa*'s pretty sick on a snowboard, huh?'

Sick! It sounded cute coming from her lips.

'Can I have a go?' Yann was winding up, his eyes brightening. 'Please can I have a go, Papa?'

Papa! His ribs went tight. Yann had just looked him in the eye and called him Papa! Was this really happening? He took a breath. He'd intended being on the slopes first thing, loosening up, giving those bindings a spin, but now…? Yann's eyes were gripping his. *Papa!* He felt his pulse going, his thoughts free riding a hundred lines at once. He could spend time with Yann first thing, couldn't he, give them all a demonstration before going to the resort? Then, he could stop in Cham on the way back, pick up a junior board for Yann, and one for Chloe too. Or maybe Simone and the kids could meet him in town. Even better! He could show them around, the kids could choose their own boards, and after, they could go for hot chocolate, soak up the Christmas vibes…

He squeezed Yann's shoulders gently. 'Of course you can, but my board's going to be too big. We'll have to get you your own.'

Yann's eyes popped. 'My *own* board!'

Yann was adorable. He really was!

He felt a smile breaking over his face again. 'Hell yeah! A serious snowboarder needs his own board!'

'But—' Simone was interrupting again '—serious snowboarders also need a good night's sleep, don't they, Dax?'

He twisted to look up at her, losing himself in the warmth of her gaze, hoping she could feel his gratitude flowing back. She was keeping him on track, reminding him that buying Yann a board was the easy part! Taking Yann back to bed, making sure he understood rules and boundaries, was harder. He felt a bitter pang in his chest. Colette had mobbed him with things, but she'd never said no to him, never given him the security of boundaries, even though he'd pushed and pushed. She'd made him feel that he didn't matter, that he wasn't worth caring about. He was never going to let Yann feel like that.

He turned back to Yann, straightening. 'Simone's right. Snowboarding is super physical, so you need your sleep.' Yann was looking up at him, seeming to take it all in. He felt a small flush of triumph. He steered Yann round slowly, propelling him gently towards the door. 'Let's get you back into bed. Maurice will be wondering where you are.'

'No, he won't.' Yann walked steadily, his small bare feet thudding softly on the floor. 'Maurice can't wonder things. He's just a cuddly toy.'

She watched them go, heart hammering. Had Yann seen? It didn't seem like it, but it had been a close shave.

Oh, God!

She went back to the sofa and picked up her glass, slugging down the last mouthful. But he could have! And then what? Disaster! She felt the cognac burning, her stomach rolling and churning. She set the glass down and pressed her fingers to her temples. What had she been thinking? She'd taken a tender moment and spun it into something else, lost control of her emotions because for a tantalising moment Dax had made her feel that it was safe to like him, because he was safe on the mountain...

Everything he'd said had made sense. About his films being showcases for the skills he'd been honing and practising for years. It had struck her that it was the same with playing the violin. When she played, she was playing more than the music. She was playing every second, every minute, every hour she'd ever played. It was all there underneath, like a huge well that rose up, powering her fingers, pouring through her. That was what Dax had, a wealth of knowledge and experience behind him and...a sense for the mountain. A sixth sense! She got that too because she'd always had a sense for music, a connection to it that she couldn't explain. It was simply there.

She stared at the fire letting the flames blur. He'd said he always turned back if it didn't feel right. He'd said he wasn't reckless. All his reassuring words and all the tidy rows in his kit room had stacked together with the tender look in his eyes, and then he'd touched her hair... She closed her eyes, feeling it again, the gentle slide of his fingers, her limbs melting, desire aching in her veins. That was the moment she should have left alone but couldn't. For three years she'd been swallowing pain and anger, plastering on smiles for Chloe's sake, but when Dax had touched her, she'd felt something warm and real unfolding, too bright and lovely to bury with all the sad bones. She'd wanted more, wanted to lose herself in something that felt good, so she'd opened the door...and he'd stepped through...and his kiss had felt so right, so perfect. Warm, tender, then wild, kindling a fire in her veins, bringing her blazing to life. It was as if everything she'd felt flowing between them from the start had found a place to be, a place that felt like home.

She got up, wrapping her arms across her front. But was it a safe home? Could she risk planting her feelings there, risk letting them grow? After everything he'd said, she felt easier about him going on the mountain, but she'd never be able to switch off her anxiety altogether. And getting closer to him, caring about him would lead Chloe in the same direction, and then what? If something bad did happen, everything would come crashing down. Bad enough for herself, but for Chloe it would be worse. Chloe had barely turned three when André died. She hadn't quite understood, but now Chloe was older, more vulnerable emotionally.

She felt her heart twisting. She couldn't not like Dax. He was warm-hearted and gorgeous. Tormented too. It felt as if they'd been through so much together already, just to get here…the bistro, his presents, that day at his apartment, that car ride back to the school. Maybe that was why her emotions were all over the place, why her feelings were so tangled? She bit her lips together. But she couldn't afford to let herself get tangled, for her own sake and for Chloe's. And there was Yann too.

Yann!

He'd called Dax Papa! He was interested in the snowboards! Good things were happening! Dax had a toehold now and they couldn't jeopardise that, couldn't risk confusing the kids and themselves. Surely, he'd see it too.

'Hey!' Dax was coming towards her, cognac bottle in hand. 'How about a top-up?'

'No, thanks.' Her mouth was dry, but more cognac was the last thing she needed. She watched him pouring a measure into his own glass. What was he thinking about? What was he feeling? Her own nerves were chiming. They'd kissed—more than kissed—and she wanted to talk about it but diving straight in didn't seem right. She needed to ease in somehow. She moistened her lips. 'You must be thrilled about Yann's interest in snowboarding.'

'Just a bit!' He dropped down onto the opposite sofa, shaking his head. 'When he said it, I was like…*what*?'

Was Dax trying to signal something by not sitting beside her? It pricked a bit, but maybe it was also reassuring. If he was distancing himself then maybe he was on the same page about the kiss.

She smiled. 'Well, I think it's great.' In spite of her nerves, she felt a little rush of warmth, a burst of happiness for him. 'It's a way in. It's exactly what you need.'

His hand went up, fingers crossing. 'Here's hoping.'

'I have a good feeling.' She took a breath, feeling her heartbeat pulsing through her skin. 'And…speaking of needs…what you don't need…' His eyebrows drew in slightly. 'What neither of us needs is to be…'

'To be what?' The light in his eyes was fading along with his smile.

Her heart panged. Maybe using the opposite sofa hadn't been a signal. Maybe he'd just been giving her some space. Hadn't he told her before that he liked to think of himself as a gentleman? *Oh, God!* She couldn't not say what she had to say, but she didn't want to hurt him. Maybe if she took it all on her own shoulders it would soften the blow. It was pretty much the shape of things anyway.

She swallowed hard. 'To be making mistakes, to be complicating things for ourselves and the kids.' Something flickered behind his eyes but trying to fathom what it was wasn't an option. She had to keep going. 'Kissing was a mistake, Dax. I instigated it, and I'm sorry. I wasn't trying to lead you on. I'm just lonely, that's all. And sad…' She felt the truth of it stinging, filling her eyes, then more truths surfacing, wanting to be free. 'I miss being touched, being held. I miss having someone…' A shadow crossed his face and then kindness bloomed in his gaze. She felt it tugging at her, tugging more out of her. 'I lost my husband three years ago… December the seventeenth.'

His eyes narrowed a little. 'I'm sorry.'

For some reason, now she'd started, the words wouldn't stop coming. 'He was just crossing the road…using a crossing…not jaywalking…' She felt a band tightening around her skull. 'The driver was texting…didn't see. André died instantly. That's what they said…'

Suddenly Dax was sitting down next to her, putting his glass into her hands. 'Here.'

'Thanks.' She took a sip, feeling the burn in her throat, feeling the band around her skull tightening. 'I shouldn't be drinking this. I haven't got a head for spirits.' He was looking at her gently, stirring something inside again that she couldn't allow to be stirred. She gave him the glass back. 'It's just a sad time of year, you know. A fragile time. I hide it from Chloe. She doesn't know when her *papa* died, and I'm not going to tell her. I don't want her to be sad.'

'I get that.' Dax shifted a little, and then his eyes came back to hers. 'Just to square things away, what happened isn't on you, Simone. I started it.' His eyes clouded. 'And I shouldn't have. It *was* a mistake, I agree.' His jaw seemed to tighten. 'If Yann had seen—'

'I know.' Her stomach dipped. If Yann had seen, he'd have been confused…troubled… And what if it had been Chloe? *Oh, God!* She drew in a breath. 'I'm glad you feel the same.'

He was nodding. 'One hundred per cent.'

'Good!' She bit her lips, feeling awkward, feeling a sudden tug of weariness. 'If you don't mind, I think I'll go to bed.' She pushed herself up. 'It's been quite a day.'

He was getting up too. 'Simone…?' His gaze was reaching in, turning her over. 'Are we all right?'

'Of course. I'm tired, that's all.' She took a backwards step, suddenly needing not to be trapped in the warm light of his gaze. 'Goodnight, Dax.'

CHAPTER EIGHT

December 13th

'DO YOU FEEL SAFE?' Simone was giving Yann a deep look.

Yann nodded, then he twisted his head up, eyes bright, voice revving like an engine. 'I want to go fast, Papa!'

'Really?' Dax felt a smile breaking his face apart. 'I'd never have guessed!'

Yann grinned a devilish grin.

He felt a glow rising inside. *This* was the lively little boy Zara's parents had talked about, the one they couldn't keep up with. Now it made sense! He felt an urge to ruffle Yann's hair but held back. A mistimed paternal gesture might dent things, and he didn't want to do that. Feeling stoked about the way things were going would have to be enough for now.

He tested his feet in his bindings, checking they were tight, then he checked Yann's feet, wedged in the gap between his own. Giving Yann a ride on his snowboard hadn't been part of the plan, but after he'd done his performing seal routine, as per Simone's suggestion last night, Yann had mobbed him, begging for a go. Saying no had been impossible.

He shifted his stance, getting ready, pinning Yann against him.

'Not too fast, Dax, okay?' Simone was looking at him, a trace of the night before in her eyes.

He felt warmth filling his chest then a pang, remembering that he'd agreed with her that their kiss and all the rest had been a mistake. *Agreed!* So there was absolutely no reason for him to be feeling tight around the ribs. It wasn't as if *Mistake!* hadn't been chiming in his ears all the way up the stairs. It was what he'd been thinking as he'd been putting Yann into bed, reflecting on the matter of seconds that had come between himself and disaster, reflecting on the fact that if Yann had seen him tearing off Simone's blouse, they'd never have got onto the subject of snowboards at all!

Tucking Yann in, he'd felt the whole weight of his mistake pressing down on him. Yann had to be his priority. He'd lost his head for a moment, lost himself in Simone's kiss, in the idea of her, but the reality was that he'd never be able to bring her happiness. He didn't do love and commitment. Relationships! He'd dangled on the strings of Colette's changing moods and whims for too many years to ever want to put anyone else through it on his own account. He didn't want anyone's happiness tied to his actions, his mistakes, especially not Simone. She was too lovely, too kind. And…he needed her to be there for Yann.

He'd had it all straight in his head by the time he'd gone downstairs. He'd grabbed the cognac—Dutch courage—and gone in, all set to be open and honest with her, but she'd beaten him to it, started talking about her husband, and Christmas…being lonely…feeling fragile…in a roundabout way telling him that she'd reached for him simply because he'd been there. So that had been that! All tidied up and tucked away, except, for some reason, he could feel a loose thread trailing, catching his feet every time she looked at him.

He threw her a smile, flashing his eyebrows. 'You know me. I *never* go too fast!' And then he rocked the board, making it slide. 'Okay, buddy, here we go…'

'Be careful!' Simone was calling out from the depths of her red jacket, her face luminous in the snow light.

'Sorry?' He put his hand to his ear, just to tease her. 'I didn't quite catch…' and then he had to face forwards because they were picking up speed and Yann was squealing.

He rode a wide arc, holding Yann firm, then wove the other way, keeping the pace easy, the arc gentle. He looked down at Yann's dark head. 'Are you okay?'

'Yes, but I want to go *faster*!'

'No way!'

'Why?'

He held in a smile. 'Because you're loose cargo! You need bindings.' He turned the board sideways, coasting to a sedate stop.

'Is that it?' Yann was looking up at him, his face the picture of disappointment.

He laughed. 'I'm afraid so. We can't go too far because Chloe's waiting for her turn. Besides, we have to walk back, remember.'

'Or you could push me?' Yann's gaze was mischievous. 'That way I get to ride by myself!'

'Okay.' He felt his lips twitching. There were certainly no flies on Yann! 'Hop off a sec.'

Yann jumped into the snow, then strode around, making footprints.

Dax watched while he freed his feet from the bindings. Could this be a Zara moment? Simone had said he needed to talk about her. If only he could think of something that would blend, not sound like he was trying too hard. He sighed. Maybe something would come, eventually. He straightened the board. 'Right, on you get.'

Yann obeyed, planting his feet wide for balance. 'Let's go!'

It was impossible not to laugh. He fitted his palm between Yann's shoulder blades. 'Brace yourself, okay...'

Yann stiffened then yelled, 'Push!'

He obeyed, chuckling. Yann was no weight at all, going along on the board. His own feet were sinking, but trudging was part of any climb, not that this was a climb, just a gentle upwards slope. He looked ahead, saw Chloe jumping up and down next to a small snow...what? *Rabbit?* Simone's idea no doubt, keeping Chloe busy while she was waiting. Simone was so great at the parenting thing. *So great!* He felt his ribs tightening again. Was it going to happen every time he thought about her, even when it was innocent stuff that had nothing to do with the way her mouth had felt on his, or the way she'd tasted, all cognac and sweetness and something that was just *her*, something that had stripped away his reason and driven him to—?

'Is it my turn now, plee-ee-ase?' Chloe was scampering up with big, excited eyes. Her facial expressions were a hundred per cent Simone, but she must have got her fair hair and blue eyes from André, the man who still owned Simone's heart.

He swallowed hard, shooting her a smile. 'Absolutely. Just let me shed this load first!' He gave Yann a boost then let go.

Yann whooped, riding the glide, then sprang off. Quick as a coin, he flipped himself over, his eyes on fire. 'When I get my own board, I'm going to go like a rocket!'

'No, you won't.' He tried adding a firm little note, Simone-style. 'You'll learn the basics and you'll go slowly to begin with.'

Simone came up. 'Yann, your *papa* is a big expert, remember.' For a beat her eyes met his, all warm. 'If you want to be as good as he is, you need to do what he says.'

'But slow is *so* boring.' Yannick was flapping his arms and legs, making a snow angel.

Snow angel!

'Is it my turn now…plee-ee-ase?' Chloe was tugging his sleeve.

'Chloe! Let Dax catch his breath, please.' The tugging stopped. Simone was raising her eyebrows at Chloe. 'You'll get a turn in a moment.'

Chloe let out a dramatic sigh then dived into the snow next to Yann. 'I made a snow bunny, see, over there.'

'Hey!' Simone was suddenly in front of him, her voice low but loaded with a smile. 'Things seem to be going well with Yann.'

Because of you. Because you came…

'Yes.' He licked his lips, trying not to look at hers. 'My son seems to have a sense for snow and a passion for speed.'

'It must run in the blood.' She chuckled. 'Like quicksilver!'

'Funny!' His ribs were going again. Something in her eyes was tugging at him, making him want to pull her into his arms and kiss her senseless. *Mistake!* He looked down, steadying himself, noticing her feet. Her boots were damp around the toe. Leaky! That wouldn't do, not at all. He looked up. 'So, last night I had an idea…'

'Oh?'

He could see the words *last night* glitching in her eyes, could feel them glitching in his own. He swallowed hard. 'I was thinking that you and the kids could come with me to Cham. You could have lunch at the resort while I'm on the slopes, then after we could hit town, do some snowboard shopping for the kids, and we need to get you some new boots…'

She seemed to falter, and then she smiled. 'That sounds great, but I don't need new boots.'

'You do! Your feet are wet!'

'They're not wet.' Her cheeks were colouring slightly. 'They're a little damp but it's fine.'

Why did she have to be so stubborn? He shifted stance. 'Please don't fight me. The deal was your fee *plus* expenses, and boots count as expenses. You wouldn't need them if you weren't here.'

'I just…' Something shimmered through her gaze, but he couldn't grasp it, couldn't make sense of it.

What he could sense, at the edge of his vision, was Chloe's pent-up excitement. He couldn't keep her waiting. 'Look, Sim. I *want* to buy you some boots, okay, so please, just let me!'

'All right.' She took a breath and then her gaze filled with warm light. 'You're so kind, Dax.'

He felt his breath catching. Had anyone ever looked at him the way she was looking at him?

'Honestly, it's nothing.' He took a backwards step, collecting himself. 'So, you're sure you're cool with me taking Chloe?'

'Of course…' Her eyebrows slid up. 'But no somersaults!'

'Aww…' He sagged, faking disappointment. 'Really?'

Her face broke apart, and then she was laughing, properly laughing all the way to her eyes. He felt his ribs loosening, his muscles, everything. This was better. The two of them getting on like before… Friends! On the way to being friends anyway, having fun in the snow with the kids on a bright, sunny morning with a great day ahead to look forward to. Looking forward was the thing. They'd made a kissing mistake, but they were pushing past it, moving on, and it was the right thing to be doing. Absolutely the right thing!

He tipped her a wink, then turned. 'Chloe! Are you ready for a ride?'

* * *

'*Vin chaud* or hot chocolate?' Dax's gaze was soft and twinkly, his hair rimmed with golden light from the Christmas stalls behind him. It was the same buttery light that was making Chloe's and Yann's faces glow, although the hefty packages under the table—two junior snowboards with boots and bindings—probably had something to do with it too. Early Christmas presents, he'd said.

Carpe diem! That was Dax. Bounding around in the ski shop, pulling out boards, running his fingers over them, scrutinising, then moving on to boots and bindings, checking the fit with the kids, being meticulous! And he didn't forget her boots, the boots that were keeping her toes toasty at that very moment, the boots she'd tried to refuse because for a split second she'd felt overwhelmed by him, overwhelmed that he'd even noticed the slight dampness around her toes when he'd been non-stop turning tricks and taking the kids for snowboard rides.

For a heartbeat, the light in his gaze had felt confusing. It had felt like something to take apart and think about, but then he'd mentioned expenses and she'd come to, remembering that they'd put the previous night behind them, that what they had was a business arrangement, a business arrangement that somehow still seemed to include warm twinkly gazes and snowboarding gear for Chloe. And now his wallet was out again. It was too much! It wasn't as if she didn't have money of her own now, thanks to him.

She reached into her bag. '*Vin chaud*, please, but I'm paying!' She pulled out two notes, offering them over with what she hoped was a firm look.

His head tilted.

'Dax, please...' He was doing that cute thing he did, that one-eye-closed scrunchy-smile thing, building up to a refusal. *Impossible!* She narrowed her eyes at him, trying not to laugh. 'Don't make me come over there.'

He fired a wild-eyed look at Chloe. 'Should I be scared?'

Chloe giggled, then nodded deeply at him. 'Yes. If you don't do what Maman says you'll be in *big* trouble.'

'Well, I definitely don't want to be in *big* trouble!' His eyes came back to hers, holding for a beat as he took the notes, making her breath catch. 'So, it's two deluxe hot chocolates, one *vin chaud*, a coffee and pastries!' He smiled a quick smile, then he was off, see-sawing through the crowd towards the hot-chocolate stalls.

She watched him disappearing, feeling all kinds of tingles. Warm ones for the way he'd been with the kids that morning. Grateful ones for his kindness over her boots and for getting them the perfect table on the viewing deck at the resort brasserie. And the usual ones that happened every time he was near. Hyper-aware tingles tuned to his contours, and the way he moved...the shift of his muscular shoulders, that physical confidence he had.

He'd been easy to spot on the slopes because he was the best. Over and over again he'd come hurtling down, flying off jumps, looping and twisting, somersaulting. She'd felt his adrenaline pumping through her own veins, felt his raw energy burning inside her. He'd looked so wild and free, so powerful. Sexy as hell...like on the couch, in his faded red shirt, with his hair still damp from swimming. She felt a tug, desire stirring. She couldn't forget the taste of him, the way his lips had felt on hers, the way they'd melted into each other, all tenderness and heat, then hunger rising and rising, oh, and the warm bliss of his hands on her body, his fingers teasing, that sweet ache—

'Simone, how long before I can do the things Papa does?'

She blinked. Yann was looking at her with serious eyes. 'How long?' She had to hold in a smile. Yann had barely touched his lunch. He'd been pressed to the rail, watching Dax. She'd stolen a picture on her phone—a son in the act of hero-worshipping his father—and texted it to Dax, just in case he ever needed reassurance about where he stood with Yannick. She took a breath, letting her smile out. 'To be honest, I'm not sure, but starting young is good and now you've got your board, and the best teacher in the world, then I think you'll learn quickly.' She looked at Chloe. 'And you will too. You'll both come on fast with Dax teaching you.'

'*See.*' Chloe was giving Yann a look. 'We're *both* going to be good.'

Yann grinned, then they started bumping shoulders, messing about. They were hungry, getting to the silly stage of tired. She looked up, scanning for Dax. The market was busy, full of glow and the sweet smell of crepes cooking, full of energetic-looking types in vibrant gear. Like Dax. 'Vibrant' summed him up perfectly. He was atomic, energetic, completely gorgeous, and—

Her mouth dried. There he was, standing near a stall, talking to a girl, a stunning girl in a bright blue parka. He was smiling and nodding, rocking back on his heels a bit, and the girl was talking and laughing, touching him, little touches, then longer ones, more like holding really, her blue-gloved hands on his forearms, her fingers going round, holding, holding on…

Simone looked down, seeing spots, hearing the blood roaring in her ears. Dax had mentioned his free-rider friends before. Pals, buddies, male friends, but of course there had to have been 'girl friends' too, and *girlfriends*… poised elegant girls like Blue Parka Girl.

Of course.

She gulped a breath, searching her mouth for moisture. Last night, after Yann had almost caught them, she'd back-pedalled, scared of getting close to Dax, scared for herself and for Chloe… And Dax had back-pedalled too, for Yann. They'd agreed that what had happened between them shouldn't have. But in spite of that, all day long it had felt that there was something still going on between them, something warm and wonderful flowing back and forth every time their eyes had met, and even though they'd agreed that the kiss had been a mistake, that bright, lovely thing shuttling between them had felt golden, like something to treasure. But now it felt as if it was being ripped away by a girl in a blue parka and she couldn't stand it… couldn't bear it!

Oh, God!

She gripped the table, head swimming. Last night, she'd told herself she couldn't let herself get close to Dax because she'd always be anxious about his free riding, because if anything happened to him then everything would come crashing down…but what was this feeling if not a crashing-down feeling? She was crashing hard, melting down, jealous of Blue Parka Girl. Feeling sick, feeling wronged, feeling too many churning emotions to count. She swallowed hard. Which could only mean that it was too late. *Too late!* She already *cared* about Dax, more than cared. *Oh, God!* She was in deep!

She drew a ragged breath and looked up. He was kissing the girl's cheeks, saying goodbye, his smile wide, his eyes all twinkly. Did they have plans for later? Her heart twisted. *Stop!* She needed to compartmentalise. Distract herself. *Fast!*

She looked at the kids, forcing out a smile. 'I think your hot chocolate is coming.' She frisked her hands together. 'Won't that be nice? Something hot to drink! Are you guys cold? Because I'm cold, freezing—'

'Perfect timing, then!' Dax was at her shoulder, sliding

a tray onto the bleached timber table. He slipped onto the bench beside her. 'Sorry that took a while. They ran out of *vin chaud*. I had to wait for them to make a new batch.'

Why couldn't she look at him? Why couldn't she stop her stomach from writhing? She passed serviettes to the kids, who were already tucking into their chocolate twists. 'It's fine. No need to apologise.' And then suddenly more words slid off some sharp edge on her tongue. 'It must have been *nice and warm* over by the stalls.'

There was a stinging silence, then the spots were flashing again, and regret was streaming through her veins. What was wrong with her? She was out of control. She had to rein it in. *Had to!* And then she felt his hand settling between her shoulder blades.

'If you're too cold we can go somewhere else.' There was a dry patch in his voice, a sort of crack, like thin ice breaking. 'We don't have to stay here...'

Her heart shrivelled. She'd hurt him. The last thing she ever wanted to do. She took a breath, trying to find a piece of steadiness. 'No, it's fine, really. I'm sorry.' She swallowed hard, forcing herself to look up. He looked bleached, his eyes loud and bruised. Her fault! But how to explain? How to make it right? She took a breath. 'I'm sorry. What I said came out all wrong...' *Breathe!* 'I'm not that cold.' She dug out a smile. 'How could I be in this lovely cosy jacket?' Something flickered behind his eyes. 'I just meant that it was probably warmer where you...' Her stomach tightened. 'But I'm fine.'

'Are you?' He tilted his head. 'Because we could go inside somewhere...' His gaze was searching, too hard to hold.

She looked at the kids, tucking in, all rosy-cheeked. They'd all had such a great day, because of Dax, because of his kindnesses. That was what she'd been thinking about before Blue Parka Girl had thrown her into a flat spin. That was what she needed to tell him, so he'd know how much he was appreciated.

She turned back to him. 'No, honestly. I want to stay here. It's lovely…the lights, and the nice smells, and the festive vibes! It was a good idea to come!' She felt warmth for him rising inside like light. 'You've given us such a fantastic day, Dax. I've loved every minute of it, the resort, Chamonix, seeing the streets and the horse traps. And now this!' The tension in his eyes was fading. She felt relief bubbling up, a smile spilling out. 'The cold might be freezing my cheeks off, but I don't want to be anywhere else.'

His gaze was clearing, warmth coming back in. 'Okay.' He picked up the *vin chaud* and put it into her hands, a smile touching his lips. 'Well, hopefully this will unfreeze your cheeks!'

'Thanks.' She slid her hands around it, nosing the warm cinnamon and clove aromas to hide the sudden wetness in her eyes. He was so lovely. No wonder she was feeling what she was feeling, but she couldn't do anything about it because he'd agreed with her, hadn't he, that their kiss had been a mistake? Yann was his priority, and, though he hadn't said it, he had his commitments to his sponsors too, the big 'adventure' he was planning. She shuddered around her glass. She'd just have to keep her feelings locked up: the deep ones, the jealous ones. She absolutely couldn't sting him like that again. He didn't deserve it. And *she* needed to remember why she was here: for Chloe, for Yann, and there was the money too.

She felt a sudden nudge, Dax's shoulder bumping hers. 'By the way, I got you this too.' A delicious-looking piece of flan slid into view. 'They said it was a special Christmas recipe…'

* * *

Yann was bouncing up and down on his bottom. 'I can't wait to try my board tomorrow!'

Full of life! Was this the same boy he'd brought back to Paris a few months ago? It didn't seem like it. This bouncy version of Yannick reminded him of himself. He pinned the duvet over Yann's knees, restraining him gently. 'Tomorrow will be here before you know it, especially if you settle down and go to sleep. Snowboarders need their rest so they're sharp on the slopes, so they don't make mistakes.'

'I was watching you the whole time today.' Yann collapsed backwards into his pillow. 'You didn't make any mistakes.'

He smiled. Just as well Yann's eyes weren't attuned to nuances yet. Being out there again had been a blast, but a few times he hadn't sailed high enough to pull off the somersaults as seamlessly as he'd wanted, and some of his landings had been a little off, but he'd been away for a while, hadn't he? So no surprise! A few more resort sessions would oil his wheels, and then he'd be good for the wild stuff. For now, he could use Yann's misapprehension to his advantage.

He shifted, tucking the duvet around Yann's chest. 'That's because I had a good night's sleep.' *White lie!* He'd actually had a restless night, thinking about Simone and the kiss and about her losing André so close to Christmas—December the seventeenth—how that must have felt, and then he'd been thinking about Yann's unexpected interest in snowboarding, feeling stoked about it. Maybe lack of sleep, and the little entourage—*his son*—watching from the restaurant deck had affected his performance on the slopes too. He'd only ever ridden for himself before—for satisfaction, for personal validation, for sponsorship money—but today he'd felt a sudden overwhelming desire to impress Yann, so that Yann would look up to him, admire him, see him as a father to be proud of. He'd never had that…a father to look up to, a father to share things with. It was the hole in his soul he'd learned to ignore, but on the slopes it had come to him that Yann's interest in snowboarding was a line he could ride, a line that might, one day, take him all the way into Yann's heart.

He finished with the duvet and sat back. It was already doing something, changing things. Yann was looking at him openly now, his eyes full of light and mystery. He felt a little pang in his chest. Zara had used to look at him like this. Could this be a Zara moment…? Could he make it into one somehow? His stomach tightened. Saying the wrong thing could mess things up, but Simone had said he should try and who'd have known better than her? She'd been there, got the tee shirt. He swallowed hard. He wasn't exactly comfortable, but this wasn't about *him*. He needed to try, for Yannick.

He took a breath and reached a slow hand to Yann's head, touching the springy dark hair that felt exactly like his own. Yann blinked but he didn't pull away. That was good. Encouraging! He licked his lips. 'Your eyes are just like your *maman*'s, you know.'

A shadow flitted across Yann's face.

His chest panged. Flitting shadows weren't good. He gulped a breath, clutching at straws. 'But I guess you know that already… I mean, people must say it…must have said it before.'

Lame!

Yann let out a little sigh.

His mouth turned to dust. Now what? He was looking at a stop sign. He swallowed hard, twirling one of Yann's curls around his finger and then suddenly he noticed Yann's eyes flickering, drooping a little. His breath caught. Had Zara played with Yann's hair like this? And then a memory surfaced. Hot nights, tangled sheets, lying in Zara's arms, her hands in his own hair, playing, twirling, always twirling.

Of course!

He felt a warm tide rising, a sudden peacefulness. 'Your *maman* liked your hair, didn't she?'

Yann nodded, his eyes drooping a little more.

He twirled his fingers for a while, then flattened his hand, stroking his son's dark curls, watching him drifting, feeling a strange tightness in his chest, an urge he couldn't contain. He leaned over, pressing his lips to Yann's forehead. 'She liked mine too.'

For a heartbeat Yann's hand connected with the place above his ear, and then he was turning, settling for sleep.

He felt a lump thickening in his throat. Had Yann's warm little touch been meant for him, or had it been a sleepy reflex meant for Zara? He breathed in slowly, deeply, feeling the weight of his mistakes pressing down on him all over again. He should have been better with Yann from the start. He'd filled Yann's room with toys, just as Colette had done with him, and then he'd given up when Yann hadn't fallen over himself with gratitude and joy. If it weren't for Simone's advice, he'd still have been getting it wrong, missing out on this strange, wonderful thing that was happening.

If it weren't for Simone...

He got to his feet, watching Yann for a moment longer, then he slipped out of the room and padded downstairs. In the hall he stood, listening to the low sound of the television coming from the den. Simone was in there, waiting for him, but he couldn't go in, not yet. He needed to be alone, needed space to think.

He went to his office and fell into the easy chair. That

edge on Simone's voice at the Christmas market and the desperate apologies that followed were niggling him. They'd moved past it, smoothed it so flat that he couldn't bring himself to ask her about it now, but still, it was bothering him. He wasn't good at leaving things alone: dripping taps, leaky boots, loaded tones.

He sighed. He just didn't get it. They'd had such a great day. Perfect weather! Buzzing resort! He'd got them a good table for lunch and, after his last run of the day, he'd taken them around Cham, pointing out the cool places. Simone had been sparkling, teasing him in the ski shop, smiling down at her new boots. In spite of the kissing mistake, it had felt as if something bright and alive was still flowing between them and he'd liked it. *Loved it!*

But then something changed. One minute she'd been all smiles, forcing money on him for the drinks, and the next, she'd been tight-lipped and spiky. A different person. It had knocked the wind out of him, killed his buzz. He'd felt flattened. *Hurt!*

He swallowed hard. It had pitched him backwards to his childhood. Colette, one minute warm and smiling, 'dying' to see the picture he was drawing for her, the next too busy with some waste-of-space loser to even look up from her champagne flute. And those soirées…taking his hand, leading him around like an exhibit, until some fawning sycophant had caught her interest. He'd been forgotten in the pop of a champagne cork. The next day, she'd be all over him again, playing the devoted mother, taking him to some fancy shop to buy him something he didn't want. With Colette, he'd never known which way the cards were going to fall. At fourteen, he'd seized the pack and dealt himself the cards he wanted. Money? Yes! School? No! Skateboarding? Yes! All day, every day! And at sixteen, he'd left, taking the credit card she'd given him when he was fifteen so he could 'sort himself out' with food or whatever during her frequent long weekends away. She'd always paid it off, no matter how much he ran up, because she was generous like that!

He got to his feet, pacing. Holding all the cards, calling all the shots was the only way not to get hurt, the only way he could be sure of not hurting anyone else. Honesty was key. With women, he always told them the truth upfront, made sure they knew he was only interested in physical kicks. No strings, no tomorrows, no heartbreak. But with Simone, he'd had to start in a different place. And he'd felt safe in her hands because she'd been kind and honest and wise, and yet still, even Simone, the only woman he'd ever trusted, had changed in a heartbeat, exactly like Colette!

He raked a hand through his hair. Except she wasn't like Colette, not at all! There had to have been a reason for the snarky tone she'd used on him, something he was missing. *Think!* She'd been fine when he'd gone off for the drinks, cool and stiff when he'd got back. There was something in between he wasn't seeing.

'*It must have been nice and warm over by the stalls...*'

Nice and warm...

Nice and warm...

His pulse jumped.

Pascale!

Had Simone seen him with Pascale? But why would that have upset her? Unless… Unless maybe she'd thought that he was *into* Pascale? But how on earth…? Was it Pascale being all over him? He blinked. But that was just Pascale. Touchy-feely! Just a touchy-feely friend, whereas Simone…

What was Simone?

He felt warmth swelling in his chest. Simone was more than a friend. Much more… She could turn him inside out with just a look, could stop his heart with a smile. Didn't she know that? Hadn't she felt it in his kiss? Or did she think, because he'd agreed it was a mistake, that it hadn't meant anything?

He felt a frown coming, confusion tangling inside. She'd said she'd kissed him because she was lonely, because it was a bad time of year. He'd got the impression that maybe, in her head, she'd been kissing André. It had stung, but if he was on the right beat about Pascale, if Simone had felt jealous of Pascale, then... His pulse quickened. Then maybe everything he'd felt in her kiss had been real after all—real for *him*, Dax, not André—the way she'd melted into him with soft little sighs, the way it had all felt so perfect...

He sat down again, heart pumping. But what to do? How to even make sense of all the things he was feeling about Simone? Like the way he loved talking to her and hearing her thoughts, even when they challenged his own. Like the way he loved spoiling her and Chloe just to see them smiling, just to feel their warmth flowing back. Like wanting Simone to believe in him, and in his sport, and in his sense for the mountain, so that she wouldn't be worried. Like wanting her to be proud of the way he was learning to be a parent.

He squeezed his eyes shut. He didn't just like Simone, he was crazy about her, but he couldn't march into the den and pull her into his arms, no matter how much he wanted to. They'd been there once and stepped back. Picking it up again would be a conscious decision, a commitment, and what did he know about commitment? It was what Simone would want, was no less than she deserved, but he didn't do love, didn't do relationships! He'd learned at his mother's knee that being close to someone only led to pain. He didn't want to feel pain or inflict it on anyone else, especially not Simone. The thought of hurting her the way he'd been hurt by Colette scared him more than riding down the steepest cliff.

He rubbed the back of his neck. And this wasn't just about him. Yann was coming out of his shell, letting him in, giving him something back…that little touch as he'd turned to go to sleep! Yann was happy, having a good time with Chloe, and with Simone, and with *him*! He couldn't risk changing the dynamic, risk embarking on something that could go wrong, that could chase away the only two people who mattered to his son.

He drew in a breath and stood up. He'd have to content himself with caring for Simone as a friend. He could still laugh with her, still talk to her, and enjoy her company. Being friends was safe. He could live with that. It was a win-win, for everybody.

CHAPTER NINE

December 17th

'MUSH! MUSH! MUSH!' Chloe was calling out to the dogs, flicking her arms for good measure.

Simone laughed all the way from her belly. Chloe was having the best time ever, and so was she, swooping through a frosted landscape behind a team of huskies. It was just like the picture on the dog-sledding website, except this was real. Completely perfect! High blue sky, sun catching at her eyes, Chloe in front, giggling. The pace was gentle, but the breeze on her face and the sound of the runners sloughing through the snow was making it feel faster somehow.

She twisted her head to look back at Dax, felt her heart filling. He'd planned this outing specially, to help her get through the anniversary of André's death. He hadn't said it, but she knew. It had been there in his eyes. It was classic Dax. Kind! Thoughtful!

His sunglasses glinted, then he was smiling, his voice coming over the swishing snow. 'Are you all right?'

Her heart filled again. He was always looking at her with that melting gaze he had, asking her if she was all right, making her feel cared for. *Cherished!* It made her want to throw her arms around him and tell him that he was cherished too. It made her want to tell him all the things she was holding inside, all the deep wonderful feelings that were growing and growing. She was a dam ready to burst. That was what it felt like.

She pushed up her sunglasses wanting him to see everything she was feeling. 'I'm better than all right! It's the best thing ever!'

He laughed, circling his hand. 'Eyes forward! You've got dogs to drive.'

She turned back, chuckling. *Dogs to drive!* The dogs seemed to know where they were going without any help from her. They were capering along panting misty breaths, tails going. It was all so lovely, dashing through the snowy pines with steep peaks rising through the mist in the distance. It was a sad day, yes, but she couldn't make herself feel sad because Chloe was in front trilling a happy little song from her favourite movie, and Dax was there, right behind her, filling her well.

She felt warmth pulsing through her veins. Dax was always filling her well, such as when he'd miraculously 'dug out' an old snowboard for her, a board that looked suspiciously brand new, so she could join in with Chloe and Yann's basic snowboard training. He'd held her waist from behind, gliding his board along with hers, keeping her straight, steadying her when she wobbled. It had felt wonderful, the board moving, his hands right there, his body behind hers, their breaths billowing and tingling, a special moment that had felt intimate even though Chloe and Yann had been watching.

That was Dax! Always giving. Even though he'd been busy on the slopes—the safe resort slopes, thank goodness—getting himself back to mountain fitness, busy with testing and reviewing kit for his sponsors and padding his social media feeds, he'd somehow still found time to organise some private ice-skating lessons for the kids, and he'd set them up with a block of skiing lessons too. All that, and what had she done? Stung him with her jealous words at the Christmas market, and even though it had happened days ago, and even though it hadn't put a dent in things, it was still a stone in her shoe, a constant irritation that she wanted to shake out.

She wanted to explain herself, open up her heart, but every time she'd tried the words had dried on her tongue, because explaining would have meant unravelling everything, going back to the kiss that they'd agreed was a mistake, and it had made her think about how she'd felt that night when Yann had come downstairs, how close a shave it had been, how it could have spoiled everything for Dax and his son. And then she'd thought about Chloe, about what they could both lose if she got tangled up with Dax and something happened to him. And when she'd thought of all that, it had seemed too big to talk about, too heavy, so she'd held it in.

But now Dax had done it again, surprised her with dog sledding, to take her mind off André. And he'd succeeded, except that it wasn't the dog sledding that was taking her mind off André. It was *him*! Everything he was. Handsome. Kind. Thoughtful. Generous. Her heart was full to the brim and there wasn't a thing she could do about it. She was deep in, falling deeper... What to do? How long could she keep these feelings in? She dropped her sunglasses over her eyes, gripping the sled handle hard. Not much longer. She didn't want to. No matter how complicated things were, she wanted to take that risk, tell him how she felt, shout it from the top of Mont Blanc. She was falling for Dax D'Aureval!

* * *

'That was so great!' Simone was all smiles. Beautiful. Radiant! Eyes, cheeks, lips. Perfect in her red jacket and the green hat he'd given her in Paris. She was perfect full stop.

He grinned. 'You're a natural musher.'

'Hmm...' She widened her eyes at him. 'Not so much at the beginning...'

The sight of her jogging—slipping and sliding—alongside the sled as the dogs fell into their running rhythm, then trying to jump on, had tickled him and Yann to bits. He felt his grin widening, sliding into goofiness. 'The getting-on part is always tricky...'

'It wasn't for you!' Her eyebrows slid up. 'You just leapt on.'

'I think we got the geriatric dogs, so—you know—slower.' He shot a glance at the kids, who were busy making a fuss of the huskies. 'They were too slow for Yann anyway.'

She chuckled. 'Actual light is too slow for Yann! He's high octane, like you!' Her hands went to the beanie, making some tiny invisible adjustment, then they fell again. 'Anyway, it was a lovely surprise. Thank you.' Her gaze tightened on his, something flickering behind it. 'You're very thoughtful, Dax.'

He drew in a careful breath. So she knew, or had guessed, that he'd organised the dog sledding to lighten her day! *This* day, the seventeenth... If she could read him that easily, what else was she reading on his face? Could she see how much he wanted to kiss her?

Her gaze softened, radiating warmth. 'Just so you know, I'm really okay about it being the day it is.' She took a little breath, a smile ghosting on her lips. 'I'm happy, you know, just being here. With you...' He felt his pulse quickening. Was she trying to tell him something, or was that just his own wishful thinking—?

'Yoh, Dax!'

She startled and he did too, but the voice ringing across the compound was familiar and dear. He threw his hand up. 'Hey, Victor!' He shot Simone a quick look. 'Victor's a buddy. He owns this place.'

'Ahh!' She took a backwards step. 'I'll leave you to catch up, then.' She smiled, dazzling him, then she grimaced, cartoon-style. 'Chloe's wanted a dog for ever, so I'd better go check she isn't stuffing a husky under her jacket!' She turned, walking away, her hair flowing from under the beanie, catching the breeze, glinting in the sun.

He felt a tug. Caring about Simone as a friend had been a good plan...in theory. The problem was, he couldn't seem to shoehorn his feelings into the friendship mould. He'd tried. He'd got her a snowboard so she could join in with Yann and Chloe's lessons but then hadn't been able to resist helping her balance by riding his board behind her with his hands on her waist, just to be near her, just to touch her. She was in his head all the time, messing with his pulse, making his chest go tight, then fuzzy, and the more time he spent with her, the worse it was getting. And maybe she was feeling it too because just now it had felt as if she was trying to tell him something significant. Victor's timing sucked!

'Hey, man!' Victor was stepping up, beaming.

'Hey, Vic! How's it going?' He held out his hand. 'I thought you'd be out skiing.'

Victor pumped his hand, then landed a few hearty slaps on his back. 'No. I'm playing midwife today.' He chuckled. 'We're having puppies!'

'Nice!'

'It's so good to see you, Dax! It's been a while, huh?' His eyes narrowed. 'What are you doing here? Don't tell me you're sledding?'

'Yep! We just got back!' He took a breath. 'Family outing.'

Victor's mouth fell ajar. '*Family* outing?'

He felt his cheeks growing warm. Victor wasn't in the loop. Very few of his buddies were. He nodded. 'That's right. I have a son.' He motioned to the kids. 'He's over there with his friend. His name is Yannick.'

Victor turned to look. 'Christ! Mini-Dax! How did—?'

He cut in. 'It's a long story.' One he didn't want to get into at that moment. 'I'll tell you another time.'

'Okay.' Victor's eyes gleamed. 'And who's the lovely lady? Yann's *maman*?'

'No. Simone's my...' He looked over. She was bending to pet the dogs, laughing at something the kids were saying. He swallowed. 'She looks after Yannick when I'm riding. The little girl is her daughter, Chloe, Yann's best friend.'

Victor swung round to look, then swung back, scratching his ear. 'I'm impressed! You've got yourself quite a little family there.'

For some reason, he didn't feel the slightest inclination to protest.

He grinned. 'You're not doing too badly yourself! Puppies, huh?'

'Funny!' Victor rolled his eyes. 'I'm planning ahead! Some of the dogs will be retiring soon. This is our second litter this winter.' He shifted on his feet. 'Hey! If you're not in a dash, maybe Yann and Chloe would like to come and play with older puppies for a while. They need socialising.' He let out a hearty chuckle. 'The puppies, I mean, not the kids.'

His heart pulsed. With the kids out of the way, maybe he and Simone could pick up their conversation. 'They'd love it, I'm sure!' He threw an arm around Victor's shoulders and started walking him towards the kids. 'Chloe's desperate for a dog, apparently, so cuddling some puppies is going to be right up her street!'

'It's like a fairy tale!' Simone was turning slowly, looking up and around, her voice hushed and full of wonder. 'There aren't even any footprints. It's like no one's ever been here before!'

She was right. The glade was pristine, shimmering with lemony light, plushily silent.

'Maybe they haven't. Victor only completed it last year.' He felt his stomach churning. So much for picking up their earlier conversation! They were out of sight of the compound now, starting along the woodland trail, a perfect, private spot, and suddenly he was tongue-tied, full of doubts, reduced to making polite conversation. *I'm happy...just being here. With you...'* It had sounded as if she was trying to tell him something, but what if he was wrong? If he blew it, it would spoil the happy day he'd planned.

She was coming round to face him again, an irresistible bundle of red jacket, and green beanie, and glossy hair, and those eyes, holding his, turning him inside out, tying his knots into knots.

He swallowed a dry edge in his mouth. 'He wants to pull in summer visitors. So there's a woodland walk. Picnic areas. He's talking about putting in an adventure playground for the kids.'

'Anything that keeps kids entertained is a bonus.' A smile touched her lips. 'Like puppies...'

Even that sounded like an oblique message. Or was he just losing the plot altogether?

She tilted her head slightly. 'So...have you known Victor a long time?'

He bit his teeth together. 'Yeah. Vic's a free skier. We used to—' He clamped his mouth shut. He couldn't do this, small-talking. He didn't know whether he was coming or going, imagining signs or not, but it was time to seize the pack, start dealing the cards he wanted. He closed the distance between them, fastening his eyes on hers. 'Look, Simone, I don't want to talk about Victor.' He could feel his pulse pounding through his skin. 'I want to talk about us.'

She blinked. 'Us?'

'Yes…' His pulse was in his ears now, hammering softly. 'You said back there that you were happy here, *with me*, and the way you said it…well…it felt like you were trying to tell me something, but I don't know…' he swallowed, trying to read the changing landscape in her eyes '…and I want to…need to.'

Her mouth was working, and then her eyes filled, gleaming, tugging his heart right out. 'What if I *was* trying to tell you something?' She took a breath. 'What if I was trying to tell you that you make me happy all the time, every day? What if…?' Her eyes were reaching in, taking him apart. 'What if I were to tell you that, that… I care about you, Dax?' He felt his ribs loosening, tenderness rushing in. 'And what if I just didn't know how to say it because I wasn't sure?' Her lips stiffened. 'Because we said it was a mistake…'

His heart pulsed. 'Oh, Simone…' He felt a powerful warmth rising inside, a slew of emotions he couldn't name. 'Maybe it just felt like a mistake at the time because of Yann.' He put his hands on her shoulders, tightening his gaze on hers, loading it with everything he was feeling. 'But now, all I know is that whatever we started, I can't seem to switch it off. I can't make myself not want to be with you.'

The gleam in her eyes turned to a bright warm glow. 'And I can't make myself not want to be with you either.'

For a beat, his breath stopped and then he couldn't hold back. He took her face in his hands and lowered his mouth to hers, wanting to show her all the things he was feeling inside, things he couldn't even name. Her lips were perfect, meltingly warm, yielding, and suddenly he was burning up inside, exploding, his senses skewing just as they had the first time. He pulled her in hard, deep kissing, losing himself in the heat of her mouth, the maddeningly sweet taste of her, until she was moaning softly, pulling him in, tangling her fingers in his hair and it was too much but not enough. He hooked his arm around her waist, lowering her into the snow, kissing her face, her neck, her mouth again, feeling his veins blazing, feeling her body moving, rising against him, and then she was holding his face, stroking his cheeks, burning his lips with hers until his breath was broken.

He pulled away, pulse racing, taking in the flush in her cheeks, the haze in her eyes. Her lips looked red and full. His felt scorched. He wanted her with every fibre of his being, but not here, in the snow, with the clock running down. When he made love to her, he wanted to do it slowly, and in comfort. He drew in a breath, combing a lock of hair away from her cheek with his finger, looking into the soft glow of her gaze. 'Are you all right?'

'More than all right.' She smiled a slow smile. 'You're always asking me that.'

'Because I always want to know.' He kissed her, feeling a fresh tug of desire. 'And since I seem to have thrown you to the ground, I definitely need to know because I might have to check for injuries!'

She started to giggle. 'No injuries!' She put her hand to his face. 'And you didn't throw me down. I think I was going dizzy, and you caught me!'

'Dizzy doesn't sound good.' Her touch and the look in

her eyes were messing with his pulse, making his own head swim.

'It was fine!' Her lips curved up. 'It was the *best* kind of dizzy.'

'Ah, that kind!' She was irresistible, almost too lovely to look at. 'I think I'm feeling it right now, looking at you.'

'And you looking is making me feel it again.'

He kissed her nose, then shifted, propping himself up on his elbow. 'We should just stay like this for a while until it passes.'

'It won't pass.' She turned her head, trapping him in a soft twinkly gaze. 'That's the problem I have with you, Dax D'Aureval. You make me dizzy all the time.'

'Right back at you.' He felt his throat thickening, something welling up inside. He swallowed. 'From that very first moment.'

'At the bistro door...' Her eyes filled with a gleam. 'Me too.'

Snowflakes melting on her eyelashes, that luminous smile. He traced a finger over her cheek, feeling its coolness, its softness, feeling a rush of tenderness. 'My first thought was: Snow Angel.'

Her eyes filled. 'That's so...romantic.' And then her lips quirked and suddenly she was giggling. 'You were Monsieur Blue Jacket, which isn't very imaginative, but I was, you know, dizzy!'

'You were perfect.'

She pulled a screwy face. 'Erm, no! My hair was a mess, and I had panda eyes.'

'I didn't notice. I just saw you.'

Her eyes held him for a beat, and then she chuckled. 'God, you're a smooth talker! Do you practise in the mirror?'

He grinned. 'Every day.'

She smiled, and then she was wriggling away from him. 'We should make a move. The kids will be wondering where we are.'

'They're knee-deep in puppies. They don't care where we are.'

'Come on!' She was sitting up, tugging at his sleeve. 'We should get back.'

He jumped up, pulling her to her feet, then he picked up the beanie.

'I'll have to say I fell.' She was looking down at her jeans, rubbing at the damp patches.

'Well, it's the truth! Kind of!'

'Funny!' She flicked him a smile that made his heart skip.

Snow Angel! God, she was lovely, and she cared about him, in spite of her misgivings about his free riding. *That* was really something! His stomach tightened. Could he be as strong for her, not cause her any pain? Was he going to be any good at the relationship thing? It was all so new, and it wasn't as if they only had themselves to think about. Was being a little bit scared acceptable?

She was smoothing her hair now, scanning the ground for the beanie.

'I've got it!'

She looked up. 'Ah!'

He brushed it off, then stepped in, fitting it to her head, feeling her eyes warming his face. He met her gaze. Scared or not, he couldn't not want her, couldn't not want to try being everything she needed. He put a hand to her cheek. 'Sim, just so we're absolutely clear, this isn't a mistake, okay?'

'I know.' She smiled, and then her eyes became serious. 'But we should talk about the practicalities.'

'You mean the kids?'

She nodded. 'We need to be discreet.'

'In case it turns out to be a mistake?'

She nodded, frowning a bit. 'Not very romantic, is it? But I suppose that's the way it is with kids...' She gave a little shrug. 'I haven't exactly been here before.'

'Me neither, but you already know that.' It wasn't romantic, but squaring things away was good. They had to protect the kids. 'I agree about being discreet.' He took a breath. 'Also, I need to tell you something...'

A shadow crossed her face. 'What?'

His chest panged. She was such a worrier. He tugged her close, looking into her eyes. 'It's nothing bad, just something you should know.' He could feel his heart drumming, a prickling at the back of his neck. Was it ridiculous to be feeling embarrassed? He took a deep breath. 'I'm a relationship virgin.'

Her face stretched. 'Really? You've never...' And then her expression softened. 'I suppose all the travelling's not exactly conducive...'

'No. No, it isn't.' He felt a prick of guilt. It was only a white lie and it could well have been true! Travelling *was* a barrier to relationships unless your girlfriend was into the free-riding scene. The truth could wait. He didn't want to be unravelling his inner psyche right now, getting into all his Colette hang-ups. Simone was in his arms in a snowy glade with lemony light catching her eyes. All too soon they'd be back with the kids. Right now, all he wanted to do was kiss her.

CHAPTER TEN

Later...

'DO YOU KNOW what I feel like?' Dax was twinkling at the kids, making their eyes dance. 'I feel like making fondue! Who'd like to help?'

Chloe and Yann both yelled, 'Me!' then burst out laughing.

Dax laughed too and then his eyes found hers, full of slow burn and the secret they were keeping.

She felt her breath catch, her insides turning to liquid. She could hardly believe what had happened between them in the woods, could hardly believe that they were starting something after all, taking a chance on each other. She felt a smile coming, a rush of pure joy behind it. 'Are two helpers enough or do you need me too?'

'You can spectate for now.' He grinned, flashing his eyebrows in that mischievous way he had. 'You're probably still catching your breath, huh?'

She felt a giggle vibrating in her belly. He was speaking in riddles for the kids' sake, but she could read him. He wasn't only alluding to their tumble in the snow and all the kisses they'd shared on the way back to the sledding centre. He was teasing her about the luge, the luge on rails alpine coaster that had been his second surprise of the day.

After they'd peeled the kids off the puppies, he'd driven them to Domaine des Planards amusement park. 'The luge is good fun,' he'd said. 'It's not as fast as the real thing, but I think you'll handle it.'

'Me?' She'd felt her stomach collapsing. She hated roller coasters, hated the feeling of not being in control, and the toboggans that were flying along the rails and screaming around the tight bends had looked insanely quick. Not her thing at all. She'd tried to put her foot down. 'I'm not going on that!'

'Simone!' He'd leaned in, squeezing her elbow, breathing words into her ear. 'I'm bigging it up for Yann and Chloe! Kids three years and over can ride this thing, but they have to be accompanied by an adult, which means you've got to ride it.' Big, brown eyes—not so innocent eyes—had fastened on hers. 'You *can* control the speed if you want to, but where's the fun in that?' His eyebrows had flickered out a challenge. 'Brakes are for wimps!'

She held in a smile. The tow up had seemed interminable. She'd plastered on her game face for Chloe's sake, fake smiling and waving at Dax when he'd turned around from the toboggan in front to throw her a cheeky grin. Chloe had been in the front seat, chattering away nonchalantly about the puppies, her little feet twitching against the footrests. Simone had made the appropriate responses, but the serene blue sky and the steady green pines ahead, and the skiers blithely whizzing past on the slopes around them, had seemed like a cruel taunt, a happy world away from the gnawing in her belly and from the rhythmic, metallic clunk of the toboggan as it went up, and up, and up. And then there'd been that jolting halt at the top, watching Dax and Yann's toboggan taking off, disappearing round the first bend at full pelt.

They'd had to wait another interminable minute before

their own toboggan had started its death dive. Instantly, Chloe had let out an excited little screech, following it with whoops and deep, rolling chuckles. Simone's stomach had been dipping and clenching, performing acrobatics, but then somehow all that had seemed to stop, and the speed had started to feel exhilarating. Suddenly, she'd been laughing too, leaning into the experience, soaking it up, going with it instead of fighting it. By the third bend, she'd abandoned the brake, had heard her own squeals soaring with Chloe's, flying free on the wind as the speed and the G-force had tugged and pulled, and it had felt terrifying and thrilling and empowering all at the same time.

When she'd tumbled off with Chloe at the end of the ride, high as kite and tingling all over, Dax had been waiting, his eyes merry and wicked. 'So, are you up for another go?'

She gave herself a little hug inside. She'd jumped at the chance! *Her!* Simone scaredy-cat Cossart! They'd ended up having three more goes, swapping round so they each got two rides with Yann and two with Chloe. Afterwards, Dax had taken them for crepes. And now, he was showing Chloe and Yann how to rub cut garlic around the fondue pot, looking every perfect inch of him like the perfect father.

'It adds a nice flavour.' His eyes lifted to hers, flickering. 'Makes the fondue even more tasty.'

Her pulse spiked. Dax could turn her inside out with a single glance. She felt a rush of happiness, a mad tingling in her belly. Everything was opening up between them, unfolding, and it felt so good. Yes, things were complicated, but the direction of travel felt right. Going forwards. Going forwards at last, after three long years of simply existing.

She looked at Chloe. She was looking up at Dax with shining eyes. André's eyes! Chloe was so like André. Her smile, her frown, just like his. She felt a tug of sadness, strangely, not for herself, but for André's parents. In spite of what day it was, she was on top of the world, but they had nothing, only photographs and emptiness. She felt a lump thickening in her throat. They could have had so much more. They could have been seeing what she was seeing now: André living on in his daughter. They'd cut off their noses to spite their faces. So sad. So stupid! How could they have let their grief shut them in like that, cutting them off from love and happiness, and all the things in life that were still good, and pure, and true? All the things she was feeling for Dax.

Dax! Supervising Yann with pouring beer into the fondue pot, and at the same time directing Chloe to a shelf in the fridge to get the cheese, smiling the whole time. He was something else!

She slipped off her stool and leaned over the island unit. 'So, where did you learn to make fondue?'

He looked up briefly, and then he was setting the pot on the hob, lighting the gas, adjusting the flame until it was a small glow. 'Colette used to make it for me sometimes when I was little…' A shadow smudged his face. 'She used to let me help. My job was adding the Gruyère.' He turned to Chloe and Yann. 'Which is what you two are going to be doing in a minute. But first, we need to chop the cheese up. Chloe! How are your knife skills?'

Chloe's eyes popped. 'What are knife skills?'

'I guess that answers my question.' His eyes caught hers, his gaze steely. 'Simone, are you okay with me teaching Chloe some knife skills?'

Her breath stopped. Was he mad? The knife in his hand was hefty, glinting with sharp intent.

She shook her head. 'No! Definitely not. She's six!'

He shrugged, frowning. 'Don't you think it's good to

teach kids this stuff when they're young? It's like snow-boarding or playing the piano.'

She felt her neck prickling. 'No! Actually…no! Playing the piano is rather different from playing around with sharp objects—'

'*Simone!*' His lips were twitching, and then he was cracking up, laughing into her eyes. 'I was joking!' He was shaking his head at her, warm light twinkling in his eyes. 'You're *so* serious sometimes.'

He was right, she *was* serious, especially where Chloe was concerned. When it came to Chloe, her protective radar was set to max. How could she even have thought he was being serious? He colour-coded his storage boxes, for pity's sake, kept his ropes and snowboards in impeccable rows. He wasn't reckless!

She shook her head. 'You got me!'

'Got you good!' He flashed a smile and then something openly seductive slipped into his gaze. 'So, I'm chopping the cheese; Chloe and Yann are going to throw it in; but we're going to need a responsible adult to do the stirring while I get on with cubing the bread.'

Responsible adult? He was up to something, luring her over. She held onto a smile, tingling inside. Being close to Dax was exactly where she wanted to be, near enough to catch the deep, warm scent of him. She moved around the island unit, watching him chopping and divvying up the cheese between the kids, until she was there at his side near the hob, standing close, feeling little sparks flying between them.

'Here.' He put a wooden spoon into her hands, his gaze steady except for a pinprick glow of mischief. 'Do you know the correct stirring action required for a fondue?'

She felt a smile aching in her cheeks. She was getting his drift, feeling a thrill of wickedness quivering in her belly. She held his gaze. 'To be honest, no, I'm not completely sure. I don't make fondue myself.'

His eyebrows flickered. 'In that case, I'll have to show you.' He moved in close. She breathed in the warm base notes of his cologne, felt the floor sliding under her feet. His eyes darkened. 'So you need to face the hob, obviously.'

She bit her lips together hard, holding onto the bubble of laughter that wanted to come out. 'Okay.' She sucked in a breath and turned her back to him. 'And I guess I put the spoon into the pot now…?'

One warm hand landed on her waist, followed a nanosecond later by the warm, gentle pressure of his whole body against her back. His voice was low. 'That's right.' His voice turned upbeat. 'Okay, kids, you can start adding the cheese… Yann! Not too much at once. Simone needs to stir it in…' His voice dropped again. 'She needs to melt it, slowly.' She felt the pressure of his body against hers increasing, felt a small gasp lodging in her throat. She looked at Chloe and Yann quickly. Their faces were fused in concentration over their separate bowls of cheese. She stirred slowly, pushing herself back, by degrees, against Dax, fighting a near impossible urge not to laugh out loud.

'Here…' His voice seemed to catch, and then it was trickling into her ear on a warm breath. 'I don't think you've got that quite right yet.' His right arm moved around hers, and then his hand was covering hers on the spoon, guiding her. 'Like this, see, round and round, so that all the cheese melts…slowly.'

'I think it's ready!' Yann was leaning over the pot, staring into it. 'I'm starving. I want to have some right now!'

'Me too.' Chloe looked up, and then her head tilted in a frown. 'Dax, did you do the bread yet?'

From behind, Dax produced a hearty cough that was full of unexploded laughter.

She stifled an explosion of her own, turning off the gas, and then she looked at Chloe. 'No, he hasn't. He's been slacking but I'm sure he's about to jump right to it.'

Dax sipped his beer, staring at the computer screen. Going over the route for his first proper free ride wasn't distracting him after all. He was still thinking about Simone, wondering why she'd disappeared into her room after they'd put the kids to bed. He tapped his teeth together. Was she all right? Had he done something wrong? He moused over the satellite picture of the couloir, zooming, and scrolling, feeling his stomach churning. She wasn't having second thoughts, surely…? *No!* She'd been warm and smiling all afternoon and through dinner, sending him looks that had stopped his heart. He sighed. Maybe the whole André anniversary thing was weighing on her, making her feel awkward about the evening ahead, about being alone with him. *Oh, God!* Did she think he had expectations?

He set his beer down, heart going. He wanted her, yes, more than anything, wanted to unwrap her, very slowly, but it didn't have to be tonight. If it was feeling wrong to her because it was the anniversary of André's death, then he totally respected that! He could give her space, time, anything she wanted. He just wanted to know that she was all right. Knowing for sure. That was his thing. His insecurity. Courtesy of Colette!

He pushed the thought away, and moved the mouse, tilting the image so he could see the view from the summit. So different from the side-on views. From the top, features flattened, disappearing altogether sometimes. It was a question of looking from all angles, holding the shape of the line in your head. In spite of his jitters, he felt a smile coming. Simone's shape was burned on his brain and he'd got a good idea of her lines when she'd pushed back against him stirring that fondue. Making fondue was relationship stuff! Having fun in the kitchen. Being naughty! It had felt as hot as…but then Chloe had called him out over the bread, and that had been that. *Family stuff!*

'Hey…'

Simone! He spun his chair and felt warmth taking him over. She was coming towards him, gorgeous in a low-necked blouse and dark jeans, her hair loose and gleaming. So *that* was what she'd been doing, trying to perfect perfection.

He got up, stepping out from the desk. 'Hey!'

She walked into his arms and lifted her face, smiling. 'I thought you might be in here.'

He kissed her, lingering for a moment, losing himself in the warmth of her lips, feeling the first hot lick of desire, and then he broke off. He was going to give her space, let *her* lead the way. He smiled. 'I was just checking something out.' He released her, stepping back. 'You look lovely.'

She tossed her hair then shot him a quirky little smile. 'Well, it's our first official date! I thought I should make an effort.' And then her eyes slid past him, narrowing. 'Meanwhile, you're playing computer games!'

He felt a smile creasing his cheeks. 'Not exactly, but I'll switch it off now.'

'No, don't.' She was going over to the desk. 'I'd like to see what you're looking at. It looks…weird.'

He followed her, catching the delicate scent of her perfume. 'It's mountain porn, only interesting to mountaineers, but if you really want to see it…'

'I do.' She sat down and peered at the screen, her brow furrowing. 'It's incredibly detailed.'

'It's a geo map. The couloir I'll be riding in a couple of days. We're doing a film, promoting a board…' He felt shy suddenly. 'It's a board I had a hand in designing so it's kind of a big deal.'

She twisted her head. 'You're a designer too?' And then she was giggling. 'No wonder you have to pack in the protein.'

He felt a jolt in his belly, laughter starting. 'You saw that, huh?'

She was wide smiling. 'It's your best role yet! I went straight out to buy that yoghurt!'

She was too lovely. All sparkling eyes and alluring neckline. But it wasn't just that. She was interested in the map, and in the descent that he was planning. It meant a lot.

'I made that advert back in my competition days. I don't advertise that stuff any more.' He tore his eyes away from hers and leaned over to move the mouse, hovering the cursor over a point at the summit. 'So…the helicopter will drop me here…'

'Helicopter?' The chair spun and his pulse spiked. She was looking up at him, giving him a bird's-eye view down the front of her blouse. Milky throat, collarbones, breasts cupped in dark lace.

He swallowed hard. 'I have to ride the line over and over so the camera crew can take different angles. A helicopter's the quickest way to get me back to the top.'

She grimaced a bit. 'I find helicopters terrifying!'

'Like the luge was terrifying?'

Her lips parted for a beat and then she smiled. 'Well, maybe I'm growing! Today, I went on a ride suitable for three-year-olds. In twenty years, who knows? I might graduate to helicopters!'

He couldn't not put a hand to her cheek. 'I'd like to be there to see that.'

Something came and went behind her eyes, and then she was rising up, sliding her arms around his neck, her gaze reaching right in, taking him all apart. 'I think we should start our date now.'

He felt a tingle starting. 'What do you want to do?'

A smile touched the corners of her mouth. 'I think you know.'

She nestled into Dax's firm warmth, smiling inside. She couldn't make herself regret this, even though it was the anniversary of André's death, even though the geo map of the couloir had stirred a dread in her belly that she'd had to hide. Right now, Dax was here, safe, in her bed and in her heart. Deep in. Secretly. She ran her fingers over his chest. Smooth. Contoured in all the right places. Was she deep in his heart too, secretly? Was that what she'd seen in his eyes when he'd said that thing about wanting to be there in twenty years to see her braving a helicopter…? Only he knew, but she'd felt something, something that had stopped her breath and drawn her to her feet.

His hand suddenly covered hers, squeezing softly. 'Are you all right?'

How couldn't he know? She hadn't held anything back, wouldn't have been able to even if she'd tried. She shifted so she could see his face. 'What would you guess?'

His eyebrows drew in. 'I think, maybe…yes…'

'Then you're right!'

'Good!' His eyes crinkled. 'I like to be sure.'

'I've noticed.'

A shadow flitted across his face. 'Does it annoy you, me asking all the time?'

'No. I just sometimes wonder how you can't tell.'

For a beat, his face stiffened, and then he sighed. 'That would be down to Colette. She messed me up good!'

She felt her stomach tightening. She had a low enough opinion of his mother already, not being 'hands-on', not helping him with Yann, not remembering his favourite toys, letting him leave home at sixteen. *Sixteen!* What else was left for her to have screwed up?

She wriggled out of his arms, settling herself on her side. 'Do you want to talk about it?'

'Not really.' He turned his head, trapping her in a pained gaze, and then he was rolling over to face her. 'Colette's flaky, okay. As a kid, I never knew whether I was in or out.' His voice cracked a little. 'The worst thing was, she could change in a heartbeat, go from sweet and smiling to not, and I'd think it was my fault, that I'd caused it.' His focus seemed to turn inwards. 'If I'd had a father around, to balance it out, maybe…'

She felt tears thickening in her throat, burning behind her eyes. André's parents had changed in a heartbeat too, but she'd only had to endure the pain once, as an adult, not over and over again as a child.

He sighed. 'I got in the habit of trying to pre-empt her, asking if she was all right, and I'd keep asking, just to be sure, because if she was all right—'

'Then it meant you could feel okay too.' She swallowed hard. He was breaking her heart.

He nodded slowly. 'I could never work out if she loved me. Sometimes she'd look at me as if she did, but then…' He shrugged. 'By the time I got to my teens, I was sick of being on the receiving end. I turned bad, cut school all the time to go skateboarding. I wanted to wind her up, get to her…'

'No, you didn't.' His eyes went silent. 'You wanted her to say stop.'

He looked at her for a long second and then he blinked. 'Deep down, I suppose that's what I was doing, yes. If she'd stopped me, it would have meant she cared but she never said a word.' He took a breath and then a smile touched his lips. 'The silver lining was that I got really good at skateboarding, which made moving to snowboarding a breeze, and that was good because from the moment I put my feet into those bindings my life started making sense.' His eyes were filling with light. 'Everything felt right. I was in my element. I won competitions. Got noticed. I went from being a rich entitled brat with "issues" to being a respected sportsman and as long as I kept delivering on the slopes, as long as I kept myself at the top of the game, the benefits flowed in. Sponsorship, travel, friends…yoghurt adverts! After Colette, it was liberating. No second-guessing. No wondering if I was in or out. I knew exactly what I had to do to earn my place.'

Earn your place! She took a needle to the heart. On the slopes Dax looked so powerful, so self-assured, but on the inside, he was absolutely not all right, and all because of Colette! She swallowed hard. 'Is Colette proud of you now? Does she watch you? Your films?' *Does she know the risks you take?* She could hear the bitter edge in her voice. 'Does she ever visit?'

He shook his head. 'I don't know what she thinks, and no, she doesn't visit. Colette hates Cham. She's not a snow person.'

Not a mother, not a grandmother, not a support, not a helpmate, and now, conveniently, not a snow person. Colette was blessed with a beautiful son, and a beautiful grandson. How couldn't she see it, how couldn't she love them?

'Hey!' He was frowning. 'Are you all right?'

'No, actually…' She sat up, heart trembling, tears thickening in her throat. 'I can't stand it, Dax, hearing about Colette… The way she is, the way she's been, not caring about you, not helping, not caring about Yann…'

He was rolling up, putting his hands on her shoulders,

taking her apart with his eyes. 'Simone, baby, where's all this coming from?'

'From bitter experience...' She clamped her eyes shut, trying to stop her tears spilling out, but it was no good, they were winding down her cheeks with all the hate and pain she had inside. She swallowed hard, meeting his gaze. 'I know how it *feels*, Dax, that's why I'm raging.' Her chest was exploding, debris flying. 'After André died, my in-laws turned on me and Chloe without warning! I'd thought they were decent people, but they shut their door on us. On *Chloe*, for God's sake, their own granddaughter! *Why?* I just can't get my head around it. My in-laws! Your mother! Behaving, like, I don't know what! What's *wrong* with them all?'

'I don't know.' His eyes were reaching in, clouding, and then his hands tightened on her shoulders. 'What do you mean, they *turned* on you?'

'They blamed me!' Suddenly, her throat was full of dust. 'For everything!'

He shifted, pulling the duvet up around her, and then his eyes were on hers again. 'Breathe, and then talk...'

His gaze was warm, bolstering. She wiped her face, then inhaled slowly, feeling her pulse slowing, moisture softening her mouth. 'André's parents are wealthy. He was an only child, their only focus. He was a violinist, like me, but super talented. His parents had thrown a lot at tuition. They were *invested*, had high expectations, and he did too. He wanted to be first violin in the Paris Orchestra...

'We were students when we met. Just before we graduated, I found out I was pregnant.' Dax's eyebrows flickered. 'We were shocked, but we were in love, so we got married. My in-laws helped us with money, paid the rent on a decent apartment. André kept on with his music. I looked after Chloe, and, when I could, I played with a string quartet, to keep my hand in. And then…it happened.' She felt her breath stalling, her eyes prickling again. 'He was carrying Chloe's Christmas present across the road when the car struck him. A huge box. A doll's house we'd picked out for her…'

Dax took her hands, folding them into his, his eyes searching. 'I still don't see—'

'Why would you?' She felt a fresh wave of anger building. 'There's no logic! His parents came unhinged, needed to blame someone and that someone was me. It went like this: I got pregnant on purpose to trap André into marrying me because… I was a gold-digger!'

His mouth fell open. 'No!'

'Oh, it gets worse.' His eyes narrowed. 'They said that if André hadn't had a child, he'd never have been on that crossing with that child's Christmas present…*that child*, thank you very much!' She couldn't stop now, her words coming, her tears flowing, everything pouring out. 'They cut us off, turned their backs. They won't see Chloe and I just can't…' She gulped down a breath. 'I just *can't* understand. She's so, so beautiful…a piece of André right there that they could be cherishing. Why don't they love her? Why don't they want her in their lives?'

Dax was shaking his head. 'Oh, Simone.' And then his arms were going around her, and she was melting into him, letting it all out, and he was holding her tight and close, stroking her hair and, after how long she couldn't tell, she felt the grip of her anger loosening, and her pain was flowing away, flowing, and flowing, and suddenly there was room to breathe, light streaming in.

Maybe he sensed it because suddenly he was nuzzling her hair. 'Why didn't you go home?'

She eased herself out of his arms, meeting his warm, brown gaze. 'I don't know… Maybe deep down, I didn't want to feel like I'd been defeated. I love my parents, but I'd always dreamed of living in Paris. I wanted to take Chloe to André's favourite places, talk about the things he'd loved, so she'd feel him more, so he wouldn't be just a face in a photograph.'

'Keeping him alive for her, like you told me to do with Zara…'

She nodded. 'It seemed even more important after what her grandparents did.' She drew in a slow breath, looking into his face. Melting gaze. Dark, dark lashes. That perfect mouth. So handsome! Talking was good, sharing things was good, but she was tired of talking now. She rose up onto her knees, letting the quilt fall, taking his face in her hands, running the tip of her nose along his. 'Are you all right, Dax?'

His eyebrows flashed. 'I think I'm about to be.'

She felt a smile coming. 'I think you could be right.'

CHAPTER ELEVEN

December 20th...

'LAST RUN, DAX.' Pierre's voice was crackling in his ear. 'Make it count!'

'Don't I always?'

'Negative!' Pierre was chuckling. 'Your last run sucked!'

He felt a smile coming. 'Take a hike, slacker!' Pierre goading him was normal. It was what they did, winding each other up, but he just wanted to get going. 'Look, I'm ready! Set me free, man.'

'Hang on—' Pierre's voice dropped out, then came back. 'Sorry, Dax. Take five, Axel's got an issue with the drone.'

His stomach dived. He was loose, raring to go. Waiting was a buzzkill! He sighed into the microphone. 'Copy that.'

He slid back six inches and pushed up his goggles. Big sky, wide vista, splintered peaks... This was his world, his stomach-clenching, heart-thumping world. He inhaled, long and slow. Yann thought he was fearless, watched his films over and over. He was always asking questions, admiration burning in his eyes. Dax felt his chest filling. Being admired by Yann felt huge. *Massive!* It crowned him king, made him feel like a real *papa*! But he wasn't fearless. His nerves were chiming as always, but that was fine. He knew the score, knew where he stood with the mountain. It was an honest relationship like…like the one he was miraculously having with Simone. *Him!* In a proper relationship! His chest filled again, fit to burst. It was insane, the way he felt around Simone. The best kind of dizzy…and special. She made him *feel* special. When she looked at him with that sweet light in her eyes, he actually felt taller. *Cherished!*

It was new, feeling cared for, and…caring in return. Feeling torn in two over what she'd been through with her in-laws. *Unbelievable!* And yet, no more unbelievable than what he had to endure at his mother's hands. He swallowed. So much hurt, so many scars… When Simone had told him last night how she'd had to sell her violin to help make ends meet, he'd felt actual relief, a giddy buzz of anticipation. A departed violin was something he could fix!

Static crackled in his ear and he flinched, coming to. Standing at the top of the mountain not thinking about the mountain was new as well. *Focus!* He scanned the slope, running his hands over his harness, tightening straps. He looked at the tracks from his previous rides, the little deviations he'd made each time, playing with the powder, innovating. He felt his pulse gathering. There was nothing like the tingling anticipation of riding a pristine slope, senses taut on high alert, the rush that came from riding into the unknown, but riding a tested slope, flying the same line over and over again was a different kind of blast. It was all about fun, and speed, and exhilaration!

'Dax!'

'Pierre!' He pushed his earpiece against his ear. 'Are we good?'

'Almost. The drone's up.'

He pulled his goggles down, letting his eyes adjust, then he coasted to the edge. The drone was rising, drawing level, and then it was above his head, hovering like a curious insect. His pulse spiked, adrenaline kicking in. He took a breath: 'I'm ready!'

Pierre's voice filled his ear. 'Go on five, four, three, two, *one*!'

He rocked back then launched himself over the edge, feeling the snow, finding his rhythm, owning the board, working it, weaving tight zigzags, spraying pow on the turns. Yann loved seeing him spray the powder. *Yann!* His six-year-old speed-freak son! He seemed to have a sense for the board, knew how to use his weight, how to move. He was already at home on the baby slopes, getting more and more confident. Yann was a natural!

He ducked his knees, crouching to touch the snow just for the pure joy of it, and then he was out of the couloir, emerging onto a wide, white expanse. *Playtime!* The tracks he'd left before were crumbling, blurring. *Track away!* He carved left, leaning hard, loving the way the pow was flying. Time to straighten, ride like the wind, take the spur head on…three-sixty spin, quick board grab. *Yes!* Crushing it!

Simone had asked him how he didn't get dizzy. A high cry tore from his mouth involuntarily as happiness crammed his heart. *Simone!* Turning three sixty in the air at fifty kilometres an hour didn't make him dizzy in the slightest, but she did. It only took one look, a flicker of one eyebrow, a single feather touch of her finger to turn him inside out and upside down. He felt heat tingling in his veins. He wanted her, wanted her as he'd never wanted anyone before. As soon as he got back, he was going to steal her away, take her to his room, lay her down and unwrap her… He could already hear her sighs, smell the warm musk of her. *Oh, God!* He was going to take her lips, then trail kisses down her throat, all the way to—

'Avalanche!' Pierre's frantic shout filled his ears, emptying his lungs. *'Get out of there, Dax!'*

He looked down, saw snow shifting under snow, coming alive. *Get out!* He felt his heart exploding in slow motion, then everything sped up. The snow was shaking, throwing him sideways, boiling and rumbling, and then it struck his back, bowling him forwards. He gasped, floundering, and then he remembered what he had to do to stand a chance. *ABS!* He yanked the strap, felt the balloon swelling around his neck and head. *Stay on top!* He covered his nose and mouth with his arm, sucked in a breath, then fought with his other arm, striking for the light. He broke the surface for a nanosecond, but then something hard socked him in the back, and he was floundering again, gagging. *Cover your nose and mouth!* He screwed his eyes shut, giving in to the drag and tumble, cartwheeling, over and over. He was boneless, like Chloe's monkey, what was he called…? *Serge!* That was it: Serge. And Yann's panda was Maurice. How could he ever forget Maurice? Lost in the airport. At least he'd found Maurice. Would he be found? *Yes!* He was wearing his tracker. It would show them where to dig… *No! No! No!* He wasn't dying. *Couldn't* die. Yann needed him. Simone and Chloe needed him. He had to fight, *had* to get back to the surface. He couldn't let all of Simone's worst nightmares come true. He couldn't. He wasn't giving up.

He blinked, trying to focus through the thundering whiteness. *There!* Brighter patches. That was the top! He lifted his arms, heavy, heavy arms. His body was being dragged, flayed by the mountain, but if he didn't get to the light, he'd be buried alive. No air. No chance of surviving. Snow set like concrete when it stopped moving, everyone knew that.

He struck upwards, arm over arm, clawing at snow and air, then air and snow, powered by adrenaline and sheer will. His muscles were screaming, but he wasn't broken. He was winning, moving up, arm over arm, fighting and then he felt the rush and rumble slowing. *No!* His pulse spiked. He tore at the snow, lunging towards the light, dragging himself upwards, driving his body forwards. One last push before the snow clamped his legs and pinned his arms. One last push! And then there was the blue, blue sky, and air to breathe, and the frantic thumping of his still beating heart.

'Scampy Dog is so funny!' Chloe was leaning against her, giggling hard. On her other side, Yann was chuckling, bumping her with his shoulder as he jounced.

She looked at the screen, trying to engage, but it was no good. Dax was out, making his film, the one that needed the helicopter, and it was all she could think about. When he'd been building up his snow fitness, sticking to the resorts, it had been easier to relax. The resorts had safety crews and constant avalanche monitoring. But now he was riding the steep couloir she'd seen on his computer screen with only a film crew and helicopter pilot to hand, and her faith in him and in his sense for the mountain seemed to be deserting her.

She felt her ribs tightening. This was the reality of caring for Dax, of *loving* him. Feeling that low hum of anxiety thrumming through her veins, dreading the worst when he was out, feeling massive relief and boundless happiness whenever he was safe and near. Three days ago she'd told herself that no matter how complicated things were, she was ready to take a risk on Dax. She'd thrown caution to the wind, told him she cared about him, but was she really up to coping with this gnawing fear? Was this relationship really doable?

Dax! Always stopping her breath, or making it catch. He could do it with just a look, with the slightest touch. From the moment he'd kissed her in the snow, she'd been walking on air, feeling something real and wonderful taking flight. Every time they made love, or talked into the night, she felt closer to him, more deeply attached, and that was making it harder to bear the thought of anything happening to him. But what could she do? In the woods she'd told Dax she *cared* about him because it had felt too soon to talk about love. They were brand new! And if it was too soon to be telling him that she was in love with him, then it was too soon to be making demands, asking him to stop doing the thing he loved, the thing that had turned his life around, given him a sense of self-worth, a feeling of earning his place. As if he even had to *earn* his place... But how to tell him that, without it sounding as if she was trying to control him, change him!

She looked at Yann. She'd hoped that *he* would be the key...that *he* would be the one to make Dax rethink things, but it was Yann who'd changed, Yann who'd come out of his shell and become Dax's biggest fan. Mobbing Dax when he came in, wanting to hear every last detail of his runs, how much air he'd got, how many somersaults he'd turned. Hero worship! To think Dax had sat in that bistro telling her he couldn't connect with his son! They were well and truly connected now. Snowboarding buddies! But Yann only saw the glory. He didn't see the danger. And neither did Chloe. She loved being out on her board with Dax, and Dax was so good with her. So gentle, so patient. He was good with both of them, a natural teacher! Exacting, meticulous—*of course*—but always making things fun. She felt a sudden warmth pulsing through her heart. Dax had so much to give, and he gave it in spades, all the time. If only he would stop putting himself in danger...

She blinked, looking at the screen again, feeling her toes curling. The movie was banal and there was another hour to go. She couldn't! She needed some air, maybe a walk around the veranda.

She extricated herself from the stew of arms and legs. 'Listen, you two, Scampy Dog isn't doing it for me.' She got to her feet. 'I'm going upstairs for a bit.'

'Okay.' Chloe didn't take her eyes off the screen.

Yann glanced up, shot her a little smile, then seeped into the space she'd left, leaning his shoulder against Chloe's.

She smiled. 'If you need anything, Chantal's in the kitchen.'

Two heads nodded.

She slipped from the room, crossing the hall, but then suddenly her feet turned to clay. Dax was sitting on the stairs, shoulders slumped, head bent.

Her heart pulsed. This wasn't him! He always came to find them when he got back, always came bounding in high as a kite. She forced her feet to move, closing the distance between them, heart going. 'Dax? Are you all right?'

He blinked, his face pale as paper, and then something raw filled his eyes, something that made her breath catch. 'I am now.' And then he was getting to his feet, grabbing her hand, pulling her up the stairs, going fast.

She didn't try to resist. He was in the grip of something, and she needed to know what it was. At the top of the stairs he caught her eye for a beat and then he was pulling her along again, powerful shoulders shifting under his shirt. At her bedroom door he turned, speaking in low tones. 'Where are the kids?'

'Watching a movie.'

'How long?' His gaze was molten, openly carnal.

Her pulse spiked. 'About an hour.'

'Good.' He leaned in, brushing her lips with his, and then he was tugging her on, past Yann's room and into his, kicking the door shut behind them. When his eyes came back to hers, she could see heat and hunger, and something else too, hiding in the shadows, a haunted look that was tearing at her heart.

'Dax... What's wrong?'

'Nothing.' He was moving in close. She felt his hands on her waist, his lips in her hair. She closed her eyes, breathing him in, fighting the dizziness she always felt around him. And then his hands were sliding under her sweater, caressing her skin in warm waves, his fingers travelling the length of her spine to her nape. She felt her pulse jump, heat rising, but around the edges of it she could feel anxiety shimmering. Dax was a confident lover, always passionate, but this was different. *He* was different.

She put her hands on his chest, pushing back. 'Dax...?' She looked up, trying to see past the heat in his eyes. 'There is something. Tell me.'

He blinked, his gaze clearing for a moment, and then he was shaking his head, his voice low, strangled-sounding. 'I just want you, okay. I want to feel you close...' A smile ghosted tightly on his lips. 'Isn't that enough?'

Her heart pulsed, then she felt it flowing out to him in waves. There was something going on, pain behind the desperate need burning in his eyes and she wanted to take it away, make him better. Suddenly it was the only thing that mattered.

She slid her hands up and around his neck, stroking his nape, looking into his face. 'Yes, it's enough.'

He made a low noise in his throat, and then his lips were scorching hers, igniting a fire in her veins, turning her insides to liquid.

'You're so beautiful.' Dax was trailing kisses along her collarbone.

Her chest panged softly. What had just happened between

them had emptied her out. She felt deliciously used. Boneless! He'd loved her hard, consumed her to the last drop. She was feeling the best kind of dizzy, but she couldn't forget that he'd been sitting on the stairs, pale as paper.

She put her hand to his face, stroking his cheek, sliding her thumb into the sandpaper zone. 'Are you all right?'

He lifted his head, a hazy smile in his eyes. 'You've stolen my line.'

Smiling Dax! She felt her own lips curving up. 'I'm only borrowing it because "I have to pack in the protein" isn't such a good fit.'

He chuckled softly. 'But actually it is…' He fell to nuzzling her neck, trailing more kisses. 'That was quite the workout!'

'Yes, it was.' She ran her fingers over the swell of his shoulder, steeling herself. 'Are you going to tell me why?'

His head came up and then his lips were on hers, teasing softly. 'Because you're irresistible. Because I can't get enough of you.'

Was he being deliberately disingenuous? She caught his face in her hands, easing him back. 'I want to know why you didn't come into the den when you got back. Why were you sitting on the stairs?'

A shadow crossed his face, and then he was rolling away, sitting up. 'How long have we been up here?'

Did he really think avoiding the question was going to work? She levered herself up, ready to pursue, but then her breath stopped. There was a livid bruise low down on his back, purple shadows ghosting around it. 'Dax!' She moved closer, felt her pulse quickening. 'What the hell happened? You're all bruised.'

He stiffened, and then he was turning himself round slowly. His face was paper again, his eyes two holes punched through. He licked his lips. 'Avalanche…'

A memory pulsed. His film...that slab cracking behind him as he'd traversed the snowfield...vertical lines fizzing either side as he'd been flying down. He'd kept ahead, and the snow hadn't come after him, not that time, but today...

She couldn't hold his gaze, couldn't breathe. What had happened to his sixth sense? She'd been wound tight with nerves all afternoon, but she'd *wanted* to believe in it, *needed* to believe in it! But now she could feel her faith shattering and ugly words crowding onto her tongue. She bit them back. Blowing her stack wasn't going to help. He didn't need *I told you so.* He knew well enough. Of course he did. That was the dark smudge she'd seen behind his eyes. She inhaled slowly, steadying herself. He was alive. That was the main thing, the thing to hold onto. But he was in shock, bruised. His confidence all dented. Right now, he needed kindness.

'Oh, Dax...' She wrapped her arms around him, felt him softening against her, holding on tight. She pressed her lips to his neck, breathing him in, stroking his hair. 'What happened?'

'I don't know...' His breath was ragged. 'It happened so fast. One second I was flying... The next, all hell broke loose. The slab...came...alive. Before I could do anything, I was caught...being dragged... The bruise must have been a rock. I remember.' She felt his body shuddering. 'I thought I was going to die.' Suddenly he was pulling away, looking into her eyes. 'I was so lucky, Sim. So, so lucky!'

She felt tears thickening in her throat. Lucky was an understatement! Her worst nightmare had almost come true, having to tell Yann that his *papa* was dead...but this wasn't only about Yann now. It was bigger. She'd let it get bigger. Falling for Dax, letting Chloe fall for Dax... *Chloe!* Letting her cuddle up to him at bedtimes...letting her get close to Dax... *Oh, God!* What had she done?

'Hey!' He was looking at her, a gleam coming into his eyes, and then he was folding her into his arms, pulling her against his chest. 'I'm still here.' His lips grazed her forehead. 'We're all right.'

Were they all right? Could they be? He *was* still here, warm and breathing, holding her close. It was what happened next that mattered. That was the thing! He knew how close he'd come. Maybe it would all work out for the best. This could be a wake-up call, especially if she underlined it.

She shifted backwards, holding his arms. 'You're still here, yes, but what about tomorrow, and the next day, and the day after that? What about Aiguille du Plan?' Something came and went behind his eyes, and then he was going pale again, the corners of his mouth tightening. She felt a prick of guilt. She didn't want to be piling on pressure when the bruises were so fresh, but she had a stake in his life now, and so did Chloe. As for Yann... Her heart panged. Yann *needed* his *papa*. She swallowed hard. She *had* to pin Dax down, for all their sakes. She looked into his eyes, holding fast. 'What are you going to do, Dax, going forward?'

For a long second, he held her gaze, and then his hand cupped her cheek, and he was stroking her cheekbone with a soft thumb, his eyes dark and liquid. 'I'm not going to die, Sim.' His lips parted for a beat. 'I'm going to have to reappraise.'

'What does that mean?'

He reached for her, pulling her in again, and she felt his lips in her hair, his breath tingling through. 'It means Aiguille du Plan is off.'

She closed her eyes, feeling wetness welling behind them, relief streaming through her veins. He was safe, was going to stay safe! She clung to him, heart filling and filling, but then he was shifting, putting her from him gently, leaning to retrieve their clothes from the floor.

'We should go down before they send out a search party.'

She looked at the purple island on his back. 'Are you going to tell Yann?'

He stiffened momentarily, and then he was pulling on his shirt. 'No. I couldn't…' He seemed to falter, and then he turned. 'I'm not sure if we'll put the film out or not, but if we do, I'll talk to him about it then.'

Her heart panged. Of course, Pierre must have filmed the whole thing. She shuddered. It wasn't a film she ever wanted to see! She pulled on her sweater. 'Did you get checked by a medic?'

'Of course.' He stood up, tucking in his shirt. 'Superficial injury! They said I was lucky.' And then he smiled, stealing her breath away. 'But we know that, right!'

CHAPTER TWELVE

December 22nd...

'HEY, DAX, HOW are you doing?'

Guilt panged in his chest. Pierre had called him yesterday too, but he hadn't been in the mood for talking. He'd been in a dip, feeling blue, which was crazy because shouldn't he have been feeling high on life? He'd survived an avalanche! Life should have been tasting sweet, but for some reason he was up one minute, down the next, churning away inside, feeling the pull of a hundred threads.

'I'm okay.' He dug out an upbeat tone. 'Sorry, I didn't call back. I was with the kids.'

'That's cool. Where are you, man? I'm picking up an outdoor vibe.'

'At ski school, watching the kids.' He moved along the rail to a quiet spot. 'Yann likes me to see how he's coming along, although he prefers his snowboard.'

'No surprise! His *papa* is the boss!'

His chest went tight. Boss of what? Messing up?

Pierre's voice was downshifting. 'Seriously though... are you okay?'

He felt a judder inside, something collapsing. 'I don't know.' He blew out a sigh. 'I'm all over the place, to be honest.'

'That's allowed. It was scary. It's okay to be feeling shaken.' Pierre paused, a functional sort of pause, as if he was sipping something. 'You should have gone back up, Dax.'

He closed his eyes, felt his gut twisting. It was what he'd been telling himself for the past twenty-four hours. He should have ridden the line again, pegged his fear right back into its hole. Getting caught by the avalanche had spooked him, but aside from the bruising he'd been fine, more than capable of going again. If he had, he could have gone home triumphant, able to face Yann, instead of skulking on the stairs, feeling like a failure. But straight after, his heart had been beating only for Simone and Yann and Chloe. All he'd wanted was to get back to them, not risk another run, just in case.

Simone's words had collected themselves around him: *'I don't want to be the one who has to tell Yannick that his papa thought riding a snowboard down a cliff was more important than being a father...'* And in the afterglow of spared life, he'd felt the full weight of them, had felt that nothing on earth was more important than his little Christmas family. Being with them, not doing anything to hurt them.

He sighed. 'Maybe.'

'You did everything right, *everything*! You didn't panic. That's why you came through. You should be proud of yourself!'

Proud? Yes, he'd remembered his avalanche drill, but before launching, when he should have been casing the terrain, he'd been thinking about Yann, feeling buzzed about the way Yann worshipped him. And then he'd been thinking about Simone, thinking about how wonderful it was having someone he could talk to properly...and just before the avalanche had struck, when he should have been concentrating on the snow, paying attention, he'd been fantasising about undressing her. That was why he hadn't noticed paradise turning to hell right under his board, why Pierre's frantic warning had given him such a jolt.

'Dax?'

'Sorry! Chloe took a tumble but she's all right.' It was a lie, but it would do. It was good of Pierre to be boosting him like this, but he couldn't cope with a full debrief. His head was cluttering, and his insides were twisting themselves into knots. He was a mess!

'It's fine…' Pierre paused. 'I was just wondering what you're thinking…about Aiguille du Plan?'

Dax's chest panged. He'd told Simone Aiguille du Plan was off, but he hadn't quite got around to telling Pierre yet. He hadn't had the chance. The previous day he'd been nonstop with the kids, then with other stuff, something driving him like a piston, keeping him going until he'd been wiped out. But he could tell Pierre now, couldn't he? Put it to bed, the line he'd been obsessing about for over a year, the line he'd come back to Cham to make his own, the line Yann had wanted to see on the computer over and over again, the line that made Yann's eyes ignite and burn…

He took a breath. 'I don't know, Pierre. Right now, I can't even think straight.'

'It's cool, man. I'm not bringing it up to push you. I'd never do that. It's your call. You've got to feel a hundred per cent.' Pierre paused. 'All I wanted to say is that the conditions are looking good for Christmas Eve…'

Simone shivered into her jacket, sipping her coffee. Sitting inside would have been warmer, but the outdoor tables with their jolly red chairs, flickering pavement heaters and little Christmas trees dotted about had looked so appealing. Besides, she'd been hoping that the happy bustling crowds and the gaily adorned horse traps going past would lift her spirits, but somehow they were only making her feel worse.

She set her cup down, feeling the knots in her stomach tightening. She ought to have been walking on air. Dax had survived an avalanche! He'd ditched Aiguille du Plan. He'd said he was reappraising. It was everything she'd wanted, for Yann, for herself and for Chloe, but something wasn't right. With him.

Yesterday, he'd coached Yann and Chloe on their boards until they'd been dead on their feet. Then he'd waxed the cars to within an inch of their lives. After the kids had gone to bed, he'd lapped the pool for over an hour then fallen asleep on the sofa. She'd watched him for a while, then covered him with a throw, thinking he'd come to her room when he woke up, but he hadn't. First thing that morning he'd had the kids out on their boards again, and now he was at the ski school. He was still smiling but there was something missing.

She picked up her cup and put it down again without drinking. It wasn't what she'd been expecting. Yes, he'd taken a knock, not just physically—although *that* didn't seem to be slowing him down any—but psychologically too. He had to have been wondering about his sixth sense, feeling shattered about the way it had failed him, but even so, *even so*, surely staring death in the face and coming out the other side should have been making him shine more brightly, should have been making him just...more! But instead, he seemed less, not on the outside, but somewhere behind his eyes, and she couldn't stop thinking about it.

She slid her cup away. Maybe she was expecting too much. The avalanche had only happened two days ago. He was probably still in shock. Maybe all his non-stop motion was just him trying to outrun what had happened in some way…

Probably…? Maybe…?

The thing was, she didn't actually know—

'Madame?' A young man was putting a flier down on her table.

She watched him weaving through the tables, handing out fliers, feeling an ache tearing at her chest. The problem was Dax wasn't talking to her about it. If he'd come to her room last night, if he'd slipped in beside her, all warm, talking into the night as they'd done before, she wouldn't have been churning away like this. Two days ago, he'd towed her up the stairs and loved her as if she'd been life itself, but since then, it had almost felt as if he was keeping her at a distance. *Why?* She felt tears prickling at the edges of her eyes. She was here for him, wanted to help him through it, but he wasn't giving her a chance.

Yet…

She drew in a long breath, wiping her eyes. Maybe this was *her* hang-up, not Dax's, because she wanted him to turn to her, not only for sex, but for all the love she had inside, the love she hadn't declared yet but wanted to. She wanted to flow into his spaces, fill him up, be his everything. And because it wasn't working out that way—*yet*—she was getting stupidly insecure. For pity's sake! Just because he hadn't come to her last night didn't mean he was pushing her away. Maybe he simply hadn't wanted to disturb her! And he'd hadn't crashed on the sofa to upset her, but because he'd worn himself out, and he'd worn himself out because it was his way of dealing with what he'd been through, which was, after all, a pretty big deal. She needed to get a grip. Stop being so sensitive!

She looked along the street, noticing the time on the pretty little clock tower. The other thing she needed was not to be wasting her afternoon. Dax had told her to take some time out, hit the spa, anything she wanted, but what she wanted, what she *really* wanted was to find him a Christmas present even though he'd made her promise not to. She felt warmth rising inside. How could he ever have thought she'd be able to keep a promise like that?

The problem was Dax had everything already!

She went for her cup but then the flier caught her eye. *The Alpine Museum!* She snatched it up. An entire museum devoted to Alpinism in Chamonix! There was bound to be a gift shop. She scanned the leaflet, felt her pulse quickening. There was a temporary photo exhibition. *Perfect!* Dax had that huge photo of Mont Blanc on his office wall! Maybe there'd be something there that could work as a companion, assuming the gift shop was stocking repro prints, and if it didn't, she could always look online. A black and white mountain landscape would be perfect!

She gathered up her things, suddenly feeling light as air. Going on a mission was way better than moping. The museum was bound to be interesting, and it might just turn up a surprise!

She glanced at her watch and gasped. Had she really been in the museum for over an hour already? She hadn't meant to get distracted, but the place was simply too fascinating. The history of the early climbers and mountaineers who'd gone up Mont Blanc had been captivating. And the gear! Light years away from the fancy kit Dax had. Wooden skis and poles, unwieldy long-handled ice axes and picks, jute ropes. And the clothes…nothing lightweight and properly waterproof. All woollen…jackets and plus fours, socks, and hats.

She scooted through the geological exhibition, sliding her eyes over the huge lumps of glittering quartz, but she couldn't not stop to look at the stuffed wolf. Grey with yellow eyes. Right up Chloe and Yann's street!

Finally she came to the photo exhibition: *Walking Through Mountain Time*. She felt a tingle shimmering between her shoulder blades. Surely, there'd be something here for Dax. She drew in a breath and stepped into the dark hall, feeling its reverential hush wrapping itself around her.

The first images were black and white. Crisp, imposing landscapes. Stiffly posed pioneering mountaineers and blurrier group photos of early tourists with smiles and sticks and canvas packs. She walked on, going slowly. It really was like walking through time, seeing the mountains change, the Savoie glacier shrinking, the town growing. Along the next row, there were colour photographs, action shots of skiers and mountaineers, but there was nothing for Dax. She moved on, turning the corner into the next exhibition space and then her breath stopped. In front of her was a huge picture of a thundering avalanche. She shuddered. Dax had said that his avalanche had been mercifully small by avalanche standards. This one wasn't. She looked at it for a long moment, feeling its immensity. Definitely not the right picture to give him.

She tore her eyes away, turning to the accompanying panel of smaller photographs, captioned *Mont Blanc avalanche claims record number of lives*. She looked along the row of pictures feeling a sick ache clawing at her stomach. Crews digging for bodies. Grave-faced mountain rescue teams. A hovering helicopter. And then, her mouth turned to dust. Dax was staring out of one of the pictures.

Dax!

She swallowed hard. It couldn't be Dax! It was a mistake! *Clearly!* They must have made a mistake. She leaned in close, holding her breath. It *was* him! Standing with a line of smiling men holding skis. *Skis?* Dax didn't ski! She scanned the caption underneath the picture, blinking away the spots that were suddenly dancing in front of her eyes.

World champion free skier Camille Deuzlier and support team perish in Mont Blanc avalanche.

She put her hand out, steadying herself against the cabinet. Not Dax, then. *No!* Of course not! Dax was alive. He was with Chloe and Yann. But if it wasn't Dax... Her pulse quickened, started roaring in her ears. She sucked in a breath, forcing herself to look at the date over the main avalanche picture again and suddenly she could feel a sob rising, filling her throat. The dates tallied. Dax was twenty-nine. The man in the picture had died thirty years ago. Could it be...could it possibly somehow be that the man in the picture with Camille Deuzlier was Dax's father?

She sank onto the step outside, breathing hard, and then she looked at the photo she'd taken with her phone. The man was the spit of Dax, or, rather, Dax was the spit of him! It *had* to be Dax's father! But who was he? She typed 'Camille Deuzlier' into her phone with trembling fingers. *There!* Same photo, but with an article. She skimmed, looking for the names of Deuzlier's team, clicking links. *There!* That was him: Gabriel Dax Guillot. Dax's father! Found!

She took a screenshot, then rolled her phone over and over in her hands. Gabriel had died on Mont Blanc thirty years ago. Two days ago, Dax had nearly succumbed to the same fate. Whatever crazy thing it was that drew Dax to the mountain, it clearly ran in the blood. Nature, not nurture! Maybe that was why he'd always felt that the mountains were his natural home. Maybe that was why his son seemed to have been born to ride a snowboard!

She drew in a slow breath, running her eyes over the jagged peaks that rose, towering over the town. What now? Should she tell Dax? Would telling him be meddling in something that was none of her business? After all, Colette had hidden his father's identity from Dax for a reason. But what reason? She closed her eyes. Unless…unless reason had nothing to do with it. Hadn't Dax said that his mother hated Chamonix? Maybe Colette hated Chamonix because Mont Blanc had taken the man she loved. The date on the picture…? She must have been pregnant when the avalanche happened. Had she gone back to Paris, had her baby, seen Gabriel in him and hadn't been able to bear it? Was that why she'd blown hot and cold with Dax his whole life, one side of her wanting to love him, the other side being too scared to in case he was torn away from her too? Hardly credible, but if that was Colette's reality then maybe it didn't have to make sense to anyone but her, any more than André's parents' attitude to Chloe didn't make sense. She swallowed hard. It was twisted sense. Warped logic. Misguided. *Wrong!* But maybe that was what grief did to some people.

She felt a shiver fingering her spine. The gift of his father's identity, and tragic fate, wasn't exactly the surprise she'd had in mind for Dax. She couldn't tell him now, not when he was dealing with his own avalanche trauma. She needed him to come right first. Until then, she'd have to keep it to herself.

CHAPTER THIRTEEN

December 23rd...

DAX KILLED THE engine and slumped back on the seat of the snowmobile. He twisted, testing his body, trying to find a patch of pain, but nothing was twinging. Not around the bruise site anyway. All the twinging was happening on the inside, torment pulling him all apart.

He drew in a long breath, felt his heart panging over and over.

What was wrong with him? Why couldn't he find a shred of peace in his soul? He'd come through an avalanche, for God's sake. He was alive. Beyond grateful. The thing was, what was he supposed to do with that gratitude? Wrap it around himself never to emerge? Stop free riding? That was the question he'd been trying to run away from for the last two days because every time he tried to answer it, he came up with something different.

Straight after the avalanche, when the snow had stopped thundering and he'd been lying there, blinking up at the sky, all he'd been able to see were the faces of Simone and Yann and Chloe, and all he'd wanted was to be with them, hold them close, never do anything to hurt them. If he'd had to answer the question at that moment, he'd have said without hesitation that he was never venturing onto the mountain again. But when Simone had asked him just hours later, What are you going to do, Dax, going forward? he'd felt a niggling doubt starting, a niggling doubt that had snowballed into full-blown chaos. And he hadn't wanted Simone to see it, so he'd kept his distance, stayed away from her bed, and then he'd felt the pain of hurting her, the pain of feeling responsible for the bruised, worried look in her eyes, and he'd felt torn in two because hurting Simone was the last thing in the world he ever wanted to do.

He didn't want to be feeling like this... Wretched. Guilty. Guilty for still loving the jagged peaks in front of him, guilty because he couldn't stop his eyes searching for lines, guilty because he couldn't seem to switch off that part of himself. He sighed. But how could he switch it off when it was the best part of him, the only part of him that had ever been worth anything? Extreme free riding had given him a place in the world where he could feel safe—ironic!—a place where he knew who he was, what was expected of him. Free riding had given him self-respect, an income of his own, a life he could believe in, but, more than that, it had given him a line to his son, a son who amazed him every day, a son who reminded him so much of himself.

Yann! When Claude had called to tell him, he'd been knocked for a loop. For a moment he'd felt resentful, yes, but then he'd remembered how it had felt, not knowing his own father. He'd felt the pain coming back, the ignominy of not having been conceived in love, of not knowing his father's name, of not even knowing what he looked like. And thinking about all that, he'd felt his heart filling with a million good intentions. He'd gone to collect Yann in love with the idea of being a father, then discovered that he had no idea how to be one. He'd failed over and over again, ached about it every day. And then…then Yann had come down that night and asked about his snowboards…

That had changed everything, set wonderful wheels in motion. Yann loved that he was Dax 'Hasard' D'Aureval, extreme free rider, with over a hundred and seventy thousand followers on social media, sponsors clamouring for his endorsement, and free-riding friends all over the world. He hung on his every word, listened to his every instruction. Yann loved watching his films, ran into his arms now with excited eyes when he came in, wanting to hear about the lines he'd been riding…how fast, how high, how many somersaults. What would Yann think of him if he gave it all up?

He pulled his phone out, scrolling through the pictures. There! He felt his cheeks loosening, warmth filling his chest. Simone had snapped it at the resort that first day he'd been out: Yann's face, rapt. Free riding had made him a hero to his son, but would he still be a hero if he stopped flying down mountains? When Simone had asked him if he was going to tell Yann about the avalanche, he'd had an immediate, visceral reaction: No! He'd hadn't wanted Yann to think he'd messed up, hadn't wanted to risk Yann thinking he was a failure, or that the mountain had beaten him. At that moment he'd felt the full weight of everything pressing down on him. He drew in a slow breath. But the mountain hadn't beaten him! It had tried, but Pierre was right: he'd stayed calm, followed the drill, done everything he was supposed to do, and he'd survived.

He tucked the phone back into his pocket. Riding a snowboard wasn't more important to him than being a father, but it was important because Yann thought it was important. Without it, who would he be, crucially, who would he be to Yann? Would Yann still look at him with admiration, would he still think he was worth listening to, or would he revert to how he'd been before? His heart panged. He couldn't bear the thought of that. Yann gave him so much now and he wanted to give back, wanted to create memories for Yann that he'd never had of his own father. Yann was already excited about the prospect of him conquering Aiguille du Plan. Could he even contemplate letting him down by not doing it?

His heart twisted. But would Simone understand? She could have torn him off a strip over the avalanche, given him the risk lecture, but she hadn't. She'd been kind. Above everything, she was kind. Snow Angel! She'd come to Cham, come to his rescue, opened him up in ways he couldn't believe. She'd said she cared about him, and he was crazy about her. More than crazy! She was making him feel things and think things he'd never felt or thought before. He couldn't stop imagining scenarios, future scenarios, like showing her the mountains from a helicopter in twenty years' time.

Twenty years...

His stomach dipped. But would he get as far as twenty minutes? Oh, God! More than ever, he needed Simone to be kind now, needed her to understand what he had to do and why he had to do it. He'd never asked anyone to be there for him before. He'd never allowed himself to get close to a woman, or to ask anything of a woman, because Colette had stolen his faith. But somehow, miraculously, Simone had kindled it back to life, opened him up to all kinds of possibilities. He had faith in her. Would she come through for him?

'Here you go!' Dax was handing her a beer. His other hand was empty.

'Aren't you having anything?' She was trying to sound casual, but she was feeling anything but. Dax seemed tense. He'd been jolly enough with the kids at bedtime, reading the story, doing the voices, his eyes twinkling, but now he was looking strained. If he hadn't been on the go so much, if he'd actually spent any time with her alone over the past two days, she'd have checked in with him, asked him if he was all right, but that hadn't happened. Last night, he'd crashed on the sofa again after another swimming marathon. She'd tried hard not to get sensitive about it, had tried to rationalise that he was still dealing with the avalanche stuff, but it had stung all the same. Now at least they were in the same room, alone, and awake.

He shook his head. 'No. I'm not drinking tonight...' He dropped down onto the opposite sofa, but he didn't settle back. He was pressing his palms together, taking a deep breath that she could almost feel fluttering in her own belly. His eyes came to hers. 'Simone, I need to talk to you about something...' His gaze was serious, a dark light inside it that she didn't recognise.

'Okay.' She felt a tingling dread winding round her veins. She folded the beer bottle into her arms, feeling its seeping chill. 'What is it?'

He blinked. 'I want to try for Aiguille du Plan... Tomorrow.'

Her lungs emptied. She looked down, seeing spots. It couldn't be true. *No!* He'd told her it was off! She set the bottle down shakily, snatching a breath, and then she looked up. 'I'm sorry...' She swallowed hard. 'Did you just say—?'

'Yes.' His eyes gripped hers. 'It's something I need to do.'

'*Need* to do!' Her heart panged, sparking anger. 'Why? Isn't it enough that you almost died two days ago? You want to, what...have another go? Do it better next time?'

His eyes went loud. 'Of course not.' He leaned forwards,

forearms resting on his thighs. 'I'm not trying to kill my-self. I'm trying to get something back.'

'What? Your sixth sense?' His face blanched. Guilt curled in her belly. It had been a low blow, but desperation was twisting her out of shape.

'No! That's still intact.'

'Really?' She could feel her pulse beating through her skin. 'So I can still believe in it—' she swallowed a sharp, dry edge on her tongue '—can I, Dax? Is it going to keep you safe this time?'

'What happened three days ago had nothing to do with...' He sighed, light shifting through his gaze. 'I made mistakes... There was a hold-up with the drone. I lost my focus.'

'And that won't happen again?'

His gaze tightened. 'I won't let it.'

She thought of Gabriel Guillot, Claude Deuzlier, André, and felt a fresh hot lick of anger. 'It's not all down to you. You can't see everything coming, can't control everything, no matter what you think. There's always going to be that one time.' Suddenly she was at a loss. 'What is it, Dax? What the hell is *so* important to you that you're prepared to risk your life again?'

The corners of his mouth tightened. 'My self-respect.'

'Self-respect?' She felt her own mouth tightening. 'Are you sure it isn't ego?' Something flashed behind his eyes. 'Maybe you just can't stand that the mountain almost got the better of you. Are you trying to show the mountain who's boss?' She felt her frustration ramping. 'Is it a man thing? Because I don't get it! You won't win, Dax. Can't you see that? In the end you won't win.' She swallowed hard. 'In case you'd forgotten, you have a son!'

He blinked and then a fierce light came into his eyes. 'He's the *reason* I need to get my self-respect back! Yann *loves* what I do…' He was pulling out his phone, tapping and scrolling, then he was thrusting his hand out, showing her the picture she'd taken herself. 'See this! Yann watching me. You took it! To show me how well I was doing with Yann, to show me how much he respects me.' He lowered the phone, looking at the screen, its light ghosting on his face, picking up a glaze in his eyes. 'He didn't respect me before. He didn't even give me the time of day, no matter what I did. But now, because of what I do, he thinks I'm a hero, and I like it. I want to live up to his expectations. I want to be someone who doesn't give up because of a setback.' His eyes came back to hers, moist and full. 'Snowboarding opened his eyes to me. It's given us a bond, given me the chance to be the father I want to be. Can't you see that? If I stop doing what I do, what happens to all that? What will he think?'

'He'll think you're putting him first. He'll know that he's more important to you than anything else. And if you're alive, and around, then you'll find other things you can bond over. Snowboarding is only the beginning…' She licked her lips. 'And no one's asking you to give it up. Only the high-risk stuff—'

'But that's what I do. It's who I am.' His eyes were filling. 'It's *all* I am, Simone. If I don't get back out there, delivering what I've promised to deliver, then I lose everything.'

'You won't lose me, Dax. Don't I count?' She felt tears burning behind her eyes. 'And Dax D'Aureval, extreme free rider, isn't all you are. You're so much more than that…' Suddenly, the distance between them was getting in the way. She went to sit by him. 'Dax, can't you see? I'm in love with you…' Something warm and intense came into his eyes, turning her inside out. Was opening her heart to him going to make him think again? She felt hope ris-

ing. She touched his cheek, flattening her palm against it.
'I love you, so much… I love you for your kindness, and
your boundless energy, and for how funny you can be,
and because you make me feel protected and safe. You'll
notice that none of those things depend on how good you
are on a snowboard… I don't want to lose you, Dax. *You!*'
She loaded her gaze with everything she could. 'I care
about *you*.'

'Oh, Simone.' His eyes were moist again, a moving
tapestry of light and shade. 'If you love me, if you really
care about me, then please…support me in this. Understand why I *have* to do it. Please…'

Her heart collapsed. Nothing she was saying was making the slightest bit of difference. She felt tears breaking
free, sliding down her cheeks. She wasn't enough. She
didn't matter enough. Chloe didn't matter enough, Chloe,
who would cry a million oceans if anything happened to
him. That momentary fire in his eyes hadn't sparked a declaration of his own, even though she thought she'd seen
love flowing through his gaze so many times.

He didn't love her.

She looked down, felt his hand settling on her shoulder.
'Don't cry, Simone. Please. I'll be fine. I don't want you
to worry about me.'

She squeezed her eyes shut. What had she done? Fallen
for a man so blind to her feelings that he actually thought
she was crying because she was worried about him? She
was worried, but why couldn't he see that she wanted
something back from him? If he couldn't see it in her,
then his feelings for her were nothing like hers for him.
In the woods that day he'd said that what they were doing
wasn't a mistake, but it was beginning to feel like one!

She took a breath, wiping her cheeks. If Dax didn't love
her, if her love for him wasn't enough to make him chang

his mind, then she had to try saving him for Yann's sake. She met his gaze. 'I can't support you. I think you're making a big mistake.' She bit her lips hard, heart tearing. 'I'm washing my hands of you, Dax!'

'No, Simone, please...' The light in his eyes was draining fast. 'Don't say that. I *need* you.'

'No, you don't.' She pushed his hand off her shoulder and picked her phone up off the low table. Was she really going to do this, hit him with the truth about his father? Her fingers were trembling, her pulse was hammering in her ears, but shock and awe was all she had left. She scrolled through the pictures to *that* picture, then turned the phone around so he could see. 'What you *need* is to see this!'

His eyes flicked to the screen, locking on, then narrowing, his mouth falling open. 'What's this?'

'It's your father. Gabriel Dax Guillot.' She felt fresh tears burning behind her eyes. 'He died in an avalanche on Mont Blanc before you were born.'

'I don't understand...' Bruised eyes gripped hers. 'How did you...? Where did you get it?'

'Photo exhibition at the Alpine Museum. I thought it was you, and then I realised...' She swallowed hard. 'You need to think about it, Dax.' He looked dazed, shell-shocked. She felt her throat filling with tears, her heart breaking for him, for herself. Suddenly she couldn't bear to look at him. She got to her feet, speaking to the floor. 'You've paid me to be here, I know, but if you ride that line tomorrow, then Chloe and I are leaving—'

'On Christmas Eve?' He was getting to his feet. 'You can't. Please, don't go.'

'I'm sorry, Dax. It's just something I have to do.' She took a backwards step, blinking back tears, dying inside. 'You of all people should understand!'

CHAPTER FOURTEEN

Christmas Eve...

HE DIALLED PIERRE'S number then pressed the phone to his ear, lifting his gaze. The mountains beyond the cemetery wall were rose-pink, turning gold as the first rays of the rising sun broke around their contours.

New day...

'Dax!' Pierre sounded primed and ready for action. 'What's up?'

He felt a small pang of not-quite-guilt. 'I'm not coming Pierre. I'm sorry if you're packed already—'

'Are you okay?'

'Yes.' He flicked a glance at the headstone in front of him. 'I'm absolutely fine, but I can't ride that line... I'm postponing indefinitely.'

There was a long silence, then Pierre sighed. 'I can't believe I'm saying this, but I'm glad. To be honest, I was surprised when you said it was a go for today... I think that avalanche really shook you up.'

Not only the avalanche.

'It did. I need to think about Yann.'

'I get that, man. If I had kids, I'd be rethinking too.'

He took a breath. 'So I'll catch you after Christmas then?'

'Absolutely!' Pierre's voice filled with a smile. 'Have a good one, Dax.'

'You, too.' He tapped his teeth together. Would he have a good Christmas? Maybe, if he could straighten himself out. He pocketed the phone and looked down at the headstone.

In Loving Memory
Gabriel Dax Guillot

He felt a lump thickening in his throat. At least they'd found the body. At least his *papa* had had a proper burial. A shiver hovered between his shoulder blades. So many avalanche victims were never found. Christ! The thought of never being found...of being buried alive, no air to breathe. The thought of never seeing Yann again, or Simone, or Chloe... He screwed his eyes shut, feeling a burn pricking behind them. What had he been thinking? What bug in his brain had convinced him that attempting to ride Aiguille du Plan was a good idea when it was, patently, the worst idea he'd ever had?

He pushed his hands through his hair. The bug that had always been there, of course. Insecurity about who he was, where he fitted, what he was for. He was a walking identity crisis! Free riding had fixed it for over a decade, but then Claude had called, and it had kicked off all over again. What was he...a father or an extreme free rider? He'd wanted to be both, and Yann's interest in snowboarding had made it seem possible. But the avalanche had kicked him back again, and for some reason, to his panicked, bent-out-of-shape brain, Aiguille du Plan had seemed like a solution, but it wasn't. He knew that now for sure. The only way he could solve his identity crisis was by choosing a side, the right side. He had to accept fully and finally that he was a father first.

A family man!

He drew in a breath, letting it settle. It sounded fine, more than fine. He felt a smile coming. But of course it did! Hadn't he felt the whole 'family man' vibe pulsing through him from the moment they'd set off for Chamonix? Rescuing Maurice! That ridiculously happy feeling he'd had concocting the whole magic Christmas tree thing… the sheer joy he'd felt seeing their faces when they'd come in…and that glow he'd felt inside showing Simone and the kids around, showing off the home he loved, that feeling of wanting them to love it too. Walking around with his phone all afternoon because he hadn't wanted to miss a second with them, not a single second…

He dropped down, running his eyes over the headstone. And it was all because Yann had started engaging with him in the car. After months of nothing, getting something back from his son had boosted him into the stratosphere, had ramped up his paternal instincts to the max, made every second feel all the more precious. He closed his eyes. And yes, if he followed that line, he could see that it had felt like that because he'd never had a single second with his own father. He'd learned to live with the pain, but it had always been there deep down, the gaping chasm in his soul. And now he was here, with his *papa* at last, closer than he'd ever been and it was too late. Too damn late! Dust! Bones! Nothing to have, nothing to hold. He felt his eyes burning again and squeezed them shut. *Crazy!* Even now he was trying to hold it in instead of letting it out. He pressed his palms to his eyes, felt a sob filling his throat.

Let it out!

The blinding shock of that photograph, spending all night searching on his computer, finding two living grand parents in Argentière, finding out that Gabriel could ski before he could walk, finding out where Gabriel was buried, that it wasn't so far away... He gulped a ragged breath, steadying himself, wiping his eyes. Shock after shock after shock. But there was a kind of peace too, trickling in. Knowing his context, knowing who he took after, not just looks-wise, but with that sense for the mountain—not the whole sixth-sense thing, which was sounding pretty arrogant to him in his head now, but that sense of belonging, that whole running-in-the-blood thing that seemed to run through Yann too.

He drew in a breath, rising to his feet. Had Gabriel known that Colette was pregnant when he'd gone off with Deuzlier's team that day? Had he stopped, even for a second, to consider the possible consequences? And could Dax really blame him if he hadn't? If Simone hadn't brought him to his senses by showing him the picture, then maybe he'd have been climbing a cliff right now.

He shuddered. Actions. Consequences. He wanted to talk to Colette. Was the way she'd been with him down to Gabriel? Had she loved his *papa* fiercely, never got over losing him? Had she seen Gabriel in him all the time and hadn't been able to cope with her emotions? Was losing Gabriel the reason she hated Chamonix, the reason why she never visited? So many questions... Maybe he could use Gabriel to open a door with Colette, find a new beginning somehow...

He inhaled deeply. Perhaps it was wishful thinking, but daring to hope was fine because he was feeling stronger now, more centered, more in control. If it weren't for Simone seeing that picture, he'd never have known all this, would never have been in this place, reassessing everything. If it weren't for Simone...

Simone!

He closed his eyes for a beat. That first moment, snow-flakes in her hair, snowflakes on her cheeks… That smile. Stealing his breath, stopping his heart…his heart. *Yes!* Last night, she'd said she was in love with him. She'd put her heart on the line trying to stop him doing a stupid thing. She'd said, *No.* No one had ever said no to him before, but she'd said it because she loved him. And he'd been so lost inside his own head and his own stupid crisis that he'd tried to use it to lever her support instead of telling her…telling her that he was in love with her too. He felt warmth puls-ing in his chest, a strong pulsing warmth growing stron-ger, streaming through his veins. *Yes!* That had to be it. *Love!* Why else would he have kept picturing her in his future? Twenty years in… Why else would she have been his first thought after the avalanche? He'd wanted to run to her with all his heart, the way he wanted to run to her now… If that wasn't love, then what was?

Simone tugged the beanie down around her ears and set off walking. There was only one way to go if she wanted to step out, and that was down the twisting private road that led away from the house. Dax always kept it clear and gritted so it was a better option than trudging through the snow on the slopes, slipping and stumbling. Her in-sides were stumbling around all over the place as it was, churning away.

She'd heard Dax leaving, the throaty rumble of his four by-four sliding out of the garage before daybreak. She hadn't been sleeping anyway, but after that, she'd been wide awake, twisting like a fish on a line. As soon a Chantal had arrived, she'd slipped out. She couldn't fac breakfast, couldn't face telling Yann and Chloe in a fak cheery voice that Dax was on the mountain. Her stomac clenched. On the mountain. Or falling off it. Or being swallowed by an avalanche...

She felt tears prickling at the edges of her eyes. What was *wrong* with him? How *could* he have gone to ride that line after seeing what had happened to his father, the father he'd missed, the father he wished he'd known, the father he'd wished had been around to offset his unfathomable mother? Gabriel's absence had impacted his life in so many ways, and he knew it, *knew it!* That photograph had been her last card. She'd thought it would bring him to his senses but he'd gone off that morning all the same.

Was it really for Yann, so that Yann would see him as a hero? Did he really believe that Yann would think less of him if he stopped doing the extreme stuff? It was so great the way the two of them had bonded. It was what she'd wanted more than anything but connecting over a love of snowboarding had backfired spectacularly! Now it seemed to have become the wind beneath Dax's wings. She'd tried to tell him that snowboarding was only the start, that they'd find other interests, other ways to connect. She'd tried telling him that he was so much more than a free rider but it hadn't worked. And now she was trapped. *Knowing* that he was out there taking massive, massive risks, *knowing* that something catastrophic could happen. Feeling heartsick and sick to the stomach.

She swallowed hard. Telling Dax she was washing her hands of him was one thing, but actually doing it was another. She couldn't switch off the anxiety that was clawing at her belly any more than she could switch off the love inside, the love she'd thought, for one tantalising instant, was going to turn him around. His gaze had filled with such a warm, wonderful, burning light, that she'd thought he was winning, but then he'd harnessed her declaration and twisted it to his own ends.

'If you love me, if you really care about me, then please…support me in this. Understand why I have to do it. Please…'

She kicked a stone, sending it scuttling across the road. Understanding wasn't the issue. She got him, got that his sport had given him a place in the world where he felt good about himself. She got what a boost to him it was that in Yann's eyes he'd gone from zero to hero. She could see the line of his thinking as clearly as he saw lines in the mountains, but just because it was a clear line, it didn't mean it was the right one. He needed to be a father first, needed to believe that he could still be a hero to Yann without pulling off the extreme stunts that could land him in an early grave. When she'd snapped that picture of Yann, Dax had been *at the resort*, a safe place where he'd still managed to blow all of their minds. Couldn't he see that flying down the resort slopes, turning tricks, was mesmerising enough? It was for her. Last night, she'd told him that all the things she loved about him had nothing to do with his snowboard, but it wasn't true. On his board, Dax was a firework, a rocket! She loved seeing him soar, and spin, throwing himself upside down, seeing all that hard, bright energy he had. It absolutely *was* one of the things she loved about him.

Love…

She felt her heart twisting, tears thickening in her throat. Dax had made her *feel* again but loving him was too hard. How could she love him on his terms? And the thought of Chloe getting even a millimetre closer to him, of herself getting even a millimetre—

Her breath stopped.

Was that his car coming up the hill? She stared, heart banging, legs suddenly shaking. *Yes!* Definitely his. But how? The climb to the head of the couloir was a goo-

three hours. It was too soon for him to be back, unless…
She felt tears prickling again. Unless he'd turned back…

The car was slewing to a halt, grit flying, and then Dax
was tumbling out, running up, his eyes full of feverish
light. 'I didn't go, Sim!' His hands were on her shoulders,
his breath coming out in little billows. 'I'm not going, ever.
It's one hundred per cent off!'

She swallowed hard, feeling anger and relief fighting
for space in her heart. 'And you were going to tell me
when…?' Tears were welling up, making it hard to speak.
'You went off… I thought you were…' A sob was rising,
filling her throat. 'I can't do this, caring about you, loving you…' His eyes were glistening, tearing her heart out.
She swallowed hard again. 'Have you any idea how worried I've been?'

'I'm sorry.' He was blinking. 'I should have left a note,
or texted. I was so deep in my own head, I didn't think…'
His gaze tightened on hers. 'But I'm going to change, Sim.
I'm going to be better at this relationship stuff.'

Relationship stuff? Did he think they were still in a relationship? She felt a small spark igniting inside, a flutter
starting somewhere. She took a breath, noticing his clothes,
regular clothes, not climbing gear. She felt a frown coming. 'So, where have you been…?'

'Argentière…' A shadow crossed his face. 'To visit my
father's grave… To pay my respects.'

Her heart twisted. 'Oh, Dax…' She blinked, felt tears
trickling down her cheeks. 'I'm so sorry about Gabriel. I
never even said that last night and I should have! I'm so,
so sorry.'

'It's all right. You had other things on your mind, like
trying to talk some sense into me…' A soft light came
into his eyes. 'But there's definitely something I should
have said to you last night…' He was cupping her face, his

hands all warm, and then his gaze turned so deep and full that it was hard to keep breathing. 'I love you and, in case you think that's not enough, it comes with a promise…' She felt her heart melting, the fluttering moving upwards in waves. 'No more risks, even if Yann thinks I'm lame. I can do other things with snowboarding…safe things… I've already got some ideas…' He took a breath. 'But the main thing is I know what I want now.' A smile touched his lips. 'It's you, Simone, and the kids… I want us to be a family, want it with all my heart. Just don't leave me…' His voice was cracking. 'Please, don't wash your hands of me.' His eyes were burning into hers, turning her inside out. 'I'll do whatever it takes.'

He meant it. She could feel it all the way to her bones, could feel happiness, love, and hope lifting her up, higher and higher, and suddenly it was impossible not to put her arms around his neck, impossible not to slide her fingers into his supremely touchable hair. 'Even move mountains?'

He broke into the smile that undid her every time. 'Now that happens to be my very particular skill…' And then she was being folded into his arms, and his lips were on hers, and the ground was sliding away, but she didn't mind in the slightest because it really was the best kind of dizzy.

EPILOGUE

Chamonix, one year later...

SIMONE WENT CLOSER to the front. The red *D'Aureval Snowboard School* banners looked great behind the small stage, but the stage was maddeningly empty. Where was Dax? And where were the kids?

Had Felix slipped his collar again? Maybe they had all gone after him, but *no*, Dax wouldn't bother himself with the puppy this close to his grand opening ceremony. She turned, searching the crowd. Maybe he was caught up with someone, signalling desperately for her to rescue him. She scanned the rows. He wasn't with Gabriel's parents, his grandparents. They were sitting in the front row, wrapped up well against the cold, their faces glowing with pride.

Warmth filled her chest. They'd been overjoyed when Dax had contacted them. They had welcomed him into their lives with open arms, told him all about his *papa*, even had their photographs of Gabriel copied for him. And they were delighted with Yann, their great-grandson!

She shifted her gaze, sliding her eyes over the groups of chattering guests. Friends, snowboarding buddies, and reps from the companies that were still sponsoring Dax to make instructional videos and safety videos, featuring their kit, of course! She held in a smile. He'd thought they'd drop him, but his face and name still had currency, even though he wasn't doing the extreme stuff any more. She bit her lips together. It was a pity that Colette hadn't come, but they hadn't really expected her to. Dax was making slow progress there, but at least Colette was beginning to open up about Gabriel. Baby steps.

She caught Pierre's eye. He winked, gave the camera a little jiggle. All set! Dax had asked Pierre to shoot some stuff to promote the school on social media, not that he needed any promotion. Being taught to free ride by Dax 'Hasard' D'Aureval was a massive draw.

Suddenly the microphone blared. 'Hello…'

She spun round, heart pulsing. Dax was on the stage after all, bang on time, and looking as gorgeous as ever! He must have slipped past her.

She threw him a smile, which he threw right back with a cheeky wink.

He leaned into the microphone. 'Thanks for coming out on Christmas Eve, everyone!' He broke into a smile. 'It's a big day…' There was an appreciative murmur from the crowd. His hand went up to his head, fingers raking through his hair. She felt a fluttering in her stomach. He did that when he was nervous, not that anyone else would know. He was squaring himself up to the microphone, still smiling. 'I almost can't believe that today I'm opening my own free-riding school, but I am, and it's all because a year ago I promised a very special person that I was going to stop riding risky lines.'

She felt her heart filling, a tear wanting to slip out.

'I loved riding those lines, I'll admit, but you should know that I've had no trouble keeping that promise because somehow, miraculously, I've been blessed with a family and…' his voice was cracking a little '…and being there for them, and with them, is more important to me than thirty-second thrill.' His eyes came to hers, full and intense. 'Why go for thirty seconds when you can have a lifetime?' She bit her lips together, feeling tears welling behind her eyes. 'Simone...' He was holding out his hand, such a look in his eyes. 'Would you join me up here, please?'

Her heart panged. What was he doing? This wasn't the speech he'd shown her. She swallowed hard and went up, feeling a blush tingling madly in her cheeks.

'And Yann, Chloe and, last but not least, Felix the disaster dog, will you also come up here, please?'

There was a movement at the front. So that was where the kids had been! Standing with Victor. Or, hiding behind Victor... They had funny little smirks on their faces, and they were looking at Dax, avoiding her gaze. She felt a brow furrowing. What was going on?

He was leaning into the microphone again, but he was looking directly at her. 'As I was saying, why go for a thirty-second thrill when, if you play your cards right, you could enjoy a thrill that lasts for ever?' A smile touched his lips. 'That's the thrill I'm after, so, Simone...'

No...

His gaze tightened on hers. 'You are the light of my life, the light of our kids' lives, and you're also Felix's favourite human, so, I think we're all agreed...'

Chloe and Yann were chuckling, meeting her eye now, except that she couldn't see very well because her eyes were all wet.

'Simone...' He was coming forwards, dropping down to his knees, his eyes burning into hers. 'Will you please, please, marry me?'

Her heart exploded softly. Only Dax could have come up with this, proposing in front of everyone, or, if Chloe's and Yann's faces were anything to go by, maybe they'd conspired. Yes! Definitely, they had. She felt a smile wobbling onto her lips, tears sliding down her cheeks. But it was perfect, because they were a family. She took a breath, fastening her eyes on his, feeling his love flowing back. 'Yes! I will…with all my heart.'

'Sick!' He was laughing, his eyes brimming too, and then he was turning to Yann and Chloe. 'Kids…*now* would be a good time…'

They bumbled forward, Felix straining on his lead with Yann hanging on for dear life, Chloe rooting in her pocket, giggling, then handing Dax a small box.

Dax popped it open, revealing a twinkling diamond, his eyes holding hers, full of smiles. 'In my head this was so much slicker.'

She couldn't stop laughing and crying. 'It's perfect.' He was sliding the ring onto her finger, and then he was on his feet, kissing her, laughing into her mouth, and the crowd were clapping and whistling, and Felix was barking, and all she could think was that it was the most perfect moment ever, the most perfect Christmas proposal.

* * * * *

COMING SOON!

We really hope you enjoyed reading this book.
If you're looking for more romance, be sure to
head to the shops when new books are
available on

Thursday 11th November

To see which titles are coming soon, please visit
millsandboon.co.uk/nextmonth

MILLS & BOON

THE HEART OF ROMANCE

A ROMANCE FOR EVERY READER

MODERN — Prepare to be swept off your feet by sophisticated, sexy and seductive heroes, in some of the world's most glamourous and roma locations, where power and passion collide.

HISTORICAL — Escape with historical heroes from time gone by. Whether your pass for wicked Regency Rakes, muscled Vikings or rugged Highlanders, the romance of the past.

MEDICAL — Set your pulse racing with dedicated, delectable doctors in the high-sure world of medicine, where emotions run high and passion, com love are the best medicine.

True Love — Celebrate true love with tender stories of heartfelt romance, from rush of falling in love to the joy a new baby can bring, and a focus emotional heart of a relationship.

Desire — Indulge in secrets and scandal, intense drama and plenty of sizzlin action with powerful and passionate heroes who have it all: wealth, good looks…everything but the right woman.

HEROES — Experience all the excitement of a gripping thriller, with an intens mance at its heart. Resourceful, true-to-life women and strong, fea face danger and desire - a killer combination!

To see which titles are coming soon, please visit

millsandboon.co.uk/nextmonth

MILLS & BOON

Coming next month

CHRISTMAS WITH HIS CINDERELLA
Jessica Gilmore

'At some point I will have to go back to real life, and I don't know how I'll survive the shock when I am the one offering tea, not accepting it. Plus, if I carry on like this, I am not sure I'll even fit in my clothes come January, which for someone who has one carefully selected travel wardrobe is a serious issue. And yet I can't stop.'

'Isn't indulging the point of Christmas?' he asked, and she shot a pointed look at his own barely touched tier of treats.

'For some.'

He laughed again as Elfie took a bite of the Yule log, closing her eyes as the intense chocolate hit flooded her taste buds, glad of the distraction. Sombre, work-focused, curt Lord Thornham she could handle, but her unexpected suite mate, the man she enjoyed making laugh, the one she was so aware of she could probably describe every millimetre of his wrists was another thing entirely.

No matter that she had her own bedroom and bathroom, sharing the hotel suite felt a lot more intimate than an anonymous bunkroom.

His laptop left on a coffee table, the book he was reading—he liked vintage crime, apparently—on a sofa arm, a bookmark denoting his spot. She saw him in his socks, in his post work version of casual, with his hair shower-wet and as he took his first coffee of the day. She saw the weariness descend at the end of another long, long day and noted how his schedule was all work and no play. Even his dog walks focused on work as she and her camera shadowed him, capturing as many moments as she could for posts, stories and the popular Walter blog on the hotel chain's website. She challenged herself to make him smile, and once or twice had found herself being gently teased in turn.

Then there were the charged moments… The times when silence descended and it was far from comfortable. The moments when she was achingly aware of every sinew on his forearms, his deceptively muscled thighs and the smooth planes of his stomach, the way his hair rebelled to fall over his forehead and the darkness of his eyes. The way he looked—or deliberately didn't look—at her. The heated caress of his eyes when he did.

Continue reading
CHRISTMAS WITH HIS CINDERELLA
Jessica Gilmore

Available next month
www.millsandboon.co.uk

MILLS & BOON
MEDICAL
Pulse-Racing Passion

Set your pulse racing with dedicated, delectable doctors in the high-pressure world of medicine, where emotions run high and passion, comfort and love are the best medicine.